Prisoner of Circumstance

Nadine Zawacki

Dedication

This novel is dedicated to my family:
Tom, Lisa, and Tom.
I love you all deeply and your support was invaluable to me.

Prologue

In a tiny cabin just outside of a small town in Tennessee, an old man was asleep. His wife of forty-eight years lay beside him. The room was unpretentious in appearance, from its simple wooden bed frame to its handmade chest of drawers.

A man reaching nearly to the ceiling stood at the foot of the bed, watching the old man sleep. He wore a simple tan tunic; his steel blue eyes could penetrate your soul. He waited patiently for the old man to come fully awake. The room was quiet and dark, except for the light that emanated from him.

The old man suddenly jolted from his sleep, momentarily startled by the sight of the man he had come to call Samuel standing at the foot of his bed.

Samuel told him he had a message for him. It was not the first time Samuel had come with a message, and the old man knew he needed to pay close attention to what he had to say. He looked down at his wife, sound asleep beside him. She never woke during these visits.

This otherworld visitor told him a story of a young woman whose life was in danger. The old man understood what he must do; he knew what was expected of him. He needed to press in, pray, and listen closely to the Lord for direction. As Samuel continued his tale of this young woman, the old man's heart filled with compassion. Samuel stood behind him as he got on his knees beside his bed and started to pray for the young woman he had never met. And so the journey began.

Chapter 1

In her penthouse in the middle of Manhattan, Regina Cavelli stood quietly by her window, staring down at the street below. She could see people rushing from one place to another, proving that New Yorkers knew two speeds — fast and faster. Often New Yorkers were known as cold, unfeeling people, but it wasn't that they were inconsiderate; it was more that they just kept to themselves, minding their own business. Regina had never known anything else.

She had the kind of beauty that stood out in a crowded room. With dark brown hair and glistening hazel eyes, she could light up a room when she smiled, which was often. She was a strong woman, with equal parts of compassion and confidence. Her strength was born out of her faith, and she needed both virtues — faith and strength — to deal with the man she was married to.

She turned around and gazed at the figure sleeping so soundly in her bed. Her husband looked sweet and innocent, almost childlike, when he slept, but she wouldn't use those words to describe him when he was awake. Physically speaking, Anthony was a very good-looking man — a fact that didn't escape him. He put on charm like a comfortable pair of jeans. His six-foot stature, jet-black hair, brown eyes, and olive skin made him very popular with the ladies. For better or for worse, marriage hadn't hindered his social life at all.

Her thoughts were interrupted by a faint knock on the door. She walked across the room and opened it to find Lilly standing there with a breakfast tray. Lilly had worked for Regina's family since she was a little girl. She'd been like a second mother to Regina, praying for her for years. It wasn't until after Regina had married Anthony that life had opened her enough to hear about God. Regina would always be grateful to Lilly for introducing her to Jesus, because a relationship with the Lord had been Regina's refuge.

With a nod, Regina thanked Lilly for breakfast and Lilly left as quietly as she could. The man currently sleeping in Regina's bed disliked her housekeeper and made no secret of it. To keep the peace, Lilly stayed as invisible as she could around him. The only reason she had stayed this long was to keep an eye out for Regina. She had promised Regina's parents she would watch over her after they were sent away. Regina and Lilly knew that without the Lord, Anthony couldn't help being the way he was. Regina had watched Lilly pray for him, over and over again, in spite of his cruelty to her.

Regina sat down, poured herself a cup of coffee, and then just sat there, staring at the steaming liquid and letting her mind wander again. Was it really a good idea for her to have caffeine in her condition? A croissant with jam was her favorite breakfast, but she wasn't quite up to eating this morning. Her stomach felt too queasy, and it might not stay down.

Two chairs and a small round table stood near the window where Regina liked to sit and enjoy the Manhattan skyline. Antique nightstands were on either side of the bed. On each stand glistened a beautiful Tiffany lamp given to her by Anthony's father, Poppy. Anthony's rolltop desk stood in one corner of the room. A gas fireplace took up part of the wall that led to the private bathroom and walk-in closet.

She started to pray, *God, give me your wisdom to do what is right. Guide and direct my every step. Protect me . . .* Her prayer was interrupted by sounds of Anthony moving about in the bed. When she heard his groaning, she wondered what type of mood he would be in when he woke up.

"Regina," he muttered, "get me some coffee."

Regina poured a fresh cup and added two sugar cubes. She walked over to the bed, her hands shaking slightly. Anthony was sitting up now.

When he saw the cup trembling in her fingers, he yelled, "What's the matter with you, woman? Be careful or you'll spill that coffee all over me!"

His response answered her question about his mood.

"I'm sorry, Anthony. I'm not feeling very well this morning. Here's your coffee, just the way you like it."

She placed the cup on the nightstand. Anthony grabbed her wrist and pulled her down to the bed. She hated it when he grabbed her, because he would often leave a bruise whether he meant to or not. He just glared at her, as if he could read her thoughts. She turned her eyes, but not her face, away from him. When he looked at her like this, it scared her. There were times she felt brave enough to stand up to him, and other times fear just got the best of her. She started to pray for strength.

"You kinda look green. I'll have Vinny take you to Doc's today to make sure you haven't got anything seriously wrong with you."

It wasn't that Anthony was really concerned with Regina's health; it was just his way of making conversation.

"That's okay, Anthony. I'm sure I'll feel better if I just get a little rest before going to the restaurant. I think I'm just overly tired. I didn't get much sleep last night."

She hoped he believed her. The last thing she needed was to go to Anthony's doctor and for him to find out that she was pregnant.

With a look of indifference, he let go of her wrist. "Suit yourself. I don't care if you get better or not. But I'll have Vinny stay here to drive you to work later."

"I'm not that sick," Regina replied as she got up from the bed. "I don't need Vinny to drive me to work. I'm quite capable, thanks." As soon as she said it, Regina realized that it had come off a bit abruptly.

"Let me rephrase that for you. Vinny will stay and drive you to work." His glare went straight through her heart. If she could have melted into the surroundings, she would have gladly done so.

She didn't feel like arguing with him. "That's fine," she said simply, then walked around to her side of the bed and slipped under the covers. She lay down on her side, grateful for their king-sized bed, which ensured that their bodies never had to touch at night.

"If you're not up by ten, I'll have Lilly wake you, okay?"

"That's fine. I should be better rested by then." She closed her eyes and silently prayed, *Lord, deliver me and my child from the danger we are in. Give me the strength to do whatever I must do to protect my child. Most importantly, please don't let Anthony ever find out that I'm pregnant.*

As Regina lay there, Anthony stared at her and wondered if she was hiding something from him. She had been acting strange lately, stranger than usual. He had a real knack for reading people; in his line of work, he had to be able to tell if people were lying to him. She was too smart to double cross him — that much he knew. Even then, it wasn't like she knew the specifics of his business. But he was sure she had overheard plenty.

Her edginess was what bothered him. He wasn't sure what was going on with her, but he knew he didn't like it. Of course, there wasn't much he liked about her to begin with.

He took another sip of coffee and then got out of bed, pulling on his robe. On the other side of the door, he found Vinny and Mario standing guard. Anthony always kept a guard or two outside his bedroom. He was able to sleep better at night knowing someone was watching the door.

With the physique of a bodybuilder, Vinny was much larger than Mario, but he was a gentle giant. Anthony liked having him around because he intimidated everyone he met with his size alone. On the other hand, what Mario lacked in size he made up for in attitude and cruelty. He was one of Anthony's most fearless men. There was no job he wouldn't do, without hesitation. He never questioned orders or thought about the ramifications to himself.

Mario's left cheek bore a scar he received as a souvenir from a fight with a drunken, six-foot-three sailor at a bar several years ago. A week later, that same man's head had been found in a dumpster behind the bar — a knife wound on his left check. The police never recovered the rest of his body. Though never proven, it was commonly known who had killed the sailor. Mario's reputation had soared.

Anthony closed the door behind him and said, "Vin, I want you to hang around here until she wakes up and then drive her to the restaurant." He never greeted his men with hellos; he wasn't interested in their personal lives. Usually he just spoke what was on his mind.

"Sure thing, Boss. Do ya want me to stay at the restaurant or go to the office afterwards?"

"I want you to stay there and keep an eye on her. I'm not sure, but I think she's up to something. I don't want her to know you're watchin'. She'll think you're there to help her out."

Vinny nodded his head to show he understood what Anthony expected.

"Did you take care of that situation last night?" Anthony asked Mario.

"Yeah, Boss. No problem; it went smooth as silk. After last night, no one will ever try that again."

"Are there any loose ends I'll have to worry about later?"

Mario seemed surprised that he would even ask. "Everything's tight, Boss."

"Good. I couldn't have my people doing their own thing and then thinking they can get away with it. That's not the kind of example I want to set. After I get dressed, I've gotta go see Poppy. Get the car and meet me downstairs in thirty minutes."

Anthony enjoyed being feared by people. He got a rush when he entered a room and knew that with one look, the largest man present would lick his boots if he asked. He relished watching them jump when he said to and bend over backward just to please him. He enjoyed being the boss and the power that came with it. For the most part, life was good to him.

He went back into his room, where Regina lay asleep. If it wasn't for his father, she wouldn't be lying there. Why had he ever agreed to marry her? He knew the answer to that, but every once in a while it helped him to say it, even if it was just to himself.

Mostly, it was all that God stuff that got on his nerves. He blamed Lilly for that. In the beginning Regina at least used to be interesting. She wasn't afraid to come back at him. He enjoyed the war of words they would have, but now she was just too nice most of the time to suit him. It had never been a marriage of love, just business. They both had agreed to it for their own reasons. Now he was trapped, and a man in his position shouldn't have to live this way.

As much as people feared him, Anthony feared no one — except maybe his father, Antonio Cavelli. Anthony had called him Poppy since he had first learned to talk, and Antonio's associates had picked up the nickname as a term of endearment. Through the years, it had stuck.

Poppy was old, but he was tough. What he said went, without discussion. They often disagreed, but Poppy always won in the end. Anthony wondered what in the world the old man wanted with him today. Whatever it was, he was sure he wouldn't like it. Poppy never beckoned unless he had something he wanted to enforce. Anthony felt like he was a teenager trying to sneak in after curfew whenever he visited his father under these circumstances. He didn't like going into a situation where he wasn't in complete control.

He'd better get ready or else he'd be late. Poppy hated it when people were late. He felt it showed a lack of respect, and the last thing Anthony wanted to do was sit through a lecture on respect.

When she heard the bathroom door close, Regina opened her eyes. She lay very still until she heard the shower running. Then, carefully, she reached behind the headboard and grabbed a small camera she had hidden there on a nail. She silently got out of bed, her eyes fixed on the bathroom door. With her heart racing, she walked over to Anthony's desk and reached underneath to the secret button. Anthony didn't realize Regina knew about it. She had seen him use it one night when he thought she was asleep. The hidden drawer opened, and she took out the little black book concealed there. The desk had been custom made with a drawer that was as big as the book but no bigger. She opened up to the middle of the book, where she had left off, and started taking pictures, keeping an eye solidly planted on the bathroom door. After snapping several pages, she stopped and placed the book carefully back in the drawer and closed it. There were only a few pages left. She figured she needed maybe one more opportunity.

The water suddenly shut off in the bathroom, and her heart missed a beat. She slid back into bed and closed her eyes.

Oh, Lord, please calm me down, she prayed as she tried desperately to steady her breathing. She nearly forgot to put the camera back but did just before the door opened. *Oh, God,* she thought to herself, *I pray he didn't see me move.* She pretended to be still asleep and rolled over to her side. She could feel his glare on her even with her eyes closed and her back toward him. *Please help my heart to stop beating so fast.*

Gradually, her heart began to calm down, and she started to feel more at ease. *Thank You, Lord.* Soon he would be gone and she could relax. She continued to lie there, praying silently.

The one-seven was full of activity. Ladies of the evening protesting their arrests. Drunks asleep on benches as they waited to be processed. Crooks of all types locked up in jail cells. The place was crowded and noisy. It wasn't one of New York's bigger precincts, but it kept plenty busy. A stale smell filled the air, the result of overcrowding bodies.

Sitting at his desk, Detective John Nelson was oblivious to the noise and insanity that surrounded him. Everything about him reflected that attitude. He dressed as casually as the department dress code allowed, which meant he was the only detective who wore sneakers with his shirt and tie. He still had dinner at his mother's once a week, and he'd been to every birthday party ever thrown for his partner's kids. He was focused, almost to a fault, and determined to catch whoever it was he was after.

In this case, Anthony Cavelli.

John's eyes were pinned to the open folder in his hands. Regina Cavelli's picture smiled up at him from the pages. He couldn't bring himself to pull his eyes from hers. They seemed kind and compassionate — yet she was married to a monster. It was well known that Regina fed the homeless and paid hospital bills for poor children. Not many people would do that. How did a girl like that get mixed up with a man like Anthony Cavelli? John couldn't help feeling drawn to her. There was something about those eyes . . .

"Hey, man. What are you doing?"

Frank Holstrum and John had been partners for the past five years, ever since John had made detective. Frank was older than John and more experienced. The father of three kids, he was married to a woman who some said was too pretty to be with a man like him. But what he lacked in looks, he made up for in charm. He was a nice guy who got along with everybody. Unlike his partner, he always dressed well — but only because his wife picked out his clothes every day.

John hadn't heard Frank come in.

"Hey, are you deaf or something?" Frank asked. It was not the first time John had ignored him with his face buried in a file.

"Oh . . . hey, Frank. I'm just looking over the Cavelli file."

A look crossed Frank's face. Leaning over, he placed his hand on John's shoulder, whispering quietly, "You know, John, people are starting to talk. You have to get a grip. You're starting to obsess about this guy. You should pay as much attention to your other cases as you do this one."

John jerked his shoulder away. "I don't need this crap right now, Frank."

"Screw you, man." Frank turned and started to walk away.

"Look, I'm sorry, Frank. I didn't mean to bite your head off." Frank turned around, so John continued, "You know how much this case means to me. I just got an idea . . . a new angle. I want to bounce it off of you."

Frank rolled his eyes and shook his head. "What is it this time?"

"I know I've said this a hundred times, but I think we've been going about this thing all wrong. Look —" John thrust the picture of Regina in front of Frank. "You see, this is the key — Anthony's wife."

Frank shook his head. "Bad idea, John. That's the kind of thing that will only get you in trouble . . . or dead."

"Listen. I think this could work. She's nothing like her husband. She doesn't seem to be messed up with the family business. So, that being the case, I bet we could get her to turn on him."

"How do you know? You've never met her. You don't know anything about her. She might be the force behind the man for all you know."

"It's just a feeling I get. She owns a nice restaurant; she gives to the poor and needy. Maybe she doesn't know what kind of guy he is, and we can enlighten her. You know, get her on our side."

"You're crazy, John."

"Come on, Frank. Let's give it a try. Just once."

Frank just looked at him a minute and then sighed. "Are you forgetting that her father worked for the Cavellis, too? Do you have a death wish? You can't go around harassing a man's wife, especially if that man is Anthony Cavelli. Did you forget what happened six years ago with your brother?"

John's complexion changed. He didn't have to be reminded. His brother, Sam, a detective, was working on the Cavelli case back when Antonio "Poppy" Cavelli was still in charge of the family. His brother's name and reputation were ruined by his death. John swore he would not rest until he cleared his brother's name and exposed the truth about his so-called suicide.

"Look. I'm not my brother! I'm going after the Cavellis with or without your help. I know they had something to do with Sam's death, and one day I'm going to prove it."

Frank studied him. "All right, you win." He paused before proceeding, "It's not that I care that much about you; it's just I've gotten used to you being around. I would feel guilty if something happened to you. So tell me the plan, and let's go catch the bad guy."

"Now that's more like it. I figure we can pay Mrs. Cavelli a visit today at her restaurant and see what's cooking." He chuckled at his play on words. Frank just rolled his eyes again. "This might work, you know. I really think she could be our one weak link in this whole thing."

"That's the big plan — that's it?" Frank saw the excitement in John's eyes and gave in. "All right, but I'd better come with you to make sure you don't do something stupid."

"Thanks." John smiled. "Okay, well — no time like the present." He grabbed his jacket and they headed out the door. It *was* a good plan . . . or maybe Frank was right and it was going to backfire on him.

But no, he had a good feeling about Mrs. Cavelli. All that information he had about her couldn't be wrong. She wasn't like the rest of the Cavellis. He could see it in her eyes.

Besides, everything else he'd tried had failed.

Before Anthony left, he took another look at Regina. She was just lying there, quietly breathing. It wouldn't take much effort, he thought, to force a pillow over her head as she slept. She wouldn't even see it coming. That happy thought lingered a bit too long in his mind; he could almost imagine it happening. He shook his head and convinced himself that it wouldn't be in his best interest, at least not yet, to give in to that desire. Poppy wouldn't be around forever, and then he'd have more freedom to do whatever he wished to his wife. He would be free of her one day.

He walked out to the front of the building where Mario was waiting. As soon as Mario saw him, he climbed out and opened Anthony's door.

"Let's go," Anthony said immediately. "I want to beat the traffic before it gets bad."

Regina looked out the window and watched as Anthony drove away with Mario. The black stretch limousine was hard to miss even from the penthouse. Anthony owned several cars, but he liked taking the limousine when he had to meet someone. It made him feel important. She walked over to the desk and opened the secret drawer, but the black book was gone, just as she figured it would be. Anthony always carried it with him wherever he went. *Tomorrow is another day and another opportunity.*

"I'd better get ready and see what is going on over at the restaurant," she said to herself. Sometimes in this hostile environment, the sound of her voice eased her nerves.

She was nearly dressed when she heard a knock on her bedroom door. "Who is it?"

"It's Vinny, Mrs. Cavelli. I just want you to know that Mr. Cavelli asked me to drive you to the restaurant. I'm ready whenever you are."

"Just a minute." Regina finished buttoning her blouse and then opened the door to find Vinny waiting for her. At six-foot-two and pushing two-fifty, he was absolutely Herculean, and it was pure muscle. He made her nervous, but she knew better than to let it show. She was the boss's wife and had to be self-assured, even if she didn't feel it.

"I'm ready." She paused a moment to assemble her thoughts. "You know, I'm feeling much better. I can drive myself to work."

Vinny smiled as he said, "Mr. Cavelli was very worried about you this morning, and he wanted to make sure you got to work safely. He also wanted me to hang around and drive you home later. I'm at your disposal today."

"Isn't that nice?" Regina replied.

"Besides, you wouldn't want me to get into trouble with the boss, would you?" Vinny smiled again.

Regina realized this was a losing battle, so she relented. "No, I wouldn't want you to get into trouble with Anthony. Let's go then."

"After you, Mrs. Cavelli." Vinny stepped out of the way to let her pass. He didn't mind the days he had to watch her. It was an easy way to make a living. She was usually pleasant and never caused any trouble. To tell the truth, he liked her. Why the boss didn't trust her was beyond him, but it wasn't his job to ask questions, just follow orders.

After his mother had died a year and a half ago from a heart attack, Anthony hadn't been sure Poppy would ever recover from the loss. It was then that Anthony had taken over the daily business operations. But now Poppy wasn't in mourning anymore, and Anthony was afraid he'd want to come out of retirement.

He arrived at his father's house right on time. He walked up the front steps, and before he could knock, Stuart opened the door.

"Good day, sir. Your father is waiting for you in his study."

"Thanks, Stuart," Anthony said as he entered the house. He always thought it was creepy how Stuart knew someone was at the door before the doorbell rang. The man had been with the family since before Anthony was born. No one knew how old he really was. His thin frame made him appear even taller than his six-foot stature, and his English accent added a touch of class to his persona. Poppy trusted him, and as long as Stuart wanted a job, he had one. Anthony knew that Poppy had offered him retirement, but Stuart refused. Since he had no family of his own, he enjoyed keeping busy. His loyalty had been proven on more than one occasion.

Anthony walked down the long hallway and found his way to his father's study. The door was open, and his father was on the phone. Poppy motioned for Anthony to enter.

Anthony sat down on one of the leather-backed chairs opposite Poppy's large mahogany desk and looked over at the pictures to his left. There were framed, smiling faces of his mother, of him, and some of Regina. It irritated him that his father seemed to care so much for his wife. Maybe that added to his hatred of her.

The entire wall to his right contained floor-to-ceiling bookcases that held hundreds of books. His father, an avid reader, enjoyed collecting books, especially first editions. He had a separate library in another part of the house that contained even more books, but he kept his favorites in his study.

Finally, Poppy finished his call and hung up.

"*Buon giorno*, Poppy." Anthony walked around the desk and greeted his father with a kiss, as was his custom. Poppy motioned for him to sit back down.

"So, my son, two things I have to ask before we get started. First, how is that beautiful wife of yours? And second, am I any closer to being a grand-father?"

Anthony hated it when his father started conversations like this. How could he explain to his father that the marriage he'd arranged for him was not one of love? And as far as he was concerned, kids would never enter the picture. It would require more than he was willing to do.

"She's a bit sick today, but I think she'll be all right."

"Morning sickness, perhaps?" Poppy asked with hope in his eyes.

"So, Poppy, why did you want me to come by today?" Anthony was determined not to talk about Regina or her having a baby. Both subjects made him ill.

"Can you think only of business?"

Anthony didn't answer him; instead, he pretended an interest in his father's books, as if he hadn't heard the question.

"Very well, then. Let's talk business. I want to discuss something with you." Poppy paused, then got up from his desk and sat in the chair next to Anthony's. "Since your mother's death, God rest her soul, I've been a little out of it. I mean, her death was so unexpected. That was why I needed some time off. I started to lose my edge. I became . . . complacent."

Anthony sighed. He did not like the direction the conversation was going.

"But I feel the time has come for me to get involved again in some of the daily operations. This is no reflection on you, of course. You've done a fine job. I don't mean to take over the whole operation again, just . . .

I would like to be kept abreast of different situations and deals that arise."

Anthony kept silent. He could feel his blood boil. *If the old man thinks I'm going to just roll over and play dead, he's got another thing coming to him.* He enjoyed the power he now possessed and would not give it up without a fight. Poppy couldn't just give him ultimate control and then change his mind on a whim.

Keeping his true feelings to himself, Anthony responded, "If it's not going to be too much of a strain on you, then I think it's a great idea. It'll be good for you to get involved again. I welcome all your experience." Anthony pressed his hands over his heart and hoped he sounded sincere. "Look, Poppy, there's some things that need my attention back at the office. If there isn't anything else, I'd like to go."

"No, nothing else."

Anthony gave his father an awkward hug and kissed him good-bye.

When he was about halfway out the door, Poppy said, "I'll see you over there later." Anthony froze mid-step. Poppy continued, "I thought I'd look over the books and see where things stand."

"Sure thing. See ya later," Anthony said, without looking back. He felt his heart start to race.

When he got back to the car, he took out his cell phone and called the accountant. "It's me. Did you finish?" He took a deep breath and yelled, "I don't want any more excuses! My father is coming to the office this afternoon and everything better be ready! If it's not, you and your family are going to wish you'd chosen a different profession."

Anthony snapped his phone shut, tired of all the delays. He took out his black book and flipped through the pages.

"Mario, when we get back, cancel all my appointments. Poppy is coming."

Concerned, Mario asked, "Is he taking over again, Boss?"

"Don't worry about it. I'm still the one in charge, and that's all you need to know."

"Sorry, Boss. I don't mean no disrespect." The last thing Mario wanted to do was get Anthony angry. He knew what would happen if he did.

The rest of the ride was spent in complete silence. Anthony still didn't speak even after arriving at the office. He just marched in, grabbed his messages off Mary's desk, and slammed his office door.

Mary, a very pretty woman in her mid-twenties, made a quite efficient secretary, which surprised most people, because her short skirts and high heels fed the assumption that she was just a pretty face.

"I guess it's not a good time to ask for a raise." Mary winked at Mario, and they smiled knowingly at one another.

Vinny pulled into the parking lot of the Long Island restaurant. He climbed out of the car and opened the door for Regina.

Without saying a word to Vinny, Regina went to the back door and unlocked it.

"Is there anything I can do for you today, Mrs. Cavelli?" Vinny asked, following closely behind her.

Regina couldn't say what she really thought or she might have to repent later. Besides, it wasn't Vinny's fault Anthony was the way he was. She hated Anthony more and more as time went on. It was eating her up inside. *Get a grip, Regina. Let it go. Forgive. Not for his sake, but for yours.*

"I'll be in my office getting some paperwork done. I really don't want to be disturbed. When the staff comes in, will you let them know that?" *If I don't get it together soon, I'll be snapping at everybody.*

Vinny nodded and then walked over to the bar, which was made of beautifully crafted oak with a dark brown finish. A dozen or so stools neatly lined the edge. Behind the bar was a large mirror with grapevines etched along the sides. To the left of the mirror, two shelves held the various types of alcohol and mixers positioned in tidy rows. The drinking glasses sat on shelves to the right of the mirror. At the end of the bar, a flat-panel television hung suspended from the ceiling. Vinny walked behind the bar and poured himself some mineral water. Then he grabbed the remote and flipped on the TV, since there wasn't anything else to do.

Regina walked to the back office next to the kitchen and unlocked the door. The key in her hand was the only one to this room, which was her inner sanctum. It was the one place she could be herself and not have Anthony's eyes watching her. She'd decorated the room with soft shades of blue and gray and had made the curtains herself; they matched the small love seat. A rectangular coffee table and a plush, round chair sat at the other end of the room. Her desk was made of mahogany, a present from Anthony's father. He loved mahogany and had given it to her when she had bought the restaurant.

The restaurant was a good distraction. Anthony's father was kind to her, but she resented him for the pain he had caused her family. She struggled with her feelings for Poppy. If it wasn't for her bargain with him, she wouldn't be married to his son. But she'd had no choice. Not then and not now.

If I hadn't married Anthony, then . . . She decided that she wouldn't dwell on the past. She had done what she'd had to do. The future of her child was at stake now, and that changed things for her.

Regina had so much on her mind that it was hard to know what to do first. Who could she trust with the information from Anthony's book? She knew Anthony had some cops on the payroll — one for sure. He'd been very careful not to reveal who it was, not even to his own men. And lately it had felt to her like Anthony was having her watched twenty-four hours a day. Both she and her baby would be dead if she gave the copies to the wrong person. *Lord? Help me find someone I can trust. Guide and direct me in this situation.* She opened up her drawer where she kept her Bible and opened to the book of Acts. Her eyes fell right on Acts 2:25-28:

> *"David said about him,*
> *'I saw the Lord always before me*
> *Because He is at my right hand,*
> *I will not be shaken.*
> *Therefore my heart is glad and my tongue rejoices;*
> *my body also will live in hope,*
> *because You will not abandon me to the grave,*
> *nor will you let your Holy One see decay.*
> *You have made known to me the paths of life;*
> *You will fill me with joy in Your presence.'"*

Regina let her breath out slowly. *Oh, Lord, thank You for Your word of encouragement to me.*

The knock on the door startled her. She wasn't expecting anyone because she had asked Vinny not to disturb her. "Who is it?"

"It's Vinny, Mrs. Cavelli." He opened the door a crack and stuck his head in. "I know that you didn't want to be disturbed, but you have some visitors that insist on speaking to you. It's a couple of cops."

"Show them in."

Vinny walked in, followed by two men. The blonde one walked over to her with a smile on his face, holding his badge in one hand and extending the other.

"Mrs. Cavelli, my name is Detective John Nelson, and this is my partner, Detective Frank Holstrum."

Frank nodded his head in acknowledgment.

Regina didn't extend her hand but simply looked the two detectives over, saying nothing. She wondered if God answered prayers this quickly.

When she didn't respond, John continued, "If you don't mind, Mrs. Cavelli, we'd like to ask you a few questions." He took out his note pad and opened it up.

Cops made Vinny nervous. He interrupted, "As I told you before, detective, Mrs. Cavelli is a busy lady, and she ain't got time for your questions."

"Does Mrs. Cavelli have a tongue, or do you always speak for her?" John asked, sarcasm sliding through his tone.

Before Vinny could protest further, Regina raised her hand to stop him. "I have a tongue, Detective. Forgive Vinny. He's very protective of me. So, what type of questions would I possibly be able to answer for you?"

Vinny gave Regina a confused look.

"Well, Mrs. Cavelli, I have questions regarding your husband and some of his business affairs."

"In that case, why don't you ask him your questions?" Before he could answer, she continued, "I'm quite sorry, because I don't know anything whatsoever about my husband's business dealings. He doesn't tell me how to run my restaurant, and I don't tell him how to run his business. So I have nothing I could possibly help you with. I'm afraid you've wasted your time coming here and now you've wasted mine as well. If that is all, gentlemen, I have work to do. Good day to you both. Vinny, please show the detectives to the door."

Conversation over, she returned to her paperwork as if they weren't there.

John was a bit surprised by her words and her cold manner. Everything he'd ever heard about her or read described her as gentle and kind. He was not expecting this forceful, strong-minded woman who didn't even give him a chance to speak. He decided he wasn't giving up that quickly.

"Here's my card, in case you change your mind."

Regina didn't look up, so he placed it on her desk.

"Good day, Mrs. Cavelli. Sorry to have troubled you. Let's go, Frank."

After the three men left, Regina picked up the card and looked it over. He had written his home number on the back. She quickly copied it and placed the number in her pocket. Vinny walked in to see her looking at the card. She pretended not to notice him standing there and tore up the card into little pieces and threw it in the trash. Vinny smiled as he watched her.

"Is there anything else I can do for you, ma'am?"

"Thanks, but no. If you don't mind, I'd like to finish up my work."

Vinny closed the office door, took out his cell phone, and placed a call. Anthony answered on the first ring.

"What's up?"

"It's Vinny, Boss. I thought you'd like to know who just paid your wife a visit. It was that detective."

"What happened?"

"He wanted to talk to her, but she just blew him off and sent him packing. She was really something." Vinny was truly impressed with the way Regina had handled herself.

"Interesting."

Anthony paused. Vinny stood there, waiting for his next order.

"I want you to bug her office phone just in case she decides to contact him."

"I don't think so, Boss. She ripped up his card."

"Don't question me, just do as I say."

Anthony hung up in Vinny's ear. Vinny hadn't meant to upset him. It was just that you would think a man could trust his own wife. *But what do I know? I do as I'm told.*

Regina sat at her desk and prayed, *Lord, can I trust Detective Nelson? Should I call him or not?* Another thought slowly began to form in her mind. *Nelson — why does that name sound so familiar?* She thought about it and then remembered that the cop who had been guarding her parents had also been named Nelson. She wondered if there was any connection. It was something she'd have to look into.

She lowered her head into her hands and sat there for what seemed like an eternity. Finally, feeling God's peace, she reached for the phone number in her pocket and dialed. As the phone rang, her heart took a flying leap. Suddenly she wasn't sure if she should do this. He couldn't possibly be home already.

His answering machine picked up. What should she do? Should she leave a message or not? She got scared and hung up the phone. Maybe she'd try again later.

Chapter 2

Driving back to the station, John didn't say much. Regina was more stunning in person than the pictures he'd seen. Maybe she'd call him when she wasn't being watched. Maybe that was why she had given them the brush-off.

Maybe she was afraid to talk to him in front of that big goon — or Frank. Maybe he should have gone alone . . .

Frank was the first to break the silence. "You see, John? I told you it would get us nowhere. She practically threw us out! If she knows anything, she's not telling. Now are you gonna give up on this crazy idea of yours?"

"I think she's just scared. That big guy works for her husband. He's probably there to keep an eye on her. At least now she knows there's someone out here who can help her."

"Have you lost your mind? Help her do what? She doesn't look like she needs any help. Do you live in some kind of fantasy world? Were we both in the same place? She's not going to call you! She seems to be very loyal to her husband. You need to just leave this alone and look for another angle, or else you're going to get yourself killed."

John was quiet for a moment. "Maybe you're right. I guess I'm just kidding myself." He didn't want to continue this conversation. Next time, he'd go see her alone. It would be less intimidating for her, and he wouldn't have to hear "I told you so" from Frank.

He changed the subject. "Hey, Frank, did you watch the game last night?"

Anthony looked at Mario. "Get the car. I want to go and have a little talk with my wife before Poppy comes over."

Mario knew that tone all too well. For Regina's sake, she better have the answers Anthony wanted to hear.

Regina could hear the staff in the kitchen. She must have lost track of time; they were probably getting ready for the lunch crowd. She needed to go and check with the chef to make sure there weren't any problems with the morning deliveries.

Anthony stepped through the restaurant's front door and walked over to where Vinny sat at the bar. "Where is she?"

Startled, Vinny answered, "In the back, Boss."

"Follow me." As they walked toward the kitchen, Anthony instructed, "While I talk to her, you go into her office and bug the phone. Use this." He dropped a small listening device into Vinny's palm.

"No problem," Vinny answered, closing his hand over it.

As they approached, Anthony saw Regina talking to the chef. He glanced toward her office door and noticed it was open a crack, which made it pretty easy for Vinny as he slipped into the room and disappeared from view.

"Hello, Darling."

Regina jumped. "Anthony, what are you doing here?"

"Chef Paul, please excuse us," Anthony said as he grabbed her by the arm and started walking her toward the back door. "I need to talk to you alone," he hissed.

Before she could protest, Anthony had her outside the building. He spun her toward him and released her arm with a shove. "I heard you had a visitor today," he said as he stood nose-to-nose with her, glaring into her eyes.

"I see Vinny couldn't wait to call." Regina took a step backward.

"He told me you handled yourself very well."

"Now, what else would I do? I know how this works."

"Good."

Anthony closed the distance between them, and she hurriedly asked, "Did you come over here just to tell me that? You could have called."

"I wanted to see your pretty face," he replied as he reached up and brushed her cheek with his hand.

Regina wiped her skin where he had touched her. She had never liked it when he stood close to her or touched her in any way, which amused him. "Very funny. What else do you want, Anthony? I have work to do."

Anthony didn't appreciate her tone and made it known by grabbing her arm again and squeezing it.

"Anthony, stop — you're hurting me! I only asked a simple question."

"Let's get something straight, Babe. You don't ask me questions, simple or otherwise. I'm the only one who can ask questions. Is that clear?"

"Crystal."

"Good." He let go of her arm and continued, "I'm here to convince you to come back to the office with me. Poppy is coming for a visit and I know he would be happy to see you." Regina would be enough of a distraction to buy him more time, in case the accountant was late.

Regina thought *convince* was an interesting word choice. Knowing he wasn't going to accept no for an answer, she took a deep breath and said, "Sure, I'll come with you. I'll go get my purse and lock up first. I also need to give the staff a few minor instructions. Is that okay?" She knew that asking him for permission would calm him down and stroke his ego at the same time.

Anthony eyed her with a superior air. He always enjoyed these little bouts for power. They ended the same every time — with him on top. "Sure, go ahead. I'll wait in the car. Don't take too long."

Regina walked back into the building, rubbing her arm where he had grabbed it. It still stung a little. What was Anthony up to? She stepped out of the kitchen just in time to see Vinny freeze outside her office, the door swinging slightly behind him. *Wait a minute . . . Did he just come out of my office?* As she approached him, she demanded, "What were you doing in my office?"

"I wasn't in your office," he replied matter-of-factly. "I was just standing here waiting for you, ma'am."

Regina didn't buy that. She knew what she had seen but decided it was best to drop it for now. Anthony hated to be kept waiting, especially by his wife. "I'm going to be leaving for a while with Anthony. Tell the staff that if there are any problems to call me on my cell phone."

"Yes, ma'am," Vinny said with a smile.

Regina went in and retrieved her purse from the desk drawer. She looked around her desk, and nothing seemed to have been moved. Still, she had the uneasy feeling that Vinny had been snooping around. Vinny *was* coming out of here — she was almost certain of it. What was he up to — and did it have anything to do with what Anthony was up to? She left and locked the door. She gave the chef some minor instructions and then went out the back way.

Anthony was waiting in the limousine. Mario saw her approaching and climbed out to open the door for her.

"Let's go," Anthony immediately instructed. They drove in silence, which was fine with Regina. It gave her time to think, time to pray, and time to prepare herself to be in her father-in-law's presence.

John arrived home tired and frustrated by his day. Captain Merrill had sent him home early, since he had come in around four a.m. to do paper work. He often did that when he couldn't sleep. John lived alone, except for some goldfish, in a small one-bedroom apartment in Park Slope, Brooklyn.

His living room was dark beige. He wasn't sure it had been painted that color originally, but years had passed since anybody had tried to do anything with the walls. John didn't mind the fading, since he was rarely home anyway. He was able to fit a recliner, a loveseat, and a nineteen-inch color television in the living room area. He had a small portable CD player on an end table next to the recliner. His bedroom was cramped with a double bed; a dresser; and one end table that held a phone, a lamp, and an alarm clock. The bathroom had a tub with a fish shower curtain.

The last area in the apartment was what some would call a kitchen; others would call it a closet. It contained a small oven with a four-burner stove, a refrigerator, a sink, and a small counter that separated the kitchen from the living room. He had two stools by the counter where he ate his meals. It was a small place, but he could afford it, and it was located only about twenty minutes from the precinct.

Out of habit, he went right to the answering machine and hit play. A familiar voice filled the air. *"John, this is your mother. I was wondering if you could stop by for dinner on Sunday. Your sister will be here and . . . well, we all miss you. I love you, Honey. Call me."*

The next message was from some salesperson telling him he'd won free airplane tickets to Florida; all he had to do was examine a time-share in Tampa. The final message was from his sister. *"John, it's Lisa. How are you doing? The kids miss you. I miss you, too. We all hope to see you Sunday. Mom says she's making your favorite — pot roast. Well, anyway, know that you're loved. Bye."*

He couldn't help but think how lucky he was to have a family who cared so much for him. They were always trying to make sure he stayed connected to them.

He felt a bit disappointed that there wasn't a message from Mrs. Cavelli. He was about to press the button and reset his caller ID box when he noticed that it read four new calls. Funny, he thought he'd heard only three. He reviewed the calls listed and noticed that one of them was from Regina's Place.

I wonder why she didn't leave a message. He thought about calling her back but quickly dismissed the idea. Too risky. He didn't want to get her in trouble. Thinking about his next move, he pulled open the refrigerator and saw there wasn't much in there: some beer, an apple, and milk that was probably expired.

"Well," he wondered out loud, "since there doesn't seem to be anything for dinner, maybe I should go out to eat. And wherever shall I go? Regina's Place seems to be as good a place as any."

Mario pulled into the garage next to the two-story office complex. It was about twenty minutes from Regina's restaurant, and the Cavelli family owned the whole building. All their businesses operated from here, each with a name that sounded respectable and completely above board, but what happened behind closed doors was another story. Anthony had his men sweep the building periodically for bugs, and sometimes they found a few. As far as the city cops were concerned, their informant was usually quite reliable. But the Feds were a different story; they planted bugs fairly regularly or positioned men outside to observe the proceedings as best they could.

As Regina and Anthony got out of the car, he asked her, "Do you think you can manage to be civil to my father?"

"Of course, I can. I forgave him a long time ago for forcing me to marry you and live in hell," Regina replied with an edge of sarcasm. She sometimes couldn't help but give snide remarks, especially when she was around Poppy. It was a shortcoming she was still working on.

Instead of being sarcastic in return, Anthony said calmly, "That's exactly what I mean. The old man thinks we are happily married. I'd like to keep it that way. Now just do as you're told and everything will be all right."

Normally he would come back at her or threaten her in some way. For the second time today, Regina wondered if something was wrong. She kept quiet, hoping to pick up on what was really going on.

Stepping into the building with Anthony and Mario at her heels, Regina tried to focus. She always found it difficult to be in Poppy's presence, especially now in her condition. He had always wanted a grandchild. It was a topic that had been on his mind, and lips, since the death of Anthony's mother. *Lord, I need You to help me keep my cool and not give myself away.*

A little prayer never hurt in stressful situations.

They walked into the outer office and a very nervous Mary greeted them. She came out from behind her desk.

"What's the matter with you?" Anthony asked. "You look like you've seen a ghost."

"Mr. Cavelli, your father is in your office," Mary said with much excitement in her voice. "He came about twenty minutes ago and just walked right in. Then he started dictating letters to me. I didn't know what to do! I didn't get a chance to call you. I was just about to now. He's been making phone calls and asking me questions . . ." Mary was very close to being frantic.

"Calm down, will you? Just bring us some coffee and type those letters like he asked. Don't worry about it. Did the accountant drop off anything?"

"No, sir, he hasn't."

This did not seem to make Anthony happy at all. Grabbing Regina by the arm, he whispered, "Don't forget what I told you."

They walked in and found Poppy on the phone, sitting behind Anthony's desk. He motioned for them to come in, as if it was his office they had just walked into. Instantly, heat shot through Anthony's body. He didn't like this situation at all. Poppy had no business, none whatsoever, appearing so comfortable in Anthony's office.

Poppy hung up the phone and, with a huge smile on his face, got up to greet them.

For a second, Anthony smirked at Regina's expression. Hugging her was like trying to hug a fence post. She never returned his father's hugs, but it didn't seem to phase Poppy or discourage him from trying.

"What a pleasant surprise! Anthony, why didn't you tell me Regina was going to be here?" Before Anthony could answer him, he went on, "My son can't seem to tell me if I will ever become a grandfather. Regina, Dear, can you give me an idea?"

"I'm sorry, not yet. You know we're still young. There's plenty of time for that in the future." *Forgive me, Lord, for telling such a lie.* It amazed her how this man seemed to forget that he had forced them to get married. He lived in some fantasy world in which they were all one big, happy family.

Mary walked in with the coffee tray and set it up on the table.

"Okay, I'll drop it for now. But I have a wonderful idea. Why don't we all go to lunch together? I would love to visit with you in a more pleasant environment."

Anthony smiled and said, "That sounds great. I guess we won't be needing that coffee, Mary. Thank you anyway." He turned to his father. "Why don't you two go out to the car? I have some instructions for Mary before we leave."

As soon as they were out of hearing distance, Anthony whispered in a low growl, "Mary, I want you to call the accountant and tell him that he'd better be here with the books before I return from lunch. Make sure he understands — wait. Forget that. Instead tell Jimmy to go there in person and pick it up. He'll know what to do if it's not ready."

"Yes, sir. No problem."

On his way out to the car, Anthony made a call. "Yeah, it's me. Can you talk? Listen, I want to know what he is up to *before* it happens, not after. Why wasn't I told about the visit? That's not what you get paid for! No more excuses — just keep a better eye on him!"

When Anthony joined them in the limousine, he was back to his pseudo cheerful self again. "So, Poppy, where to?"

"Mama Rosa's Seafood Palace. I'm in the mood for some fish."

"Great. Mario, you heard him — Mama Rosa's."

Regina started to pray. *Lord, give me strength to hold down my lunch. And help me to behave in a way that would please You.* It really didn't do her any good to be upset. Nothing ever seemed to change.

John settled down to watch some TV and unwind until it was time for him to go to the restaurant — it was still way too early for dinner. He'd been feeling a little edgy lately, and he hated having time on his hands like this; it made the loneliness seem more apparent.

Most of the time, he didn't consider being sent home early much of a gift, but today it had given him some much-needed time to think. Spread across his lap lay his file on Regina Cavelli. He'd discovered some interesting information about her in the past few months.

For one thing, she had married Anthony during a break from college and had never returned to finish. Her father had worked for Antonio Cavelli as his accountant and had been in police protection when she had suddenly married Anthony. Antonio Cavelli had planned an extravagant wedding for his son and new daughter-in-law. The press was invited to attend, and it was front-page news in all the papers. That was where it got interesting. After the wedding, Michael Palmetto, Regina's father, had "lost his memory" and would no longer testify.

John's brother, Sam, was working on the case at the time.

Sam had been very frustrated by the whole thing. All his hard work had gone out the window with Mr. Palmetto's memory. But as frustrated as he had been, Sam had had so much to live for; he never would have gotten mixed up with drugs. A short time after the Cavelli wedding, Sam had been found in his apartment, dead from a drug overdose. They had ruled it an accidental suicide, but John would never buy that. He knew his brother too well.

The doorbell rang and roused him from his thoughts. *Who can that be?* John slid the folder under the couch cushion and walked over to the door. "Oh, hi, Frank. Come on in."

"Hey, John. I'm here on an important mission from Annie."

"What's up?"

"She told me and I quote, 'Don't come home unless John is with you.' She says she misses you and so do the kids. They've been asking for their Uncle Johnny. They want to spend some time with you this afternoon since there's no school today."

"That's sweet, but I plan on having Chinese food later. I have a craving. Then I was going to turn in early. I haven't been sleeping so good lately."

"Are you trying to get me into the doghouse with my woman? You know how Annie gets. Come on — you know I can't go home without you. Besides, Annie is a great cook. You know she'll want you to stay for dinner. Come on; we'll drive over together." John didn't respond, so Frank continued, "I promise you, I'll get you home early enough to get a good night's sleep."

John realized that if he didn't go, it would look suspicious. "Okay, but I'll take my own car. I'll meet you downstairs."

"All right, but if you're not down there in ten minutes, I'm coming back after you." Frank left with a big smile on his face.

Maybe an after-dinner drink then . . . John grabbed his keys, shut off the lights, and went out the door.

The ride to Mama Rosa's was harmless enough. What Poppy said out loud didn't worry Regina as much as what was going on in his head. As they arrived and were seated, her worry only worsened. Poppy might be old and retired from the business, but men like him always retained their power: the power to harm, to control, and to ruin lives. That was what these men did. She just couldn't have them influencing the future of her child; that could not be allowed to happen. This baby was innocent and helpless, and it would be up to her, and her alone, to hold on to that innocence for as long as she could . . .

"Regina," Poppy repeated. "Regina."

Regina startled. She barely remembered getting to the restaurant, much less being seated. "I'm sorry, Poppy. How rude of me. I was thinking about some plans I have for the restaurant. What do you think about live entertainment?" It was the best save she could come up with; she knew asking it would make him feel important, and because of that, the question would please Anthony as well.

"Well, my dear, that sounds like a very good idea. I knew if I bought you that place you would make it successful. You should be very proud of your wife, Anthony." Poppy's face glowed with pride.

"Of course I am, Poppy," Anthony said with a plastic smile. This was his own doing; for whatever reason, he had chosen to endure an afternoon of hearing Regina's praises sung from the rooftop, and he wasn't going to enjoy it. Regina could see his smile's insincerity from across the table and wondered how Poppy didn't.

"After lunch, Anthony, I would like to go back to the office with you and look over the books. That's still okay with you?"

Anthony's hesitation was barely discernable. "No problem," he responded with the same brittle smile.

Just then, the waiter came over to the table. "Good afternoon. My name is Carmine, and I will be your server today. May I take your order, or do you need some more time?" He looked about fifteen, but Regina knew that he was more than likely a college student. He was tall, thin, pimple-faced, and had a huge smile.

Anthony seemed grateful for the interruption. "No, I think we're ready. I'm getting hungry. Sweetie, do you know what you want?"

Regina hated it when Anthony called her names like *sweetie* or *honey*. She just had to grin and bear it when Poppy was around. But she knew one thing for certain now: Something was up with Anthony. He was so edgy.

He always acted like this around Poppy, but it was more noticeable today than usual. They placed their order.

"Would anyone like a cocktail or an appetizer?"

Anthony said, "I'll have a scotch on the rocks."

Poppy glanced at him. "Don't you think it's a bit early to have a drink, son?"

Anthony ignored him. "Just bring it," he told the waiter.

Quiet, Regina put her napkin in her lap and pretended not to have noticed how much he had just given himself away. *Edgy*, apparently, wasn't the right word; Anthony was downright moody. What was his problem?

"Anyone else?" Carmine asked.

"Espresso," Poppy said.

"I'll just have water," Regina added. Carmine left.

Poppy returned his attention to Regina. "When was the last time you saw your folks?" he asked, casually overlooking the way his son had just dismissed him.

"Last week. They're doing fine." She paused. "Thank you again for keeping them safe and hidden so well." She said that only because she knew you could catch more bees with honey than with vinegar. He acted like she saw them regularly, when she was taken to see them only twice monthly — if she was lucky.

How could she leave Anthony . . . and still keep her parents safe? She was not allowed to call them; they could call her once a week, but the calls were always monitored. She hoped that one day, she'd be able to save them completely and have them home again. It was a situation she tried to change whenever the opportunity came up, and now seemed as good of a time as any.

"Poppy, do you think all of this secrecy is still so necessary?" As soon as the words came out of her mouth, she realized this hadn't been a good idea. Anthony shot her a look. Questioning any Cavelli could be dangerous. She knew she took a chance every time she asked about her parents, but Poppy genuinely seemed to enjoy her and her company, so, perhaps, she wasn't as afraid of mentioning it as Anthony would like her to be.

"Regina, my dear," Poppy started, "I do believe we have been over this before. It's for their protection and for yours that I have them hidden.

Realize that if the unpleasantness of the past did not get in the way, things would be very different now. We would all be here having lunch together. But, of course, that is not possible. You know there are people out there who want to hurt the family. As a matter of fact . . ."

He paused as the waiter came back with the drinks and salads. When he had gone again, Poppy continued, "As a matter of fact, I hear you had some interesting visitors today."

Poppy gave them a moment to absorb what he had said.

Regina was not surprised. Of course, he would know; he was Poppy. But Anthony seemed a bit taken aback. He stared at his father, a line between his brows.

"Two detectives came to see if I knew anything about the family business. I told them I didn't, and then they left. That was the end of that. It really wasn't a big deal." Regina made note of Anthony's reaction and realized that Poppy hadn't gotten this information from his son. Interesting how father and son didn't trust each other; each played games to impress the other.

"I'm proud of the way you handled yourself. You have been an asset to this family from the beginning. I always knew that you would be. It was nice to see how you and my son have gotten along. Who says arranged marriages don't work?" Poppy smiled broadly and continued on that subject for what seemed like an eternity. They finished their salads, and the waiter came over with their entrees.

"Thank you, Carmine. This smells wonderful." The rest of the meal was spent in idle chitchat, mostly dominated by Poppy. Regina and Anthony nodded and smiled often to show they were paying attention.

Both wished they were elsewhere.

John pulled into the parking space behind Frank's blue sedan as his partner climbed out and headed toward him. *All right, let's get this over with.* John opened his door.

"Thanks for coming. I wouldn't hear the end of it if I showed up here without you," Frank said, sounding relieved.

"No problem. Annie is a terrific cook, and I always enjoy seeing the little rug rats."

As they walked up to the front door, Frank's youngest child, Nick, came running out of the house, shouting, "Daddy's home! Daddy's home!" He launched himself into his father's arms. "Oh, looky! It's Uncle Johnny, too. Hi, Uncle Johnny!"

Nick left his father's embrace and ran to John. At five years old, Nick already wanted to be a detective like his father and Uncle Johnny. He thought they were the best. His dark hair and big, brown doe eyes could convince you to do just about anything. As they got to the door, Frank's middle child, Lynette, greeted them. She was a twelve-year-old beauty with long, reddish-brown hair and green eyes.

"Hi, Dad. Hi, Uncle Johnny. I'm helping with dinner," she said with pride. Then she turned and yelled at the top of her lungs, "Mom! Dad and Uncle Johnny are here!"

"Where's your sister?" Frank asked.

"You mean her highness? She's upstairs in her room. She's too cool to associate with us mere peasants. She's in high school now, you know."

"Now, Lynette, that's not very nice, is it?"

Lynette just shrugged her shoulders.

"Nicole, I'm home," Frank yelled up the stairs as Annie entered the room and welcomed them both with hugs. Annie was a very beautiful woman with shoulder-length red hair and green eyes. She looked much younger than her age. People often thought her eldest daughter, Nicole, was her sister.

"Oh, John, it's so nice to see you. I'm so glad you came. We've missed you around here. Sit and make yourself comfortable. Lynette, go check on the sauce. Nick, Sweetheart, go wash your hands — they're filthy. Honey, would you go see what's keeping our elder daughter? I want her to set the table."

Now looking back at John she said, "Do you want a drink? We have soda, wine, beer, water . . ." Annie said all of this without even coming up for air. She sure was a fast talker, but John didn't mind at all because she usually could carry the conversation by herself. All you ever had to do was nod once or twice so she knew you were paying attention.

"Soda is fine, thanks," he answered.

Finally, Nicole descended the stairs as if she were royalty making an entrance at a ball. A younger version of her mother, she had the greenest eyes and the reddest hair. Frank always told John stories about her latest boyfriends. "Hello, Uncle John. Hello, Father. Did you guys kill anyone today?" she asked sarcastically, with a smile.

"Very funny, kiddo. Give Daddy a kiss?"

She walked over and greeted him with a peck on the cheek.

"You get prettier every time I see you, Nicole," John said. It brought a smile to her face and she graced him with a peck on the cheek.

"So who's this week's heart break?" John asked with a sly smile.

"Daddy! You talk way too much about us at work." Nicole rolled her eyes at her father, but she smiled at John to let him know she had liked his question.

Annie re-entered the room with drinks for her men. "Nicole, please go set the table," she requested firmly.

"Mom, dinner isn't for another hour. Can't I do it later and visit with Uncle John and Daddy?"

Annie, a very structured and organized woman, preferred things to be prepared in advance. "Just do it now and get it over with. You'll have plenty of time to visit later when all the work is done." Nicole left, looking unhappy. "Why don't you fellas go into the living room and sit and relax? I'll be back after I check on the girls, and we can have a nice visit."

Regina sat in her office and tried to figure out what Vinny could have possibly been doing in there earlier. Anthony obviously didn't trust her. She wondered if he somehow knew about the copies she'd made of his private book, but she doubted it. If he had, he would have made her life much more miserable than it already was, if not worse. She had been surprised to find out at lunch that Poppy wanted to get involved in business again; that would make Anthony even more difficult to live with.

But back to the matter at hand — Vinny.

Think, Regina, think. Use the brain God gave you.

Her gaze landed on the antique phone on her desk, and for some reason, she felt a draw to it. She lifted the receiver, unscrewed one end, and was not surprised to see a tiny electrical device hidden inside. This wouldn't be the first time he had done something like this. Instead of being angry, she wondered if she could use this to her advantage. Anthony had no idea she'd discovered his little bug. Of course, if he'd bugged her office phone, what else had he bugged? Was her car or even her home safe?

But who was she kidding? Home was never safe. *Lord, show me the way out.*

The knock on her door startled her. She quickly screwed the receiver back together.

"Come in."

The door opened, and it was Dave, one of the bartenders. "Mrs. Cavelli, I thought you might like to know that we're out of gin."

"Did you check the cellar? We were supposed to have gotten a shipment today. Didn't it come in while I was out?"

"No, I've already checked the cellar. We don't have any. I guess I can stretch out what we've got."

"No watered-down drinks. If you run out, then apologize and give a free drink of something else."

"No problem." Dave started to leave, but then he hesitated, and a frown pulled across his forehead. "Mrs. Cavelli, is everything okay?

"Sure, Dave. Why do you ask?"

"You look like something's bothering you."

"This is the third time this has happened in the past two weeks. I'll have to change suppliers. I don't like firing anybody."

"Don't worry, Mrs. Cavelli. If you'd like, I'll call them for you."

"Thanks, but no. I'll take care of it. Thank you for your concern, Dave."

Dave was obviously not satisfied with her answer, but there was nothing for him to do if she didn't want his help. An ex-con, he was as big as an ox but as gentle as a lamb. Regina had hired him six months ago, believing that everyone deserved a second chance. He was a very hard worker and was getting married for the first time at thirty-five. Lauren, his fiancé, led the Bible study Regina sometimes attended.

Dave was very loyal to Regina because she had done so much for him. He didn't like Anthony, or his men. More than once, Regina had broken up some near skirmishes between Dave and some of Anthony's crew. She would hate for anything to happen to him because he was defending her.

Sitting in his semi-dark office, Anthony was on the phone. He wasn't happy and was getting more upset by the moment. "Look, you moron, what saved you today is the fact I had lunch with my father, and by the time we were back, you had the books ready. If he finds anything amiss, you can kiss your family good-bye."

Anthony slammed down the receiver. He had bigger problems on his hands than that idiot, like what to do about his father. He'd grown accustomed to being the boss; his men had grown accustomed to his being the boss, too, and he didn't relish being sent back to second place. That couldn't be allowed to happen.

Mario knocked then stuck his head in the door. "Hey, Boss, is everything okay? I heard you yelling. You want me to take care of something or somebody for ya?"

"No. That moron accountant won't make the same mistake again." He rubbed the back of his neck, scowling. "Poppy is starting to . . . Poppy is starting to breathe down my neck. He wants back in, and I know he wants full control again. The old man didn't fool me for a minute. I won't let it happen! I'm in charge, and that's the way it's going to stay."

Mario couldn't believe how Anthony was talking about his own father. He knew Anthony was ruthless, but he almost sounded like he was threatening Poppy, something Mario had never thought possible, even for him. Mario didn't know what to say or what to do, so he remained silent and just stood there, waiting for further direction.

"You know," Anthony began, "if only I could find a way to distract him from this idea of coming back to work . . . but what?" He got up and started to pace.

"Well . . ." Mario began, but then, after getting that one word out, he wasn't sure he wanted to continue.

"Well, what?"

"Well, Boss, if Regina was pregnant, he'd be busy with the grandchild he always wanted. He wouldn't care about the business then. He'd be too consumed with chasing after a grandkid."

Anthony looked at Mario like he had ten heads. "Are you crazy? That would mean I would have to . . . ya know. That only happened once, and

I was drunk at the time. That won't work. She hates my guts as much as I hate hers." He hesitated for a moment and then continued, "But you know . . . Regina could be the key. I don't get it, but the old man acts like mush when she's around. It really bugs me. The thing is, how do we use that to our advantage?"

"I don't know, Boss."

"Maybe between the two of us we could come up with something. You hungry?" Without waiting for an answer, Anthony continued, "Let's go get some pasta, okay?"

"Sure, Boss. I'll get the car."

Before Anthony left, he looked at the picture of Regina on his desk. He kept one there for appearance's sake. Every man had a picture of his wife on his desk, and he didn't want to cause suspicion with Poppy.

Anthony picked up the picture of Regina and said, "You're going to help me get the old man off my back, whether you know it or not."

Sliding onto a barstool, Regina told Dave, "I'll have some water."

"Sure thing." Dave poured her a glass of bottled water and then looked at her with concern. "I wish you would tell me what's wrong. I might be able to help."

"Not yet. Just pray for me, okay?" Changing the subject with barely a pause, Regina said, "Did you see the ad in the paper about the auditions?"

"Yeah, I did. It looked good. What type of entertainment are you looking for?"

"I'm not sure yet — a band, a singer, a piano player? Whatever."

Regina turned around in time to see Detective John Nelson walking through the front door. Her heart stopped. "Oh, no," she said as she quickly turned back around.

"What's the matter, Mrs. Cavelli?"

Panicking, she asked, "Where's Vinny?"

"He left about fifteen minutes ago. He said he had an errand to run and he'd be back in an hour. Why?"

That made Regina feel a bit more at ease, but her mind started to race. She had to find a way to arrange a less-public meeting. *What am I thinking? That's not going to work. Lord, what am I going to do? He's heading my way. Help me find the right words to say to him.*

John walked over and sat down two stools away from Regina without looking at her. To Dave he said, "I'll have a club soda with lemon please."

Dave poured the drink and dropped a healthy slice of lemon in the glass. "Will that be all, sir?"

"Yes, thank you."

"That'll be two bucks."

John reached for his wallet, but then Regina suddenly said, "The drink's on the house, Dave."

"Yes, ma'am."

"That's very nice of you, Mrs. Cavelli," John said, without looking in her direction.

Dave walked down to the other end of the bar to serve another customer. Regina glanced around to make sure no one was watching. Aware that her heart was still pounding like mad, she looked down at her water, trying not to draw attention to the fact they were about to start a conversation.

"Detective Nelson, what are you doing here? I thought I made myself quite clear when you were here earlier that I have nothing to say to you."

"Yes, ma'am, you did. I thought that maybe you'd be more willing to talk to me if we were alone." He took a drink from his glass. "I've been reading about you."

"You've been investigating me?"

"No, I just wanted to learn more about you. It seems that you're a kind woman with a good heart, and you help people."

"Oh, I see."

"So what puzzles me is how someone like you is married to a monster like Anthony Cavelli."

"Look, this conversation is dangerous for both of us. Maybe you should leave."

"I need your help. You can trust me."

"I can't trust anyone. Trust is expensive." She paused then continued, "If I decide to help you, you need to understand that no one must know. I would be risking everything."

"I promise. Does that mean you'll help me?" John glanced at her. The possibility sent butterflies through his stomach.

"Look, I'm deadly serious. I need your word that you will keep this just between us, or else no deal. You can't even tell your partner, understand?"

Without showing any of the emotions he was feeling, John responded simply, "Yeah, I understand. And I promise."

"Now please leave before someone notices that I'm talking to you."

"Thanks for the drink, Mrs. Cavelli." John got up and started toward the door. As he stepped through it, he passed Vinny coming in. He tried to keep his head down, but he knew that Vinny had seen him. *I hope this doesn't cause her any trouble.*

Vinny walked over to the bar and sat down next to Regina. She was startled to see him but tried to disguise that by saying, "Oh, it's you. Thank God. You wouldn't believe who had the nerve to drop by *again.*" She made certain she emphasized that word.

"You mean Detective Nelson."

"Yes, how did you know?" she asked, as if surprised. "Did you see him?"

"Yes, I did. Is everything okay?"

"He came in for a drink. He sat over there. I think he just wants me to know that he's watching me, to keep me on my toes."

"Mrs. Cavelli, I would appreciate it if you didn't mention this to the boss."

"Why would you want me to keep something from him, Vinny?" Regina knew how to play this game. Now it seemed she had an advantage, and she was about to take it.

"Well, he told me to watch out for you, and if he finds out I left, even though it was just for a little while, I could get in a lot of trouble. I would appreciate it, ma'am, if we kept Detective Nelson's little visit between us. Okay? I mean, nothing happened, right? You're okay and all — no harm done."

"I wouldn't want to get you in trouble, Vinny. I don't think this will be a problem. Besides, you're right; it's no big deal, anyway. This is a public place and anyone can come in for a drink. Right?"

"Yes, ma'am. Thank you."

Vinny seemed appreciative that Regina had agreed, and Regina was so grateful it was Vinny's idea that she didn't even stop to think about his motives.

Driving home, John started to smile to himself. He turned on the radio to relax.

He was so excited. This could be the break he'd been waiting for, and he wanted to make sure everything went smoothly. Seeing Anthony Cavelli in jail would bring this chapter of his life to a rather satisfying conclusion.

Chapter 3

Regina was still asleep when Anthony left for the day. It was nice to wake up to a peaceful house. They lived in a two-story penthouse apartment, but most of the time Regina felt like she was living in a museum more than a home. Anthony had decorated it with expensive furniture and works of art, none of which he knew anything about. Regina loved art and Anthony often sent her to auctions to build up their collection, but he didn't care about the details; he just enjoyed having a rich man's home.

Making her way to the kitchen, Regina slipped into a chair at the table and sipped the mint tea Lilly handed her. Lilly believed mint tea helped settle the stomach and was a decent cure for just about everything else.

"I worry about you, Regina. You've been so sick lately." Lilly paused. "If I didn't know better . . . you aren't pregnant . . . are you?"

The look of horror on Regina's face spoke volumes. For a moment, both women were at a loss for words. Lilly just stared at Regina, wide-eyed and amazed.

All Regina could do was nod her head. She placed a finger to her lips so Lilly wouldn't say anything else. "Lilly, you have such a sense of humor," she said, laughing.

After finding the bug in her office phone, she couldn't be certain that even her home was a safe place to speak. She motioned for Lilly to follow her. They went out and walked down the hall to the incinerator room. It wasn't very spacious and the two of them barely fit inside together, but it was the safest place Regina could think of on short notice.

Once there, Regina spoke in hushed tones. "I don't want you getting involved. It could be dangerous for you, Lilly. I haven't told anyone except my parents, and I haven't been to a doctor yet. I just couldn't risk Anthony finding out."

"Did this happen because of that night?" Lilly asked quietly.

"Yes, but it's not this child's fault who his or her father is, or how it came to be."

"Regina, you need to get away before he finds out," Lilly begged her, reaching for her hand in the shadows.

"If I run away, he'll hunt me down. If I stay, I'll endanger my child. I'm stuck between a rock and a hard place."

"You do realize it's better to leave than to stay, though — right?"

Regina looked away and didn't answer her.

"I'll do whatever you need me to do. I'm not afraid. The Lord will protect us. I couldn't help you that night, but . . ."

Lilly had a hard time finishing her sentence. They hadn't spoken much about it, but Regina knew her old friend still felt guilty that she hadn't been able to protect her from Anthony's advances the night Regina was raped.

Regina placed her hand on Lilly's shoulder. "There was nothing you could do that night. The door was locked and guarded by his men. Besides, if you *would* have gotten in, what do you think would have happened to you?"

Lilly didn't respond.

"But there is something you could do for me. I need you to go to a pay phone and call this number." She handed her John Nelson's phone number. "It's the detective who came to my restaurant."

"Are you sure about this? What if he's working for Anthony?"

"There's no chance of that. I've checked him out. You won't believe this, but he's Sam Nelson's brother. Do you remember him?"

"Oh, yes, that poor man who was guarding your father."

"I doubt that he would work for the man he probably blames for his brother's death. I'm sure he wants to get to the truth of what really happened. We both know that wasn't a suicide, accidental or otherwise. I'm pretty sure I can trust him."

Lilly nodded her consent. "What do you want me to say to him?"

"I want to meet him alone tomorrow at five thirty a.m. at my parents' house in Brooklyn. It's been empty since they've been away. Tell him to park his car around the corner and go through the alley to the back of the house. I'll leave the back door open. Do you remember the address, Lilly?"

"I'm not getting that old," Lilly replied with a smile. "Are you sure you can get away that early?"

"Tonight Anthony plays poker. You know how he gets — he plays all night. If I meet the detective that early, I can still get back in plenty of time before Anthony comes home. He won't even know I've been gone."

"What about the man he has guarding your door at night?" Lilly asked.

"When he goes out, it's usually just Jimmy. I'll slip him some of Anthony's sleeping pills."

"Regina, promise me you'll be careful."

"Please, don't worry. I'll be fine." Regina tried to reassure her.

"Before we go back to the apartment, can we pray?" Lilly asked, almost pleading.

"That's a good idea. I know it'll make me feel better."

So they prayed right there in the little incinerator room. It wasn't a long prayer, but God knew their hearts. They felt His peaceful presence and strength to continue with what lay ahead.

Mary walked into the office, placed her bag in her desk drawer, picked up her steno pad and a pen, and knocked on Anthony's door.

"Come in."

"You're in early today, Mr. Cavelli."

"With the FBI always breathing down my neck, and now my father, this is the only place where I can think. Is there any coffee ready?"

"No, sir. I just came in, but I'll go make some. I saw your car when I got in and wanted to see if you needed anything."

"I need coffee!" Anthony snapped.

"Right away, Mr. Cavelli." Mary quickly left the room. He was more irritated than usual, which wasn't a good sign for the rest of the day.

When she returned with the coffee a few minutes later, Anthony was absorbed in the book in front of him and didn't seem to notice she was there.

"Is that anything I can help you with?" Mary politely asked.

"No! If I want your help, I'll ask for it. Go file or something. Can't you see I'm busy?"

"I'm sorry, Mr. Cavelli. I'll be at my desk if you need anything."

She rushed out of the office, determined to stay away from him for the rest of the day. Whenever he got like this, he was dangerous to be around. She wiped the tear from her cheek. Why did she put up with his treatment of her? The money was good, but it really wasn't worth it anymore. She was afraid to quit, because she knew too much of the Cavelli business dealings, and the last thing in the world she wanted to do was make a man like Anthony Cavelli angry. She couldn't help wondering what in the world he, of all people, was doing with a book of herbs and natural medicines, but she wasn't about to ask. Being a secretary meant that you pretended not to notice things you weren't supposed to see in the first place.

John was just about halfway out the door when he heard the phone ring. Should he answer or let it ring? It could be Mrs. Cavelli. He rushed to the phone and picked it up. "Hello?"

"Is this Detective John Nelson?"

It sounded like a woman. He didn't recognize the voice. "Yes. Who's this?"

"That doesn't matter. I'm calling for a mutual friend."

"What friend is that?" John asked.

"Look, I can't say over the phone, but trust me; you'll want to meet her."

It was a *her.* Maybe she was talking about Mrs. Cavelli. It had to be — who else could it be?

"This friend wants to meet you tomorrow morning at five thirty in Brooklyn. Do you have something to write with?"

John saw a pen on the table but had no paper nearby, so his hand would have to do. "Okay, where?"

"The address is 563 Avenue N, in Brooklyn. Park your car a block away and go through the alley to the back of the house. The back door will be left open."

"I'll be there."

"On a personal note, detective, please make sure nothing happens to our mutual friend. She is very special to me."

The phone went dead before he could respond.

Sudden excitement overwhelmed him. Whether it was the woman herself or the very real prospect of a break in the case, he wasn't sure, but he felt almost giddy about seeing her again and it surprised him. His mind filled with images of their last encounter. She seemed so confident, yet her sad eyes told a different story.

The phone rang and Regina's assistant, Kelly, answered. "Good morning — Regina's Place. May I help you?"

"Kelly, it's Lilly. Is she available?"

"Yes, hold on, Lilly." Kelly pressed the intercom button and said, "Regina, it's Lilly on line two."

In her office, Regina picked up the phone. "Lilly, what can I do for you?"

"I just wanted you to know that I was able to pick up the cleaning for you today. I'm about to go to the market, and I wanted to know if you needed anything special."

"There isn't anything. Thank you, Lilly. I appreciate your help this morning. I'll see you later."

Knowing the phone was bugged, Regina and Lilly had worked out a system. If she hadn't been able to contact Detective Nelson, Lilly would have said that the cleaning wouldn't be ready until tomorrow. But as it was, Regina knew the meeting was set for five thirty tomorrow morning. She probably wouldn't be able to finish taking pictures of Anthony's book before then, so what she had would have to be sufficient.

It was too dangerous for her to try to develop the film herself. She was sure Detective Nelson could take care of that. *Oh, Lord, I hope I'm right about him. If Anthony ever found out I'm helping the cops . . .* She didn't want to think about it.

Kelly entered and said, "Regina, the acts are ready to audition. Are you ready, or do you need some more time?"

"No, I'll be happy to see them now. Would you mind helping me?"

"My pleasure." After a short pause, Kelly said, "Are you okay?"

"Yeah, I'm okay. I'm a bit tired is all."

"The first act is almost done setting up their equipment."

"Okay then, Kelly, let's do this."

Regina was so glad she had someone as dependable and hardworking as Kelly to assist her. She knew how hard it had to be for Kelly as a single mom, and so she had been certain to help her out in any way she could, such as allowing her sick leave when her son had become ill. She had paid the doctors' bills that the insurance company hadn't covered and wouldn't let Kelly pay her back. In return, Regina could not have asked for a better, more dedicated, more faithful employee. There was nothing Kelly wouldn't do for her.

Regina and Kelly took a seat at one of the front tables. After a few minor adjustments, the first group was ready. The singer introduced everyone. "Hello, my name is Jacqueline, and our bass player is Frenchie. Roger is our guitarist, and our drummer is Tommy Z. We're called Passion." The up-beat song they performed was positive and inspiring. Regina couldn't help but notice the Christian overtones in the words. When they were done, she thanked them.

Most of the acts that showed up were not the type Regina would want to represent her restaurant, but there were a couple of good acts, a comedian, and a piano player who also caught her eye. It was hard to make a decision between three different performers. After talking to Kelly, Regina decided to have Passion work on the weekends. The comedian, who was funny in a clean, family-friendly way, would open for the group and entertain between sets. The piano player she decided to use during the week to play during the dinner rush. This way she could offer a variety and didn't have to choose among them.

"You know, Regina, I think this is going to work out really well."

"If they agree to our terms, then place an ad in the paper to announce it. We'll start this new lineup next weekend."

"Yes, ma'am."

Antonio's limousine hummed down a narrow, curvy road lined with trees on either side. He'd been traveling for over two hours, and much of that time had been spent deep in thought. He always chose his words carefully. He believed much could be accomplished if it were spoken with quiet authority. If people believed you meant what you said, then action needn't always follow.

Here, today, that was especially important, because he needed to have her believe him.

Stuart made a turn onto a dirt road most people wouldn't realize was there, and followed the path through the trees until the limo reached a tiny blue house with white shutters. Stuart slipped out and opened Antonio's door. "Any special instructions, sir?"

"No, Stuart. Just wait here. This shouldn't take very long."

"As you wish, sir," Stuart replied.

Antonio went up the stairs and knocked on the door. A few quiet moments later, it opened, and there stood Sophia Palmetto. *As beautiful as ever*, he thought to himself. It had been so long since he had last seen her. Time had been very good to her. She was a beautiful woman, with soft brown eyes and dark brown hair that was only slightly gray.

"Hello, Sophia," Antonio said, his voice just above a whisper.

She stood there looking at him, as if she couldn't fathom what he was doing on her doorstep after all these years. Words seemed to escape her.

Before Antonio could speak again, Michael came to the door. He, unlike his wife, had changed quite a bit. He'd grown thin, and his hair was completely gray.

"Sophia, honey, who is . . . ?" He stopped.

For a second, no one said a word. Then Michael's voice deepened, and he demanded, "Antonio, what are you doing here?"

The words and tone were no harsher than Antonio had been expecting. "If it's all right with you both, I'd like to come in and talk." He was not fazed by Michael's reaction to him. It was to be expected, after he'd kept Regina from them all these years.

Another moment passed. Then Michael said, his voice still unforgiving, "Come in."

"I just wanted to talk to you about Regina."

"Is there something wrong with her?" Michael quickly asked.

"No, no, nothing like that," he answered as he settled onto the couch. "I had lunch with her and Anthony yesterday."

He didn't miss Sophia's sudden glare. She resented the fact that he could see her daughter whenever he wanted. *I didn't come to rub it in your face*, he thought, frowning. Out loud, he said, "I see how much she misses both of you. I've been thinking that maybe we can make different arrangements."

Sophia spoke up for the first time. "Are you saying we can come home?"

"I thought we could discuss the possibility. I would need to be assured that what happened the last time would not happen again. Regina asked if you both could come home. At the time I said it wasn't possible, but maybe I'm being too harsh. The kids have been married for many years now and soon we will become grandparents."

Sophia's eyes widened. "A-Are you trying to tell us something we should know?"

"Unfortunately there are no babies on the horizon." He took a deep breath. "To tell the truth, Regina is not the only one that misses you." He was looking at Sophia when he said it, but before she could flush, he continued, "I mean the both of you, of course. There was a time we were also friends, Michael."

Michael didn't respond. He didn't need to.

"I've written down the terms, and if you're willing to live by them, then we can work something out."

He handed Michael the paper. Michael looked it over carefully and then gave it to his wife. She read the contents.

"If you decide that you will agree to this, I'll make arrangements for you to come home by the end of the week."

"What about Anthony? You know how he feels about Michael."

"Don't worry about Anthony; he's my concern." Antonio got up from the sofa and headed for the door. "I'll wait for your answer. Good day."

His visit didn't last very long, and he was gone as suddenly as he came.

Michael and Sophia looked at each other. Wordlessly, they went out to the porch and watched as the limousine drove away. When they could no longer see it, they stepped onto the path in front of their house and took a walk.

"What do you suppose he's up to, Sophia? Do you think he knows about the baby?"

"I don't know," she said, shaking her head. She reached over and took his hand in hers. "I'm so sorry. I know that my past is what has gotten us in this situation." Her voice trembled. "I hope you know how much I do love you."

Michael stopped walking. He turned to her and touched her face gently. "Sophia, we've been over this a hundred times. I forgave you long ago. It's time for you to forgive yourself." He took her hand, and they continued their walk. "It's my reaction to the past that finds us in this mess. It's my fault. I should have known better. If I hadn't tried to testify against him . . . and now it's Regina who is paying the biggest price."

"I know," Sophia said simply. Regina, their little girl, was the one suffering for their mistakes. She looked down at the paper in her hand. "I guess the promise to not ever cooperate with the police is easy enough. But 'family dinners' at his house on occasion — what do you suppose he's up to with that? Does he think we will become one big happy family? That we can forget about the exile we've been in for so long or the fact that his son threatened to kill you? I can't believe he's foolish enough to think that Regina and Anthony's marriage is for real after she made a deal with him."

"I don't know what's going on, Sophia, but wouldn't it be nice to see Regina more, especially now? She's in more danger now than ever. What happened to her is my fault. I put her in a situation where she felt she had to protect me."

She squeezed his hand. "Michael, don't do this to yourself. Playing the blame game will not help Regina. If we can be strong and cooperate for now, then we can get close to our daughter again. Maybe we can help her. Besides, Antonio would never allow any harm to come to her. I think we should go inside and start to pack."

"You're probably right, but Antonio's not the one I'm worried about. I'll call him tonight to let him know."

Anthony's voice blared over the intercom. "Mary, is Mario out there?"

"Yes, sir, he is. So is Vinny. Do you want to see them?"

"Just send in Mario."

Mario got up, smirking like an eleven-year-old. "You heard him." He loved it when Anthony excluded Vinny on anything. He went into the office, closing the door behind him.

Obviously, Vinny didn't appreciate being shut out. There had been several instances lately, just small things, where the boss had seemed to prefer Mario over Vinny, which didn't make sense, and Vinny didn't like being kept in the dark.

He frowned at the door a moment, and then, becoming aware of Mary's sympathetic expression, he asked, "Hey, Mary, would you mind getting me a bagel with cream cheese? I'll buy you one, too, if you go pick it up. I want to stay close by in case the boss needs me."

"Sure thing, Vinny. Since it's your treat, mind if I get a cappuccino to go with that?"

In response, Vinny took out his wallet and handed her some cash.

"Would you mind covering the phones for me?" Mary asked.

"No problem." Vinny gave her a wink.

"I'll be back in a bit."

Vinny walked over to her desk and sat in her seat. "I'll keep your seat warm, Mary. Thanks again." He made sure she was out the door before he lowered the volume on the intercom and turned it on.

"So you understand, Mario. I need your discretion on this one. Arsenic isn't hard to find and we don't need much. It just can't be traced back to me."

"I understand, Boss. Are you sure it won't kill her?"

"Yeah, I'm sure. I'm not stupid; I did my research. Her getting sick is enough of a diversion for the old man. Timing is everything."

Vinny had heard enough. Keeping an eye on the door, he shut off the intercom and took out his cell phone. Whispering he said, "Yeah, it's me. We've gotta talk. It's getting out of hand. Okay, I'll meet you there later."

He knew Anthony was talking about Regina. He couldn't believe he would hurt her.

This job was getting harder all the time.

John walked into the precinct feeling better than he had in days. Grinning like a little boy with a frog in each pocket, he knew he had to try to contain himself or everybody within shouting distance was going to know something was up. Frank was already at John's desk.

"Hey, man, what are you smiling about?" his partner asked, folding his arms and leaning against the front of John's desk.

"Oh, I had a good time last night. I'm glad I went. Tell Annie I appreciate the home cooking."

"She'll be happy to hear that. I'm happy you came, too. Maybe next time you won't give me such a hard time about it." Frank chuckled and then continued, "You know the kids also enjoy seeing ya. That reminds me — I have something for you." He reached into his jacket pocket and pulled out what appeared to be braided string. "Lynette forgot to give this to you yesterday. She made it in school and wants you to have it."

"What is it?"

"It's a friendship bracelet. If you ask me, I think Lynette has a little crush on you, and she was too embarrassed to give it to you herself."

"Lynette embarrassed. Now those are two words I never thought I would hear together. Will you thank her for me? And tell her I'll wear it all the time. Give me a hand, will you?"

Frank helped John tie the bracelet around his wrist. John smiled to himself again and thought what a lucky man Frank was to have such a wonderful family. Maybe one day he'd try having a wife and kids himself. But not just yet.

"So tell me: Are you still hot on the trail of Regina Cavelli this morning?" Frank asked, only half joking.

"No," John lied. "I've decided you're right. It wouldn't do the case, or me, any good. Besides, she seems so straight-laced. She probably didn't know anything. It looks like she's very involved in her restaurant."

"Good. You know men like Anthony Cavelli don't mix business with pleasure. We just have to wait. He'll mess up sooner or later. We have a lot of good informers out there and time is on our side."

"Yeah. You're right." John wanted to tell Frank the truth, but he had promised Regina. Maybe he could convince her Frank was trustworthy. But for now, it was better if the conversation ended.

"Hey, the captain gave us a new case. Here's the profile." Frank handed him a folder.

Great, that was all he needed now — another case. There was only one case on his mind, but he grabbed the file and said, "Thanks," anyway.

A man sat on a bench near the gazebo in Prospect Park, reading his newspaper. He was surrounded by the usual afternoon activities: Runners jogged by; fallen leaves danced in the breeze; and nearby an elderly couple was feeding some pigeons.

Vinny took it all in as he walked over to the water fountain next to the bench. As he bent down to get a drink, he spoke quietly. "He's planning on poisoning her. I'm not sure when. I overheard him say he's not trying to kill her, just make her sick. I'll keep a close eye on the situation and let you know if he really acts on it."

"Just make sure nothing happens to her," the man with the newspaper replied.

Vinny finished drinking and walked away.

The man behind the paper stayed there until Vinny was long gone.

Regina enjoyed mingling among her clientele. She made a point of greeting each table and making sure people were satisfied with the service they received. Her personal touch kept them returning over and over again.

Today, speaking with a couple who were celebrating their twenty-fifth wedding anniversary, Regina felt teary-eyed. She wondered if she would ever be happily married. Would she ever celebrate being married to someone she loved for twenty-five years?

"Yes, we have three girls and one boy. You can just imagine how the girls spoil their baby brother," the wife proudly proclaimed as she held out a picture for Regina to see.

"You have a beautiful family." Regina signaled their waitress to come over to the table. "Make sure you bring a special dessert and a bottle of champagne to this lovely couple after their meal, compliments of the house."

The waitress nodded, and the couple smiled at Regina's gesture.

"Thank you," the husband said. "That is so nice of you."

"You're welcome. Enjoy your meal, and happy anniversary."

Regina had no sooner uttered those words than she turned around and noticed that Poppy had entered the restaurant and was being seated at his regular table. These unexpected and unannounced visits made her nervous. *Oh, Lord*, she prayed quickly, *give me strength. Let there be nothing wrong.*

She mustered up a smile as she went over to greet him. "Poppy, what brings you here? Is everything okay?"

"Yes, Dear, everything is fine. Do you have a moment to sit with me?"

She hesitated but then thought better of refusing him. "Sure." She sat down in a chair opposite him and folded her hands on the table. "Yes?"

"I have some good news for you."

He paused, and Regina waited for him to continue, making certain her expression didn't change, even at the prospect of good news. He finally said, "I've decided to allow your parents to come back home."

For a second, Regina thought her mind was playing tricks on her. She had waited to hear those words for so long that she almost couldn't believe them. "Are you serious? Do you mean it?"

"Yes, I mean it. I spoke to them last night, and they will be back home by the end of this week."

Regina couldn't contain herself at such good news. Before she realized what she was doing, she was out of her seat and giving Poppy a quick hug and a kiss on the cheek. This not only surprised her, but it caught Poppy very off guard. He stiffened up like a post. She had never shown him any affection before, even though she always tried to be polite to him. There was an awkward moment while he seemed unsure what the best course of action would be, and then she felt his arm go around her, almost too tenderly, as if he were afraid he would break her. His eyes welled up a bit, and Regina knew how much the spontaneous hug had meant to him. This was Poppy, Anthony's father — the man never cried; it would be sacrilegious. Yet here he was, blinking to keep his eyes dry.

She sat back down. "Thank you! I've missed them both so much." Wiping tears from her face, she hesitated, unsure whether or not to ask this question, but then went on, "May I ask what made you change your mind? I mean, at lunch you seemed to be quite certain about not allowing this."

"I started thinking about what you said. This exile has lasted long enough. After all, we are family."

Regina suddenly thought of Anthony and what his reaction likely would be, and her joy momentarily stumbled. Poppy noticed the change.

"What's the matter? You look upset."

"Please don't take this the wrong way," she said, trying to choose her words carefully. "But I mean . . . um . . . what about Anthony?"

"Don't worry about Anthony. I'll tell him myself. It will be all right."

The prospect of what Anthony might do when he found out scared Regina. Anthony hated her father for what he did, or had tried to do. Anthony wanted him dead for his betrayal and didn't keep that fact a secret.

"Don't worry, Regina. Let me take care of Anthony. This is what I want and think is best for the family. Trust me; he will accept this. I wanted to tell you first. Your reaction makes it all worth it. I know I have made the right decision. Until I tell him, let this be our little secret."

Regina smiled. Maybe God was changing his heart. She prayed for Poppy as she did for his son. "Have you eaten yet, Poppy?"

"Yes, but you know I always have room for some of Chef Paul's cheese-cake. Will you join me?"

"Yes, it would be my pleasure." Regina signaled one of the waiters over to the table. "Two pieces of cheesecake, Alfredo. An espresso for Mr. Cavelli and some milk for me."

"Yes, ma'am. I'll be right back."

"Milk?" Poppy seemed puzzled by her choice of beverage.

"Yes, I've been trying to eat better. Milk makes me feel less guilty about the cheesecake." She laughed. All she could do was thank God silently in her heart for this miracle. She could really use her folks and their support at a time like this.

The apartment was dark, except for the small lamp Lilly usually left on in the hallway. *Lilly must have gone home*, Anthony thought as he entered the penthouse and closed the door behind him. He hadn't seen Regina's car downstairs.

He walked into the kitchen and looked around. Finding the sugar bowl on the counter, he took out a small plastic bag from his pocket and opened the top of the bowl. He was about to sprinkle a pinch of the pow-der into the sugar bowl when a thought occurred to him, and he paused. This wouldn't work — other people on the staff might use this bowl. Not that he cared what happened to them; he just didn't want to raise suspi-cion if everyone got sick. He would just have to put this in her food or drink directly somehow. A little tricky, since they didn't spend much time together.

Anthony startled at the sound of the front door opening.

"Regina, is that you?" he called out as he slipped the plastic bag back into his pocket. He walked into the hallway and pretended he was surprised to see her. "You're home early."

"I'm tired, Anthony. I don't have . . . oh, never mind. I'm just tired." Anything she said would end up in an argument, and Regina didn't want to argue with him right now. She had so much to be grateful for today. After what God had done for her, the least she could do was work on her attitude toward Anthony.

"I'm going to make some herbal tea and go to bed."

As she passed him, he reached out and gently touched her arm. The gentleness startled her. Her skin crawled. She pulled away from him.

"You look tired. Why don't you go up and get ready for bed? I'll get your tea," Anthony offered, to Regina's surprise.

In his tiny cabin just outside Tennessee, the old man was sitting at his kitchen table and eating a snack before going to bed. Suddenly he felt a presence in the room. He wondered quietly if Samuel had returned.

He looked around but didn't see his angelic friend. It must be the Lord. He placed his cup of tea down on the table and closed his eyes, asking God what He wanted him to do.

Regina paused, looking at Anthony in disbelief. She didn't know what to think. He was never this nice. The sweet tone he was using sounded so strange coming from him. She felt ill at ease about the whole thing — so much so, in fact, that she began to think the Spirit was trying to warn her of something.

"No, thank you. I prefer to do it myself. You don't have to trouble yourself."

"It's no trouble. I insist. I know I don't usually do nice things for you, but maybe I should start. After all, you've been so nice to Poppy."

The smile he gave her sent a shiver down her spine. He was trying too hard. Something didn't feel right about all of this. She could sense it, but she didn't know what it was. Her mind felt cloudy, and she couldn't seem to think straight. If she didn't want an argument, she had no choice but to relent.

"Well, then, if you insist."

"I'll be right up with your tea," Anthony said as he headed for the kitchen.

John stared at the ceiling fan turning slowly above him as he lay in bed. Sleep eluded him. He had so much on his mind, especially the meeting with Regina that was coming up in just a few hours.

He reached over to the end table for the remote and started flipping through channels. Nothing interested him. Most of the channels were having commercial breaks. Some movies were already in progress. He came across one of those TV evangelists. He paused at that channel and wondered, as he sometimes did, whether God was truly out there or not. Maybe being a cop had made him cynical.

He shut off the TV and made sure his alarm was set for four thirty a.m. He didn't want to be late, and he needed extra time to find the house. If only he could turn off his brain and get some rest.

Antonio was in his kitchen pouring himself a cup of milk. He looked in the cookie jar and took out an oatmeal raisin cookie that the cook had made. It wasn't as good as the ones his wife used to make, but it would do the trick.

He sat down at the kitchen table, thinking back on his day. Regina was definitely the best part of it. Maybe his plan would work; maybe now she would soften toward him. At least it was a beginning. Enough of a start to put a smile on an old man's face and hope in his heart.

The old man got up from his kitchen table. He knew God was asking him to pray for the woman again. He went into the living room and sat in his favorite rocking chair. For some reason, God's presence was stronger in this part of the house.

He listened quietly. He sensed the woman was in danger . . . grave danger. Standing up from the chair, he proclaimed forcefully, "In the name of Jesus, I come against the forces of darkness that are out to destroy this woman of God. Father, protect her and keep her safe in Your hands." He continued to intercede, marching back and forth as he prayed.

Regina changed into her nightgown. She still wasn't able to shake off this ill feeling she had. *Lord, help me. Direct me and give me wisdom.* The only thing she seemed to do lately was ask God for wisdom, protection, strength, and peace. He must think she was a broken record.

Anthony stepped into the bedroom, a cup of tea in his hand, and all of a sudden it dawned on her: *Don't drink the tea.* He placed it on the table.

She walked over to it, praying silently, *Wisdom, Lord, wisdom.* Near the table, she pretended to trip, grabbing hold of the table edge with one hand and knocking over the teacup with the other. As tea ran across the table and onto the carpet, Anthony looked like he was about to yell, but he managed to contain himself.

"I'm so sorry. How can I be so clumsy?" Regina said as she started to clean up the mess.

"It's okay," Anthony stiffly replied. "I'll make you another cup. It won't take very long." She could easily see that he was still trying to contain his anger.

"Oh, please don't go through any more trouble. I feel bad enough you made it in the first place. You have been very sweet, but I'm really tired." She yawned. "I think I'll just go to sleep. Are you coming?" She knew what he was going to say before he opened his mouth.

"No, I have my poker game tonight. I came home to change."

"Oh, that's right. I must have forgotten. Have fun."

"Yeah, see ya later." He left.

Regina sighed. "Thank you, Lord," was all she could whisper. She wasn't sure what was in the tea, if anything, but she had the overwhelming sense she'd just dodged a bullet.

In the hallway, Anthony glared at the closed door and said to himself, "You'll get what's coming to you yet. There's always tomorrow."

The old man stopped praying, for the urgency was now gone. He was not sure what role God wanted him to play in this woman's life, but he would continue to seek Him on her behalf and wait until God's appointed time.

Chapter 4

The house felt cool, and to Regina, the darkness seemed a bit eerie. Looking around, she could almost hear echoes of the happier times she had spent here growing up. The house had been empty since her parents had moved out. She had been taking care of it for them, in case one day they returned. At last, it looked like that day was very near — which was one more reason to do what she was doing now.

Waiting for the detective, she made some hot chocolate and poured herself a cup, carrying it into the living room.

Anxiety began to get the best of her as time ticked on. She wondered if the small canister of film in her hand was enough to rid her and her baby of Anthony. Was there enough information on it to send him away forever? She hoped so, with all her heart; she couldn't live like this anymore.

She heard the back door open. Taking a deep breath, she prayed, again, that she was doing the right thing. Then she stood from the couch and walked into the kitchen to meet him.

"Hello," John called out, closing the door behind him. All of a sudden he noticed her standing there. Unexpectedly, his pulse started to race at the sight of her, and, without meaning to, he again noticed what a beautiful woman she was. Her soft eyes seemed to penetrate his soul, an effect with which he was not familiar or even very comfortable. Forming complete thoughts took a peculiar amount of effort. "Hello," he repeated, more quietly this time.

"Hello again. Why don't we go into the living room where it's more comfortable?"

He nodded and Regina led the way, asking over her shoulder, "Would you like some hot chocolate?"

"No, thanks. I'm a black coffee kind of guy."

"I'm sorry I don't have any."

"That's okay. I'm fine."

They stepped into the living room, and she turned to face him. An awkward moment passed. She didn't seem sure how to proceed with the conversation. Eventually, she took a deep breath and handed him a small canister.

"I hope this will be helpful."

"What is it?"

"I took pictures of Anthony's private book. He writes things down and keeps it with him at all times. It appears to be coded, but I figure you will know who to give it to. If I'm right, there could be enough information on it to help put Anthony away for a long time."

John found himself staring at her as she spoke. He was totally captivated by her mannerisms. Her awkwardness was charming. She looked around the room as she spoke, as if trying to avoid eye contact.

But then, rather suddenly, she looked at him head-on, and, startled, he finally said, "You must have taken a lot of risks to get this information." He hesitated before continuing, "You can say it's none of my business, but . . . why are you doing this?"

Regina almost whispered her response. "I have my reasons."

"I'm sorry; I don't mean to pry. It's just that most wives wouldn't double-cross their husbands, especially if they're married to a man like Anthony Cavelli. You must know what he's capable of . . . don't you?"

She slowly sank down onto the couch. He sat beside her, giving her as much space as the couch would allow.

"Believe me — I know firsthand what he's capable of, but sometimes in life you just have to . . . ."

Regina's mind trailed off to a time she didn't want to remember and to a night that had caused her entire life to change. She realized that she had left off in mid-sentence and continued, "Let's just say things change. I don't mind for myself, but . . . never mind. I have very good reasons for taking these risks. It's important to me that Anthony is stopped. I know how to be careful, but you need to be careful also. Anthony wouldn't think twice about going after you, if he felt threatened."

She paused, glancing down at her hot chocolate. "There is . . ." She hesitated. "I don't know if I should tell you this or not."

"There is . . . what? Come on; you can trust me or else I'm sure I wouldn't be here. Believe me — I want to see your husband behind bars as much as you do. Maybe more so."

"This has more to do with you on a personal basis."

Now he was intrigued. "Go on. You can't leave me hanging here."

"Well, you see . . . one of the reasons I feel I can trust you is . . ."

"Just say it, Mrs. Cavelli."

"Please don't call me that. I would prefer that you just call me Regina."

"Okay, then you can call me John. Now that all of the formalities are out of the way, please continue."

"A long time ago, I overheard Anthony talking about your brother."

He paused. "What about my brother?"

"Well . . . right after we got married is when the . . . um . . . tragedy with your brother happened. Anthony thought I was asleep when the phone rang late one night. I overheard him talking, but I'm not sure to whom. He said something like, 'Did you make sure the cop looks bad?' I wasn't sure what he was talking about until the story came out in the paper the next day. I just kind of put two and two together. I know it's not much to go on." Regina could see by his expression that he was upset. "I'm sorry. I know this must be hard on you."

For a long moment, John stared into space with a glazed look in his eyes. Then he got up from the couch. "I knew it," he said softly. "I knew he didn't kill himself."

"What I heard is not enough to prove anything. We both know what that comment meant, but in the hands of a good lawyer, which Anthony has about a dozen of, it could be made to sound like something else. If what I overheard was enough, I would have been to the police sooner. I want you to know that I didn't want to risk exposure until I had something solid."

"Maybe there's proof on this film." John looked down at the canister in his hand and then placed it in his jacket pocket for safekeeping. "I know you're scared, but with what you know and a little bit of proof, we could have a case."

Hearing the hope in his voice, Regina couldn't help but feel a little sorry for what he and his family must have gone through. She could tell that his brother's death was still very painful. "I hope for your sake, and for mine, that you're right. I don't know how much more help I can give you. Other than the film, I don't have any solid proof that could stand up in court."

The only thing he could think about was the risk she was taking; he didn't want her to be another casualty like his brother. He walked back toward the couch, dismissing the urge to take her in his arms and comfort her. *Why am I feeling like this?* He didn't want to scare her or push her away. He sat down again, closer to her this time, and placed his hand gently on top of hers, hoping to convey his support in a friendly, brotherly way.

"Do you think you'll be safe? If Anthony finds out what you did . . . I mean, your life would be in danger. I can protect you."

The look in his eyes was both tender and caring, two things she hadn't seen a man direct toward her in a long, long time. Without warning, she found herself thinking things she hadn't thought for an equal length of time. The warm touch of his hand awakened something within her that had lain dormant for many years. It was so strange to her how her heart jumped when he looked at her. She hadn't experienced this before with anyone, and she could only sit there and wonder at it.

But she was married and pregnant — what was she doing? She withdrew her hand and looked away.

A slight flush stole across her cheeks. Suddenly self-conscious, John pulled himself away and stood up. He had made her uncomfortable; that had not been his intention. "Maybe it would be best if I leave now. Can we meet here again?"

"I'm not sure. My parents are coming home this week."

This news surprised him. "Really? Rumor is that they're dead." He realized that hadn't come out the way he'd intended. "I'm sorry. I meant to say . . ."

Regina interrupted. "It's okay. They're both alive. Poppy had them sent away, but now he's randomly letting them come home. I'm not sure why he changed his mind, but I'm glad they're coming back."

This was all news to John. It wasn't the Cavelli style to banish people. Kill them — yes. "Are you sure they're going to be safe?"

"It's a long story, but it's really only Anthony that poses a problem. He hates my father, but Poppy and my father used to be friends a long time ago. Poppy promises me they will be in no danger."

As he pondered her words, he looked around the living room. It reminded him of his own parents' home, with dozens of family pictures everywhere on the walls and tabletops. He noticed a picture of a baby on the end table next to him and picked it up.

"Is this you?"

"No, it's my younger brother," Regina said quietly.

"Your brother? I thought you were an only child."

"I am now."

"I'm sorry." He'd been a cop too long. It was hard being sensitive sometimes. He should work on that.

"Shortly after that picture was taken, he became ill and died. I was about five when it happened. My parents haven't really spoken of him much since then."

An uncomfortable silence filled the air.

John had to ask his next question, but he wasn't sure if this was a good time. At least it would break the awkward silence. "I'm wondering about something."

"Wondering about what?"

"Again, you can tell me it's none of my business, but . . . did you marry Anthony because of your dad?"

The look on her face spoke volumes. "Yes. I married Anthony so that my father wouldn't testify."

She couldn't believe she had just said that, that she had just exposed the truth with barely a pause. But she felt safe with this man for some odd reason. How ironic was it that she felt safer with a stranger than with her own husband?

"Why?" John asked, with more compassion than she had expected.

Regina hesitated. How much did she truly want to tell this man? Lifting her gaze off the floor, she looked him in the eyes and answered, "Because Poppy convinced me that they could find my parents no matter where the government hid them. Anthony wanted my father dead. It was a matter of honor to him. He was betrayed and couldn't let that go unpunished. Marrying Anthony would be the only acceptable alternative for Poppy. This way, he knew my parents would get the message. He knew my dad wouldn't testify if I were married to his son and under their control. For some odd reason Poppy always wanted me to grow up and marry his son. I never liked Anthony, even when we were kids. He was cruel then, and he still is. He has no redeeming qualities that I can see. God forgive me, but the bottom line is that I just . . . let's just say I dislike him intensely. He isn't very fond of me, either, but for some reason he went along with the whole thing."

She knew that holding onto hate wasn't good for anyone, but she couldn't quite follow that through when it came to Anthony. Hatred was easier to deal with than fear.

"The FBI protected them. After the trial, they would have been in the witness protection program. You could have been part of that deal."

"You don't understand. It is while they were under heavy protection that Poppy came to me, when I was at school. He offered me proof that he could get to them anywhere, anytime."

"What kind of proof?" John asked.

"He handed me my mother's wedding ring. The only time she takes it off is when she sleeps. He could have killed them then, but didn't. He wanted me to know that they would never be safe. That no matter where they hid, they would be found. He promised me they would be safe if I did what he asked, and from time to time I could visit them. I had no choice. It was either marry Anthony or live with the possibility of my parents being killed. I wouldn't be able to live with myself if something happened to them. But the crazy thing in all of this is Poppy expects Anthony and I to be happy and live like normal married people."

"How does this keep Anthony from . . . doing what he wanted to do?"

"His father's approval means more to him. He pretended that the marriage was what he wanted also. He convinced his father that he was in love with me from afar. Anthony knew his father wanted us to get married. He thought making Poppy happy in this small way would make it easier for him to take over the family business one day. Family is very important to the Cavellis."

Regina paused for a moment to collect her thoughts. She wasn't sure if she should continue, but after coming this far, it was hard not to finish. "Once, after Anthony told me we had to pretend to be happy in front of his father, I told him I wouldn't do it, and he hit me so hard in the stomach that I threw up. He knew better than to hit me where it would be noticeable. Violence is the only way he knows how to get what he wants. I tried to fight back, but he's stronger than I am. I have no choice but to do as he says. We came to an agreement: He leads his life any way he likes, and I pretend I can stomach him in front of his father."

She stopped and looked at him, blushing a little as she said, "I'm sorry. I don't know why I said all of that."

Compassion for her and the situation she found herself in grew in John's heart. Every instinct he had wanted to protect her. Her pain touched him. The man inside of him wanted to hold her until she felt safe; the cop inside of him wanted to shoot Anthony in the head.

Obviously, either action would create some problems.

"How do you stay married to a man like that if you're not in love with him?"

"God. He gives me strength. I pray daily. I even pray for Anthony. Now, don't get me wrong — it's not always easy to pray for him, but I try to. Unfortunately, he hasn't changed yet." Looking at her watch, she said, "We should probably leave. You go first. I'll clean up and then go."

"I won't let you down." He realized how dorky that must sound. "I'm sure I don't have to tell you to be careful. But remember, if there is anything at all I can do, please don't hesitate to call me, day or night."

Once again he handed her his card. "This has my cell number on it. If you get in trouble, just call me."

"Thanks."

She began to feel that, maybe, her instincts had been right. God may have answered her prayers for help. Maybe He had arranged for them to meet like this, and had worked it out, and would continue to do so. Perhaps the quiet voice in her head was right — perhaps she really could trust this man.

Anthony sat in his office, sipping coffee from a black mug and looking out the window. He wasn't really looking at anything in particular; it just helped him to process things. He was feeling so much pressure from so many directions.

How was he ever going to rid himself of Regina? His girlfriend wanted to get married and have children. If the truth were known, he wouldn't mind having kids, just not with his wife. Poisoning her was risky, but he was willing to take his chances.

Then there was Poppy. He had to find a way to get him off his back.

The intercom buzzed, startling him.

"What is it, Mary?" he demanded.

"Sir, I know you don't want to be disturbed, but your father is here to see you."

Anthony paused a moment. "Tell him to come in."

Poppy walked in with a smile as he greeted his son. "Anthony, I apologize for just dropping in today."

Anthony got up and greeted him. "You don't have to apologize. I always enjoy seeing you, Poppy. Sit down and tell me what brings you here today. I hope there's nothing wrong."

"Well, it depends on how you look at it. I think it's good news."

Anthony wasn't sure he liked the sound of that. "Okay, tell me."

"I've decided to bring Regina's parents back home."

"Are you kidding me?!" Anthony rose to his feet with anger that was palpable.

Poppy's brows lowered. "Sit down. You will not raise your voice to me. I am still your father and the head of this family, even if you're running the business *for now*."

Anthony sat down and glared at his father. He was not going to stand for this. "For now"? What was that supposed to mean? He knew Poppy took his failure to show restraint as a sign of weakness, so he tried to change his tone. "I'm sorry, Poppy. But why would you change your mind now? Isn't it bad enough you let that man live?"

"I had my reasons back then, and I have my reasons now. I've thought it over and enough time has passed. I know he won't make the same mistake again. You and Regina are married now."

Anthony thought about this for a moment. Why bring Michael back, except to rub it in Anthony's face? There was no sense arguing with the old man, though. Once he'd made up his mind, that was that. "Can I ask you something?"

Poppy nodded, stone-faced.

"Since you made up your mind to do this without talking to me, does this mean you're planning to come back and take over?"

"I told you already that's not my intention. I just want something to do. It's not like I have grandchildren to run after." Poppy seemed to enjoy throwing that into the conversation whenever he got a chance. "Look, you're still in charge of the business, but I'm head of this family. I want you to know that I think this will help bring our family together. You're married to Regina and one day will have children. I think this is for the best and I want you to back me up. I've guaranteed their safety. You need to respect that, understood?"

Anthony couldn't believe what he'd just been told. He took a deep breath, trying to buy himself enough time to cool down. If he was still in charge, why was this decision made without his input? He definitely had to re-think some things. "Understood."

"I'm glad I've made myself clear. This new arrangement will be best for everyone. You'll see." Poppy stood up to go, but before he left, he added, "I hope that Regina is well?"

"Yes, she is."

"That's good. You know how I worry about her sometimes. I've grown very fond of her over the years. From the time she was a little girl she captured my heart. If anything were to happen to her, I would stop at nothing to get to the bottom of it. You give her my best." With that, he hugged Anthony and left.

Anthony sat back down at his desk. What was that all about? And what was with him and Regina anyway? What did he mean by "stop at nothing"? He stood up and began to pace around his office. Maybe poisoning her was not such a good idea. It seemed a little risky now. Maybe he could arrange for an accident . . . no, that wouldn't work. If Poppy found out he was behind it, Anthony wasn't sure what he would do. Being the old man's son didn't seem to carry as much weight as being his daughter-in-law.

Suddenly, a light bulb popped on in his head, and he froze, his hand on the windowsill. He'd been going about this all wrong. If Regina *did* get pregnant, Poppy would be happy, and then, if something were to happen to her after that . . . it would be a tragedy, yeah . . . but Poppy would have a grandchild to dry his tears. It was perfect. This way he could get rid of her for good.

There was only one problem, and that was getting her pregnant. She would never go along with it willingly. She hated him as much as he hated her, but it didn't really matter what she wanted, did it? She would get pregnant one way or another.

This was one of his more enjoyable ideas. He always won out in the end.

Regina sat at the kitchen table, sipping warm milk. She'd heard that it helped you sleep, and these days she needed all the help she could get. She'd been anxious all day about how Anthony would react to Poppy's news. He hated her father and made no secret of it.

The meeting had gone well with John. Very well.

Too well, perhaps. In fact, there was a bit of a problem. These unexpected and entirely inappropriate feelings she seemed to have toward him not only embarrassed her, but they made her feel ashamed. He was very handsome. Not to mention compassionate. At this point in her life, those weren't a good combination. What was wrong with her? Why couldn't she get him off her mind? *I can't afford any romantic fantasies.*

She was about to take another sip of milk when she suddenly noticed Anthony standing in the kitchen doorway, staring at her. He had a huge bouquet of red roses and baby breath in his hand.

"Anthony, you startled me. I didn't hear you come in. How long have you been standing there?"

"I'm sorry to startle you. I've been home for just a few minutes. I bought you some flowers." He went over to the cupboard and pulled a glass vase from the top shelf. As he filled the vase at the sink, he continued, "I just couldn't help noticing how beautiful you look sitting there."

Regina's heart stopped for a moment. What was he up to? He didn't appear to be drunk, but she didn't like the look in his eyes. *Oh, Lord, whatever it is, I pray You protect me.* She didn't know what to say or how to respond, so she just sat there and looked at him.

"I called the restaurant and they said you came home early. I hope you're not sick."

"No. I'm fine, just a bit tired. I didn't sleep well last night, and I've been working hard to kick off the new changes at the restaurant." This idle chitchat was starting to unnerve her.

Anthony came over and placed the vase of flowers on the table. He sat in the chair next to her and tenderly took her hand. "Poppy tells me your folks are coming back."

Now she understood. *Okay, Regina. Get ready for the bomb to go off.*

"I think it's a great idea. I thought I would tell you that and assure you not to worry. I'm fine with the whole thing. Poppy is right — it's time to move on and look to the future, for the sake of the family."

Regina pulled her hand away from his and got up from the table. Setting her cup in the sink, she said, "That's good. I'm glad you're all right with the whole thing." She knew he was lying. Did he honestly think he was fooling her with this phony sweet talk?

She wasn't sure what was going on, but she didn't want to stick around to find out. "I'm so tired." She yawned. "I'm going to turn in early. I'll see you in the morning. Thank you for the flowers."

As she walked toward the door, he stood up and gently grabbed her around her waist. "I think I'll go upstairs with you. Maybe we can talk a bit," he said playfully.

Regina forcefully pushed his arms from around her waist, looked him right in the eyes, and said, "Anthony, I don't know what you're up to, but let me explain something to you. I'm going to *sleep* and I have no interest in 'talking.' I'm tired — and keep your hands to yourself."

"I'm so sorry, Darling. I don't mean to upset you."

Regina looked at him and shook her head. She walked out of the kitchen and headed up the stairs toward their bedroom. Anthony caught up to her halfway up the steps and slipped in front of her, both hands lifted in surrender.

"Regina, I just want to talk. I've been thinking about something for a while. Since we *are* married and nothing is going to change that, we should consider the future. I mean, being hostile to one another is no way to live. I think it would be a good idea if we started a family."

All the color drained from Regina's face. He must have lost his mind.

They had an arrangement. And now he wanted to . . . The thought made her ill. Maybe he was trying to get closer to his father or something . . . Whatever the reason was, she was not going to play this game with him. He would never, ever touch her again.

"No! No! No! We have an agreement! You promised me after the last time . . . You said it wouldn't . . . You disgust me. The thought of you touching me is repulsive. Just get out of my way!"

She shoved his arm back and started running up the steps to get away from him. But Anthony was determined not to let this conversation end and grabbed her arms, forcibly jerking her back down toward him.

"Now, Regina —"

"Let me go! Have you lost your mind?"

As she wrestled to break free from his grasp, her feet slid off the steps. Anthony's grip loosened as she spun to grab the rail, but she missed and felt herself plummeting down the stairs. Anthony tried to catch her but couldn't get a hold of her. Pain jolted through her skull and hip as she hit the bottom steps.

Lord . . . remember the baby . . .

Chapter 5

Anthony couldn't believe what just had happened. Stunned, he stood there halfway up the stairs and gaped at Regina lying motionless on the first floor. He expected her to sit up and glare at him, but she didn't. She didn't do anything. Then he snapped out of it and ran down the steps to see if she was still breathing.

He took out his cell phone. "Hello, this is Anthony Cavelli. My wife had an accident and I need an ambulance . . . Yes, she's still breathing . . . Nine twenty-six Third Avenue. It's on the corner of Sixty-ninth Street. Hurry."

He dialed again. "Mario, meet me at the hospital. Regina's been in an accident. Tell Vinny to get there as soon as possible . . . Don't question me, you putz. Just get there!"

I can't call Poppy until I know what's going on. After all, why upset him if she's going to be okay?

Mario and Vinny arrived at the hospital before Anthony, both of them filled with questions. All Anthony had told them was that Regina had been in an accident; they were well aware that could mean a whole variety of things. When he arrived, he told them what had happened, and while they were waiting for the doctor to return, Poppy appeared in the doorway of the waiting room.

His tone made the three men freeze momentarily. It was the first time Mario and Vinny had been happy not to be in Anthony's shoes.

"I want to know what happened."

"Poppy, it was an accident. She was going up the stairs and somehow tripped and fell. There was nothing I could do. I called for an ambulance right away — they got there within minutes."

"You were there? And yet she just *somehow* tripped and fell."

Anthony didn't appreciate the way his father was talking to him. He didn't like the look in his eyes, either. "Yes. We were talking as we went up to bed, and she suddenly lost her footing. I tried to grab hold of her, but it happened so fast. The next thing I knew, she was at the bottom of the stairs."

Before Poppy could respond, the doctor came into the waiting room. "Excuse me, Mr. Cavelli."

Anthony was glad for the interruption and hoped, rather desperately at the moment, that the news would be good. He got up to greet the doctor and shook his hand. "Is my wife going to be okay?"

"I have some good news for you. Your wife is going to be fine. She has a concussion, but it's really amazing she wasn't more seriously hurt, considering the bump on her head. She's in good shape, strong and healthy. And the best part is, there's nothing wrong with the baby."

The words hung in the air.

Anthony nearly fainted. *Baby! What baby?* The news disrupted all coherent thought, and a moment passed before he could whisper, "Baby?"

"Yes, the baby has a good heartbeat. If you'd like to see her, you can, but we'll be keeping her overnight for observation."

Poppy grabbed his son by the arm before he could leave. "What baby? How come you didn't tell me about this? You know how much I wanted grandchildren. I don't appreciate your hiding things from me. If anything would have happened to her tonight . . . I will get to the bottom of this."

"Poppy, I swear I didn't know! I don't know why she didn't tell me. Maybe she didn't even know herself."

"Let's go see Regina together. I'm very curious to hear what she has to say about this whole situation." He had several questions, beginning with her being pregnant and why he, as well as her husband, hadn't been told.

But he was especially curious to hear Regina's side of what had happened with the staircase.

John had been thinking about Regina since his first meeting with her; his last meeting with her had cemented her in his thoughts to the point of distraction. He couldn't seem to get her out of his head. He found himself attracted to her with a . . . completeness unlike any other attraction he'd experienced. She was unbelievable — he doubted he would be able to be as strong as she if their roles were reversed. He'd left her parents' house feeling an unfamiliar closeness to her that had surprised him, a closeness he never had felt with anyone else, male or female. At one point in their conversation, she had completely let down her walls and been wholly transparent, and that had impressed him.

Her beauty had drawn him at first; it would have drawn anybody. But after he'd spent just this small amount of time with her, the woman herself was drawing him now, and he definitely had much to think about.

And probably shouldn't think about. She was married. To a man he despised for several strong, irrefutable reasons. Right off the bat, this was all messed up.

Frank called out his name, interrupting his thoughts. "John, are you listening?"

"I'm sorry. Go ahead."

"I just got a phone call from a friend at the hospital. They brought in Regina Cavelli tonight."

"What? Is she okay?" John felt his heart stumble. What if Anthony had found out what she had done? If that man had hurt her in any way . . .

"She fell down the stairs at her penthouse, but it seems she's going to be okay."

"I gotta go."

"Wait, John. There's more."

John stopped and looked at him. "What?"

"She's pregnant. No wonder she kicked us out — she's going to have his kid."

Frank's words totally derailed him. John slowly sat down on the desk with a look of bewilderment on his face. There must be some mistake. She told him they didn't have that type of marriage. Was she lying to him? Was she playing him for a fool? Was she setting him up for a fall? No, he couldn't be *that* wrong about her.

He had to go and see her.

"Hey, man. Are you okay?" Frank asked.

John snapped out of his fog and replied, "Oh, yeah. I'm fine. I'm wondering how she fell down the stairs. Maybe she was pushed. Maybe we need to go and investigate it. What do you think? I mean, if she and her husband got into a fight of some kind and he pushed her, then . . . well, we should go and make sure. Hey, at this point, does it matter how we get him, just that we do?"

"Maybe you're right. Why don't you go to the car and I'll meet you there in a second, okay? I want to put away some papers I'm working on."

"Okay," John answered.

Anthony's phone rang. Antonio raised his brow. Without looking at him, Anthony just shut it off and dropped it back into his pocket.

The moment Antonio turned his attention to Regina, he felt his anger soften. She was lying so still on her bed. She looked beautiful and innocent, like an angel sleeping. He had heard that phrase used before, but for the first time, he experienced what it meant. She could have died today; the doctor had expressed amazement that her injury wasn't more serious.

Antonio's emotions felt incredibly mixed up at this point, but he would get to the bottom of this.

Anthony tried not to look at his father. Regina had to be okay. She had to tell Poppy the truth. Why didn't she wake up? He couldn't stand the way his father kept looking at him.

Regina lay on the bed, trying not to move. If her eyes fluttered even the tiniest bit, it would give her away. She sensed Poppy and Anthony at her side, waiting for her to wake up. She knew she would have to open her eyes eventually, but first she needed to pray and come up with an appropriate defense.

She was almost certain that the doctors had told them she was pregnant. How was she going to explain it to them? If ever she needed some divine intervention, it was now! Maybe she just could lie there and never open her eyes. Maybe they would go away.

But who was she kidding? She prayed until she could feel the Spirit's peace come over her. Slowly, her stomach began to calm, and the peace began to swallow her fear.

She might as well get this over with. Holding her breath, she opened her eyes.

John and Frank entered the hospital and found out what room she was in without any difficulty. As they approached, they saw Vinny and Mario waiting outside, guarding the door.

Does that guy get bigger every time I see him, or is it just my imagination? John took out his badge to identify himself, even though both of them already knew who he was.

"What are you doing here?" Mario demanded, the more aggressive of the two.

"None of your business, punk," John replied.

Mario glared at him. "The Cavellis *are* my business, cop."

"We've come to investigate the accident. We always investigate accidents, to make sure that's what they really are."

If they weren't irritated before, that insinuation sealed the deal.

"You can't go in there now. Her husband and father-in-law are in there," Mario stated, blocking the door with his body.

Poppy spoke first. "Regina, how are you feeling, my dear?"

"A bit sore, but I'm okay. Did you call my parents?"

"No, my dear, we haven't had a chance. We wanted to make sure you were okay first. The doctor tells us that both you" — he paused for effect — "and the baby are fine."

There it was. They both knew.

Before she could come up with a response, she heard loud voices outside the door. "What's going on out there?" she asked.

Anthony tersely answered, "I don't know, but I'm going to find out."

He walked over and yanked open the door to find John Nelson and his partner arguing with the boys. Regina's throat tightened when she saw John standing there.

For a second, Anthony seemed caught off guard, and then he demanded, his annoyance evident, "What's going on here? What do you two want?"

"Official police business. We understand there has been an accident, and we'd like to ask you some questions," John said with total professionalism.

"Oh, give me a break. Nobody called you. Why don't you just leave?"

"I'm here to question your wife first, if you don't mind."

The implication infuriated Anthony. "Well, I do mind. She's still weak. I don't want you upsetting her in her condition."

At that point, much to Regina's surprise, Poppy stepped in and interjected, "Anthony, that's enough. Why don't we ask Regina if she's up to answering questions? The detectives are only trying to do their jobs."

For the second time in two minutes, Anthony was clearly caught off guard. He stared at his father as if he couldn't believe he had just said that. He looked as if he wasn't going to allow it for a moment, but what could he do? Poppy had okayed it. Anthony had no choice but to let John and his partner have their way.

With a glare, he stepped back and motioned for them to enter.

"Regina, are you up to answering some questions about what happened?" Poppy asked with such care in his voice that Regina was taken aback. She assumed it was because of the baby. She nodded, wondering whether or not John knew she was pregnant, too. Maybe she should have said something to him.

"Mrs. Cavelli, can you please tell us what happened? How did you fall?" John asked.

Regina took a deep breath, all eyes fixed on her. Only Anthony's gaze bothered her, because his was an out-and-out glare that promised retribution if she said the wrong thing. Poppy didn't seem to notice. Choosing to ignore it, she looked right at John and answered, "It was an accident. I was going up the stairs to bed and I tripped. I just lost my footing and fell. The next thing I knew, I was here. I just woke up." It was the truth. She knew that John wanted more than that, but this time Anthony was innocent.

John tried to push the situation a little by asking another question. "Where was your husband when this took place?"

Anthony objected. "What the —"

"Anthony!" Poppy forcefully interrupted. "Watch your mouth."

Regina felt the tension level spike as Anthony bristled beneath his father's reprimand. His tone as smooth and cool as ice, he rephrased the question. "What are you trying to say — that I had something to do with her accident?"

"I'm just trying to investigate what happened. The way I do that is by asking questions," John condescendingly replied. He smiled when he saw the reaction in Anthony's eyes.

Regina just wanted them to stop. "Look, it was an accident. Anthony had nothing to do with it." She hated having to defend this man, but it was the truth. How much she wanted to lie and say he had tripped her or that he had thrown her down the steps. That would solve so many problems! But it just wasn't something she could do and live with herself. The truth was the truth.

"Are you satisfied?" Anthony asked.

"Well, if that's the story, then I'll have to be satisfied."

"Then leave," Anthony barked at him.

"I'm sorry to have bothered you." Then, to the surprise of everyone in the room, he added, "I hope you and your baby will be just fine, Mrs. Cavelli."

"How did you find out?" Poppy demanded.

"When we were told about the accident."

Both detectives said nothing else and left the room.

All Regina could think about was how she was going to explain this to John. He had looked so upset. He must have thought everything she had told him was a lie. But would he believe her if she explained what really had happened?

And then again, why was it so important to her what he thought? She looked at Poppy and Anthony standing beside the bed and knew they were both expecting an explanation about the baby.

"I know you must be wondering why I didn't say anything about the baby before. I just needed some time to make sure everything was okay with the pregnancy before I said anything. I know how much a baby would mean to you, Poppy, so if something went wrong . . . Well, anyway, it was probably wrong of me to keep this a secret. I was going to tell you both really soon."

Poppy spoke first. "Regina, all that matters is that you are going to have a baby. Congratulations! I can't begin to tell you how pleased I am about becoming a grandfather. We're going to take good care of you until this new addition arrives. Aren't we, son?"

"That's right. We're going to take real good care of you."

"Millions of women have had babies before me. Please don't make a fuss."

"Yes, that may be true, but none of them had *my* grandchild."

So it began. Regina was now truly trapped. The look in Anthony's eyes was anything but reassuring. She tried not to focus on it, but even with her head turned, she still could feel his glare on the side of her face. More than ever, it was so important to put him away. Poppy seemed to be softening somewhat, so maybe he wouldn't be a problem, but Anthony would be. She knew God would help her. Somehow, He had to help her.

John and Frank drove back to the precinct in silence. John didn't know what to think. Regina had looked so helpless there in that bed surrounded by men who had no understanding of how special she is. He wanted to go to her, to comfort her, to hold her — he must be going crazy. She was married and having her husband's baby. Things couldn't be *that* bad if she was pregnant. But still, she had given him that film.

He felt so mixed up. He needed to find a way to talk to her alone again.

Why was he so captivated by this woman he barely knew? He was getting far too emotionally involved, but he didn't — and couldn't — care. She had to have a good explanation. He wasn't wrong about her. He couldn't be.

Chapter 6

In the weeks following Regina's release from the hospital, Anthony had been so pleasant it was nauseating, not to mention unnerving. He'd been hovering over her, making sure she didn't "strain herself," as he put it. She felt suffocated. The only peace she got was when she visited her parents.

Anthony insisted that Mario or Vinny drive her everywhere once she got out of the hospital. Usually it was Vinny, mostly because she preferred him; he was nicer than Mario. But this morning, she didn't want any company. She wanted to visit her parents alone and wasn't taking any chances this time. It was Jimmy's turn to guard her bedroom door. Late last night when he'd stepped away for a moment, she had dropped a couple of Anthony's sleeping pills into his soda. She had asked God to forgive her; she had mostly meant it.

She got up early, left a note for Anthony, and slipped past Jimmy, who was sprawled in the chair outside the bedroom, his chin on his chest. Those sleeping pills really worked. It would be a couple of hours until Anthony got up. He would surely send one of the guys to look for her as soon as he found her missing, so she wanted to make the most of her time.

She had so many things on her mind. How would she get away now that all eyes were on her constantly? Would she ever be free and safe from the Cavellis in order to raise her child? She hadn't been able to contact John, and she hated to imagine what was going on in his head. She prayed he didn't get the wrong impression of her.

As she drove to her parents', she dreamt about how her life could have been different. What if her brother hadn't died? What if her father had worked for honest people? What if she had never married Anthony? That was the biggest wonder of all. But she knew it wouldn't do her any good to dwell on the past, or on what could have been. All that accomplished was heartache — she knew because she'd been there. Instead, she needed to concentrate on the present.

Deep in thought, she arrived at her parents' home more quickly than she had anticipated. Pulling into the driveway behind her father's car, she noticed the federal agents in the unmarked car across the street. Ever since her parents had come home, there had been an agent or two parked there, watching. Even though her father didn't work for the Cavellis anymore, they still watched him. She didn't see the point. Her father had told them he wouldn't testify.

Sophia opened the front door to retrieve the newspaper and saw Regina starting up the walk. "Oh, Honey, I'm so glad to see you! What a pleasant surprise. You're here so early . . ."

"Good morning, Ma. Is Daddy up yet?" Regina asked. She greeted her mother with a warm embrace and a kiss on her cheek.

"Not yet, Honey. Come in and I'll fix you some tea, just the way you like." It suddenly dawned on her that Regina stood on the front step completely alone. "Where is your shadow today?" she asked out of curiosity.

"I sneaked out. Instead of tea, I would much rather go for a walk."

Her mother understood immediately. "Let me grab my jacket, Dear." As she pulled it over her shoulders, she spotted the federal agents across the street and sighed. "Do you think they'll ever leave us alone?"

"I don't know, Ma."

They started to walk. Some distance from the house, when they saw that no one was following them, Regina asked, "Ma, what am I going to do?"

"I've talked to Father Thomas, and he thinks he can help us."

"Really? But how can he help? He's a priest, not a cop."

Father Thomas was the parish priest of Saint Mary's, where her parents attended church. Regina had often worked with him in the past, helping with the children's charities he had started. She had never met anyone so loving or giving of himself. There was a real call of God on his life, and it amazed her how much he had accomplished, even as such a young man. He was only a few years older than she was but had wisdom beyond his years.

"There is a retreat house he goes to that's part of a monastery. It's in Georgia, in a remote area with no people for miles around. He thinks that if we can get you there, then Anthony won't be able to find you. We could all go, but that would be tricky. We have everyone watching us, from Anthony to the Federal Government. He told me that we could stay there for as long as we needed to. It could be a safe place to be until the baby is born and then we could see where God leads us."

Regina tried to digest her mother's words. Running meant leaving everything — her home, her restaurant . . . and then there was the fear of being found. It meant raising a child in a place where he or she would have to be watched constantly. When would it be safe to come out of hiding — one year, five years, never? She knew that Anthony would never stop searching for his child. Neither would Poppy. He was so excited about this child that he would gather all of his resources to find her. And then there was John. She wondered if he had been able to decode the book yet. When that happened, they wouldn't have to leave.

They walked in silence as Regina contemplated all of this. Her mother didn't seem to mind the quiet. They didn't have nearly as much time together as they would have liked, so any time spent together, silent or not, mattered. As they turned the corner onto Avenue N, Regina was surprised to see a car with a familiar man inside parked by the curb under a large tree. She stopped dead in her tracks.

"What is it, Dear?" her mother asked.

"Ma, that's the detective I've been telling you about." Regina tried to swallow the lump in her throat.

"What's he doing here?" Sophia asked, quickly glancing up and down the street.

"I don't know, but I think we're about to find out." Regina looked back nervously to see if anyone was following them, but she still saw no one.

John got out of the car and approached them.

"Good morning," he said, as if greeting old friends.

"What are you doing here? How did you know I would be . . . ?" She stopped, not wanting to waste words; she just wanted to know what he could be thinking, meeting up with her like this out in the open.

"Don't be mad, but I've been following you. I've been keeping an eye on you since you got out of the hospital and this was the first time you've been semi-alone. When I saw you going for a walk, I drove past you and waited."

"I see." She paused. "Have you lost your mind?"

Sophia interrupted, "Honey, have you forgotten your manners? Aren't you going to introduce me?"

Regina couldn't believe her mother wanted introductions. This conversation was craziness. "I'm sorry, Ma. This is Detective John Nelson. John, this is my mother, Sophia Palmetto."

"Nice to meet you." They spoke almost simultaneously.

Regina rolled her eyes. It wasn't as if they were regular people running into each other. She gruffly pointed to an alley she saw on their left between two small apartment buildings, and they walked into it. Sophia stayed near the end to keep watch, while John and Regina walked a little further and then stepped behind a dumpster to talk.

"Did you get the film developed and decoded?" she asked desperately.

"Yes and no. Yes, it has been developed, but no, it's still not decoded."

Regina was very disappointed, but she knew by his eyes he had something else on his mind. It wasn't hard for her to guess what it was. She didn't want him to get the wrong impression about the baby. He was too considerate to ask the question she knew he wanted to ask.

"It's not what you think."

"What's not?"

"The baby. Yes, it's Anthony's child, but . . ." Unexpectedly, her eyes welled up, and she wasn't sure if she could continue.

He took her hand and said, "It's okay. You don't have to explain it to me if you don't want to. You don't owe me any explanations."

"No, I want to. It's just that . . . I didn't lie to you. Anthony and I do have an arrangement. His dad is always pressuring him about us having children, and one night after an argument with his father, he got very drunk. He came home and I was already asleep."

Now tears were running down Regina's face; unexpectedly, she just couldn't hold them in any longer. For months, she had tried to be strong about it. She hadn't wanted to upset her parents, so she had tried to get over what had happened, to just brush it away. And no matter how her baby had come to be, it was so important to her that her child didn't feel unwanted.

John gently wiped her tears and asked softly, "Did he rape you?"

All Regina could do at this point was hang her head. Feeling a greater response than he'd anticipated, he placed his arms around her, and she started to weep against him. "I'm so sorry this happened to you," John said as he held her tenderly in his arms. After a moment, her tears started to subside and he continued, "I know this might take time, but I promise to work as fast as I can."

She pulled herself away, her face reddening. "I'm sorry. This is all wrong. I'm still married and pregnant, and I can't . . ." She rambled.

"Can't what?" He slowly drew close to her. He had never wanted to kiss anyone as much as he wanted to kiss her at that moment.

Regina stopped him. "I can't. I'm still married, regardless of the circumstances." She stepped away from him. "Please don't make this any harder than it already is."

The rebuke caught him off guard, even though, perhaps, it shouldn't have. John nodded his head, knowing she was right. "I hope you don't think I'm trying to take advantage of you. I don't know what came over me. I don't know what comes over me every time I'm near you . . . I'm sorry; please forgive me."

"I didn't mean to make it sound like it's all your fault."

This endeared her to him even more. And as much as he hated to admit it, he had no business even considering what had nearly gotten him in trouble just a second ago. He needed to keep a clear mind. He had to stop thinking about himself and start thinking about what was best for Regina and her baby.

"You have to get away from him until we can get the evidence we need. You need to be someplace safe."

"I know. My mom has an idea, but it will be tricky."

"Can I help?"

"I don't know. It requires my parents and I escaping and going to a new location without being followed. It could be dangerous. I know you're a cop, but I still . . ."

"You don't have to do this on your own. I can make sure you get there safely."

For a moment, she seemed to consider the risk factors of his involvement, and then, frowning at him, she continued, "You need to contact Father Thomas at St. Mary's Catholic Church. He knows of a safe place for us. After today, I know Anthony will keep a closer eye on me. I kinda ditched his guards."

"I hate the thought of you going back to him. Why not make the break now?"

"There's no time. He's probably up by now, wondering where I am. I really have to get back. Don't worry. I'll be in touch."

Regina walked quickly to where her mother was standing and turned back to smile at John one last time.

John stood there for a while after she left, leaning against the wall of the building and thinking about what had just happened. With all that she had gone through, there was no bitterness. The only thing on her mind was doing the right thing, and she was more concerned with the safety of others than her own safety. *What an incredible woman.*

It was a good thing he had been following her. *Father Thomas must be a close friend and someone she trusts. I guess if you can't trust a priest . . .*

St. Mary's — wasn't that the church his sister, Lisa, used to go to before she moved? She was always inviting him to go with her and her family on Sundays or Wednesday nights for some type of Bible study. That was who Regina reminded him of — Lisa. Both of them had deep convictions and complete trust in God, something John didn't comprehend.

Anthony opened his eyes and looked at the time. It was still early. He rolled over and realized the other half of the bed was empty; Regina was gone. Maybe she was downstairs.

He got up and found Jimmy, sleeping like a drunken sailor, in the chair outside the door. He barely stirred even when Anthony said his name.

Muttering beneath his breath, Anthony went down the stairs and immediately spotted Regina's note on the hall table.

That sneaky little . . . He reached for the phone and dialed her parents' number. Michael answered the phone.

Great. Now he had to talk to that traitor. "This is Anthony. Is my wife there?"

"Yes, she's sitting here having breakfast with us. Is there something wrong?"

"No, just put her on the phone."

Regina took the receiver from her father. She drew in a deep breath. "Hello?"

"What are you doing there? Why didn't you tell me last night if you wanted to go somewhere? You know I don't like you driving in your condition. You should really take better care of yourself."

She rolled her eyes. "Anthony, it's not a big deal. I'm fine. The doctor has given me a clean bill of health, and there is no reason why I can't drive. I just wanted to visit with my parents. I came straight here. I'll be home shortly."

"No, you wait there. Vinny doesn't live far from your parents. I'll send him to pick you up."

"What about my car?"

"Don't worry about it. I'll make sure you get it later."

He hung up the phone and called Vinny.

"Vinny, go to Regina's parents' house and pick her up. Do it now!" He hung up the phone without waiting for a response. It didn't concern Anthony if Vinny was up, dressed, or in the middle of making love. He expected him just to do as he was told immediately.

Now . . . what to do about Regina? He couldn't believe that sneaky, stupid . . . Well, he needed to do something about this. He couldn't allow her to think she could do as she pleased. *First she goes where she wants without telling me. What's next?* He didn't like the feeling of not being in control. She needed to be taught a lesson. There was nothing he could do to her until she had the baby, but he did have another plan. He picked up the phone and dialed.

"Yeah, it's me. Do you remember the conversation we had the other day? Good. I want you to put it into action. Not later, right now. Stop whatever you're doing and take care of it. Call me after it's done."

Perhaps his reaction was a bit harsh, but he had been waiting for this opportunity for years — far too long. Besides, he didn't need an excuse; he could do as he pleased. And this pleased him greatly.

Regina didn't want to leave her parents' house, which felt more like home to her than any other place. They had spent so many years under a microscope. When they could get away from here, how wonderful it would be to live as they had lived before all of this craziness. Even though she had reservations, her mother was right. Getting out of here was the only way. She couldn't wait for the police anymore. When this child was born, Regina's life would be as good as over.

She didn't trust Anthony. All his concern was just a front. She knew better than to believe it was real. Despite his recent displays of kindness, she could sense his disdain more and more. He believed he could hide his true feelings, but he was not as good of an actor as he thought. Behind the smile and kind words, his dark, hate-filled eyes gave him away.

"Well, Ma . . . Dad, I guess I'll have to go. Vinny's been waiting outside for a while now. But I don't want to go. I love you both so much! I'll come again soon to see you." Regina got up from the sofa. After giving them hugs good-bye, she walked out the door.

Vinny was patiently waiting. He threw his cigarette on the ground when he saw Regina approaching and walked her across the street to his car. She was just about to get in when she realized she had left her keys.

"I forgot my keys on the table. Would you mind getting them for me?"

"No, ma'am, I don't mind," Vinny replied.

She climbed into the back seat, and he closed the door after her.

But then her father came up to the car. "Hey, Honey, you forgot your keys."

Regina rolled the window down. "Thanks, Dad. I was just going to send Vinny in to get them."

Down the street, a black car with tinted windows turned the corner and began coming toward them. Regina barely noticed it as she took the keys through the window, and Michael leaned in to give her a kiss. Smiling at her, he headed back across the street.

Regina suddenly looked up again as she heard the black car gun its engine, heading straight toward her father.

"Dad! Watch out!" she screamed.

The car struck him, tires skidding. He rolled off the hood and landed on the street. As the black car raced off again, the federal agents took off after it, roaring around the corner in pursuit.

Regina jumped out of the car and yelled at Vinny, "Call for an ambulance!"

Sophia came running out of the house. She screamed when she saw Michael lying in the middle of the street, Regina kneeling by his side.

"Daddy, Daddy, can you hear me?" There was no response.

In a daze, Sophia walked into the street and stood behind her daughter. She asked softly, "Is he okay?" She stood there stunned, tears running down her cheeks. Regina looked at her mother's face, and all the color drained from it. This was their worst nightmare coming to life.

Regina checked for a pulse. *Oh, Lord! Please help us.* She found it. "He's alive, Ma. He'll be all right! I just know it."

She had never felt more helpless in her life. Trying to keep a strong front for her mother, she resisted the tears and prayed that the ambulance would get there quickly. A crowd was starting to form. *A miracle, God,* she asked silently. *A miracle.*

By the time the agents returned, the ambulance had arrived. The agents cleared the crowd to give the paramedics room to work. Quickly checking Michael's vital signs, the paramedics secured him on the stretcher and loaded him into the ambulance. Sophia and Regina wanted to ride with him, but they were not allowed.

As the ambulance was leaving, one of the agents approached Regina. "Mrs. Cavelli, I'm sorry. We lost the car. It didn't have any plates. But I promise we'll get to the bottom of this. I would have to say, however, that at this point it appears to be a professional job. I've never lost a car so fast."

Regina could feel her anger growing as she helplessly watched the ambulance take her father away. Everything was happening so quickly. There was no doubt in her mind who the "professional" behind all of this was. *Lord, forgive me for the anger and hatred I feel right now.*

"Vinny, will you take us to the hospital?"

"No problem, Mrs. Cavelli."

"Come on, Ma. Vinny is going to drive us to the hospital. Don't worry. Daddy's going to be okay."

Sophia said nothing. After asking if her husband was okay, she just stared into space with tears running down her face. She felt numb. In her heart, she knew who had done this and that he would pay.

How could she have been so foolish to have believed him in the first place?

John was driving back from another call when he heard the news about the Palmettos come over the police radio. He couldn't believe it. Anthony had to be behind this, but how would he prove it? Regina must be going crazy.

He had decided to go to the hospital before reporting for duty, just to see how she was doing, when another call came in over the radio for him to report to a crime scene in Marine Park. Unfortunately, the hospital visit would have to wait.

Poppy and Anthony arrived at the hospital at the same time. They greeted each other outside the entrance.

"Anthony, how did this happen?"

As they entered the building, Anthony answered, "I don't know. Vinny said some crazy person ran him down. Unfortunately, Regina was right there and saw the whole thing. She's very upset. But don't worry — I have some people working on it. I'll get to the bottom of this if it's the last thing I do."

Poppy said nothing until they were on the elevator. Then, away from the eyes of others, he said quietly, "I gave my word that he would be safe. If I find out you had anything to do with this . . ."

"I swear, Poppy. I had nothing to do with this."

Poppy didn't respond. He just glared at him, sending a very clear message.

Surely my own father wouldn't threaten me over someone like Michael Palmetto.
"I had nothing to do with this," Anthony repeated again. There was still no response from his father, so he pressed, "Why would I endanger my own child? Can you imagine how upset Regina is right now? I wouldn't do anything that would upset her like that."

Very calmly, Poppy replied, "I hope not."

Regina was sitting in a chair in the hall with her head in her hands, praying that God would save her father. The doctors said he was in really bad shape; there was a lot of internal bleeding, and he still hadn't regained consciousness. They'd tried to repair the damage in surgery, but he was still in critical condition. She heard footsteps approach and looked up to see Anthony and Poppy coming toward her.

"Regina, how is your father? Will he be all right?" Poppy asked. At first glance, he seemed genuinely concerned.

Regina didn't respond; she just glared at his son.

"I want you to know, I have some boys out looking for whoever did this. I will get to the bottom of this, Babe. Someone will pay." Anthony walked over and knelt by her side. He tried to put his arm around her, but she jerked away from him.

Poppy gave Anthony a look. "She doesn't like to be held when she's upset," he said, as if he would know.

Regina got up and looked at Anthony in a way he had seen only once before. She spoke calmly and distinctly. "Get . . . out . . . of . . . here."

"Regina, what's the matter?" Poppy asked, seeming confused by her anger.

"I want him out of here," Regina repeated. She couldn't believe the rage that was roaring through her. If she had a gun in her hand, she wouldn't have hesitated to shoot him.

"Why?"

"Ask your son. He knows why!"

"Hey, Babe, I don't know what you're talking about. I know you're upset about your father, but don't take it out on me. I'm just trying to help."

The sound of his voice was making her crazy. She couldn't stand it anymore and lunged toward him to slap him in the face. A stunned Anthony caught her hand before she could make contact. Spinning around, Regina attempted to slap him with her other hand, but Anthony grabbed that one, too, and stood there trying to keep her back. Poppy stepped in the way and separated them. He held Regina away from Anthony, who was still stunned. Neither one of them, apparently, knew she had it in her.

"Regina, calm down! Tell me what's the matter!"

A few paces away, arms folded, Vinny watched the whole scene in disbelief. He had never seen Regina act this way before. It looked like she had gotten in a few good shots before Poppy separated them.

He knew it would be best if he just stayed out of the whole mess. Poppy looked like he had everything under control. Vinny leaned against the wall and watched in open fascination, as well as a little bit of suspicion.

He had never seen Regina act this way before.

The door to Michael's room opened, and Sophia looked at them incredulously. "Take your hands off my daughter, Antonio! Have you no respect at all for my family or me? My husband of over thirty years is in that room fighting for his life, and you show up here to cause trouble? It is not good for Regina to be upset in her condition. I think it would be best if you both left."

"Sophia, I apologize. This is not as it appears," Poppy replied, letting go of Regina. "I didn't mean any disrespect to you or Michael. I came here to see if there was anything I could do. Regina is upset with Anthony, for some reason, and I was just trying to get to the bottom of it."

Regina angrily interrupted. "Not *some* reason — many reasons. The latest being my father was run down right in front of me! Any guesses on who's responsible?"

"What?! I never heard of such a ridiculous thing. Why would I do that?" Anthony replied, as if she was crazy for even thinking such a thing.

"Because you hate him and have never forgiven him. You saw an opportunity to get rid of him by making it look like an accident. The federal officer who witnessed everything even said it had to be a professional hit. You're the only professional I know with a reason to harm him."

"No, he's not," Sophia said, looking at Poppy. "Is he? You waited all these years to get back at him, didn't you? Why go through the charade of having us come back here? Why not do it years ago, instead of having my daughter marry that animal you call a son?"

Anthony didn't appreciate her tone. He could feel the rage rise up inside him, but he fought to keep calm in front of his father. That old woman was asking for it. She'd better watch her step.

"Sophia, on my honor, I did not do this, nor did Anthony. It could have been one of our enemies trying to make it appear as if we did. I'll get to the bottom of it, I promise you."

"Honor? How dare you speak of honor! You have no honor. Now leave us alone. Come, Regina. Let's go sit with your father." She took Regina by the arm.

Regina turned around and looked at them, saying, "I mean it — get out, and stay away from me with your false sympathy."

They walked into her father's room and closed the door. It had been a long time since she'd spoken to Anthony like that, and it felt good to release the anger she felt toward him.

Antonio stared at his son.

"I'm telling the truth, Poppy. It wasn't me."

"Let's go." Antonio wasn't sure if he believed him, either. But he made up his mind to think him innocent until proven guilty. After all, Anthony *was* his son.

Father Thomas stepped off the elevator as Poppy and Anthony were getting on. They had no idea who he was, but he knew who they were. He nodded a greeting to them as he would to anyone and then waited until the elevator doors closed before starting to walk toward Michael's room.

He saw a huge, burly man sitting outside the room and figured him for Vinny, one of Anthony's men. Sophia had mentioned him. He said hello, and Vinny stood up. Father Thomas, not a short man, instantly felt dwarfed.

"May I help you?" the big man asked.

"Is this the room of Michael Palmetto?"

"Yes."

"My name is Father Thomas. I've come to pray for him and see if I can be a comfort to his family."

"I'm afraid I can't let you in until I see some identification." Vinny was not impressed with the priest outfit. Any idiot could rent a collar at a costume shop, and after what had happened today, he wasn't taking any chances. For all he knew, this could be the same guy who had run Michael down.

The door opened, and it was Regina. "Father Thomas, I'm so glad you're here. Vinny, it's okay. Father Thomas is a good friend of the family. Please, come in."

Vinny relaxed. "Sorry, Father. A person can't be too careful under these circumstances."

"That's quite all right."

Vinny still felt rather shocked about what had happened just a few minutes ago. Mostly, he couldn't help but feel sorry for Regina. She was such a nice lady. She had always been kind to him, and the fact that she would lunge at Anthony scared him. No one had ever done that and lived. He wasn't sure if Anthony had anything to do with her father's hit-and-run or not — and for Anthony's sake, he hoped he didn't. Poppy was not some-one to cross, even if you were his son.

But the real surprise was Sophia. She was one tough broad to go up against Poppy like that. He'd never seen Poppy react so gently in the face of someone so angry. He wondered what that was all about.

He never thought he would see the day when two women would get the best of the Cavellis.

Michael was still unconscious when Father Thomas took his hand and started to pray. "Father, I come before You and ask for mercy. Touch Michael with Your Holy Spirit. Let Your healing power flow through him. I pray, Lord, we can speak to him again. Help him come back to us. Help him open his eyes."

He continued to pray silently as Regina and Sophia joined in. After several minutes, he said, "Amen."

Regina wiped her eyes, putting on a brave face for her mother. "Thank you so much for coming. This means so much to my mother and me. We appreciate your support and your prayers."

"I'm so sorry for your pain. I want you to know that I'm here for you in any way that you might need."

He had barely finished speaking when Michael unexpectedly cleared his throat. The noise startled them.

Sophia leaned over him, squeezing his hand. "Michael, can you hear me?"

He slowly opened his eyes. "What happened?"

"You got hit by a car, Daddy."

"Who . . . ?" That was as much as he could ask.

"No, Daddy, they haven't found out who hit you. How are you feeling?"

"Sore." He moved his head and saw that Father Thomas was standing nearby. "Thanks."

Father Thomas nodded and smiled at him.

"Daddy, I'm going to get the doctor. He'll want to know that you're awake."

"No . . . not yet." Michael was growing more alert now, and the words came a bit more easily. "I'd like to talk to Father Thomas alone."

"Okay, but don't take too long. I don't want you to tire yourself." Sophia turned to her daughter. "Come on, Regina. Let's find the doctor and let him know that your father is awake now." She kissed Michael on the head as they left.

A moment passed in silence. Father Thomas waited for Michael to speak.

"Father, I've made many mistakes in my life," Michael finally whispered. "I don't normally go to church unless Sophia drags me. I can feel it . . . I'm dying."

Father Thomas wanted to tell him otherwise, but he sensed by the Spirit that Michael might be right. As tempting as it would be, lying to a dying man was not in his nature. His job now was to prepare the soul for the afterlife. "I'm afraid that's a possibility."

A doctor and a nurse came into the room. The doctor examined Michael, asking, "Mr. Palmetto, how are you feeling?"

"Like I just got hit by a truck." Michael chuckled softly and then winced at the effort. He'd have to remember no more jokes. They hurt too much.

"Well, it's good to see you have a sense of humor. I'll be back in a bit to check on you." He turned to Father Thomas. "Don't tire him out too much, okay?"

"No problem, Doctor."

The doctor and nurse left, closing the door behind them.

Michael could barely wait to get out the words. "I want to confess my sins," he said abruptly. "I want God to forgive me."

"Michael, God loves you very much. I know the hard life you have led. I will listen to your confession, but it's God who forgives and gives you eternal life. May we talk for a few minutes first?"

"Yes."

So Father Thomas started telling Michael about Jesus and His sacrifice on the cross, how He died for him so that he might live eternally with God the Father. He told him about God's mercy and grace and especially about His forgiveness. He listened as Michael confessed his sins, repented for them, and asked God to forgive him.

There in the hospital bed, Michael began to understand Sophia and Regina's love for God. The words he'd heard them say and the way they had led their lives came flooding into him, affecting him in ways they never had before. The accident had caught his attention. He remembered a song from his childhood, one he hadn't heard in years:

Jesus loves me, this I know,
'Cause the Bible tells me so.

Why this came to mind now, he wasn't sure. But he'd come this far; before it was too late, it was time to finish the race. With Father Thomas' guidance, he prayed to Jesus and asked for a relationship with Him. When they were done, it was as if a giant weight had lifted from his shoulders.

Michael had one final prayer: He asked God to forgive him for wasting so many years not serving Him.

"Promise me you'll look out for Regina and Sophia. Help them get away. I suspect that either Anthony or Antonio is behind this *accident.* I forgive them, or whoever did this to me. They don't know any better."

"Don't worry about Sophia or Regina. I'll do all that I can to help them."

"Will you get them for me?"

"Yes. Bless you."

Father Thomas smiled at him once more before stepping out. Regina and Sophia were pacing the hallway and came to him immediately.

"He wants to see you both. Before you go in, I want you to know he just gave his life to Christ."

They grinned and hugged him, thanking him for all his help.

Father Thomas was getting off the elevator in the lobby when a man bumped into him. He recognized him as the cop who was trying to help the Palmettos, but in his rush, John didn't acknowledge Father Thomas.

"Detective Nelson, how are you?"

"Okay, Father. I'm sorry, but I gotta go. Talk to you later."

He certainly was in a hurry. He always looked so troubled. The priest began praying for him, asking God to bring him peace.

Regina and Sophia stood on either side of Michael's bed. Regina tried not to cry as he turned toward her. He looked in her eyes, and he didn't have to say a word; she knew what he was thinking. All those years wasted. How she regretted the time they had lost. Especially now.

"Regina, I want you to know how much I love you. A man couldn't ask for a better daughter."

The tears started again, and Regina couldn't get them to stop. "Daddy, please don't talk like that. I know you love me. I love you, too. Don't say it like it's the last time, okay?"

"Please listen. Take care of your mother and that grandchild of mine."

Silent tears rolled down Regina's face. The thought of losing her father crushed the breath out of her. She was not sure she had the strength to say good-bye.

He looked toward Sophia, the one woman who had captured his heart. His eyes started to well up with tears. He opened his hand and she placed hers inside it. He gave it a gentle squeeze, silently reliving all the good times they'd shared. If it weren't for her, the last several years would have been unbearable. There was so much he wanted to say, and so little time.

"Sophia. How can I express in mere words my love for you? After all our years together, I hope there is no doubt in your mind about my love."

Sophia held back her tears. "I don't deserve you. I never did. You are the best thing in my world. For the rest of my life, I will love you." She bent over and kissed him. She held his face tenderly in her hands. He looked at her, smiled one last time, and then closed his eyes.

His monitor flatlined. Suddenly the room was filled with nurses and doctors rushing about trying to revive him, but it was too late. Their valiant efforts didn't change the outcome. He was gone. The only sound was the monitor's piercing, final toll.

Regina and Sophia just held each other and wept. The doctor called the time of death, and that was it. They were left alone to say their final good-byes. The two of them came out of the room, holding each other and crying.

Vinny watched the love between them and couldn't help but feel their pain. He thought about how he would feel if this were his father. The big, strong man fought back the sting in his eyes and pushed down the lump he could feel forming in his throat.

When John got off the elevator, he saw them in the hall. Regina was crying, and he figured there wasn't good news. He didn't want to intrude. Instead, he went over to the nurse's desk and showed his badge. "Excuse me. I'm Detective John Nelson. I'm here to investigate Michael Palmetto's accident. I need to ask him some questions."

"I'm sorry, Detective, but he just passed away."

John wanted to go to Regina and comfort her, but he knew that wouldn't be appropriate. Not now. He saw the big guy who worked for Anthony and didn't want to cause her any trouble. He found it interesting, however, that neither Anthony nor his father was anywhere to be found.

The family deserved some time to grieve. The last thing they needed now was questions.

Chapter 7

The rain fell softly on the tent roof, somehow comforting and almost like music to Regina's ears. For a time, it was the only sound she was aware of in the entire cemetery.

The service was small and private. Some of the press was there to cover the funeral, perhaps not so much because of who Michael was but because of those attending — Antonio and Anthony Cavelli. Anthony's men kept them at bay. The press had been in love with Regina ever since she had married Anthony. She always smiled for the camera and understood they needed to make a living taking her picture, and, since she cooperated, they really didn't bother her. It was all part of the game.

The game she played because she was married to Anthony. The game that had cost her father his life. All those years being married to a monster, trying to protect the very person she now was burying.

Father Thomas spoke about Michael's love for his family and for life. Her parents had been gone from the area for so long that they had few friends left. Regina saw some of those familiar faces now; a few neighbors had come to show their support as well. The flowers were colorful and in abundance. Regina was surprised by the vast variety of them, some surrounding the casket, some on the ground, and others on stands. She hadn't known there were so many different types. Before the service had started, she had looked to see who had sent them and discovered, somewhat to her surprise, that Poppy had sent them all.

Her mother hadn't said a word to Poppy since that incident at the hospital. Regina couldn't recall ever seeing her mother that angry before.

She was staying at the house with her to keep her company and help make all the arrangements. Anthony hadn't put up a fuss about Regina's staying there. He was playing the part of the understanding husband, who would sacrifice for his beloved mother-in-law in her hour of need. Maybe he thought time away would change Regina's mind about his being responsible for her father's death. She didn't really care about his motivation at this point; her mother was her main concern. She'd have to worry about his responsibility later on.

As Regina sat there, she only half listened to Father Thomas speak. Her thoughts wandered again to her father — how much she loved him and now he was gone. It felt so strange to know that she would never hear his voice or give him a hug ever again. That hurt almost more than she could bear. But she was worried about her mother. Sophia hadn't eaten much lately. All she seemed to do was clean the same things over and over. She hadn't moved anything that belonged to her husband; those things she didn't touch. She had left the coffee cup right on the kitchen table where he'd set it. Regina had tried once to clean it up but had been heartily rebuked.

The police and the FBI were both investigating the hit-and-run death of her father. So far, the only thing they had come up with was the car. They had found it abandoned downtown, but, of course, no prints could be made out and the car had been stolen days before the accident. One thing was certain: The driver had been very careful to cover his tracks. That only confirmed what Regina already knew: This wasn't a random accident, and the person driving had been deliberately aiming for her father. There were only two people she could think of who would want him dead.

The words, "And now, let us bow our heads and say a prayer in silence," roused her out of her fog. There was silence for a few minutes, and then Father Thomas concluded with, "Amen." He walked over to Regina and Sophia and placed his hands upon theirs, speaking words of encouragement. When he removed his hand from Regina's, she could feel a piece of paper between her fingers. Not wanting to draw attention to it, she reached into her purse for a handkerchief and dropped the piece of paper in at the same time.

During the entire service, Anthony had been sitting beside her and trying to continue his role of supportive husband. Occasionally, he had reached over to place his hand on Regina's, but she pulled hers away every time, and he had finally given up.

As the service concluded, those in attendance took turns walking by the casket and placing a rose on it. They, too, expressed their sympathy to Regina and her mother.

Poppy waited to speak until they were alone. "Sophia . . . Regina, let me express my deepest sympathy for your loss. I know what it's like to lose someone you love so much. I am here if you need anything."

Sophia sat without moving and did not reply. She didn't even look at him as he spoke. Regina didn't know what to do or say, so she just kept silent.

Poppy hesitated and then followed Anthony out of the tent. After he'd departed, Sophia got up slowly from her chair. She took a rose from the nearly empty vase, kissed it, and placed it lovingly on the casket. "Good-bye, Michael. I'll love you forever." She looked at Regina and then walked toward the car. Vinny opened the door for her, and she slid inside and waited.

Regina, with care, took a rose and placed it on the casket near her mother's. With tears rolling down her cheeks, she said, "You've been the best father a girl could ever have or hope for. I will always love you, Daddy." She started to walk away but then realized she had one more thing to say. "I promise to tell your grandchild all about you. You would have been a wonderful grandfather."

A short distance away, Antonio waited with his son beneath a tree and overheard every word Regina said. He wanted to go to her and comfort her. He wanted to tell her the truth, but he knew he never could.

He came up behind her. "Regina, wait."

She stopped walking.

"Regina, please, you must believe me. I had nothing at all to do with your father's death. You must tell your mother for me."

She turned around, looked him in the eyes, and spoke directly and calmly. "With all due respect, I don't know for sure what happened, but I am sure of this: Either you or your son did this."

She started to walk away again. Antonio caught up to her and gently grabbed her arm. She stopped and looked at him.

"What can I do to convince you?"

"Nothing you do or say will convince me. But what you can do for me now is let go of my arm."

He quickly did as she asked.

"I'm working on forgiving the person who caused my father's death because it's not good for a person to hold on to hate. As for my mother — just keep away from her. She wants nothing to do with you, and nothing I can say will change that. And frankly, I don't want to change that. I don't want to see her hurt any more than she has been. And if I never see you or your son again, it won't be too soon."

She walked away, leaving Antonio and Anthony behind. Anthony started to follow her, but Antonio stopped him. Regina needed to be alone. He understood her pain and her anger. Her words hurt him, but there wasn't anything he could do about it. Time would soften her heart again, or so he hoped.

John pulled up to his parents' house and sat in the car for a few minutes, wondering how Regina was handling everything. Hopefully, Father Thomas had had an opportunity to give her his note.

He noticed his sister's car parked in the driveway. *Good. I could use her advice, too.* He walked up to the house and before he could knock, his mother opened the door.

"Hi, Honey. I saw you sitting in your car, and I was wondering how long you were going to stay there!" She paused, and when he didn't answer, she asked, "Are you okay?"

John surfaced from his thoughts enough to say, "Hi, Mom. Sorry. I was just thinking."

"Come on in. Lisa! Your brother is here."

"Oh, John, it's so good to see you." Lisa came in from the kitchen and embraced him warmly. She always knew how to make him feel special. They had been close as children and had become even more so after Sam's death.

Their mother looked puzzled. "What brings you here this time of day?"

"I wanted to talk to you."

"Do you want me to leave?" Lisa asked.

"No, please stay. I'm glad you're here."

They sat down at the kitchen table by the window. The kitchen wasn't very large, but it was a comfortable place to be. Many lively discussions had taken place at this table, as well as fun-filled family meals. When he was growing up, they would gather together and eat as a family almost every night. They would recap their day and laugh at each other's stories. It was a special time, and he couldn't help thinking of it and feeling rather nostalgic whenever he came for visits.

John's mom poured everyone some coffee and sat down. The women waited patiently, sipping their coffee and giving John time to speak. He wasn't sure how to begin.

"I've been working on this case that has me a bit confused." He paused for a moment, but when neither Lisa nor his mom spoke, he continued. "There's this woman . . . She's married to the suspect and she's pregnant. It was an arranged marriage."

Lisa and his mom just looked at each other.

"Anyway, she's very religious and living with him has become quite dangerous."

He found himself rambling, not making much sense. He could tell by the look in their eyes that they weren't following him. He finally took a deep breath and just blurted it out. "I think I'm falling in love with this woman, who's married to a suspect in a case I'm on, and I don't know what to do."

There. He had said it out loud. He looked from one to the other, trying to gauge their reactions.

There was silence for a moment. This would be the first time his mother and sister had ever heard him say he was falling in love. In fact, most likely, they had never even suspected him of being so before. He had had women in his life previously, but he had never been all that serious about any of them.

His sister spoke up first. "So, is she in love with you, too?"

"I'm not sure. I haven't asked her. She's an amazing woman. She's brave, sweet, and very caring. Her husband raped her and that's how she became pregnant. I don't think she would ever express her feelings for me, if she has any, because she's married, even if it's in name only. That's just the type of woman she is." John wished he could stop blabbering every time he spoke.

His mother finally introduced her opinion. "Oh, John. This is not a good situation for you. You must realize that you're playing with fire. Who is she? Would we know her?"

John had a hard time keeping the truth from his mother, but he knew he couldn't tell her. He just shook his head.

"Please, tell me."

John trusted these two people with his life, but it couldn't be helped. "I'm sorry, Mom. It would betray my promise to her. I can't tell you."

Lisa stared at him. Her eyes betrayed her thoughts. John wasn't sure of this — right now, he wasn't sure of anything — but she couldn't possibly know who he was talking about. "John, you're insane if it's who I think it is."

He didn't respond. He couldn't even look at her anymore.

"It's Regina Cavelli, isn't it?"

His eyes widened in surprise. How did she know? He tried to cover it. "No, Lisa, you're wrong."

"No, I'm not. You should have seen your face when I said her name."

John just stared at the table. He hadn't intended for the conversation to go this far. "I'm sorry I came here. This was a huge mistake."

Lisa shook her head. "You are insane. What are you thinking?"

"Lisa, if you met her, you would understand. I've kept this bottled up for so long. I don't understand my feelings at all, and all I can do is think of her. I think about her first thing in the morning when I wake up, and she's on my mind at night right before I go to bed. During the day it's hard to stay focused. I feel like I'm losing my mind. So yeah, maybe I am insane."

"John, Honey, it's okay. We understand." His mom shot Lisa a disparaging look. "I want you to know that I love you, and I'm glad you came here today and told us."

She wished she could make his pain go away and didn't know what else to say. John seemed so flustered and fragile. She couldn't recall him ever being this way before. It seemed to be affecting his work as well, which concerned her. He couldn't afford to make mistakes in his job, and she couldn't lose another son.

She couldn't.

Lisa realized her mother was right, so she kept to herself the rest of her concerns over his involvement with this woman. After a few minutes of silence, she said, "The only thing I can think of that would help you at this point is prayer. May I do that?"

"I'm not much for praying . . ." He paused. "But I guess, right now, I've got nothing to lose."

So Lisa took his hand and her mom's. She closed her eyes and started to pray, "Lord, come now and fill us with Your presence. I pray that You will help John come and know You. Lord, give him Your strength and Your wisdom to work this situation out. We ask that You protect Regina Cavelli and her unborn child as well. In Your name we pray. Amen."

She kept it short and sweet. She didn't want to overwhelm him. "You know, God does love you, John. He'll give you all you need."

He'd heard this all before, and he just didn't want to get into the whole "God" thing again. Besides, he had somewhere to be. "I've gotta go. Thanks for listening."

"John, be careful," his mom urged.

"Don't worry, Mom. I'm always careful," he said with a smile.

Regina was sitting on her mother's sofa, watching Sophia as she stared into space. She prayed for her silently because she didn't know what else to do.

"Ma, do you want some tea?" Sophia didn't answer. "Maybe you should go lie down?"

Sophia finally responded. She studied her daughter a moment then got up and headed for the door. She turned around and motioned for Regina to follow. They stepped outside and started to walk.

"I want you to promise me something."

"Sure, Ma. What is it?"

"I want you to promise me that you will get as far away from here as possible. I want you to go to Father Thomas' now."

"Not without you, Ma. You have to come with me."

"No. I'll stay here to make sure you get away and keep them from finding you. Don't worry about me. I'm not a threat to them now."

"It's not safe for you. You know that. I hate to think of what they would do to you to find out where I'm hiding."

"Don't worry about them. They wouldn't hurt me. It's your father they hated."

"What about Anthony? I know he's the one responsible for Daddy's death. Who's to say he wouldn't try to hurt me by hurting you?"

"Anthony can't hurt me. Antonio won't let him. I know what I'm doing. You need to trust me."

Regina stared at the ground. Sophia could sense her sorrow. "Regina, don't look so sad. It's more important now for you and the baby to be safe. If these men would go back on their word about your father, what do you think your husband will do to you if you don't get away before this child is born? Regina, don't you see the hate in his eyes when he looks at you? I'm worried for your safety. Now, don't argue with me — I'm still your mother. You are all I have left, and I couldn't bear it if something were to happen to you."

Regina didn't want to face a future without her mother. She had already lost her father. The sad thing was that she knew her mother was right, as much as it scared her. How would she face all of this alone — getting away and staying hidden, living a life in secret? Yet she knew she wouldn't be completely alone, no matter what happened, for God was with her.

Suddenly she remembered the note Father Thomas had slipped her. It was back at the house in her purse.

"Ma, we have to go back. I forgot that Father Thomas slipped me a note at the funeral. I don't know what it said. It might be from John."

Sophia didn't miss the excitement in her voice as she said the detective's name. "Regina, you're in enough danger. Don't complicate things by falling for this detective."

"Don't be silly, Ma. I don't have time for that. I'm not falling for him. He's just trying to help me."

Sophia stared at her, feeling somewhat suspicious, and didn't say anything else.

Regina hurried to explain further. "Father Thomas told me he would be the go-between and relay messages back and forth. Maybe I won't have to go away if Anthony is put in jail."

As they got back to the house, they saw Anthony's limousine parked in the driveway.

"What's he doing here?" Regina asked flatly. Her question was soon answered.

Anthony stepped out of the car and with concern in his voice said, "Darling, where have you been?"

"I went for a walk with my mother. She needed to get some fresh air."

"Well, Sophia, I hope you're feeling better. But I've come to take my wife home. It would be better for her and our baby if she were with me. I want you to know that you're welcome to come with us, if you don't want to be here by yourself."

Sophia didn't know what to say. When she looked into Anthony's eyes, all she saw was pure evil. But what choice did Regina have? If her husband "suggested" something, he wasn't asking her; he was telling her. She didn't want her daughter to go alone. As she spoke, Sophia tried not to choke on the words.

"Anthony, I think I'll take you up on your offer. I need to be near Regina right now. She's such a comfort to me. Give me a few minutes, and I will go inside and pack some things."

Sophia looked at Regina and smiled, letting her know that everything would be all right. She then walked inside, leaving them alone.

"Why? What are you up to?" Regina asked.

"It's starting to look bad. It seems like you want to stay away from our home, and from me. And you being pregnant . . . Well, let's just say I can't have that any longer. Besides, I've missed you." Anthony grinned.

"Let's not play this game where you pretend to be concerned for my well-being. I know you had something to do with my father's death. Why in the world would I go anywhere with you?"

"I've told you before that I didn't have anything to do with what happened to Michael. Besides, you're not stupid." Anthony smiled at her again. He placed his hand on her shoulder and squeezed it slightly as he said, "You know it's better for you and your mother if you come with me now. Don't disappoint me, Regina."

Regina looked at him and knew right then, her fate was sealed. She had to get away — and fast. "I'll be out in a while. I have to get my stuff and see if Ma needs any help."

"Don't be too long. I'll wait in the car until you ladies are ready. I've got some phone calls to return anyway."

She went inside, knowing that unless she could get away soon, she might not live to see her child grow up. She fished the note out of her purse, unfolded it, and read:

> *I deeply regret the loss of your father and extend my sincere sympathy to you and your mother. We have to talk. I'll meet you at your mother's house later. I'll come in the back way like the last time.*

Oh, no. Your timing is horrible! Was he crazy? Didn't he know how dangerous it could be? Anthony was outside. She had to hurry up and leave before John could get here. Her mother came down the stairs with her suitcases.

"Honey, I packed your things for . . . Regina, what's the matter?" Before Regina could respond, there was a knock at the back door. Sophia glanced toward the kitchen. "I wonder who that could be."

"No, Ma." Regina grabbed her mother's arm and whispered in her ear, "It's John. That's what his note said. We have to go before Anthony catches him here!"

Sophia whispered back to her, "No, this is perfect. Regina, go. Now is the time. I'll go outside and stall Anthony. Just go with him. Let him take you to safety."

"No, Ma. I can't leave you," Regina said, tears in her eyes.

But Sophia would not allow her to argue. She handed Regina her bag and led her to the back door. She opened it, and before John could utter a single word Sophia whispered, "Take her to Father Thomas' house *now*!"

John looked stunned. He didn't know what was going on.

"Please take my little girl to safety. She's all I have left. There's no time to waste. Please, before it's too late." She looked at Regina's face soaked in tears and hugged her quickly. "Darling, go, please. I'll be all right. God's watching over me."

Trying to stay strong for her mother's sake, Regina turned and left with John through the back alley.

Sophia closed the door and took a deep breath. As her heart began to slow, she walked back into the living room and looked around. On the fireplace sat a picture of her and Michael. She went over to it and just stared at it. "It doesn't matter what happens to me now, Lord," she whispered at last. "Just watch over Regina."

She picked up her suitcase and walked out the door. Mario took her bag from her and put it in the trunk as she walked slowly down the front steps to the car. He opened the door and she climbed inside.

"Where's Regina?" Anthony asked.

"She's using the bathroom. You know how pregnant women are. She should be out shortly. She told me to go ahead and wait in the car."

Anthony just looked at her, but Sophia didn't flinch.

They reached John's car without either one of them saying a word. John dropped her bag on the backseat, and they drove away, leaving her mother behind. Regina kept looking back to see if they were being followed, but she couldn't tell.

"Don't worry. Nobody is following us." He looked at her briefly and asked, "So what was that all about?"

Panting and out of breath, Regina replied, "Anthony came to take me back. My mom thought it was better if I left."

"Are you okay?"

"Scared and worried about my mother, but okay. This is happening so fast."

"Don't worry. I'll take you to Father Thomas' house, okay?"

"No, not yet. Anthony will look there for sure. He knows I won't trust anyone else. I need a safe place that he won't think to find me, until I can leave town."

"I know just the place."

"How long does it take to go to the bathroom? Mario, go see what's keeping her!" Anthony barked.

Before Mario could move, Sophia interrupted, "Let me go. If there's a problem, I can help. I'll be right back."

It'd been about fifteen minutes since they had left. *Let that be enough time*, Sophia thought as she went into the house, calling out Regina's name. She walked up the stairs to the bathroom and opened the door. Then, hearing Anthony enter downstairs, she took a deep, trembling breath and ran back down the steps, calling for her in a panic.

"I can't find her! I think she's gone. Where do you suppose she went?" Sophia said with as much panic and fear as she could muster, which wasn't hard considering Anthony's expression.

"I don't know, but I'll find out. Mario!"

Mario quickly answered the summons.

"Get the boys together — Regina disappeared. I want her found!"

"Yeah, Boss."

He looked at Sophia with great anger in his eyes, but she just returned his look and said, "I hope to God she is okay. Why would she leave like that?"

"Did she tell you anything, Sophia?"

"No. All she said was what I've already told you. She told me to wait in the car because she had to use the restroom." She walked over to a chair, sat down, and started to weep. "O Lord, protect my child! Protect my child!" She cried until Mario stepped back inside the house.

"I sent some boys out, Boss, and I called Vinny to check the neighborhood. How do you suppose she left without us seeing her?"

"Through the back door obviously, you moron! Go out and see if you can pick up any trace of her."

"Do you think we should call the police, Anthony?" Sophia asked, sounding desperate.

"No, Sophia, let me handle this."

"Well, how about your father?" Sophia pressed, knowing she was pushing his buttons. She wanted him off guard in order to give Regina more time. She also didn't want his suspicious mind thinking she had anything to do with this.

"I've got it under control. There is no need to tell my father anything until we know something for sure. Don't worry. I'll find her."

"I'm sure you will. Thank you, Anthony. First her father and now Regina." She started to cry again and, putting her hand over her mouth, escaped upstairs for privacy. Walking into her bedroom, she closed the door, leaned against it, and prayed silently for Regina's safety. She knew she was in good hands. The way that cop looked at her, he would protect her with his own life.

She heard the back door slam as Mario returned. "I'm sorry, Boss," he said, his voice floating up the stairs, "but there's no trace of her outside."

"We've got to find her, do you hear me?!" The kitchen table rattled as Anthony crashed his fist on top of it. Sophia winced. "We've got to find her before Poppy finds out."

Regina fell asleep in his car. John knew he needed to be careful, in every way, because she was so vulnerable right now, but he couldn't help glancing over at her from time to time. *She must be exhausted.* Was he dreaming, or was she really in the car with him? So much had happened and so much was at stake. Yet he couldn't stop looking at her as he drove. She was beautiful when awake and almost breathtaking when asleep.

He took out his cell phone and called the department. "Yeah, it's Nelson," he whispered, trying not to wake her. "I won't be in for the next few days. Tell the captain I'll call him tonight. Yeah, it's one of the cases. Thanks."

At some point he'd have to figure out what to actually tell the captain and Frank. All he knew right now was that he wanted to take care of her and keep her safe.

He used his cell phone once more. "Yeah, it's me. Look, I need a big favor . . . Please don't ask any questions now . . . I need you to have a house-guest . . . You promise, no questions . . . Okay, I'll see you in a bit. Yeah, we're almost there."

Regina should be safe there until he got a chance to talk to Father Thomas again.

"Look, Poppy, I don't know what's going on! I didn't say a word to her. No — why don't you ask Sophia? She was as surprised as I was. Maybe all the hormonal changes made her crazy in the head! I have the boys on it. I'll call you back as soon as I hear anything."

Dropping the phone in its cradle, Anthony grabbed the picture of Regina that he kept on his desk and threw it against the far wall. She was going to pay big for this. Poppy had been calling him nonstop since it had happened. How had he found out? *I bet Sophia called him just to cause trouble.* That old woman hated him.

Mary came in when she heard the crashing noise. "Mr. Cavelli, is everything okay? I heard something break."

"Yeah, fine. That picture fell."

"I'll clean it up right away."

As soon as Mary saw the picture, she knew it was the one he kept on his desk and that it didn't just *fall* all the way across the room. She said nothing as she cleaned up the mess. She had seen Anthony mad before, but today he brought it to a new dimension. Sweeping up the shards, she made her decision: This was her last day of work. She didn't want to deal with this stuff anymore. She was not married and had no family, so disappearing would be easy. She could start anew somewhere else.

She went back to her desk and discreetly started gathering her things.

Vinny came up to Mary's desk and asked quietly, "How is he?"

"Enter at your own risk."

He smiled and took a deep breath. He didn't have good news for the boss, so, prepared for the worst, he knocked and popped his head inside the door.

"Hey, Boss, I'm sorry, but the boys can't find her. It's like she's disappeared into thin air."

"Get out! Don't come back until you have that witch with you!"

"Yes, sir." He quickly closed the door and looked at Mary. "You were right. I'll see you later."

Actually, no, you won't. "Yeah, bye." She had always liked Vinny. He didn't seem as harsh as the others, or as cold. Lately, he appeared to have mellowed even more.

"Mary!" Anthony roared over the intercom. He didn't need to use it, for he could have been heard in the Bronx, she thought.

She went into the office. "Yes, sir?"

"I want you to check all the hospitals, just in case she was in an accident, and also the hotels. Put a trace on our credit cards to see if she's used them and where. Then you can leave for the day."

Mary just nodded and left. That was going to take her all day. She went to her desk, opened up to the yellow pages, and started dialing numbers.

"We're here." John gently shook Regina awake. He had already gone into the house and explained everything to his sister.

Regina opened her eyes, and, blinking, she sat up in the seat and looked around the two-car garage. "You brought me to a garage?"

"No. I just pulled in so no one would see you going inside. This is my sister's house. You'll be safe here until we can make arrangements with Father Thomas." He saw her start to frown, and he reassured her. "She's just like you. I mean, she prays and stuff. Anyway, she used to go to Father Thomas' church when she lived in Brooklyn. Don't be afraid — you can trust her."

They got out of the car. The garage had a door that led to the kitchen, and Lisa was waiting inside.

"Hey, Sis. I want you to meet Regina. Regina, this is my sister, Lisa."

They exchanged greetings. To break the immediate, awkward pause, John asked Lisa, "Where are the kids, Sis?"

"Next door. I figured you didn't want anyone to know she was here, so I made the attic up for her." She turned to Regina and said, "It's quiet. No one goes up there. Its main use is storage. Come. I'll show you."

They followed her upstairs. The attic was accessible through a walk-in closet in Lisa's room. It had a ladder that pulled down from the ceiling. With John's help, Regina managed the ladder, and right away, she noticed how large and spacious and clean the attic was, especially considering Lisa had said it was just for storage. In one corner stood a desk, a chair, and a cot for a bed. On the other side was one small window. Boxes were neatly stacked against the wall. Regina was impressed by how neatly organized everything was.

"You can stay up here. I'll bring you something to eat. You can use the bathroom downstairs in my room. This way the kids won't know you're here. Tomorrow you'll have the whole house to yourself. We're taking the kids to the zoo for the day. There's some towels over there on the chair and an extra blanket on the desk."

Regina reached over and touched Lisa's arm. "I want to thank you for your kindness. I won't be staying long. Just long enough to travel safely away."

"It's no trouble. I think you're brave." Lisa thought that must have sounded stupid to Regina, especially when she didn't reply.

Regina didn't know what to say. She didn't feel brave, especially at the moment. She felt afraid and unsure of her future. "I'll be very quiet. Your family won't know that I'm here."

"I'll go get your bag out of the car. I'll be right back," John said as he disappeared down the ladder.

He left them alone in a silence they didn't know how to fill. Feeling out of place, Regina walked over and sat down on the cot. She could sense Lisa staring at her, and eventually the woman said, "My brother is right. You are beautiful."

Regina smiled at the thought of him calling her beautiful. "That's very nice of you to say. I don't feel that way, though."

Lisa found it hard not to say what was on her mind. "Understand this — I don't want to lose another brother because of your husband." As soon as the words came out, she regretted how harsh they sounded.

Regina's face darkened. "I wouldn't do anything to hurt John. As soon as I get away, I'll probably never see your brother again."

In a much softer tone, Lisa replied, "I doubt that. You must know how he feels about you. By the look in your eyes when you speak of him, he's not alone in those feelings, is he?"

Regina looked down at the floor and then back at Lisa. "I don't know how to answer that question." She took a deep breath. "If I have feelings, I can't act upon them . . . I wouldn't do anything . . ." She couldn't finish her sentence.

Sensing her confusion, Lisa said, "Please forgive me. I don't mean to be harsh or pushy; it's just that I'm worried about him. I've never seen him . . ." Before she could finish her thought, they heard John coming up the ladder.

"Hey, I'm back." He saw that they both looked a bit uncomfortable, and he realized they must have been talking about him. "Hey, Sis, do you mind leaving? I need to talk to Regina before I go."

"No problem. You must be hungry, Regina. I'll be back with something for you to eat. Oh, I almost forgot. There's a cooler over there with some bottled water in case you get thirsty."

"Thank you so much again for your kindness. You've thought of everything."

Vinny drove around almost aimlessly, not knowing where to look anymore. He'd been everywhere, including the restaurant twice. He had talked to everyone he could possibly think of, and no one had seen her.

His cell phone rang. He recognized the number.

"Hello, sir . . . No, I've had no luck . . . Well, to tell the truth, he's really mad . . . Yes, I think we do have reason to be concerned for her safety." Listening to the other man deny that possibility — again — Vinny grimaced and told himself, *Just go along with whatever he says.* "No, I agree with you; I don't believe he would harm her while she's pregnant. Yes, it would be better if we found her first . . . No need to worry, sir. I'll be careful." He hung up.

How did I ever get myself in this position in the first place? One wrong move to either side . . . No one would ever find my body.

"Look. I pay you good money for information. I don't pay you to give me excuses. Just get it back! Name your price. I need those copies back! Don't forget about my *loving* wife." Anthony listened a moment and then snapped, "Fine, it's a deal — you get them back, and I'll give you the sum you ask for. But your freedom we're leaving on the back burner for now."

Anthony hung up the phone. No wonder she was running. *I thought she was smarter than that. Didn't she know I would eventually find out about her betrayal? She had someone helping her.* The question was, Who? It could be more than one person.

The more he thought about it, the more he figured Sophia would be as good a place to start as any. *My sweet, innocent mother-in-law, I'm not as stupid as you think I am.*

"May I come in?" Antonio asked.

Sophia stood there right inside the door, not moving, not speaking, just staring.

"Please, Sophia. I need to talk to you. I promise I won't stay long."

What was he doing here? But the situation being what it was, she couldn't risk just kicking him out. At this point, Regina didn't need any added difficulties. Scowling, she knew she should at least *try* to humor him, for Regina's sake, as much as it pained her to do so. Opening the door wider, she let him in and then went over and sat on the couch, folding her hands in her lap.

Antonio sat across from her in a chair. "I'm really sorry about Michael. I want you to believe me — I didn't have anything to do with his death. If I had wanted to hurt him, I would have done it years ago."

"What do you want from me, Antonio?" Sophia asked with gritted teeth.

"I want to help Regina."

"The best way you can help her is to allow her to stay missing."

"I can't do that, Sophia. She's carrying my grandchild, and you know how I feel about her. I loved my wife, but she was barren. As much as I love Anthony, well . . . it is not the same as your own child."

"I've told you hundreds of times — she's not yours! No matter how many times you say she's yours, it doesn't make it so. I just want you to stop all of this craziness!" Sophia demanded.

Antonio got up from the chair. He walked over to the window and stared outside, watching the children play stickball in the street. Sophia had been watching them herself, before this very uncalled-for interruption. Without turning around, he said, "I know what you've said, but in my heart I know she could be. You have never offered me any proof that she isn't." He turned around and said softly, "I think you know the truth, but you don't want to admit it."

With tears in her eyes and anguish in her voice, she said, "Why are you doing this now? I loved Michael and I made a big mistake with you. It's something I'll always regret because of the pain it caused my husband."

"Sophia, you don't mean that. What we had was much more than a casual encounter. You know how much you still mean to me."

"Enough! I don't want to talk about this anymore with you. As a matter of fact, I don't ever want to talk of this again." Sophia stood up with determination and stated calmly, "I'm tired and I'm worried for the safety of my daughter — *my* daughter. She has been and always will be mine and Michael's." She walked over to the door and opened it. "Now, just leave me alone."

Antonio felt defeated. Her words hurt him more than he would let show. "I'll leave for now." He headed toward the door and stepped out onto the porch. He turned to face her. "A part of me will always care for you. Remember I wouldn't do anything to hurt you or Regina." He turned and walked to his car.

Sophia closed the door and started to weep.

John sat on the cot next to Regina and desperately tried not to look directly into her eyes. "I'll go see Father Thomas and get the directions to the monastery."

"You've done so much for me. How will I ever repay you? It's not such a good idea, my being here. It endangers your sister and her family. I don't want anyone to get hurt because of me."

"No one knows you're here. Believe me, it's okay. Besides, you seem to forget that I'm a cop."

"So was your brother."

Silence filled the air and she realized she'd hurt him with her comment.

"I'm sorry. I shouldn't have said that." Tears filled her eyes as she continued, "I'm just . . . so scared. I don't want anyone else to get hurt or killed. I know Anthony killed my father. My mother stayed behind and . . . there's you, and now your sister and her family . . . It's all very overwhelming." Regina felt so totally helpless at the moment.

"It will all be okay. You need to stay calm. Let me get you to safety first." He wiped the tear coming down her cheek. He realized this was yet another inappropriate move on his part, so he got up quickly. "We can probably leave tomorrow, if I can get in touch with Father Thomas tonight." He headed for the ladder. "I'll check on your mom for you if that will make you feel better."

Regina smiled and said, "It will make me feel better if I know she's okay. Thanks again for your help."

When John had gone, she lay down on the cot and started to cry. As the tears rolled down her cheeks, she prayed, *Lord, I pray for protection for all the people helping me: for my mom, John, Lisa and her family, and Father Thomas. I ask that You give me strength and courage to do the right thing.*

For the first time, she suddenly felt the baby move inside of her. She caught her breath. Her mind knew she was going to have a baby, but to actually feel the child move within her brought that fact into new dimensions. Immediately, she knew she would never tire of this. She placed her hand on her belly and continued to pray. *Lord, protect this child within me. Let him or her have the chance to grow up safely. I pray that You give this child all that he needs to grow healthy and strong. Let him feel how much he is loved. Thank you, Lord.*

Chapter 8

In a completely quiet house, Regina sat in Lisa's kitchen and sipped tea. She had heard the family leave about an hour ago and now was waiting on John. She hadn't slept very well last night. All she could think about was the events of the last several days: her father's death, her mom being left behind, her feelings for John, and her running from Anthony. She wanted to scream, but that wouldn't solve anything. Running from Anthony was bad enough, but what about Poppy? Was she crazy enough to believe he wouldn't send his own people after her? He had found her parents — why wouldn't he find her? There didn't seem to be any progress in the case against Anthony. What if all she did was for nothing?

But thinking like this wouldn't help her situation. She asked the Lord to help her through this mess and to keep her mom safe. She continued to sit, wait, and pray, because that was the best she could do.

Vinny played the tape for Poppy, giving him a running commentary. "You see, this part is very muffled, and what is said isn't clear. Someone comes to the back door, and you can hear Sophia urging Regina to leave with whoever it is. She's got someone helping her, and it's obvious Sophia knows who she left with. Maybe she knows where they were heading."

Vinny stopped the tape and waited for a response. He was glad they didn't have to meet at the park anymore. Anthony had him keeping an eye on Poppy now, so there was no more need for secrecy.

"Did you play this for Anthony?"

"No, sir. I thought you should hear it first and tell me what you want done. He asked me to check the tapes at Sophia's, and when I heard it, I knew you would want to know immediately. This is the original, and I made a copy as you've instructed."

"Good job, Vinny. I can't push Sophia or she won't help at all. But you were wise not to let Anthony know. He would be giving Sophia a hard time if he knew she had helped Regina in any way. We'll just keep this our secret, okay?"

"That's fine, sir, but there's some other things . . ." Vinny didn't know how to bring it up. He had heard the conversation Poppy had had with Sophia, and Poppy knew it.

After a moment, Antonio said, "It's about time you know the truth. Keeping things bottled up gets to a person after a while. It was foolish of me to talk that freely. You're a good man. Thank you for protecting me."

Antonio was grateful that he had Vinny to keep an eye on Anthony. He'd had a good feeling about Vinny all those years ago, and it had proven to be a smart move. The man had been very loyal.

"Sir, may I ask a question?"

"You may ask anything you wish." At this point, there was nothing to hide.

"Does Anthony know he's really not your son?"

"Anthony doesn't know we adopted him. No one does. I loved my wife very much, and at the time she had difficulty getting pregnant; the doctors said she would never have a child. When she did get pregnant, I was thrilled. But then she lost the baby at home in her eighth month. It was stillborn — a boy. She was devastated. It pained me to see her in such a state. She barely ate or spoke for weeks. I was so worried because she was getting so lethargic. She just stayed in bed. It was as if she lost the will to live. We told no one about what had happened. I arranged privately to adopt Anthony. No one was the wiser. Everyone thought Anthony was the baby she was pregnant with. The doctor has never told a soul. I had helped his family with a situation, and he owed me." Antonio had watched his words for so long that it felt liberating to speak so freely now.

"I see. What about . . . ? Never mind."

"Vinny, it's okay. You mean, what about Sophia? Well, that is a much longer story. Maybe someday . . . Right now we need to find Regina before my son does. Who could be helping her? Who does she know that we don't?"

"The people at the restaurant, maybe? Or how about that priest . . . ?"

"Father Thomas, the one who spoke at the funeral? Very good, Vinny, very good. I'll pay him a visit. You keep an eye on Anthony and keep me informed about what he's up to."

"Yes, sir."

Before Vinny left, Antonio added, "Hey, be careful. If my son finds out . . ." He didn't need to finish his sentence because Vinny knew what would happen to him.

Anthony sat in the car for a moment. Looking at Sophia's house, he realized he had to proceed with discretion. He wanted some answers from her, but Sophia was an intelligent woman and getting her to talk wouldn't be easy. Unfortunately, he wouldn't be able to use his normal tactics because he knew it wouldn't sit well with his father.

Speaking to Mario, he said, "Wait here. If you see anyone else coming, call me on my cell phone."

Anthony walked up the stairs and rang the doorbell. Sophia opened the door and he said, "Hello, Momma Sophia. May I come in?"

"If I said no, would that stop you?"

Anthony laughed. "You have a great sense of humor. I guess that's where your daughter gets it. And speaking of your daughter, that's why I'm here. I want to talk to you about Regina." He walked in without invitation and sat in a chair in the living room, where he waited for Sophia to join him.

Anthony watched Sophia closely as she sat down on the couch. She seemed very cautious and even a little afraid. If he played this right, he could get her to crack under pressure.

Anthony got up from the chair and sat next to her. He spoke very softly. "Where's my wife?"

"I don't know. I was as surprised as you were that she left. She told me she had to go to the bathroom; that's where I thought she was."

"As time goes on, I'm finding it hard to believe you don't know what happened to her. She is very close to you. You both spent so much time together right before she left, and you're telling me you didn't know she was planning this?"

"I don't know where she is. But if it will put your mind at ease, if I should happen to hear from her, you will be the very first person I call. I promise."

Did this old woman think he was stupid? Did she have any idea who she was speaking to? He decided to approach her in a different way. "You wouldn't tell me, even if you did know, would you?" The muscles tightening in her jaw, Sophia did not answer him. He looked deeply into her eyes and gave her a sinister smile. "No reply for me?" He leaned in closer and said, "I'll promise you something also. If I find out you helped her, you'll be seeing your husband sooner than you think. Do you understand me?"

Without batting an eye, Sophia said, "A threat, Anthony? That's not very wise, is it? Let's see if you understand this — I'm not afraid of you. Now, get out of my house." She stood from the couch, walked to the front door, and opened it. "Get out now."

He stood up, snickering to himself. When he got to the door, he looked at her and said, "I haven't decided if you're a gutsy old broad or just insane for standing up to me. For the record, either way, I don't like it. You need to have more respect, old woman."

Anthony looked at her, and Sophia could sense his hatred. But for some odd reason, she genuinely did not feel afraid; more than ever, she was glad her daughter was gone and safe from this madman.

Before leaving, he added one more thing. "And if you should happen to hear from my wife, it would be in your own best interest, and hers, if you convinced her to come back before I find her."

He walked to the car and turned around, looking at her once more and shaking his head.

John let himself in with the extra key Lisa had given him. There sat Regina at the kitchen table, reading a book with a flower on the cover. Since no one was home, she had ventured out of the attic.

"Hi. How are you doing today?" he asked.

"I'm at peace."

John thought that was a strange response to his question. How could she possibly be at peace? Regina must have read the puzzled look on his face because she continued, "I was reminded today, while I was praying, of a plaque that sits on my desk. *Sometimes the Lord calms the storm. Sometimes He lets the storm rage and calms His child.* You must think I'm crazy, but I really do feel His peace today — but tomorrow could be another story."

She laughed, and he smiled. It was good to see her more relaxed. "So, what you're telling me is that just believing in God is helping you in this nightmare that you're living in."

"It's more than that."

John hadn't meant it to be an in-depth question, and he didn't really want to continue this conversation. Talking about God made him a bit uneasy, and he was sorry he had brought it up. A change of subject was needed. "Hey, we'd better hit the road. We have a long trip ahead of us, and I'll feel much better after we put some more distance between you and Anthony. Father Thomas says hi, by the way. He told me he'd be in contact with you."

He picked up her bag and they went to the car, parked in the garage once again. As he opened the door for her, Regina couldn't help but smile. These simple, thoughtful gestures, like carrying her bag and opening her door, were things Anthony never did. How different these two men were. After John got in the car, she looked at him and said, "Thank you."

Vinny got to the office and noticed that Mary wasn't at her desk. Maybe she was out running an errand. Anthony's door was ajar and Vinny heard him call, "Mary, is that you?"

Vinny went in. "No, Boss, it's me. Is she sick or something?"

"Who knows? She didn't call and she's not answering her phone. But I can do without her for a day. I want you to go to Brooklyn and check the tapes. There's something I want erased from it."

"What am I looking for?"

"I paid Sophia a visit and I want the conversation erased."

"No problem, Boss. I'll go right away. The tape is as good as gone." The phone rang, and as Anthony picked it up, he said to Vinny, "Hey, close the door behind you."

"Okay, see you later."

After the door closed, Anthony said, "Hey, talk to me. Hmmm . . . I see. Where is he? What do you mean you don't know!? That's not what you get paid for." He realized he was yelling and took a deep breath to calm down. "What do you plan to do about this? You better come up with something! Keep me informed."

He slammed down the phone and had gotten up to refill his coffee mug when the phone rang again. "Yeah?" He changed his tone when he heard who was on the other end. "Hey, Baby. I miss you, too. I will as soon as I get a chance." He listened to her complain some more and tried to reason with her. "Now, Baby . . ." His girlfriend hadn't been happy ever since she'd learned that Regina was pregnant. Anthony hadn't seen her now in a couple of weeks, and reasoning with her was getting to be difficult.

Vinny shut the intercom off and tiptoed out of the office. He climbed into his car and drove away as he placed a call to Poppy. "I'm on my way to check the tape again. I thought you might want to know he paid Sophia a visit. I don't know what happened, but I'm supposed to destroy the tape. I will. Yes, sir. I'll see you later. Yes, that's understood."

Vinny wondered how much longer his luck was going to hold out, playing both sides of this dangerous fence. He just hoped he was on the winning side in the end.

The precinct was quiet today. Leaning back in his chair, Frank frowned toward the door and wondered where John could be. He'd tried calling his apartment. John wasn't answering his cell phone, either. He'd been acting kind of funny lately, Frank thought and decided to go ask the captain if he knew anything.

He found his office door ajar. "Hey, Captain, may I come in?"

"Sure, Frank. You need something?"

"Well, sir, I was wondering if you'd heard from John. I've been calling him all day, and he's not answering his home phone or cell."

"Yeah, he called me last night. I'm sorry. I was supposed to tell you about it. He's discovered some lead and asked permission to pursue it."

"In which case?" Frank wondered.

"The Hammerstein case. He told me an informant gave him a solid lead but that he had to get to California right away."

"California?" Frank's frustrations got the best of him. "Isn't he supposed to be my partner? Why didn't he call me? Why didn't I go with him?"

"Hey, calm down. He was running late and had a plane to catch. That's why he didn't call you. He wanted me to let you know. The case didn't need two cops with expensive expense reports. He's going to hook up with the LAPD when he gets there. Do you remember Detective Washington? He moved out there and is working for the LAPD, and John's going to contact him. He'll be back in a few days, more or less."

"Sorry, sir, for overreacting. It's just that John's my partner, and something just doesn't sit right with this whole thing." Taking a deep breath, Frank changed his tone and said, "Excuse me. I have paperwork to do."

Frank was not happy with the captain's answer. What was John up to? When he got back to his desk, he called a friend who worked for the airlines out at JFK. "Hey, Billy, it's me. Yeah, I need a favor. All right, you first . . . How many tickets are you talking about? Hey, man, haven't you heard it's cheaper to put quarters in the meter? Okay, I'll take care of it for you. Now can we get back to me? I want you to find out which flight a friend took to Los Angeles last night. I'm not sure which airline . . . Yeah, I know. Well, do you want the tickets to go away? Thanks. You're a pal. The name is John Nelson. Yeah . . . got it . . . good. Call me as soon as you find out."

Regina was sitting quietly in the car, looking out the side window. They had been driving for a while now. She'd discovered that she didn't know what to say to him, or even how to act. It had been very hard to keep her emotions in check lately, even when she wasn't doing anything, like now.

She decided to break the silence. "I appreciate all that you've done for me. Thanks for checking on my mom, too. It's good to know that Anthony didn't bother her after he found out we'd gone."

"No problem," John answered.

"I miss her so much." Regina smiled when she felt her child move. She placed her hand on her stomach.

John looked over at her and asked, "If you miss her, why are you smiling?"

"The baby just moved." She reached over and took his hand that was resting on the seat and put it on her belly. The baby kicked again and John began to smile.

"Wow. That's unbelievable. You know, when my sister was pregnant, she let me feel her kids kick, too. It's really something to know that there is a little person growing in there. I hope to one day have this same experience with . . . well, to feel my own baby move."

What was he doing? Pulling his hand away, he realized how much he wished this was his baby — his baby, his wife — and it frightened him just a bit. Where were all these thoughts coming from? What was wrong with him? Whenever he was around Regina, he felt so out of sorts. He had better start getting a grip on reality.

"Let me know when you need a rest stop, okay? If I remember correctly, my sister needed lots of those." What a stupid thing to say. He felt like a geek back in high school. He got around this woman, and his words fumbled and his stomach ached.

"Thank you. I will." *It is nice to share this moment with someone*, she thought to herself, *especially someone who can appreciate it for what it is.* She realized how much she wanted her child to be anyone's but Anthony's. She wanted it to be John's. In the short time she'd known him, without even trying he had managed to awaken feelings she thought were dead.

But she was only fooling herself. A relationship with him could never be. She had to stop thinking and feeling things that would never come about. How could she expect any man to want her with all the baggage that came with her?

Sitting behind his desk with his back to the door, Anthony gazed out the window, not really looking at anything in particular. He had a lot on his mind. What was he going to do about Regina? If he did find her and bring her back, Poppy would be keeping a close eye on him. The old man already suspected him of Michael's murder.

Poppy had warned him about not harming Regina before. If he knew his father, he probably had his own men looking for her, too. The trick would be finding her before Poppy did and then getting the baby. The baby would be Poppy's consolation prize and maybe enough of a distraction to keep his mind off Regina's untimely demise during childbirth. If he could keep Regina away from Poppy until the baby was born, then . . .

There was a knock on the door.

"Hey, Boss." Mario cleared his throat. "I have some bad news for you." Since Anthony didn't respond or turn around, Mario continued, "We still can't find Regina, but I have guys on it twenty-four seven. The other thing is that it appears that Mary skipped town. I sent some boys to her home, and it was cleaned out. No one has seen her since the other day. Her car is gone and her bank account closed. Do you want me to send a couple of guys to look for her?"

"No. I have bigger fish to fry. If she stays gone, then I have no problem with her. Call the agency tomorrow and get another girl set up." Turning his chair around, he continued, "As far as Regina goes, I have a plan to fish her out. Come in and sit for a while. I need to talk to you."

Vinny played the tape, and Antonio was not pleased with what he heard. "Enough! I have heard enough! That son of mine is getting out of hand. He just can't be trusted. Before anyone else gets hurt, I'm going to have to take over again. Before you go back to work, I want you to send some boys to guard Sophia's house. If anything looks suspicious, I want you to tell them to take care of it. Is that understood?"

"Yes, sir. What should I tell them about Anthony?"

"If Anthony tries anything personally . . . then have them bring him to me. And, Vinny, please make sure you don't send over any hotheads."

"Yes, sir, I'll take care of it." Vinny left.

Antonio picked up the phone and dialed the number from memory. It rang, but there was no answer. Finally the machine came on; it was Michael's voice, which spooked Antonio at first. Sophia hadn't changed the greeting yet. At the beep, he left this message: "Sophia, it's Antonio. We need to talk — it's important. Please call." He hoped she would call him back. He was worried about Regina also. Maybe it was time to step up his search efforts. He had to find her before Anthony did.

Anthony had become very unpredictable lately. Antonio had never thought the day would come when he couldn't trust his own son. It saddened him that life had gotten so out of control. He wished sometimes that he were a plumber, or a lawyer, or anything else. But he was not because he had chosen to live his life this way. It was truly too late to go back and change anything.

Regina woke up a bit startled, but she quickly got her bearings. Sitting up, she looked around the motel room and didn't see John. The light was off in the bathroom, and the blanket he had slept on was rolled up and sitting in the corner chair. He had been such a gentleman. He had slept on the floor the whole night, if he had slept at all. It couldn't have been very comfortable. They had decided to share a room because John wanted to keep a close eye on her.

They had arrived late the night before. John had carefully chosen an out-of-the-way place and had paid for the room in cash. Credit cards could be traced to them, and the last thing he wanted was to leave a trail, even if it was his. He had thought of everything.

For the first time since she had married Anthony, she felt safe.

The door opened and John entered, carrying a brown paper bag in his left arm.

"Hello. Did you sleep well?" he asked.

"Yes, a lot better than you did, I'm sure. What do you have in the bag?" Regina was hoping he had something to eat. She felt famished.

"I have some coffee for me and some tea for you, decaffeinated of course," he said as he handed the to-go cup to her. "I didn't know how you liked it, so I have milk, lemon, and sugar just in case. If you're hungry, I also bought some donuts. I didn't know what kind you liked so I have jelly, powdered, cream-filled, plain, chocolate . . . Well, anyway, I have a few different types."

"Yes, I am. Thank you." Regina sipped her tea. It tasted so good and the cream-filled donut was delicious. It really hit the spot. At least this morning, she didn't feel like throwing up.

"I probably should have gotten something more nutritious for you and the baby, but donuts were the only thing I could find. If you like, we can stop somewhere later to eat something more nutritious."

John knew he was rambling again. This felt so awkward. But one thing he knew for sure: He could no longer ignore this. He just had to tell her before he exploded.

Finally, he said, "Regina, we need to talk."

Regina hesitated but asked, "Okay, what about?"

"Us."

"Oh." *Great.* Regina had struggled to keep herself focused on other things, and now he wanted to talk about the very subject she was trying so hard to ignore. Instantly, all her calm, relaxed, good feelings left. "I don't know if that's a good idea. It doesn't serve any purpose at this time." She glanced at him. "Do you understand what I'm trying to say?"

"Yes, I do. But I have feelings for you, and they're getting stronger all the time. I'm not trying to make life more complicated." He walked over to her and took her hand. And then, without any hesitation at all, he continued, "I love you. I know you're pregnant, I know you're married, and I know nothing can come of this right now. I'm not asking for anything. I just need to say it to you out loud before I go crazy."

John couldn't believe he had just said all of that. Until the words actually came out of his mouth, he hadn't realized that he had fallen in love with this woman, whom he barely knew.

She must think he was crazy. Maybe he was.

Stunned, Regina pulled her hand away. For a moment, she couldn't think of anything except that he felt the same way she did. When her heart had slowed enough to allow other thoughts, she realized she couldn't tell him that. It would be too dangerous for him, for both of them, if she said what was on her heart. She was not sure she would be able to stop her emotions if she allowed them the slightest leeway.

"I see. I . . . um . . . don't know what to say. I wish I could tell you . . . but if I do, then . . . Look, after you drop me off, it would be best for both of us if you just forget about me."

"I don't think I can do that. I've tried, but not thinking about you isn't an option. I will promise you this: Anthony will pay for his crimes. Then maybe we can . . ." John noticed how red her face was growing. "Never mind. I don't want you to feel uncomfortable. Maybe we should just hit the road. We still have a long drive."

He could have kicked himself. What was he thinking pouring his heart out like that? He wished she could have given him some tiny, little hope that she felt the same. Maybe she did, and that was why she didn't say anything. But he was going to make himself crazy if he didn't stop wondering what was going on in her head. He grabbed their things and headed out to the car.

Vinny entered the office and noticed that a new girl was sitting behind what used to be Mary's desk. She was very young, probably fresh out of high school. Right away Vinny couldn't help but notice her blonde hair, blue eyes, and cute little figure. She smiled when she saw him and said, "Hello. May I help you?"

"What's your name?"

"My name is Emily. Today is my first day. Do you work here, too?"

"Yeah, I'm Vinny. Is the boss in?"

"Yes, he is. He's in there with some other gentleman. Hold on and I'll tell him you're here." She pressed the intercom to announce Anthony's visitor, but before she could finish, Vinny was already on his way in.

"Hey, guys," he said.

"Good. It's about time you got here. Where have you been?" Anthony snapped.

"I'm sorry, Boss. I took care of the stuff you asked for and then I got some food. Sorry, I was hungry. What did I miss?" Vinny played innocent.

"Have a seat. We were talking about a plan to fish Regina out of hiding."

"So did you come up with anything?"

"Yeah, but I don't think my father is going to like it, so this will have to be our little secret, okay?"

"What has to be your secret?" Poppy asked as he entered the office, startling everyone.

Anthony felt himself pale. Completely flustered, he wondered how long Poppy had been standing there. "Poppy, what a nice surprise. Come in. I was, um . . . talking to the boys about setting up a nursery in the penthouse for when we find Regina." *Nice save,* Anthony thought to himself. He hoped the old man bought it, even though the explanation sounded a bit lame, even to him. Before his father could go one way or the other, Anthony stood up, greeted him properly, and continued, "Come and sit, Poppy. The boys were just leaving."

Taking their cue, they got up and left.

"We still have no trace of her, but I'm hopeful we will find her," Anthony continued.

"Anthony, this is not a social call. I think you're going through a lot right now, with your wife missing. Looking for her and your unborn child should be your first priority. I can help you do that by coming back to work for a while. To keep an eye on things and see that everything goes smoothly. This way, you'll have more time to concentrate on Regina. Today is as good a day as any for me to start."

This couldn't be happening. "Are you saying I can't run the business and look for my wife at the same time? I knew you would pull something like this! You've been waiting for just the right moment. I've been in charge, and I am still in charge. You can't just come in here and demand to take over! I've done nothing to deserve this. We've made more money than ever since I took over. And it's because of my way of doing things."

Anthony finished his tirade and stood his ground, huffing and puffing. Antonio didn't appreciate what his son was saying to him, or the way in which he was saying it. He was not going to be talked to this way by anyone, especially his son.

As calmly as he could he said, "Are you forgetting who I am? How *dare* you talk to me with such disrespect. I will not put up with this. Now, you listen very carefully because I will say this only once. Your behavior proves to me that there are too many distractions going on here. I will be here to oversee things. The first task I have for you is to check up on the restaurant. I want to make sure it's running smoothly so Regina has a business to come back to. If you need me, I will be in the office down the hall. Whether you like it or not this is the way things are — get used to it." Antonio left.

Anthony started to pace. Now what was he going to do?

Well, he had to be careful. His next move was vital.

Mario had heard the shouting, and he stepped back in. "Hey, Boss, is everything okay?"

"No, but I want you to proceed with the plans we talked about earlier. Just be very careful because now we have Poppy watching us on a daily basis. He may think he's in charge again, but that will happen over my dead body. Let him pretend that he's the boss, but nothing changes. Is that clear?"

Mario nodded. He got the message.

Frank hung up the phone, and for a minute, he just sat there and fumed. His friend at the airport had been quick getting back to him. There was no trace of John taking any flight leaving any airline, which meant he had lied. To make matters worse, he still hadn't called. Where was he? What was he up to, and why didn't he trust him enough to tell him about it? Maybe the captain knew something he wasn't telling him. The phone rang again.

"One seven, Detective Holstrum speaking. Oh, hi, Honey . . . No, I still don't know what happened or where he is. If I find anything out, I'll call you. Yes, I know you're worried. I love you, too . . . Bye." Frank decided it was time to go to the captain.

Captain Merrill was on the phone when Frank knocked on the door. He didn't wait for a reply as usual; he just walked in. The captain cut his phone conversation short when he saw his expression. "Hey, Frank, what can I do for you?"

"Well, Captain, I'm worried about John."

"Why?"

"I've checked the airports and he didn't get on a plane to Los Angeles. I have no idea where he is. What if something has happened to him, and that's why he didn't make the plane?"

"I'm sure he's fine. But in any event, he's got some explaining to do when he gets back. Do you think he's in some kind of trouble?"

"I don't know. I could go to his apartment and check it out. What do you think?"

"That's a good idea. You do that. I don't like being lied to — if that's what happened. If you hear from him, tell him to come back from wherever he may be!"

Anthony picked up his cell phone and said, "Yeah, you have something for me? I see. I wonder . . . never mind. Just find him, okay? Let me know what you find out."

He was beginning to wonder whether or not Regina had company on her trip. Maybe she was a bit chummier with that cop than he had first anticipated. Perhaps the copy of his ledger wasn't the only thing she had given him. Up until this point, he had assumed the baby was his, as she had implied, but maybe he'd been too trusting. His mind started to wander.

He called Mario's cell phone. "Listen, I want you to bring in Lilly for questioning. Yeah, maybe she knows what's going on with Regina. They're real close. Do you have someone watching that priest? I don't want to talk to him yet; just keep some men on him. I want a full report. How's that other project coming along? Good, just wait for the right moment. That's right, just as we discussed."

Hanging up, Anthony began to feel a little better. Contrary to everything his father thought, Anthony still had plenty of control where it counted. At least some things were working out the way he wanted; at least some people knew how to do their jobs.

Maybe that connection at the precinct was becoming unnecessary and useless. He hadn't been much help lately, and Anthony was getting information after the fact.

Yet, giving it further thought, he decided to hold on to him for the time being. He had learned not to make these types of decisions abruptly.

Chapter 9

Sophia pushed her shopping cart down the supermarket aisle. Her cart was still empty, even though she had been there for at least thirty minutes. She just couldn't seem to decide on what to buy or how much. She had been cooking for Michael for so many years and now there was no one but her. What was she to do? She paused in the fruit section and just stood there staring, wondering where Regina was right now. She said a prayer for her and for John. More than anything else now, she just wanted her safe and away from the Cavellis, who had cost them both so much in life. She still struggled with forgiveness, not only toward them but also toward herself.

She had been so young, foolish, and confused when she'd gotten involved with Antonio. And Antonio was smooth talking, sophisticated, refined, polished, and powerful. She had allowed herself to fall for the lie of this earthly world that there was something better out there than what she had. And what did she have? A man who worked too hard and for too many long evenings. A man who had so wanted to give her everything that he had sacrificed his principles in order to make money. When she thought about how she had almost lost Michael and the price they had paid for her affair with Antonio, she felt like dying. If Michael hadn't found out what had happened all those years ago, he never would have turned against Antonio. She regretted any moment of Michael's life that had been spent in agony over what she had done.

"Lord," she prayed quietly, "please help Regina not to make mistakes that she can't live with. Help her to stay focused. Give her Your strength."

Well, she had to make a decision about the groceries, so she placed some apples, oranges, and bananas in her cart and moved along to the fresh vegetables section. She wished she hadn't forgotten her list; now she had to try to remember what she was out of at the house, and thinking was something she wasn't doing very well at the moment.

"Sophia."

She recognized his voice all too well. She turned around and saw Antonio standing there. *Not again.* What was he doing here? She wanted to ask, but she seemed to have lost her ability to speak.

"Sophia, please — I need to talk to you about Regina. It's important. Will you come out to the car with me?" Antonio pleaded with her.

She didn't know why she followed him, but she did, leaving her cart right there in the aisle. As they approached Antonio's car, she saw Vinny in the driver's seat, not Antonio's regular driver, and briefly she found that strange because Vinny usually worked for Anthony. Why she noticed this or even cared she didn't know.

Vinny took his post outside the car and scanned the parking lot as, in a fog, Sophia climbed inside the vehicle, still not exactly sure why she was letting Antonio do this to her. She blamed him completely for what happened to Michael. *Oh, God, will I ever awaken from this nightmare?* She took a deep breath before asking Antonio, "Did you find Regina? Is that why you asked to speak to me?"

"No, and that's why I've come to you now. Sophia, I'm worried for the safety of our daughter."

"Don't call her that! She's my daughter! If you can't get that straight, then we have nothing else to ever say to one another. Is that clear?"

"I'm sorry. Please don't be angry with me. I'm just worried for her. Anthony is getting out of control. I've gone back to work fulltime in order to oversee things again. Basically, I just want to keep an eye on him, which also means I will be keeping a close eye on the search to find her."

She didn't trust this man and never would, but he was correct about this one issue: His son was completely out of control.

When she didn't respond, Antonio cautiously continued, "I want to help her. I want to keep her safe. I want her to have the best care for her child. Please, I beg you — if you know where she went, tell me. Help me find her before Anthony does."

"Why do you think I would willingly deliver my child into your hands? I've been in exile for years. I've missed being there for her and now when she needs me the most — I still can't be with her. I blame you. I blame your son. It's your fault she married him in the first place. You forced her to marry that monster! You made her choose to live in hell with your son in order to save her father's life. What kind of man are you? Never mind — don't answer that because I already know. And now you plead for my help in finding her. Antonio, understand me when I say this . . . I don't trust you to guard my purse, much less protect my child. If I knew where she was, you would be the last person I would tell."

Sophia couldn't help her hostility. She felt as if she had nothing to lose anymore. Had she really just said all that to him — finally? It was about time. She needed to get away from him. "I'm going back to my shopping." She got out of the car and slammed the door behind her.

Antonio watched her go, deciding he should give her some time to cool off before he approached her again. But as she disappeared back into the store, emptiness filled his heart. *What am I doing here?* he thought.

Vinny climbed back into the car and sat silently until Antonio asked, "Vinny, have you found out yet what Anthony has planned?"

"No, sir. He keeps me busy with other matters. He's more concerned with me keeping an eye on you right now. Mario is heading up whatever it is he's got planned. He never got the chance to tell me, and I didn't want to question him about it. It would cause him to be suspicious."

"You have people watching Sophia, correct?"

"Yes, sir. They are with her now. They're the best at what they do. She won't even know she's being followed."

"How about the house?"

"Yes. Everything is covered, as you asked. No need to worry, sir."

"Good. Why don't we head back to the office now and see what Anthony is up to?"

Anthony paced back and forth, wondering what was going on. Why didn't he call? The phone rang and he grabbed it. "Yeah, talk to me. What do you mean? Who was it? That's a shame — I'm going to miss him. I bet my dad placed him there. When was it set to go off? Good. Just get back here."

Anthony hoped this didn't backfire on him, but there was no other way to get the results he was looking for. This had to work. He had gone through a great deal of expense to make it look like an accident.

John and Regina stopped at a gas station a few hours from Atlanta to fill up the car and take a break. The ride had been very pleasant, and there had been no more talk about feelings and emotions.

After all the time in the car, Regina needed to stretch her legs. She also had a craving for some chocolate. "I'm going to get a candy bar. Do you want anything?"

"No, thanks. But answer me this: Is the baby wanting some chocolate, or is it Mommy?" he asked with a smile.

"Both," she replied, smiling back at him.

She went inside the station on a serious chocolate mission. She picked something out, then grabbed a second one just for good measure, and went up front to pay for them, but the young man behind the counter didn't see her right away. He was too engrossed in what was happening on the television.

"Excuse me? I would like to pay for this." She had to repeat it because the man didn't seem to hear her.

Finally he spotted her and said, "I'm so sorry, ma'am. I was just watching a news flash from New York. I used to live there, so anyway . . . Okay, let's see what you got."

Regina could see the small set behind the counter and noticed all the commotion on the screen. A house, maybe several houses, appeared to be on fire. Her curiosity got the best of her. "So what's going on in New York?"

"Oh, man, there was a big explosion and a bunch of people got killed."

"That's terrible. Where in New York?"

"In Brooklyn somewhere. Some house blew up, and the fire spread to the houses nearby. So far, five people are dead, and they're still digging through the rubble."

Regina felt the color drain from her face. It couldn't be. Before she could ask where in Brooklyn, she saw the reporter and where she was reporting. *LIVE* flashed across the screen. She took a closer look and recognized Mrs. Dunway's house down the street.

By this time, John had finished filling the tank and had walked inside to pay the cashier. Regina looked at him with horror in her eyes. "We have to go back." Panic constricted her throat and made it difficult even to breathe, much less talk. "We have to go back now!"

"Wait a minute. Calm down. Why do we have to go back?"

She pointed to the screen. He saw the news story. Without another word, he paid for the gas and they left.

In the car, Regina repeated, "We have to go back. What if my mom . . . ? I just have to go back. If I don't, who will be next? I know he's behind this somehow."

"Look, we don't know if your mom was hurt or even at home when this happened. Let me call the precinct and find out what's going on. Your mother wouldn't want you to endanger your life or your child's by going back now. Trust me, okay?"

Regina took a deep breath. Realizing that John was right, she gave in. "Okay." *Oh, Lord, let my mom be okay. Protect her, please! I can't lose her, too.*

When Father Thomas realized that the explosion had happened in a neighborhood where some of his parishioners lived, he grabbed his coat and rushed out the door, praying on the way to his car. Maybe there was something he could do. Some might need a place to stay while their homes were being repaired or rebuilt. Some might need comfort and prayer.

Then realization hit him. *Isn't that Sophia's neighborhood?* What if this wasn't just a gas explosion? Oh, no — what would he tell Regina? He ran out to his car and drove until he reached the police blockade. After explaining who he was, Father Thomas was able to pull his car over and park. Heading toward the fire engines, he spotted the fire chief, whom he knew.

"Hey, Roy, is there anything I can do?"

"No, Father, not right now."

"Do you know what happened yet?"

"At this point, it appears that house number four thirty-six just blew up. Probably a gas leak. We got the fire out, and we're looking through the rubble to see if we find anyone else."

"So who lives there?" Father Thomas already knew the answer to that, but he wanted the confirmation. He needed it.

Roy looked over his clipboard and said, "Let's see. It said Sophia Palmetto. Do you know her, Father?"

"I know her and her family." He took a deep breath and asked a question he wasn't sure he wanted to hear the answer to. "Was she inside?"

"We're still not sure. We haven't gotten through all the debris yet."

"Where are they taking the survivors from these other homes?"

"They're taking them to Coney Island to check them out. Some are in shock. And there are some we don't know will make it."

"Thanks, Roy." Father Thomas looked at the destruction in front of him and could not believe his eyes. How could this happen? All he could do now was pray. Perhaps he would be more helpful at the hospital. There wasn't much he could do here; maybe he could offer some comfort to those who survived this mess.

He decided to wait for confirmation of Sophia's whereabouts before he called Regina. She was probably still on the road. Besides, he didn't know anything for sure. Why worry her needlessly?

Frank had gotten the call at home, and by the time he arrived the fires were almost all out. The ambulances were taking some survivors away.

The captain wanted him to investigate the cause. Apparently, they had found the remains of a man's body next to the house that had blown up. Not much was left; they would probably have to identify him with dental records.

He saw some guys from the precinct. "Hey, Jonesy, anything yet on the cause?"

"I only have some initial findings. It looks like this house here had a gas leak and it blew. Since the houses are attached in this neighborhood . . . Well, let's just say they didn't stand a chance. The fire spread down the block. It's a big mess. So far the count's up to ten confirmed dead and six in the hospital; three are critical. If this had happened during the day, most of these people would have been at work or something."

"What a mess. What about the guy they found next to the original house? Do you think this could be foul play?"

"It's not definite yet. The jury's still out."

Frank's cell phone rang. Glancing at the screen, he said, "Hey, excuse me. I've got to take this call." He walked away from the crowd and answered, "John, I don't believe it. Hey, man, where are you?"

"Didn't the captain tell you?" John asked.

"You mean that lame story you told him? I know you didn't go to California. Don't lie to me, man — where are you at?"

"I'm sorry, Frank. I can't tell you. I'm asking you to trust me. I called because I need to know what's going on there. I've seen the news."

"You mean the explosion? Is that the only reason you called?" Frank was a bit miffed at this conversation. Did John think he was stupid or something?

"Yes. I want to know if the house that blew is Sophia Palmetto's. Was she hurt in the blast?"

Now Frank understood. There was only one reason he would be asking that question. He decided to do some fishing himself. "I hear Regina Cavelli is missing. No one knows where she is, and her husband is pulling out all the stops trying to find her. You wouldn't know where she is, would you?"

"Are you nuts — how would I know anything about that?" John asked defensively.

There was silence. Frank decided not to tell him what he really thought. "Yeah, it's Sophia Palmetto's house. Be careful, John. If you're with who I think you are, then you're playing with fire."

"I don't know what you're talking about, man. I'm helping my sister with some personal stuff. I just can't talk about it, okay? I lied because I know how much the captain hates me taking time off for family things. I heard the news on the radio and was just curious to see what's going on. Do you know if she was in the house or not?"

"No, she hasn't been found yet."

"What does that mean?" John pushed for a more direct answer.

"They're still going through the rubble. No one is certain if she was at home at the time of the blast or not."

"Okay, thanks for the information. I gotta go. I'll call you later."

Before Frank could say anything else, John hung up. *What is he thinking? Does he honestly think I bought that garbage about his sister?* The phone rang again. He answered it without looking at the name. "John?"

"No, it's Captain Merrill. Did you hear from John, Frank?"

"Well . . . yes. I thought you were him calling back."

Captain Merrill wanted a straight answer. "What did he want? Where is he? Did he say when he's coming back?"

"He didn't say, sir. He just called about the explosion. He said he heard about it on the radio and wanted to know what was going on. He told me he was helping out his sister."

"So he lied to me about the case."

"I think he's heading for some trouble. I think he might be with . . ."

"With who?"

"Never mind. I don't know what I'm saying. It's kinda crazy out here. There's lots of noise and . . . did you call me for a reason, sir?"

"Yeah, I want to know if you found anything out yet. The mayor has been calling here and wants answers. He's making me crazy."

"Nothing new, sir. As soon as I know anything I'll call."

"Frank, I want to know what is going on. What is John up to?"

"Captain, I'm not sure. I just don't want to see him get hurt." The line was quiet a moment. "Captain, are you still there?"

"Yeah. So, Frank, who do you think John is with?"

"Uh, no one. I misspoke, really."

"Okay, if that's how you want to play it. Keep me updated about the explosion."

Lilly sat in Anthony's office and looked like she half expected him to pull the pistol from his top drawer and put a bullet between her eyes. This was the first time Anthony had seen her since Michael's death; Lilly had been staying with her mother.

"Mr. Cavelli, I don't know where she is. I haven't seen her since the funeral."

Anthony just stared at her. He wasn't sure yet if she was lying; if she wasn't, then all this was fruitless. Yet, even if it was, he enjoyed watching her squirm in her seat and decided he would do so for a little longer. At the very least, maybe he could make her . . .

His cell phone rang in the middle of his thoughts. Never liking interruptions, he snapped it open and barked, "Yeah? Oh, it's you — hold on. Lilly, if you wouldn't mind waiting outside while I take this call?"

Lilly didn't mind. She got up as quickly as she could and skittered out of the office.

With a grin, Anthony returned his attention to the phone and said, "Talk to me . . . yeah . . . interesting. So you think our little detective friend is with my wife. Are you sure or just guessing? Do you know where they are? Call me if you find out anything else. How's the investigation going? Well, you just make sure the end results are in my favor. Of course, there will be a bonus for you if this gets done in a timely fashion."

Maybe things were starting to look up for him. He pressed down on the intercom and ordered Emily, "Tell Lilly she's free to go."

He'd heard enough; he didn't need her now. There were bigger fish to fry. If that detective *was* with Regina, they both were going to regret it. He would make sure of that.

The emergency room was filled with people trying to find loved ones. Some were elated to discover them; others had to be consoled at their loss. Father Thomas tried to find Sophia, but she wasn't there. He did his best to comfort family members who were mourning and victims who had survived with injuries.

What a mess! What would he say to Regina if he couldn't find her mother? First she had lost her father and now this. He was also concerned about her baby. He didn't want her to get upset in her condition. Maybe he should go to her and talk to her in person if the news was bad; he couldn't give her news of this magnitude over the phone.

He did everything he could for those in the waiting room and then knew he had to leave them, as much as he hated to do so. He needed to get back to the church and prepare for some of the people who would be staying with him in the rectory.

But then he heard someone ask, "Excuse me, but are you Father Thomas?"

He looked up to see a very well-dressed man standing before him. He wasn't all that tall, but he had a menacing look about him that immediately made Father Thomas wonder if answering him would be safe. But finally he said, "Yes, I am. May I help you?"

"My name is Mario Malotti, and I work for Anthony Cavelli. I do believe you know his wife, Regina. If you can come with me, Mr. Cavelli would like to speak to you."

Father Thomas wasn't sure this guy was going to take no for an answer. But he had things to take care of, and it was worth a shot. "I'm sorry, but right now isn't very convenient. I was about to go back to the church and make arrangements for some of these people who are without a home. If Mr. Cavelli would like to speak to me, please tell him he is welcome to come to the church anytime."

Mario wasn't quite sure what to do now. No one had ever turned him down before, and if they tried, it didn't take much to convince them otherwise. But this was a priest. He couldn't strong-arm a priest, at least not in front of all these witnesses, yet he couldn't go back empty-handed, either. That left him in a predicament.

"Excuse me, Father, but I know Mr. Cavelli would greatly appreciate you coming back with me, and I assure you it won't take very long. I will take you back personally as soon as you are done."

"I'm sorry, but I can't right now."

A policeman, Sergeant Matthews, approached them. Mario had had some run-ins with him before and he didn't want any trouble now.

"Father Thomas, how are you?" the sergeant asked, giving Mario a warning look. "Do you need any help?"

"Good evening, Sergeant. No, I'm fine. I was just telling this nice gentleman that I have to get back to the church and set things up. Some of these people need a place to stay for a while."

"Well, I'm off duty now, Father. I would be more than happy to drive you back and help in any way I can."

"That's wonderful, but I have my car. If you want to follow me, I could certainly use an extra pair of hands — thank you. Mr. Malotti, please extend my apologies to Mr. Cavelli."

Mario had no choice but to nod in agreement. He knew Anthony would not be pleased, but what else could he do with a cop standing right there?

About an hour from their destination, John and Regina drove in silence. Once she had calmed down enough to be reasonable about the whole situation, she had spent the time praying for her mom's protection. When her mind raced and her heart throbbed, it was so hard to hear His voice. With every concentrated breath, she could feel her heart slowing down.

With her mind clear, her heart at peace, she was able to allow God to minister to her. Philippians 4:6–7 came to her:

> *Do not be anxious about anything, but in everything, by prayer*
> *and petition, with thanksgiving, present your requests to God.*
> *And the peace of God, which transcends all understanding, will*
> *guard your hearts and your minds in Christ Jesus.*

John noticed the change that came over her. He was curious as to why, in the midst of all the craziness around her, she looked peaceful. "Are you okay?"

"The Lord reminded me of His promises, and I know in my heart that my mom is fine. I have peace about it."

He shook his head, not knowing what to think. She heard God talking to her? John just didn't get it. How could someone hear God? "You're running for your life, your father has been killed, and your mom's house just blew up and you have no idea where she is. Yet you're at peace because of God? I don't get it."

Regina thought about this for a moment. How do you explain to someone who is not a Christian how God makes a difference in your life? How do you explain His peace without sounding like an idiot or a religious fanatic?

And how do you do that when, lately, you've been having your own trouble understanding God's ways?

"That's a good question. I don't know quite how to explain this to you. Right now I'm not sure about much. I can only go by what I do know. I know that God is good and that He loves me. He gives me strength to get through every day. All I know to do is pray and ask for His help. When I prayed for my mom, this incredible peace came over me. There are times God speaks to me. It's not an audible voice, just a feeling I get. He sometimes uses the Bible to give me words of encouragement and hope. Don't get me wrong — I'm not perfect at this. I don't always react perfectly. There are times I feel hopeless about what's going on around me. I just know it gets better when I pray."

"So, how do you explain your father's death? Wasn't God watching over him? Didn't you ask Him to save his life?"

Regina glanced at him as he drove. "I miss my dad very much, but I can't blame God for his death. He's not the one who ran him over or ordered someone to do it. Whether God could have stopped it is not something I question. But bad things happen in this life to good people and to bad people. There are other forces working in this world, and our own choices have plenty to do with what happens to us. But God is good regardless of the circumstances."

John continued to stare straight ahead, his face blank.

"I know you're probably thinking about what Anthony did to me, but it's not this child's fault how he or she came to be. Anthony could have killed me that night, but he didn't. He could have beaten me up worse, but he didn't. I believe in heaven and in hell. Some people would like to forget about hell or deny that it exists. They don't understand that Satan's domain is here." She paused. "I'm sorry. I don't mean to sound preachy."

"You're not. If I didn't want to know, I wouldn't have asked. I admire your faith. In my line of business, it's hard to have faith in anything or anybody."

"That's sad. Is that why you haven't gotten married?" The second it came out of her mouth, Regina could have hit herself. Why in the world had she asked that? Slightly mortified, she hurried on, "I'm sorry — I don't mean to pry. You don't have to answer that."

"It's okay. I don't mind. The simple truth of it is that I haven't found the right girl yet. It appears all the good ones are already taken," he said as he smiled at her.

His comment didn't register as he intended it, and she smiled back at him as she turned to look out the window. As silence filled the car, she reached for the radio dial and tried to find a music station.

Yelling an expletive, Anthony snapped his phone shut. Who did that priest think he was? Nobody turned Anthony Cavelli down when he requested to see them. He didn't care if he was a priest — that meant nothing. No more Mr. Nice Guy. He picked up the phone and dialed. "Paulie, I've got a job for you. It's a bit sticky. Yeah, I want you to bring someone over to the warehouse on Eighth Street. He needs a lesson taught to him. Father Thomas over at St. Mary's. That's right — you heard me. If you have to use force, then do so." He hung up the phone and wondered if everyone around him was getting soft.

The door suddenly slammed shut behind him. Anthony startled and spun around in the chair. Poppy glared at him as he approached the desk. It was a look Anthony had learned to placate or run from as soon as possible. But today Anthony was angry enough that he didn't feel afraid. For the first time in his life, his father didn't frighten him.

"You're out of control," Poppy said.

"What are you talking about?" Anthony replied innocently.

"Sophia's house. It just randomly blew up by itself? Do you think I'm senile? Do you not listen to me when I speak?"

"I saw that on the news — what a tragedy. They say it was a gas leak of some kind. But I didn't realize it was Sophia's house. Do you know if she's okay?"

Antonio looked at his son and suddenly realized, for the first time, that what sat before him was a person he didn't recognize anymore. Sophia was right. Anthony *was* a monster. A monster Antonio had created by the lifestyle he had led and brought Anthony up in. And considering what had happened this evening, it appeared to be too late for change.

"You're through," Antonio said very calmly. "I want you to pack up your things and go home and stay there."

"What do you mean I'm through!? Let me tell you something, old man. I'm through all right, but it's not in the way you think. I'm through with you and your rules! I'm a grown man, and I've been taking care of the business a long time now. I know what I'm doing. Business is at its peak thanks to my leadership. I will not roll over because you say so. Now, if you don't mind, I need to get back to work."

Anthony stood and started to stomp past him, but Poppy grabbed his arm. For an old man, he surely had a grip. Anthony couldn't back down now. He had to completely step through this door he had opened, or else he never would.

"With all due respect, Poppy, let go of my arm. I'm not a kid any-more."

Poppy didn't let go; instead, his grip just hardened, pulling Anthony around until he now stood face to face, eye to eye with his father. "Do you really want to travel this road with me? Do you think because I'm old you should no longer respect me? How *dare* you. I will not repeat myself again. Just be grateful you are my son. I can't believe who you've become." He shook his head. "I have no one to blame but myself."

He glared at him with more anger than Anthony had ever seen from any-one, and slowly, he realized he might have gone too far with his challenge. Anthony's anger was such that if he didn't get it calmed pretty quickly, he was going to explode. He couldn't have that. Not yet. He couldn't allow his father to know what was truly in his plans.

"Now, do you have something you want to say to me?"

Anthony took a deep breath, hoping it would settle him down. If there was one thing he'd learned, it was not to overplay your hand. Timing was everything in this business. "I apologize for disrespecting you."

Poppy let go of his arm and Anthony continued, trying to sound as meek as he could, "I've been under a lot of pressure trying to find Regina. She's carrying my child. You're taking away the only thing I have left — this job. You probably think I had something to do with Sophia's house blow-ing up, but I didn't. The news said it was a gas leak. Why would I do such a thing?" He looked imploringly at his father, who said nothing. "It pains me that you think so little of me. I'm telling you the truth. Poppy, you must believe me. Don't take the only thing I have left away from me."

It was better to humble himself than start a war with his own father. He didn't want to divide the family that way, especially before he was properly prepared. How many men did he really have under his control? If it came to war between them, who would stand with him? He must be certain of his position before making his move.

What choice did he have now but to play nice? All that mattered was that in the end, he was on top. For now he must convince Poppy that he was sincere. He hoped the old man would buy it.

Watching the regret spread across his son's face, Antonio began to re-think his decision, for more than one reason. Maybe it would be best to keep Anthony around; if he was out there with no one watching him, there was no telling what he might do. For now he would keep an eye on him.

"Fine, but let's get this straight. I'm in charge and nothing happens that I don't know about. Understand?"

"Yes, Poppy. I wouldn't dream of it. Now, if it's okay with you, I have an appointment I have to get to."

"Where are you going?"

Anthony bristled at the question, but he had no choice. "To the ware-house. There's been some difficulty with equipment disappearing there. This matter shouldn't take very long."

He wasn't about to tell him the truth. Poppy had changed so much since his mother's death and not for the better, in Anthony's opinion. He had grown soft, and weak. This business called for the strength to do what was necessary, which was why it flourished under Anthony's control. He had what it took, while Poppy was becoming a liability. He couldn't be-lieve he was thinking this, but maybe one of these days . . . No. He couldn't start to think that way. Even he was not willing to cross that line.

With tears rolling down her cheeks, Sophia stood in the middle of the street, looking at the blackened, charred rubble that used to be her home.

It wasn't safe to shift through the mess. The damage to the foundation was severe.

The city had people checking the other gas lines in the neighborhood. Sophia didn't seem to notice the workers all about her. Vinny stood at a distance, watching her. He felt so sorry for this woman who had lost so much in so little time.

Jimmy approached him and said, "Hey, Vin. What's the job?"

"The senior Mr. Cavelli wants you to stay at a distance and keep an eye on her. Follow her but give her space. George will come and relieve you in eight hours. If you see anything suspicious, call me right away. You're to report to me and to me alone. I want a full report at the end of your shift."

"No problem."

Vinny touched Jimmy's shoulder. Jimmy turned to look at him. With a somber tone he added, "This job is not to be discussed with anyone except me. I hope I've made that point clear."

"Yeah, I understand. No one but you."

Vinny slowly approached Sophia. "Excuse me, ma'am." She didn't turn around. "Mrs. Palmetto, Mr. Antonio Cavelli has sent me to be of service to you." Still no response. He went closer and gently touched her on her shoulder. "Ma'am, are you okay?"

Sophia slowly turned around and looked at Vinny, her eyes glazed. Her knees suddenly gave way, and he caught her as she fainted.

"Get the car, Jimmy!" Vinny shouted to him. Jimmy ran for it, and they took her to the hospital.

Chapter 10

Sitting at his desk, Frank sifted through his paperwork and felt like groaning. He'd been buried in this stuff ever since John had been out helping "his sister." The stack didn't seem to be getting any shorter. A mug of coffee sat cooling beside his monitor, but the caffeine wasn't helping; he was having trouble focusing.

Finally, a messenger came by with the final medical reports on the dead from the explosion. Frank grabbed the folder and thumbed through it, looking for the one about the guy they'd found by the house. Who was he, and what had he been doing there?

The phone rang, and he jumped, nearly spilling the folder across the floor. "Yeah. Hey, Arnie, what's up? Are you kidding me? That's great! How is she? I'll be right there. Yeah, I want you to keep a guard at her room. I'm not convinced the explosion was an accident." He hung up the phone and walked into Captain Merrill's office. "Captain, I've got some good news. Sophia Palmetto was just brought into the hospital."

"Is she okay? Who found her?"

"You won't believe it, but it was one of Cavelli's men who brought her in. She was unconscious at the time."

"Go to the hospital and keep me posted on her condition. Call me if she wakes up."

Anthony arrived at the warehouse to find that Father Thomas had come in with a bit of a struggle. A small cut still bled on his lower lip. He was sitting in a chair with two of Anthony's men guarding him. Each had a hand on one of Father Thomas' shoulders, making sure he stayed seated. As Anthony approached, his men greeted him with nods.

"Father Thomas, how good it is to see you again," Anthony said as he extended his hand in greeting.

Only out of his own sense of common courtesy did Father Thomas shake his hand. Anthony gave his men a look, and they let go of the priest's shoulders and took a step back.

Father Thomas started to pray. He had heard many things about this man who stood in front of him, and the look in Anthony's eyes told him that evil lived there. He knew that only God could get him out of here alive, and he asked Him for wisdom in what to say.

"Mr. Cavelli, there was no need for these two men to force me to come here. There is much work I need to do back at the church. But now that I'm here, what is it that I can do for you?" Father Thomas tried to proceed with caution.

"I see you like to get right to the point. Well, so do I; small talk doesn't interest me. I must say, I was quite disappointed you didn't come to see me earlier when I sent Mario to pick you up."

Father Thomas just kept silent and waited for Anthony to get to his point.

"It takes either a strong man or a stupid one to refuse me. Which one are you?"

Father Thomas knew where Anthony was heading with his questions. He decided to cut to the chase and go there first. "Mr. Cavelli, I understand your wife has been missing recently. I'm sorry for your loss. I have had the pleasure of knowing her and her family for many years. She has a kind heart. The death of her father was hard on her, and now her mother's home has been destroyed. Sophia still has not been found."

Anthony interrupted, "Yes, it's a shame how accidents and tragedies happen to good people. As far as Sophia is concerned, I understand she was brought to the hospital. One of my men found her. She fainted right in his arms. I'm still waiting to hear how she is doing. But I did not bring you here to discuss Sophia — rather, Regina." Anthony paused and stared at him coldly. "So tell me. Do you have any idea where she is?"

Father Thomas didn't like lying, but this time, it was to save not only one life but two. He knew God would understand and forgive him for bending the truth. "I'm sorry, but how would I know where she is?"

Anthony bent over, looked him squarely in the eyes, and responded, "I thought lying was a sin, Father. Doesn't the Bible say that the wages of sin is . . . Now, what is the word I'm looking for . . . ? Oh, yeah — *death.*" He emphasized it for effect.

Father Thomas knew exactly where Anthony was going and the intimidating message he was trying to convey. He could not let himself be frightened by this man. This close to his eyes, he could almost see the demons that controlled him.

Father Thomas tried to find a way to reach him. "I see your pain, Mr. Cavelli. It doesn't have to be this way. If you open up your heart to Jesus, He will set you free from the demons that haunt you."

Anthony straightened. He didn't like the way this man spoke to him. Or how it made him feel. In a weird, perverted way, it almost frightened him, though he didn't understand how it could. He couldn't allow this man, priest or not, to get to him. Especially not in front of his men. He approached him again and slapped him as strongly as he could across the face.

Father Thomas hadn't been expecting that, and he couldn't remember a time he had been hit this hard before. The throb lingered. He didn't say a word.

Anthony stared at him. He could feel the hatred being stirred up in him like never before, so he slapped him again.

"Get up!" he yelled in frustration. "Get up and face me like a man without hiding behind your God and your collar. I asked you a question and I want a direct answer! Do you know where my wife is?"

That slap hurt more than the first. Father Thomas was determined to be strong. He couldn't allow this man to get the best of him.

He stood up slowly. "There is nothing I can tell you about your wife's whereabouts."

That remark seemed to anger Anthony even further. Hissing a curse, he punched him in the stomach, the force of the hit making Father Thomas double over. He fell back into his chair but didn't cry out or make a sound, though it took every ounce of self-control not to do so.

"So how much longer will you keep being stubborn about this?" Anthony demanded as he started to pace in front of him. "Why don't you save me time, and yourself pain, by telling me what you know? I never met a priest before so hell-bent on keeping a loving husband from his wife. You should know better than to encourage Regina's rebellious nature."

Father Thomas decided not to engage in a war of words. Or fists. Before becoming a priest, he had been an amateur boxer, and right now, he was trying hard to forget that fact. He painfully stood back up, struggling with his own feelings of hate for this man he hardly knew. For Regina's sake, he had to behave better than this man.

"Mr. Cavelli, I'm sorry for your loss. I don't know how you came to your conclusions, but the only thing I can do is pray that God will keep your wife safe from all evil and harm, wherever she is. I will pray the same for her unborn child. I do not know where she is."

Anthony didn't like the way this man was holding his ground. He was getting nowhere fast, and it was putting him over the edge.

Did he not understand who he was dealing with? Anthony took out his gun and pointed it directly in Father Thomas' face.

Anthony's two men exchanged a glance and took a step forward. Killing a priest was not in their job description. They wouldn't be able to look their mothers in the eye again. It was hard enough not to do anything when Anthony was beating him; actually killing him would be like signing a contract for rental property in the deepest level of hell. But they weren't sure if they could do anything to stop the situation. When Anthony got like this, he could not be reasoned with.

Father Thomas was without fear. "I'm ready to meet my Maker. Are you?"

Anthony's breathing grew ragged.

With the gun still pointed at his head, Father Thomas continued, "You can pull that trigger, but it won't do any good. I have no information for you. There is nothing I can tell you."

Father Thomas was stunned that he didn't feel any fear and thanked God for that. The more he stood and prayed, the more he felt Anthony's rage diminish.

Anthony lowered his arm and took a deep breath. He had never felt this way before. He just couldn't pull the trigger. He didn't understand what was going on, and completely weirded out, all he wanted was to put distance between him and this priest.

"You're not worth it, priest. I wasted enough of my time on you." To his men, he said, "Get him out of here."

They escorted him away. As they passed Anthony, Father Thomas said, "I'll pray for you."

"Don't bother. I like who I am. I don't need some priest or anyone else praying for me."

Antonio had been sitting beside Sophia's bed for half an hour. Vinny, who had been keeping post outside the door, entered the room and said quietly, "Mr. Cavelli, there's nothing you can do here. Why don't I take you home so you can get some rest? Jimmy is here, and he'll keep an eye on her for you."

"No, I'm all right. This is all my fault. My sins are finally catching up with me. All of this is my fault." His voice tightened. "She's gotta wake up."

Vinny was at a loss for words. He didn't know what to say that would comfort him. "I'll be outside this door if you need anything."

As Vinny stepped back into the hall, he saw Mario walking toward him. Frowning, he figured Anthony had sent him there to find out what was going on.

"How's she doing?" Mario asked.

"The same."

"How's the old man?"

"Worried. Does Anthony want me for anything?"

"No. He sent me here to see what was going on. You can go home. I'll stay and keep an eye on things."

Great. Leaving Mario here was not an option. He didn't trust him and didn't want to leave Poppy alone with just him and Jimmy, who wasn't strong enough to handle Mario on his own. "Don't worry about it. I don't need to be relieved. I feel fine. I can stay."

But Mario never took no for an answer. He didn't like being refused. Ever. Higher in rank than Vinny, he raised his voice and repeated, "I said that I will stay and you can go home. That wasn't an offer."

"Hey, man, don't get in my face. I wasn't trying to buck you or nothing."

The door jerked open, and Poppy stepped out of the room, glaring at them both. "What is all this shouting about? Don't you have any idea where you are?"

"Sorry, Mr. Cavelli. Vinny here wouldn't listen to me, and Anthony wants him to leave and for me to stay."

Mario's explanation sounded pretty whiny, and Vinny rolled his eyes. He felt as if he was back in grade school. *Gimme a break.*

"Well, you can tell my son that I want Vinny to stay, and you can go home. He was the one who found her and brought her here. I want him to finish what he started."

Mario scowled. Vinny was relieved Poppy had come out because he wouldn't have been able to win this argument otherwise. Mario didn't make it easy — that was for sure. He didn't understand why Anthony sometimes seemed to prefer him; dealing with the man was nearly impossible.

Before Mario could respond, somebody else joined them. Detective Frank Holstrum. As he walked over, Vinny tried to control his urge to punch somebody.

"Well, well," Holstrum began, "what an interesting gathering we have here."

Glaring at him, Poppy demanded, "What do you want?"

"I'm here to see how Mrs. Palmetto is doing. I want to ask her some questions." Frank didn't feel the need to explain himself but did so anyway.

"Well, she's not even conscious, so she won't be able to answer any of your questions," Vinny stated, as if that would dismiss him.

Frank walked up to Vinny and glared at him. In response, Mario and Jimmy came and stood on either side of Vinny, making him appear even more menacing than usual. He already stood about a foot taller than Frank, but this didn't intimidate Frank in the least. He had gone up against men who were just as big as Vinny before.

"I remember a time when they didn't allow you guys to speak up at all. I miss the good old days. I suggest you keep your mouth shut and speak when spoken to, boy." Frank hoped Vinny was as insulted as he intended him to be.

"Are you the man that's going to make me shut up?" Vinny asked.

Antonio couldn't take another minute of this testosterone-filled war of words. "Enough! How old are you men? We're in a hospital, in case anyone is wondering. I just want you all to leave. What matters now is that Sophia gets better. Should she wake up to this fighting outside her room?"

Vinny and the boys knew better than to ever question Antonio. They backed down and separated.

But Detective Holstrum was not about to leave that easily. "I don't mean any disrespect, but I have an investigation to conduct. Not to mention, I don't work for you. I have questions I want answers to, Mr. Cavelli, and you're as good a place to start as any."

"What can I possibly tell you? I wasn't there when it happened."

"That may be true, but the interesting thing is that one of your men was. The body was just identified as Al Nichols. It appears that he was outside the house at the time of the explosion. What do you suppose he was doing there?"

This was news to Antonio. He had liked Al very much. A moment passed before he could quietly reply, "He was a good man with a nice family."

"I'm sure he was, but what was he doing there when Mrs. Palmetto wasn't home? Do you have an answer for that?"

Antonio started to shake his head. He felt very bad about losing a man like Al. He didn't realize he had been killed. "It's all my fault. I had Al keep watch over Sophia and her home. I was worried about her after her husband was killed and Regina disappeared."

"Why would you care?"

"That's really none of your business, but if you must know, I've known her and her husband for a very long time, and their daughter is married to my son, which makes her family. Now, I've had enough of you and your questions, and I want you to leave."

Antonio was not about to play any more games. He was done.

Frank had been investigating this man for years. At this point, he was getting to where he could almost read him. Almost. But there was one thing he had never been able to understand. It surprised him how Antonio Cavelli took such care looking after Regina and her mother. Regina he could understand, but what was up with Sophia Palmetto? Even today, he found it a bit odd that he'd be camping out by her bedside. "I'll be back later when she wakes up," he said finally.

As Frank started to walk away, Antonio added, "Detective, please let me know the results of the investigation. I need to know how this happened."

That surprised Frank, too. He studied him a moment, then said, "Well, I'll see what I can do."

John and Regina arrived at the monastery that night. The monks greeted them with excitement. They were not used to many visitors, especially those who arrived at such an hour. Father Thomas had explained the special circumstances involved with Regina's coming to stay with them, and they were very willing to help in any way.

They had traveled for two full days, and John thought it would be a good idea for him to get some rest before heading back to New York. Brother Steven showed them to their rooms.

"Would either of you like anything to eat?" he asked. He was a kind-hearted man who spoke softly despite his large stature.

Regina didn't feel like eating anything and shook her head, but John replied, "Thank you, Brother. That would be great. I think it would be good if Regina ate something, too. She hasn't eaten much today."

Regina knew he was probably right, so she begrudgingly agreed.

Brother Steven smiled at her. "Follow me and I will show you to the kitchen."

They went downstairs and had some of the most delicious stew and homemade bread they had ever eaten. The cook was pleased that they enjoyed their meal so much and left them alone to finish in peace.

He was exhausted; he was concerned, and he couldn't help but look at her. John realized that tomorrow he would be on his way back and may not see her again for a long time. It made his heart ache. He reached over and touched her hand.

"I want you to know that I've really enjoyed getting to know you more on this trip. I'm sorry I have to leave and go back without you." He pulled his hand back. He didn't want to say anymore because he knew he would make her feel uncomfortable. In fact, he probably already had.

Regina didn't know what to say. She knew what her heart wanted to say; she knew she wanted him to never leave, but that was impossible. She ached for him to hold her in his arms and tell her everything would be okay, but she pushed the ache away.

"I'm really tired. Sleep will feel good tonight. I feel safe in this place for some reason." She paused, looking down at her stew, then finally asked, "Will you please check up on my mom? I'm worried about her. I won't be able to really rest until I know she's safe for sure. And you won't forget to tell me the moment you have anything on Anthony?"

Regina could feel herself wanting to ramble. The conversation was managing to head straight into their feelings again. Just then, she didn't know if she would have the strength to contain her own emotions.

She must have made at least a little sense because John smiled. "Of course, I will. I wish I could be noble about this, but I have my own selfish reasons for you to return."

The only light in the office was a desk lamp that cast a cool yellow glow through the room. It was late, but Anthony had nowhere else to go. His girlfriend was driving him nuts; her demands were getting out of hand.

He hated it when women became too clingy or too high-maintenance. She would just have to go.

He wouldn't have trouble finding a new one. So far this one had lasted the longest, and if he could have loved anyone, it might have been her. He had thought that maybe he would even marry her one day, if he ever could get rid of Regina.

As always, that subject left a bad taste in his mouth. Maybe he shouldn't have put the hit on her father; it had started a chain of events that he had not anticipated. Perhaps he should have been more patient. Maybe if he had waited to make it look more like natural causes . . . But no, he was not going to start second-guessing himself now, not when he was so close to getting what he wanted.

Why was he even thinking about this, anyway? It must have been that priest — there was something creepy about him. It was the same feeling he would get whenever Regina was around. He didn't know what it was, but being in the same room with her was like knowing there was a tarantula somewhere in your bed but not being able to find it. He couldn't stand her presence.

The hour grew later and later, and feeling miserable, he just sat there and stared out the window at the traffic.

The knock on his door didn't budge him. "Enter," he called. He could see Mario in the window's reflection and didn't bother to turn around. "You have something to tell me?"

"Yeah, your father is at the hospital. He's keeping a close eye on her. What do you want me to do, Boss?"

"Nothing. Let it rest for now. Did you see anybody else?"

"Yeah, Jimmy and Vinny were there." Mario hesitated for a moment, not knowing if he should go on. But he figured it would make him look good, so he cautiously proceeded, trying to plant seeds of doubt in Anthony's mind. "I don't know how to say this, but have you noticed that Vinny's been acting funny lately?"

Anthony finally turned his chair around. "Funny — how?"

"I can't put my finger on it. He just seems . . . I don't know . . . chummy with your dad lately. Wherever the old man is, it seems so is Vinny."

"My dad likes him, which works to my advantage. Besides, I told him to keep an eye on him for me and let me know what he's up to."

"Oh. Sorry, Boss. I guess all the stuff going on lately has made me a bit suspicious of everybody."

"No problem. Why don't you wait for me outside? I'll be leaving here soon. I just want to make a call first."

Mario left without another word. Oh, well. So much for that. At the very least, his question had showed the boss he cared and was looking out for his interests. So it still had worked to his advantage.

Anthony picked up the landline and dialed. He tapped his fingers on the desk until the person on the other end answered. "Is there any news on my wife?"

"Nothing new," the voice answered calmly. "He should be returning soon and when he does, I'll try to find out what is going on. Don't worry — I've got it under control."

"Really now. How about the investigation? Have they decoded my book yet?"

"No, not completely, but I'm afraid they're getting close."

"You're afraid they're getting close. Um, what you *should* be afraid of is me if they do. You know if I go down, I will not be going down alone. I'll have you to keep me company."

"What do you want me to do? If I interfere, I risk exposing myself. That wouldn't do you any good."

"Well, it's either that or something worse."

"Are you threatening me?"

"Now, we both know I don't make threats. I make promises. You know what I expect from you. Don't pretend that you don't know the type of man I am. Don't make me wait too long."

Anthony hung up the phone. He couldn't believe how stupid some people were. It wasn't like this cop didn't know him. He knew what would happen to him and his family if he decided to double-cross him.

Saying good-bye to Regina had been harder than John expected. He was determined to do all that he could to nail that so-called husband of hers. He hoped they would be closer to decoding the book by the time he got back.

Even though he had hours and hours left to drive, the ride home seemed to pass more quickly than the trip down. Maybe he had just wanted the time to last longer before, when she was with him, so he hadn't driven as fast as he could have. But now, the silence was beginning to drive him nuts, and he had so much to take care of when he got back. He didn't want to think about that just yet. He turned on the radio to see if anything else had developed with the explosion case back home.

He couldn't find a clear station at first. "Finally," he muttered after fiddling with the dial for a few minutes. They were just switching to a commercial. When the newscaster got back on the air, he read the local news and then switched to national news. The top story was still the explosion in Brooklyn.

"The death toll is now at twelve. Two of the burn victims on the critical list died a half hour ago, and Sophia Palmetto, wife of former mob accountant Michael Palmetto, has finally been located. She's recovering from posttraumatic stress disorder. According to hospital staff, she opened her eyes this morning but is not responding to anything or anyone. The doctors believe she's in shock. It was the Palmetto home that exploded in a residential district yesterday, from an apparent gas leak. The late Michael Palmetto died recently from injuries he received when he was involved in a hit-and-run in front of the same house. Their daughter, Regina Cavelli, is married to reputed mobster Anthony Cavelli. And now a word from our sponsor."

That was enough. He shut the radio off. What if Regina were to hear this? At least she would know her mother was alive, but she would worry herself sick. He had to try to reach her some way. He also needed to get to the hospital to see Sophia. Maybe if she knew that Regina was safe, she would come around.

But even if he drove all night, he still wouldn't reach the hospital until tomorrow.

Finally, Antonio allowed Vinny to drive him home. There was nothing he could do for Sophia and he needed to get some rest, but he clearly wasn't happy about it. They drove in silence until Vinny said, "Mr. Cavelli, you won't do her or Regina any good if you don't take care of yourself. She's well guarded night and day. I've handpicked those men and believe me, they can be trusted. I've also talked with Anthony, and he still believes I'm keeping an eye on you for him."

Still Poppy didn't say anything. He just stared out the car window. Vinny stopped trying.

When he pulled into the driveway, Stuart came out to greet them. "Sir, I've prepared something for you to eat, and I've taken the liberty to lay out some bedclothes for you."

"Thank you, Stuart. I will have a bite to eat, but there is no need for the bedclothes. I don't plan on going to bed. After I eat, I'll change and go back to the hospital. Make sure Vinny has something to eat also. He's a growing boy, you know."

"Yes, sir." Stuart left to do as he was told. Like Vinny, he knew better than to argue or discuss anything with Poppy when he gave orders. They knew he just wanted his commands followed whether or not anyone agreed with him.

"Vinny, go and eat something. I think I want to shower first and get out of these clothes."

"Yes, sir. Thank you."

"Oh, I wasn't thinking. You've been in your clothes all night also. Before we go back to the hospital, we'll stop by your place so you can shower and change. I don't think I have anything that would fit a big guy like yourself."

"Thank you, sir."

Vinny was a bit puzzled by Poppy's concern for him. He had never been this thoughtful before. Maybe he was getting soft like Anthony said, or maybe he was just trying to make up for all the bad he had done in his life. But it didn't matter. He needed to call Anthony and let him know what was going on. He went over to the phone and dialed Anthony's cell number.

"Yeah, Boss, it's me. I'm at your father's house. He's taking a shower, but after he eats, we'll head back to the hospital. Yeah, she's being well guarded. Be careful with these guys; they're really loyal to your dad."

After he hung up, he thought that last bit of information had been good. This way, Anthony wouldn't try anything, and it would make Vinny look good. He had been thinking that after this crisis was over with, he might just retire. Disappear to some island somewhere.

Regina sat in her room, reading her Bible and praying. She felt her child move within her and knew in her heart she was doing the right thing. Her mother was alive. She knew she was — just in what condition she wasn't certain. But no matter what, she did have peace about it.

She had just finished reading Hebrews 10:23: *"Let us hold unswervingly to the hope we profess, for He who promised is faithful."* He had brought her this far; He would bring her the rest of the way, too.

There was a soft knock on the door. "Come in," she called.

Brother Steven opened the door with one hand. With the other, he carried a tray holding a dish of mixed fruit and a glass of milk.

"I thought you might be hungry." He placed the tray on the small desk beside her.

"You have been so kind to me. I don't need special treatment. It's very considerate of you to be thinking of me, but you shouldn't go to such trouble."

"It's no trouble. We all understand that you are going through a hard time. Right now, it's important that you take care of yourself. The doctor will be here this afternoon to examine you as Father Thomas has arranged."

"Brother Steven, how much do you know about my situation?"

"I know what is important. I know what has happened to your father and who you are married to. I know the importance of keeping your presence here a secret for your sake and your unborn child."

He knew enough. He smiled at her and left the room.

John had given her a radio to listen to, and she thought some music would help calm her nerves while she ate. The reception wasn't very good in such a remote area, and she turned the dial until it cleared a bit. It was a news bulletin.

"Yes, the tragedy in Brooklyn continues as another victim dies in the hospital, which brings the total to thirteen dead. The official cause of this tragedy is a gas leak that ignited the house of Sophia Palmetto, wife of the late Michael Palmetto, the former accountant of alleged mob boss Antonio Cavelli. She has been hospitalized for posttraumatic stress syndrome. More after these messages."

"I can't believe it!" Regina whispered. "What am I going to do?"

If she went back, they were sure to find her. Her life would be forfeit. And perhaps even the baby's. But how could she stay here with her mother in such trouble? Her mother was all the family she had left. She paced back and forth, her mind racing over the ramifications of what she was thinking about. She had to think this through and couldn't act too hastily. What was best? She didn't know the answer to that question. But thirteen people were dead now because of her. This couldn't continue. It couldn't happen again.

Father Thomas entered Sophia's room to find her sitting up in bed and staring straight forward, her eyes glassy and her look far away. He prayed that he would be able to reach her. The news media had been reporting nothing else but the explosion. He was afraid that if Regina heard about it, she might do something foolish — like come back.

He was still a tad sore from his earlier encounter with Anthony and his men. His face was swollen on the right side and his stomach still ached. A man who looked like he did, especially a *priest* who looked like he did, caused people to ask questions. He didn't want to lie to Sophia, but he couldn't exactly tell her the truth, either. It would only make the situation worse.

He walked quietly to Sophia's bedside and placed his hand on hers. She didn't respond and felt almost cold to the touch. "Sophia, I'm here to help. Your family members are all fine, and they want you to get better. I know you've been concerned about them. Where are you, my friend?"

The only thing he could do was pray. He decided to do so out loud. He must have been there for about half an hour when suddenly he felt her place her other hand on top of his. He opened his eyes and started to praise God for this miracle.

"Father Thomas," she whispered, looking up at him.

He called for the nurse, who returned with the doctor to examine her. Father Thomas stepped outside to wait until they were done.

The doctor returned presently, smiling and obviously relieved. "She's coming around nicely."

"That's really good news. Doctor, I know this request is going to sound strange coming from me, but can you hold a press conference right away to report her recovery?"

"I suppose so, but I would rather wait until I have more information."

"No, it's vital that you do this now. Please trust me."

"Sure, Father. If I can't trust a priest, then who can I trust?"

"Thank you. Thank you," Father Thomas replied.

Regina kept the radio on as she started packing her clothes. She knew she was probably making a mistake, but she had to go to her mother. Perhaps it was irrational — she knew it might be — but what kind of daughter would she be if she didn't? She had no one outside her mother. She needed her more than ever, and she couldn't just leave her like that. Regina had suffered alone too many times in her own life to be okay with it happening to the only family she had left.

Maybe she could disguise herself somehow. It would be okay.

She left the room with the radio on. She missed the announcer saying, "Sophia Palmetto's doctor announced just moments ago that she's well enough to be released from the hospital."

Chapter 11

John pulled up in front of his apartment building, amazed that he had managed to find a parking space so easily. Tonight of all nights he was grateful he didn't have to circle the neighborhood. He was tired and just wanted to go to bed. Twice he had stopped and slept on the side of the road for a couple of hours, but it hadn't been nearly enough. Come morning, he knew he would have to explain where he had been and what he had been up to, and he needed to do it with a clear head.

He locked his car and walked through the front double doors of the building. His landlady, Mrs. Fieldworth, greeted him. She was a widow who didn't have any children of her own, so she treated her tenants like family. She was truly pleasant, but getting away from her once she'd started a conversation wasn't an easy task.

"Detective Nelson, how good it is to see you!"

Exhausted, John was far too tired to carry on a long-winded conversation, but it was too late to escape. "It's always good to see you, dear lady," he said, trying to be his charming self.

"I should be mad at you."

"Why, Mrs. Fieldworth, what have I done?"

"Well, first of all, you go on a trip and don't even tell me that you're leaving, and when you finally get back, you don't even stop by to say hello! You don't need to worry, though; I've forgiven you already." She smiled at him to let him know she was joking with him.

John was a little puzzled by her reaction, since he had just gotten home. "Well, I haven't had a chance to see you, Mrs. Fieldworth. I just got home today. Right now, actually."

"Really?" Confusion wrinkled her forehead. "Who was it, then, that I saw going into your apartment yesterday, when I was leaving Mrs. Hensen's across the hall from you?"

John tried not to react. Casually, he asked, "Someone was going into my apartment yesterday? Are you sure?"

"I know I'm getting old, Detective, but the man looked like you from behind. Same hair coloring, same build. I called you . . . Well, you know, I thought it was you . . . but he just went in and ignored me. You don't suppose someone broke into your apartment, do you?" Mrs. Fieldworth tended to ramble at times, especially when she was worried. "I hope we don't have a rash of break-ins. You know how many elderly people we have living here. That's why we're all grateful you live here. We all feel safer."

If John didn't find an opening soon, she would continue worrying about this for at least another hour. He had to get to his apartment and see if someone really had been there.

"You know what? I bet it was my partner. I asked him to feed my goldfish while I was gone."

That was as good an excuse as his tired and now distracted brain could come up with, and it worked. Mrs. Fieldworth instantly brightened and dropped the subject. "You have a goldfish? That's sweet. You know, I would be more than happy to feed your fish for you."

"I didn't want to bother you, Mrs. Fieldworth. If you'll excuse me, I do have to go and get some rest. I'm a bit tired from my travels. So, my dear lady . . ." He leaned down and kissed her hand. "I bid you farewell."

She laughed and blushed whenever John did that. He had found it was the easiest way for him to end a conversation without hurting her feelings. He had to get upstairs. What if someone was on to him — or Regina? He was more concerned for her than himself.

When he got upstairs, he looked closely at his lock and saw that somebody had taken a sharp object to the keyhole, trying to pick it. And apparently, he had been successful, according to Mrs. Fieldworth. Pulling out his duty revolver, he slowly opened the door and entered with caution, just in case the intruder had returned.

But that didn't seem to be the case. He walked in to find that everything looked the way he had left it. He checked his bedroom and the bathroom, and no one was there. He replaced his gun and took a deep breath. Maybe Mrs. Fieldworth had imagined the whole thing. But if she hadn't . . . who had been here and what had he wanted? That was the question of the day. He walked over to check his answering machine.

The first message was from his mom. The second one was from Frank, and he didn't sound very happy. The third was from the captain, who sounded like he was going to hurt somebody. The next one was Frank again, apologizing for the earlier message. The final one was from his sister.

"John . . . um, this is Lisa. I'm just calling to see if you're okay. Call me. Bye."

That was strange. He picked up the phone and dialed his sister's house.

"Hello?"

"Hey, Sis, what's up?"

"Oh, am I glad to hear your voice. Can't you pick up the phone from time to time to call?" She sounded agitated.

"Hey, what's the matter?" John asked. "Why are you so upset?"

"I'm worried about you. I've been watching the news, and I can't believe all the craziness out there."

"Look, Lisa, don't worry about me, okay? I've gotta go. I'll talk to you soon."

"First, promise me you'll be careful," Lisa insisted.

John shook his head. Lisa gave him a harder time about things than their mother did. "I promise, Sis. I've gotta go. Love ya."

He hung up the phone. He didn't feel like getting into a long conversation with her now. There was too much on his mind. But first, what he needed was rest.

He went into his bedroom, pulled off his clothes, and tossed them across the chair in the corner. He set his watch on the nightstand next to the phone, right beside the second Caller ID box, and settled down to get some much-needed sleep.

Suddenly, he opened his eyes again and sat up in bed.

The light was flashing on the Caller ID box, as it was supposed to when he got calls. Jumping out of bed, he went back into the living room and checked the box next to the answering machine. That one wasn't blinking. He didn't remember checking it.

Someone had been in his apartment.

He opened some drawers in his desk and everything seemed to be in order — but not quite as he remembered. He picked up the phone receiver, opened it, and found a bug. He looked underneath tables and chairs, checked the lamps, and found another one behind his sofa.

So, someone wanted to keep an eye on him. The question was, Who? He couldn't sleep now. He had to get down to the station.

Father Thomas sat in Sophia's hospital room and tried to find words to comfort and reassure her, but apparently he was having some trouble saying the right thing. "Sophia, she's going to be okay. You need to get better now. You can come and stay with me at the rectory until your house is repaired."

"Repaired? *Repaired?*" Sophia stared at him in disbelief. "With all due respect, Father, it was blown away. There is nothing to be repaired. All my memories are gone. Nothing of my life with Michael remains. The only picture I have of him is the one I keep in my wallet." She started to weep.

He didn't know what to say to this poor woman who had lost so much in such a short period of time. He didn't want to try to console her with cliché religious expressions of comfort. So in the end, he just let her cry on his shoulder for a few minutes and then started to pray silently for her. As he prayed, she began to calm down.

"I'm sorry — I know that God loves me. I haven't lost my faith in His ability to help me. It's just that . . . Thank you for understanding that I just need to grieve."

"I understand, Sophia. It's good to cry. It's better than keeping it bottled up. The doctors say you will be released tomorrow. How about my offer?"

"What offer is that?" The question came from the doorway, startling them. Unnoticed, Anthony had quietly entered the room. He stood just inside the door with his arms folded, frowning at Father Thomas as if he resented the air he breathed.

Sophia blurted, "None of your business. Get out of my room!"

"Now, Momma Sophia, is that any way to treat your son-in-law? I've come here today to see what I can do for you. I want you to come and stay at the penthouse with me until we have your house rebuilt."

Sophia started to laugh so loudly and so hard that she surprised not only Anthony but Father Thomas as well.

"What's so funny?" Anthony asked, obviously annoyed.

The laughter stopped as suddenly as it started. "You," she replied. "You think I would go anywhere with *you*? If you think I would live under the same roof as you, it's more than funny — it's crazy."

"Sophia!" Father Thomas interjected. He knew personally what this man was capable of and didn't want her to make him upset. "Mr. Cavelli, I have offered Mrs. Palmetto the use of my home. It might be best in this situation."

"Why don't you stay out of it? This doesn't concern you," Anthony barked.

"Don't you talk to him like that. You have respect for no one, not even for a priest. I'm going to accept Father Thomas' offer. As for you, stay away from me. I don't need anything from you. I can have my own home rebuilt without any help from you."

Father Thomas could see the irritation building inside of Anthony. His concern for Sophia grew as Anthony tried to remain respectful and calm. "Momma Sophia, I apologize if I have upset you in any way. I only come here out of concern for you as my wife's mother."

Sophia sighed. "Do me a favor, will you? No, actually, two favors."

"Anything," Anthony replied.

"First, don't call me 'Momma Sophia' ever again. I hate it. And secondly, stay away from my daughter. She is much better off without you in her life."

Anthony paused before replying. Then he smiled slightly and said, "I can do the first, but I'm afraid I can't do the second. Your daughter is carrying *my* child, and she is *my* wife. For a religious woman, I thought you would want me to honor the vows I made before God and family. You know

I will find her and bring her back to live in *my* home again. I would think after all these years, you would have gotten used to that fact."

Sophia was about to speak again, but Father Thomas touched her hand and shook his head. Tight-lipped, she kept quiet, and he knew it was only out of respect for him, nothing else.

"Mr. Cavelli, maybe we should both leave. Sophia has had a trying time and is quite tired." He turned to her and said, "You rest, and I will be back tomorrow to pick you up."

"Thank you," she replied to Father Thomas and then glared at Anthony.

Perhaps it was the lighting or the way he'd been holding his head; at any rate, as she turned back to Father Thomas, Sophia suddenly noticed what he had been trying to keep hidden from her.

"Father Thomas, what happened to your face?"

He didn't know how to respond to that.

Anthony looked at him and asked, "Yeah, Father, what happened? You run into something?"

Father Thomas couldn't believe the nerve of this man. He knew no good would come of Sophia knowing the truth. It would only add fuel to her fire. "It's really quite silly," he began. "I was reading over my sermon notes while I was walking, and I tripped and landed on my face." He chuckled to make light of the situation.

"You need to be more careful. Did you hurt anything else?"

"Just my pride. No, really, I'm fine. Well, then, I believe I will see you tomorrow. You rest now. Good-bye." Giving her a smile, he walked quickly out of the room and heard her call, "Good-bye," to him as he exited. He couldn't bear to see the smirk on Anthony's face.

On the other side of the door stood one of Antonio's men. Father Thomas briskly walked past him toward the elevator. Anthony caught up with him just before he reached it.

"Father Thomas," he said, as if giving a command.

Father Thomas stopped and, with a grimace, turned around to look at him. "Yes."

Anthony came close and whispered, "Nice cover job in there. You're not as dumb as I first thought."

Father Thomas started to leave again.

"Just one more thing . . ." Anthony paused, his stare piercing through Father Thomas soul. "Don't ever interfere with my family or me again. It's not a healthy or wise thing to do."

"I'm more worried about answering to God, Mr. Cavelli. My intentions are not to interfere with you or your family, but I am called to help those who ask. I cannot and will not turn anyone away."

Anthony really hated this man. Was everyone around him stupid? First Sophia, now this priest. How much more was he expected to take? He was about to tell him exactly what he thought of that last remark when the elevator doors opened, and he saw Poppy and Vinny about to step onto their floor.

Forcing a grin, he left Father Thomas and went to greet his father. "Poppy, I'm so glad to see you," Anthony said as he embraced him.

"What are you doing here?" Poppy looked at Anthony with suspicion in his eyes.

"I've come here to offer some comfort and a place to stay to Sophia, but she refused. She's going to be staying with the priest."

"Did you upset her?" Poppy asked.

Anthony resented the question. What was this? A coup against him? "No, I only offered her a place to stay. Instead, she's staying with that priest friend of hers. Why do you choose to think the worst of me?"

Poppy didn't answer, so Anthony decided a quick exit was in order.

"Since you're here and I've already seen Sophia, I'll be getting back to work. Vinny — walk me downstairs."

While Anthony's head was turned, Antonio nodded to Vinny, giving his permission, and he and Anthony left. Father Thomas observed the silent exchange from a short distance away and decided to take the stairs.

"Excuse me, Father," Antonio said as he passed.

Father Thomas tried not to wince. He turned toward him. "Yes, may I help you?"

"Aren't you the priest who did the funeral for Michael Palmetto?"

"Yes, I am."

"And you're also the one Sophia will be staying with for a while."

"Yes."

"If you don't mind, may I have a word with you?"

Father Thomas felt mildly intrigued, but he wasn't sure if he wanted to deal with another Cavelli, especially right now. According to the news, as well as more personal sources, Antonio Cavelli was fierce and evil, just like his son. However, this man didn't appear to fit that description. He seemed significantly less harsh than his son. Since this Cavelli had been more respectful than his junior, Father Thomas decided to listen to what he had to say.

"I have a few minutes."

"Good. I'm very concerned about Sophia. With your permission, I would like to place one of my men at your church to keep an eye on her."

"She will be quite safe in the church, I assure you, Mr. Cavelli."

"Yes, I'm sure of that, but it would give this old man peace of mind." Antonio's face expressed concern, but unlike his son, he didn't seem overly determined to get his way.

"I think it would make Sophia uncomfortable," Father Thomas finally responded.

"What if I promise that he would not interfere in any way with her or church activities? You wouldn't even know he was there." Antonio tried to reassure him. "I won't send someone unless I have your permission."

Father Thomas couldn't believe the difference between father and son. Maybe time had softened this man. Why was he so caring when it came to Sophia and Regina? He wasn't sure what was going on, but after his encounters with the son, Father Thomas wasn't about to ignore caution when it came to the father. "If Sophia gives her permission, then I will allow it. I need to get back now. Good day."

"Thank you for your time, Father," Antonio replied.

As Antonio approached her door, he hoped Sophia would receive him well. He hoped she would see past her anger and distrust and realize he was only trying to help. That was sincerely the only motive of his heart. He greeted his man standing outside her room and entered to find her sitting up and looking out the window. She heard him enter, but when she saw who it was, she looked away again.

"Sophia, I am so glad to see that you're doing better." She didn't turn in his direction. "Do you like the flowers in your room?" When there still wasn't a response, he tried a different route. "I met Father Thomas outside. He is a very nice man. I hear you will be staying with him, and I think that's a wonderful idea."

She sighed and turned to look at him, her eyes full of skepticism.

"I'm truly sorry about all that has happened to you. I want you to know that I will get to the bottom of this. I'm certain this was an accident, but I assure you that if it wasn't, I will find that out also."

She stared at him and finally said, "I don't know if you're lying or telling the truth, but I know firsthand how good you are at lying. I just want to be left alone. If you cared for me or Regina at all, you would let us be."

"How can I? She is my . . ." He stopped himself from calling her his daughter just in time. "She is carrying my grandchild. I care for her, and I would never allow any harm to come to her. You must believe me."

"That I do believe. But look at how little control you have over your son. Can't you see the destruction he has caused in my life and in my daughter's?"

"He loves Regina. She is carrying his child." Even though he recently had grown to distrust his son, Antonio still tried to stick up for him; he loved him, despite his failings.

Sophia laughed sarcastically. She found it hard to believe she was actually having this conversation. Had the years made him dense? "Sure, he does. Do you have any idea how she conceived that child?"

"I assume the natural way."

"Oh, so you call . . ." She clamped her mouth shut. She had promised Regina she would never repeat what she'd told her about the rape. She had given her word, and even though Sophia was angry, she couldn't betray her.

"Go ahead and finish what you were saying," Antonio urged, his face like stone.

"Forget it," Sophia replied with disgust.

"What are you not telling me? Sophia, if there is something I need to know, then just say it."

"I'm not telling you anything, but I am asking you to leave."

He studied her a moment in silence and then decided to let her have her way. "Okay. I didn't come here to upset you. But before I go, I would like to ask you something. I asked Father Thomas if I could place one of my men at the church to keep an eye on you. He said I needed your permission."

"Since when do you ask permission for anything?" Sophia demanded.

"I understand your anger and your distrust, but don't you know how much I still care for you? I'm asking for your permission. Do I have it?"

"No. I don't want your men around spying on me. I don't even want that one that's outside my room. Why don't you just leave me alone? Just leave me alone!" Sophia yelled.

"I didn't come here to upset you. I will not bother you again. Once you are with Father Thomas, you will not see me or any of my men."

Before he left, he added, "But I promise you this. I will find Regina, and when I do, I will return her to you safely."

Brother Steven came running out the door. "Mrs. Cavelli! Mrs. Cavelli! Where are you going?"

Regina stopped, bag in hand, about to head down a dirt road in the middle of nowhere. She was further from civilization than, perhaps, she had ever been in her life. She was a New Yorker. On the other side of the stone fence, there were no bus stops in the trees. No cabs. As Brother Steven came toward her, she frowned at herself and wondered what, exactly, she had been thinking. Concern for her mother had blocked out all rational thought. Where *was* she going? Nowhere fast, at least not here.

She set her bag down, looked at him, and said, "I have to go back to New York. My mother is in the hospital, and she needs me. Where is the nearest airport or train station?"

"My dear, you can't leave," he said tenderly. "Have you forgotten why you are here? I promised Father Thomas that I would watch over you. How can I do that if you leave and go back into the lion's den?"

She didn't know what to say. She had no answer for him, or for herself. Helplessness washed over her, and she started to cry. Brother Steven picked up her bag and gently guided her back toward the house. They didn't get very far. Regina sank down onto the front steps, and he sat next to her.

"It's okay to cry, you know. It's not a sign of weakness or lack of faith. I can see that you are a very brave woman, one who carries God's Spirit within her. Draw near to Him and let Him comfort you."

They sat there for a long time, and Regina cried all the tears she had. She told him the whole story of how she had come to marry Anthony, who his family was, and how she'd become pregnant. She told him about her dad, mom, and finally about John. He listened, not judging her or even appearing shocked by anything she said.

When she had said everything she could ever possibly tell him, he took her hand and prayed for her. Ever so slowly, the fog began to lift. Feeling the first tendrils of God's peace come over her, she sat there and promised both Him and Brother Steven she would stay until they could find out from Father Thomas how her mom was doing.

When John entered the precinct, all eyes immediately latched onto him. He didn't like the way it made him feel — like a kid about to be hauled off to the woodshed. Choosing to ignore them all, he went straight to the detective squad, where he saw Frank sitting at his desk doing some paperwork and talking on the phone. As soon as Frank noticed John standing in front of him, he hung up.

"Am I glad you're here, Frank. We have a lot to talk about," John said.

Frank frowned at him, but before he could say a word, the captain stepped out of his office, saw John standing there, and said gruffly, "Nelson! Well, it's nice of you to grace us with your presence. Get in here! You, too, Holstrum."

The rest of the room pretended not to have heard. John followed his captain and partner into the office and shut the door behind him — not that it would help drown out the captain's voice. When he was mad, he could be heard down the block.

John started to explain, "Captain, I just got back and — "

But the captain cut him off. "Back from where?"

"Well, you see, I've been working on this case and . . ."

"What case?"

"You know, that one I had to go to L.A. for . . ."

"The one you didn't go to L.A. for, you mean. Frank already told me he checked out the airports, and you weren't on any flights going to L.A. As a matter of fact, no flights anywhere."

John looked over at Frank, but Frank had taken a sudden interest in the plaques on the wall and didn't return his gaze. "You see, I got another lead at the last minute . . ."

"Yeah, what lead?"

As the captain stared him down, John came to a realization: This was, perhaps, the perfect spot for an immediate change of subject. "Well, before I get into that, you won't believe what I found when I got home today. My apartment's been bugged." He was somewhat surprised he was able to complete his thought without being interrupted again.

The diversion worked. Both Frank and the captain gave him a funny look.

"Bugged?" The captain squinted at him.

"Yeah, I found one in the phone and another one behind my sofa. I don't know if there are anymore anywhere."

"Who would bug your apartment?" Frank asked.

"I don't know. It's a good question, but that's not the worst of it."

"What do mean?" The captain, much to John's relief, was now totally distracted from the point he was trying to make.

"The bug I found in my phone is the same type we use for surveillance." John pulled them out of his pocket. "If someone from the department is bugging my phone, I would like to know who and why."

The captain took one of the bugs out of John's hand and examined it more closely. "It's one of ours. I didn't order this." He picked up his phone and called someone in the supply department. "This is Merrill. I want you to check your sign-out sheets and find out if anyone recently, say within the last few weeks, checked out any of our surveillance devices."

"Wait a minute," John interrupted, leaning forward. "Have him just check the last couple of days. I believe this was placed yesterday."

"Just check the last couple of days, then get back to me." He hung up the phone. "What makes you think this happened yesterday?"

"My landlady said she saw someone going into my apartment yesterday. As a matter of fact, she thought it was me."

The captain suddenly remembered why he'd summoned them. His brows lowered, and he said, "That reminds me — where were you?"

John hesitated, knowing he couldn't tell him the whole truth even if he wanted to. But he didn't know what else to say, now that Frank had totally blown his L.A. story. He glanced at his partner again, who was frowning at him, and then said, "If I tell you, it would endanger the life of a source on one of the cases I'm working on. I can't take that risk."

"What case? I know everything you're working on."

"I can't tell you. You gotta trust me. I've never had reason to suspect this before, but I think there is someone from this department working for this individual. I realize you could force me to tell you more, but I'm asking for a little bit of time."

The captain and Frank both stared at him. The captain looked a little perturbed but a little curious as well, which gave John some hope.

"Just a little bit of time," he repeated.

Before the captain could reply, the phone rang. He turned in his chair and answered it, listened, and then hung up without saying a word.

"Supply checked the log, and there isn't any surveillance equipment signed out. However, when they checked the inventory, they discovered there were some items missing. Maybe you're right, John. I'll have to turn this over to Internal Affairs, you know."

"Captain, please — not yet. If we tip our hand too quickly, this guy can hide and cover his tracks. So far he's been very careful. If he knows we're on to him, he might just lay low."

"Yeah, John's right," Frank said. "We'll need to smoke this guy out."

John was grateful for his partner's support. For a little while there, he hadn't been sure he would get it.

"Okay. I'll give you guys some time, but you have to let me know which case you're talking about."

John didn't know what to do, but he was sure he could trust these two men. Frank had been his partner and friend for so long, and both men had been there for him when his brother had died.

"The Cavelli case. I think it might be Anthony Cavelli who has someone on the inside. Who knows — a guy like him could have more than one cop on his payroll, but my instincts feel like it's just one guy. That's all it takes."

"Why do you think it's only one?" Captain Merrill asked.

"Well, Captain, from my study of Anthony Cavelli, he doesn't trust anyone. I don't think he trusts his own father. How many of his own men have come up dead since I've been working on his case? If there were more than one person, that would mean he would have to trust more than one person. Whoever he has working for him is very slick. It's probably someone who's had some financial trouble."

"I agree. Who on the Cavelli case are you protecting?" the captain asked.

"I'm sorry, but I gave my word," John said.

The captain wasn't happy with that response, but he chose to let it go for now. "All right, get out of here. You two have work to do."

As soon as they'd left the captain's office, Frank grabbed John's arm and said quietly, "Sorry I didn't cover for you better, but you should have told me what was going on instead of that lame family excuse."

He was completely right, but John was in a bind here. Keeping secrets was a first for both of them. "I'm sorry, too." And he truly was. "But come on. We've got work to do."

"I'll go up to Supply and see how many bugs were stolen. Then we'll know if there are any more in your apartment," Frank said.

"Good idea. I think I'll check into some of the backgrounds of the guys who have helped with this case — some of the other people around here, too."

"Well, be careful. If these guys find out you're checking on them for something like this, it will be rough to work here. You know what I'm saying?"

"Yeah, I do. I'll be careful."

"Tell me, Vinny — have you found out why my dad is so obsessed with the women in that family?" Anthony asked as they walked out of the building.

"No, Boss. Your father is starting to trust me, but you know how he is. He's very secretive and keeps things to himself. I never know where we're going until I get into the car. He's been getting even more secretive in the last couple weeks since Regina's been gone."

"Yeah, my wife. She causes me more trouble than she or that brat she's carrying is worth. I can't wait to get my hands on her." Anthony pretended his hands were around her neck.

"You know, Boss, I may not know much, but I know this — we can't hurt her. We need to be careful. Your dad is really attached, you know."

"Yeah, I know. You let me worry about my dad." Anthony had his own plans, and he was not willing to share them with Vinny right now. He never let the men around him know too much too soon; more than once, that level of caution had saved him.

Just as they reached the car, Anthony's cell phone rang. When he recognized the voice on the other end, he walked away from the car, motioning that Vinny should wait for him. "So, what's going on?"

"Look, I have to lay low for a while."

"Why?" Anthony asked.

"They're on to me. They found the bugs in his apartment. An investigation is starting. I can't risk being found out."

"Well, they don't suspect you, do they?"

"No, but if I keep giving you information, they might."

"Did you get the book?"

"Yeah, I got it."

"Does he know yet?"

"No, he just got back. He hasn't had a chance to check his messages. Look, I gotta go. I'll destroy the copies I have and the film."

"No way! I want you to bring me everything. The usual place, tonight at eleven," Anthony demanded.

"I can't get away tonight. Let's do it tomorrow. It's really dangerous. You know you can trust me to do the right thing."

"I don't trust anyone!"

"Well, you're going to have to trust me until tomorrow. I've got this family thing. Believe me, I would be there tonight if I could."

Anthony was not pleased. He was not about to let this cop think he was allowed to change the rules.

"Tomorrow night will be fine. There is a situation that needs my attention tonight, anyway. Bring me all the copies, the film, and anything else you've got. Same time and place. No excuses. I'll have something to tide you over for a while."

He snapped his phone shut and walked back to the car. "Vinny, you better get back upstairs. If the old man asks you what I wanted, tell him that I want you to do some collecting for me. Got it?"

"Yeah, no problem." Vinny turned and walked back toward the hospital, wondering what "usual place" Anthony was talking about — and who he had been talking to. He hadn't caught much, but he'd heard enough to know that something was up. He needed to tell Poppy.

The phone rang in the rectory and the housekeeper, Nancy, answered. She was a very pleasant woman in her late sixties who had been taking care of the priests in this parish for thirty years. Retirement was the last thing on her mind. Father Thomas often asked her if the job was getting to be too much for her, but Nancy always waved him off with a flick of her hand. Father Thomas was her favorite. She told him all the time that she would have nothing to do all day if it wasn't for him.

"St. Mary's Rectory. May I help you . . . ? Hold on, please, and I will get him for you." She placed the phone on hold and walked down to Father Thomas' study. Knocking lightly on the door, she poked her head through the opening and said, "There is a phone call for you, Father, on line one."

"Thank you, Nancy," he said as he gave her a smile. He chuckled to himself because after all these years, she still refused to use the intercom.

He picked up the phone. "Hello, this is Father Thomas. May I help you?"

"Yeah, Father. I work for Antonio Cavelli, and he wanted me to call ya. He sez that you don't hafta worry about any of us guys hanging 'round your church 'cause Mrs. Palmetto didn't give her permission."

That was all the man said, and then he hung up. Father Thomas didn't even get a chance to ask a question or say anything at all. He wondered why Antonio Cavelli would go through so much trouble for this family. Apparently, something *was* changing with him, at least where the Palmetto women were concerned. That, of course, made him think again of Regina, and he picked up the phone to do what he had sat at his desk to do just before Nancy had knocked on his door.

"May I speak to Brother Steven? This is Father Thomas calling." He waited while Steven came to the phone.

"Hello, Father Thomas. It is so good to hear from you," the monk said enthusiastically, which made Father Thomas smile all over again.

"Yes, it is good to hear your voice also. I was wondering if you enjoyed the package I sent you."

"Oh, yes. It is just wonderful of you to remember my birthday. How is everything with you?"

"Oh, things here are fine. I am going to have a visitor stay with me. She recently lost her home and her husband. She will stay here while her house is rebuilt."

"That sounds just like you, to extend yourself to someone. I'll say a prayer for her. It's been nice talking to you, but I need to go to afternoon mass now. I hope to talk with you again soon."

"Yes, and I with you."

He trusted that this would give Regina hope. Before she'd left, she'd insisted that he never make reference to her by name over the phone. They didn't know whose phone Anthony would bug next.

Poppy came out of the first-floor elevator in time to meet Vinny in the lobby. "How did it go?"

"Interesting. It appears your son is meeting someone tomorrow night at eleven. Something about some film and copies that Anthony wants. It might be his informant, but he didn't call him by name, and I was pretending not to listen."

"You did good, Vinny. I wonder if this has anything to do with Regina. I know this is dangerous for you, but I want you to see if you can go along with him. Maybe ask him to go out, and when he says he has something to do, see if you can tag along."

"That's a good idea, but . . . he usually takes Mario, not me."

"Okay, if he doesn't fall for that, then follow him, but be careful. If you think he spots you, let it go. Go and rent a car, because he would recognize yours or one of mine."

"No problem, sir."

"Oh, by the way, what's the story you're supposed to feed me?"

They smiled at one another as Vinny repeated what Anthony had told him to say.

Chapter 12

Sophia got up early and dressed. There wasn't much to pack. The hospital had given her some of the necessities, such as a toothbrush, toothpaste, and slippers, and the ladies from St. Mary's had brought her some clothes and shoes. She had nothing except what their generosity had provided for her, and she was so grateful for their kind hearts.

At least the insurance was going to cover the cost of everything, including rebuilding the house and replacing its contents. But she hated the thought of starting all over again, of putting price tags on memories and items she knew she couldn't replace. Her head started to spin whenever she thought about it. If Regina were here, she would be able to help her. But — thankfully — her daughter and grandchild were safe. That was all that mattered.

Maybe one of these days she could get away and go be with her. But right now, that was out of the question. Even though Antonio had promised he wouldn't have anyone watching her, he could be lying. He'd certainly done it before. And there was always Anthony. Who knew what he was up to now? If she was followed and Regina was found because of her . . . No, she couldn't let that happen. It was best if she stayed put for the time being.

A knock on the door interrupted her thoughts. "Come in."

Father Thomas stepped inside.

"Oh, Father, how good it is to see you today."

"It is good to see you smiling, Sophia."

"You are such a kind man. If you weren't already married to the church, would I find a girl for you."

He blushed almost scarlet, and she smiled to herself. She was kidding, but deep down she longed for Regina to have a normal life filled with love and security, one in which she could rest and spend her days with someone like Father Thomas, who was honorable and trustworthy.

"Thank you. That's one of the nicest things anyone has ever said to me." Walking over to her, he leaned down and whispered, "She is safe and doing fine. I was able to get word to the monastery that you're staying with me so she won't worry."

Sophia felt her eyes begin to sting again. He stepped back, grabbed her bag off the bed, and extended his arm to her. "Shall we go, then?"

Wiping her eyes, she got up and took his arm. "Yes, we shall," she said and felt so relieved that she wasn't exactly sure why she was crying this time.

As they walked out the door, she saw Antonio's guard heading toward the elevator. "I guess Antonio is . . . keeping his word about not having me watched."

The moment she mentioned his name, the tears came on afresh, and she whispered, "Oh, Father Thomas, I've made so many mistakes in my life."

"You know, I've heard that God is in the mistake-forgiving business."

With sudden sadness, Sophia said, "I've made some serious mistakes, and this is why my daughter is in the mess she's in. She doesn't even know."

"We can talk about it later if you wish, but I don't want you getting upset right now."

"It would be good to let go of this burden I've been carrying for so long."

The nurse came over with a wheelchair. "Here you go, Mrs. Palmetto."

"Is it really necessary for me to sit in one of these? I feel fine," she protested.

"It's hospital policy, ma'am." The nurse smiled at her.

"She's just trying to do her job, Sophia." Pointing to the wheelchair, Father Thomas continued, "Your chariot awaits."

John switched on the computer. Maggie in personnel had told him in no uncertain terms that if he got caught, he was on his own. She was known throughout the precinct for being a tough, by-the-book kinda gal. But John knew she was a bit sweet on him, and he used that to his advantage when necessary. He didn't mean any harm, and she knew what he was doing, but they both liked playing their games.

She had looked at him slyly as she handed him the access code.

"Now, remember, you never got this from me. I have a rep to uphold."

"Maggie, my dear, should I get caught, I promise you I'll take the full blame for it. They'll never know you were here."

He felt like a slug, snooping on his own like this, but it was necessary; maybe there was something in the personnel files that would give the informant away.

Twenty minutes later, his time was almost up and he had found nothing of interest when suddenly Frank's record popped up on the screen. He knew Frank wasn't the guy, but he decided to take a quick look anyway. Maybe there was something in his file that he could hold over his head. He chuckled to himself — he could use some good ammunition.

There were the typical things about family and how long he had been on the force. But only ten seconds later, John frowned. Frank came from a family of six? He'd told him he had four brothers and sisters, which would make only five. Why would he lie about one of his siblings?

Maybe he or she had died. Looking further, John read that the youngest sibling was in an institution. She was severely handicapped and had kidney and liver damage, requiring twenty-four-hour medical care. Medical care at that level cost an enormous amount of money. John knew that Frank's father had died a few years ago, which meant that incredible financial commitment no doubt had fallen to his mother.

John sat there staring at the screen. His mind started to wander, but then he shook his head. *What am I thinking?* Frank had other brothers and sisters who could help also. John couldn't allow his imagination to get the best of him. There was no way on earth it was Frank. Regina's words suddenly came to the forefront of his mind: *Don't trust anyone.*

But this was Frank. Frank was like part of his family. He probably didn't want to talk about his sister because he didn't want any sympathy.

He was a proud man who wasn't big on showing emotion. John closed down the computer and returned to his desk before the personnel staff could get back from lunch.

His landline rang right as he was sitting down. "Detective Nelson. Oh, yeah, I hope you guys have some good news for me. I know . . . I've been away. What message? Well, tell me. Did you guys decode it?"

John paled. He couldn't believe what he was hearing. There must be a mistake. "When did this happen? Well, you did make copies and keep them somewhere else, didn't you? What about . . . ? Oh, no, not . . . the film, too. What about the computer file? The backup also. I see. No, I don't blame you. I'm sure you had it very secure. Yeah, it's a shame, especially since you were so close. Okay, thanks."

He slowly hung up the phone. Those copies had been his last hope. Now what was he going to say to Regina? The evidence she worked so hard to get was gone and probably in Anthony's hands.

"Man, you look like you've seen a ghost. What's wrong?" Frank asked, coming to stand next to John's desk.

"You won't believe it. I had some strong evidence against Anthony Cavelli — but it was stolen. Probably by our informant."

"Oh, man, that's terrible! But don't worry about it — we'll still get him somehow. These guys always make mistakes eventually." He stood there a moment more and then said, "Hey, let's go grab some lunch. You look like you could use some food, and I'm starving."

"No, thanks. You go ahead. I've got to go visit someone this afternoon."

"You want me to bring something back for you?"

"I'll grab something while I'm out. Thanks."

After Frank left, John realized he hadn't remembered to ask about his sister in the institution. But maybe it was for the best. Frank was the only one he trusted right now, and he didn't want him to know he'd been spying on him.

Brother Steven hadn't thought he would ever find himself in this position — waiting for an update on a pregnant woman's condition. Her story had touched something deep inside of him, and his heart had gone out to her. With everything in him, he wanted her situation to work out well.

A few minutes later, the doctor stepped out of Regina's room, closing the door behind him. A line formed between his eyes, and he wasn't smiling like he had been earlier.

Concerned, Brother Steven asked, "Is there something wrong, Doctor?"

"Well, the baby appears to be smaller than normal at this stage, and the heart rate is not as strong as I would like to hear." The doctor continued, "I don't have the right equipment here, Brother Steven. I need to take her to the hospital and have some tests done — an ultrasound for one. However, bringing such equipment here would cause too many questions for me, and for her. Someone might find out that she is here; and obviously, it would be hard to sneak that kind of equipment out of the clinic."

"What do you suggest we do?" Brother Steven asked.

"I've talked with our patient about this, and she agrees with me. Bring her to the hospital in a disguise or something, at night when it's not as busy. We can run the tests then. Her real name doesn't have to be used. We can call her Mrs. Jones."

Brother Steven wasn't happy about this development, but if the doctor wanted to take her in, how could he argue? The baby's life could be at stake.

"Okay, I'll bring her in myself. When do you want her to be there?"

"Tonight around ten thirty. You may enter the hospital through the staff entrance in the back. I'll leave word with the security guard. He is a dear friend and doesn't ask any questions. It will be all right. I promise."

"Tonight, then, at ten thirty. Thank you for coming."

When the doctor had gone, Brother Steven poked his head into Regina's room. Sitting quietly on the bed, she appeared a little pale. "So, how are you?"

"I'm worried about the baby. I didn't like the look on the doctor's face. I'm praying everything is all right."

"I don't want you to worry about it. The doctor is an old friend, and he is quite trustworthy. He has arranged for us to go tonight to the hospital, and I will even get you a wig to help disguise you. It will be just like an adventure!" Brother Steven tried putting a positive spin on the situation.

"I don't want you to risk being seen with me. I can go myself, if you lend me a car and give me directions."

"I will not hear of it. Please let me do this. I don't get to have many adventures." He tried not to seem overly desperate to help, even though he knew he would never let her walk out that door tonight by herself. He would be with her whether she wanted him to be or not.

"Adventure, huh? That's a unique way of looking at it. I just don't want you to get hurt. You have no idea how ruthless Anthony is."

"No one knows you're here. Believe me, you will cause less suspicion if I go with you."

"I don't know how to thank you for all that you've done for me and my baby. You're really sweet."

Brother Steven smiled and felt himself blush a little. "That's what all the gangsters' pregnant wives who hide in my monastery say." They laughed.

Brother Steven was different than how Regina had imagined monks to be. She had never met one before, but the movies always portrayed them as proper, quiet, holy men of God who led secluded lives in order to serve Him better. Brother Steven was all of those things, and yet he was more than that, too. "I'm feeling a bit tired. I think I'd better rest now. I'll see you later."

"Yes, that is a good idea. I'll go to town and get you a wig. But first, I'll change into some street clothes. A monk buying a woman's wig would raise some eyebrows." Again they laughed.

Anthony slammed down the phone in anger. Vinny and Mario looked straight ahead, not saying a word. They knew better than to catch his eye when he was mad. If he wanted them to know what had happened, he would tell them.

"I sometimes think I am surrounded by idiots! How hard is it to plant a few bugs in a priest's house?" He looked at both of them and asked, "Which one of you is man enough to do this?"

Mario spoke up first. "I can do it, Boss."

Vinny couldn't believe how much of a kiss-up Mario was at times. He would stop at nothing to be the top man on Anthony's list.

"Well, then, what are you waiting for?" Anthony snapped. He wanted things done the second the order came out of his mouth.

"Okay, Boss. I'll go right now." Mario left.

His exit gave Vinny a potential opening to tag along with Anthony. As nonchalantly as he could, he asked, "Hey, Boss, you want to do something tonight? Maybe go to the club? You know, relax and unwind."

"I've got an errand to do tonight," Anthony responded plainly.

"That's too bad. You look like you could use a night out. You've been under a lot of stress lately," Vinny said, trying not to cause suspicion.

"What are you — my mother?" Anthony growled.

"No, I just thought . . . never mind. Do you want me to come with you on this errand and then maybe we can go out later?"

Anthony paced a bit. He *had* been pretty stressed lately; a little fun might be just what the doctor ordered. "Okay. You can stay in the car while I take care of some business, and then we'll go do something."

"Anything you say, Boss."

Vinny was relieved. At least he wouldn't have to tail Anthony tonight. Living with this level of danger was starting to put a strain on him.

Antonio sat in his living room with his robe on, sipping coffee. It was nearing noon, but he still hadn't gotten dressed because he wasn't planning on going anywhere.

Stuart entered the room. "Pardon me, sir, but I do have lunch ready for you. Where would you like it served?"

"I'm sorry you went to such trouble, Stuart, but I'm not hungry. Maybe later."

"Sir, if you don't mind, may I speak freely?" Stuart asked.

Antonio glanced up. "Go ahead."

"Well, sir, I have observed your behavior lately and am quite worried about you. You're not eating as well as you should. It won't do Miss Sophia or Miss Regina any good if you become ill. Then who would look after them?"

"It doesn't matter. Neither of them wants anything to do with me. I can't find Regina, and if Anthony finds her first . . . well, I just don't know anymore. He's changed so much lately. It's sad when a father can't trust his own son. I have only myself to blame for the way he turned out."

"Have you checked with the priest with whom Sophia is staying? Does he know where she is? I do recall you saying you were going to pay him a visit."

The light bulb went off in Antonio's head, and he climbed to his feet. "Yes, you're right, but so much has happened that I never did go to see him. Stuart, I'm glad you listen so well. After I get dressed, we're going to the church."

"Yes, sir, as you wish."

Stuart always knew what was going on, yet he spoke only when the time was right. Antonio was very grateful that the quiet, efficient Brit had worked for him all these years. He appreciated Stuart's honesty and loyalty.

John was sitting at home in front of the television and watching some old movie he'd found while flipping through channels. He didn't even know its name. He'd checked again for bugs, and the apartment was completely clean, but he couldn't help being paranoid about the whole thing. The television aided in keeping his mind occupied, especially when it came to the one thing he was more concerned with than bugs.

Thoughts of Regina consumed his every waking moment. Her eyes and smile caught him off guard each and every time she looked his direction. The way she tilted her head when she was processing what she wanted to say nearly made him stop breathing. What he wanted more than anything was to protect that beautiful face, which led him to think again about Father Thomas. John had managed to talk to the father and had been relieved to hear that everything was fine and that Regina knew her mother was okay.

Anthony had to have caused the explosion. He wouldn't care if one of his men had gotten caught in the flames. It would be just a casualty of war to him. Maybe he had been keeping an eye on Sophia and unfortunately had been caught in the wrong place at the wrong time. John didn't care that it had been ruled an accident — a leak in a gas line. *Whatever.* He knew better. This was no accident, and all those lives and homes had been lost because of it. He felt terrible for Regina's mom.

But as terrible as he felt about the explosion, what disturbed him the most was the loss of Regina's film and its contents. It could mean only one thing — that Anthony knew Regina had betrayed him. It was a good thing she was far from here and safe. He had to come up with another way to put Anthony in jail, or none of this would ever be over.

A thought occurred to him. The FBI was also working on finding evidence against Anthony; maybe he should give his friend Bobby a call. Bobby had been working there for several years and their relationship dated back to grammar school.

Muting the television, he looked up Bobby's number and dialed it. He hoped the man was home.

"Hello?" a female voice said.

"Hello, is Bobby Lewis there?" John asked.

"Yes, who's calling please?"

"My name is John Nelson. I'm an old friend." John could hear the woman calling for Bobby in the background. Must be his wife.

"Yo, Johnny, what's up?" Bobby answered cheerfully.

"Bobby, it's good to hear your voice, man. How are you doing?"

"Fine, fine. How you doing? I haven't seen you since . . ."

"I know. Since my brother's funeral. I'm okay." John decided to get to the point quickly. They could catch up on old times later. Right now, Regina was the only thing he could focus on. "I've taken over the Cavelli case since I made detective."

Bobby's tone changed. "You think that's a good idea?"

"Yeah, it's fine. I'm calling because I need your help. It's just that I've come across a bit of a snag. I think Cavelli has someone working for him inside my department. Some evidence I brought in has disappeared, and it's got to be an inside job. My place has been bugged, and there's more, but I can't get into it over the phone."

"So, what can I do for you?"

"I know you guys have your own investigation going, and I thought maybe you could look into some things for me. Maybe we can have an exchange of information. It's real important to me that we nail this guy. I should have come to you before this, but . . . well, it's an issue of pride." John didn't care if he looked weak. It was no longer important to him that he catch Anthony single-handedly — he just wanted the man to be caught.

"I don't know, man. It's not even my case." Bobby paused, and John hoped that he was at least *thinking* about helping him. "Since we're old friends, I'll tell you what — I'll look into it for you. I'm not promising nothing, okay? I know the guy heading up the case, and if I find anything out, we'll talk."

"Thanks, Bobby. Anything you can do would be great. I gotta go. I'll talk to you later."

"I'll give you a call when I find something out," Bobby said before hanging up.

At least he was trying to do something. That made John feel better. A little relieved. What he really wanted to do was go see Regina, despite all the hours involved. But that would be dangerous for her, and he knew he couldn't risk that.

He had been thinking about writing her a letter. She might enjoy hearing from him. But maybe that was a bad idea, too. He was so confused; he hadn't known what to think or do lately. Sleep was probably his best bet for now.

Antonio stood at the door of the rectory and rang the bell. The woman who answered the door seemed surprised to see him. She hesitated slightly before speaking.

"May I help you?"

"I'm looking for Father Thomas. Is he here?"

"Why don't you step inside and I'll see if I can find him, Mr. Cavelli?"

"How do you know who I am?"

She laughed at his question. "Are you kidding? Everyone who watches the news or picks up a paper knows who you are. Just wait here."

Sometimes Antonio forgot how often his picture was in the news. His lifestyle was something he was starting to regret.

When the woman returned, she said, "He's in his study. Please follow me."

"Fine, thank you."

At the end of the hall, she opened the door to a small but functional study. The bookshelves stood ceiling-to-floor on the right wall. There was a couch, a couple of chairs, and a large oak desk that was simple and plain, suiting the atmosphere. Father Thomas stood up as they entered.

"Mr. Cavelli, won't you come in and have a seat?" He motioned toward the couch and Antonio sat down. "Thank you, Nancy. That will be all."

Nancy left quietly, closing the door behind her.

"Well, I'm a bit surprised to see you here. I thought you said . . ."

"I know. I promised Sophia I would not bother her. But I didn't come to talk to Sophia. I came here to talk to you."

A bit curious, Father Thomas sat in the chair opposite him and replied, "Well, then, what can I do for you?"

"I have many things on my mind. I'm getting older, and life is getting shorter. I've been doing a lot of thinking lately, and I want you to listen to my confession."

His candor surprised Father Thomas. Here before him sat a man who had done much evil in his life, and now he was choosing confession. He wasn't sure whether to believe him after all the things Sophia had told him about her past with this man, so he began to pray for guidance.

"I hope you don't think this question rude of me, but I have to ask. Why me? This is not your parish."

"I know that. I've come to you because of your closeness to the Palmetto family. I need to confess to you so that when I ask you what I came here to ask, you will believe my sincerity."

"I see." So there was an ulterior motive after all. He wasn't surprised. "I'll listen to your confession, but I don't know if I can help you beyond that."

Antonio proceeded to tell Father Thomas about his past — the crimes he had committed and the crimes he'd had others commit for him.

He explained how and why he'd come to adopt Anthony. He mentioned the affairs he'd had with other women and told him of his affair with Sophia and how he had used her back then. He talked about how he felt that Regina was his child and went into some detail about how much she meant to him. He wanted Father Thomas to know he hadn't had anything to do with Michael's death or the explosion at Sophia's house.

"I've told you every sin I have ever committed. I have held nothing back from you, so that you may know that I'm telling you the truth about this. I love Regina with all my heart and would never harm her. She means more to me than words can express. Please, if you know where she is, let me help. I can protect her."

Father Thomas didn't know how to respond to this man. He had sat here for nearly two hours, listening to his confession. Antonio had done some terrible things in his life, yet Father Thomas sensed his genuine care and love for Regina. At the same time, he wasn't about to break his confidence with Regina and her mother, regardless of the circumstances. He decided to be as frank with Antonio as Antonio had been with him.

"Mr. Cavelli, are you confessing so that I will help you, or are you here seeking forgiveness from God for the sins you committed?"

Antonio was stumped. This man was the best lead he had; in order to obtain the information he wanted, he first needed to win him over by convincing him that he was not trying to hurt Regina. So he had confessed his sins completely. That way, the priest would know he wasn't holding anything back and would have no reason to lie. But forgiveness from God? He was not so sure about that.

"Were you listening when I told you of the evil I inflicted upon people? God can't forgive someone like me. It's too late for that."

"It's never too late. Why are you here revealing your whole life to me? It's not just because of Regina. I want you to know that God can forgive all sins, regardless of their severity. Repentance is a wonderful thing. It's not as complicated as people make it out to be. First, you confess and ask for forgiveness and promise not to keep sinning. Then God forgives."

Forgive even him? Antonio was having a hard time with that concept. He didn't dwell on the choices he had made, and he couldn't allow himself to feel hope for a different future, because he knew better. The path he had chosen was sealed forever and there was no turning back. No redemption for his sins. He knew that.

But now this priest was telling him something different. He was not sure what to make of that.

Father Thomas sensed his struggle. He asked the Lord to help him find the words to reach this man.

"God can forgive even you. In the book of Romans, there is a verse that explains God's great love for us. Romans 5:8: 'But God demonstrates his own love for us in this: While we were still sinners, Christ died for us.' God sent his only son, Jesus, to die on the cross so that we could have eternal life. He paid the price so that you and I could be redeemed. We don't have to be perfect to come to God, because if we were, we wouldn't need Him to die for us in the first place."

This whole situation was fast becoming uncontrollable, and in his occupation, Antonio had learned to get out at the first hint of chaos. "That can't be right. I've told you all the terrible things I've done in my life. I've had people killed — did you not hear me say that? So many times I've lost count."

"Yes, I did hear everything you said. But God loves even you, and He wants to be part of your life. All you need to do is say yes."

Unexpectedly, tears began to run down Antonio's face. He blinked in mild horror and wiped them away, standing up quickly. He had crossed the line. "I have to go now. You've given me quite a lot to think about." He shook Father Thomas' hand. "Thank you for your time, Father Thomas. If you know where Regina is and ever speak to her, please let her know I just want to help. Tell her that I would never allow any harm to come to her or her baby. Maybe you can let her know I will do whatever she wants if she comes back here."

"Mr. Cavelli, if you want to finish our conversation, please call me. I want to reassure you that what you've told me will be kept in strict confidence."

"I knew that before I started. I figured that if Sophia and Regina trust you, that's good enough for me. Good night."

As Antonio was leaving, he saw Sophia coming down the stairs. He nodded and continued out the door.

Sophia went to Father Thomas' study and knocked. She entered when she heard him answer.

"I just saw Antonio leaving. What was he doing here? He promised me he would stay away. I knew he couldn't be trusted!"

"It is not what you think, Sophia." Father Thomas didn't elaborate.

She huffed. "Do you mean he came for confession?"

The priest didn't answer her. He just looked down at his desk and fiddled with a pen.

"Are you kidding me? He came here for confession? It must be a trick."

"No, Sophia, it isn't a trick. He's sincere."

"He told you everything?"

He would not look at her directly, and she knew right then that Antonio had, indeed, told him everything, including the details of her past with him. "I'll bet he told you what a rotten woman I am and how I betrayed my husband."

"No, he didn't speak of you in any way that was disrespectful. I cannot talk about this with you, Sophia. I cannot tell you the things he said to me. But I *can* tell you that God is softening his heart. I believe he truly wants to help Regina."

"No! Don't trust him. Please, Father Thomas, listen to me. I have known him much longer than you have. How can you sit there after talking to him for such a short time and believe his lies?" Sophia was visibly agitated.

"You also know me, Sophia. I listen with my heart. I listen to God. Do you want to talk about your feelings? I can listen to you, but I can't share anything with you that was said to me."

"I still have a lot of anger in me. I don't know what to think anymore, but I do trust you." She frowned. "I'm so tired. I just need to get some sleep. Can we talk later?"

"Sure. I'll be here when you're ready. If you need anything, let me know." Father Thomas couldn't help but feel pain for this family who had suffered so much.

Vinny drove Anthony to the loading docks. Whenever Anthony wanted to meet someone secretly, this was the perfect place to do it. The docks were secluded from prying eyes; most of the buildings were abandoned.

Anthony had him pull up near an old brick building covered with graffiti and turn the car off. They waited for about ten minutes. The man was late, which did nothing to improve Anthony's mood. Finally, Vinny saw a dark-colored Ford pull up. It was too far away for him to make out what type of Ford, but he could tell it was an older model. A man climbed out of the car and pulled a medium-sized cardboard box from the back seat.

"I'll be right back. You wait in the car."

Anthony got out and walked toward the man. The lighting was terrible, and Vinny couldn't make out who the person was. While they had been waiting, he had rolled down his window to get some air. If he was lucky, maybe he could overhear something.

"You're late! I don't like to be kept waiting. Is that it?" Anthony demanded.

"It's all here."

The man handed Anthony the box. Kneeling down, Anthony placed it on the cement, pulled up the flaps, and examined the contents.

"It's all there. I'm not stupid, you know. You got something for me?"

Anthony clearly didn't appreciate the man's tone. He straightened up and raised his voice a bit. "I'll have something for you — like a pine box if you don't watch it! You get here late and now you're rushing me. No one rushes me."

He grabbed the man by his jacket, and the man tried to shove him away, swearing at him. Vinny got out of the car and started to walk toward them, but then Anthony commanded, "Stay back. I'm okay."

Slowly, Vinny returned to the car, but this time, he stayed by the door in case he was needed.

"I thought I told you never to bring anyone," the mystery man said. Vinny believed he had heard that voice before, but he couldn't place where. "This is the last thing I do for you! I'm out!"

Anthony just laughed at him. "You crack me up. You really think you're in control of this arrangement we have? You're wrong. *I'm* in control, and when I need you again you'll do as I say, or else there is a package that will go to the police commissioner. I believe he will find it quite interesting."

"You wouldn't. You would lose, too. I'd talk."

"Yeah, I would. Killing you would be too easy. Giving you up would be much sweeter." Anthony smirked. "You have more to lose — or should I say, more *people* to lose — than I do." He took out a thick manila envelope from his inside jacket pocket and handed it to the man. "There's a little extra this time. Don't say I don't do nothing for ya."

Anthony laughed, picked up the box, and turned around. In the dark, Vinny saw the other man reach into his coat, but without missing a beat, his back still to him, Anthony said, "Oh, and I wouldn't point that gun at my back. You see, my guy over there is a real good shot, and I doubt you would make it out of here alive." He walked away slowly.

After a second, the man went back to his car, turned it around, and drove away. Vinny had hoped the car would pass him so he could get a better look, but it didn't. He was, however, able to take note of the large dent on the left side, behind the rear tire.

Anthony's informer drove away, feeling trapped and frustrated. Maybe he should have just shot him in the back and taken his chances. He had to find a way out of this mess. He couldn't do this anymore.

Wearing a red wig, Regina walked into the back of the hospital with Brother Steven. He was dressed in jeans and a blue shirt and looked like a normal man, which seemed a bit funny to Regina at first. This whole situation, with her needing a disguise and Brother Steven dressed like a businessman on his day off, was *almost* a distraction from the real issue — why they were here. Almost.

They were greeted by the doctor himself, and he showed them into the room. Brother Steven waited outside while the doctor ran his tests. He did them personally so that Regina wouldn't have to come in contact with anyone else.

Seeing her baby on the monitor for the first time, Regina began to feel incredibly lonely. A wave of emotions washed over her. She had always imagined this moment with the man she loved by her side, both of them smiling at the small figure on the screen. A tear rolled down her face as she watched the baby's heart beat. She tried to wipe the tear before the doctor could see it, but she was too late. She noticed him staring at her.

"How's my baby?" Regina asked.

"The baby appears small for this stage of your pregnancy. I'm going to run some other tests. If there's a problem, we'll find it. What about the baby's father?"

"There's no need to worry about that, Doctor. For your own safety, I think it's for the best."

"Well, then, I need to tell you . . . I'm not 100 percent about this yet, but there appears to be a cardiac malformation. Again, I'm going to run some other tests, and if there's a problem, we'll find it." He paused. "Don't worry, Mrs. Jones. We'll do everything we can."

A nurse came into the room. She seemed startled to see the doctor and a patient she knew nothing about. Regina turned her face from her when she entered.

"Excuse me, Doctor. I didn't know you had a patient in here. She's not on my schedule. Is this an emergency that came in?"

"Don't worry about it, Miss Jensen. This has all been taken care of. You can go. Thank you."

The nurse left and Regina felt uncomfortable about having been seen. The doctor reassured her, and she tried to relax as he continued with his tests.

Chapter 13

John sat up in bed, rubbing his eyes. He had tossed and turned most of the night. All his nights seemed to be restless lately — when he slept at all. Something wasn't right and he wasn't sure what; he couldn't seem to put his finger on it.

So much had gone wrong lately. Maybe it had been stupid not to hook up with the FBI before now. Was he foolish for thinking he could have taken on the Cavellis on his own? His brother's death *had* made him a bit obsessive about clearing Sam's name and proving the Cavellis were to blame. But . . . now what?

He walked into his kitchen to make some coffee. But when he opened the canister, he found it completely empty. He had to make time to get some groceries one of these days. He decided to shower and get ready for work, then stop at his favorite diner for a cup of coffee, maybe some eggs, and to read the paper. He wasn't due back at the station for a couple of hours.

Until Bobby got back to him, he would have to be patient — a virtue he had yet to fully develop, but he knew enough not to hound the man. He needed his help too much to tick him off by being overly aggressive.

He was almost out his building's front door when Mrs. Fieldworth stepped from her apartment and spied him. "Good morning, Detective," she called with a big smile on her face.

"Good morning. How is my favorite landlady today?" John replied as he gave her a playful wink.

She giggled like a schoolgirl. "Oh, stop it. You're such a flatterer. I'm your only landlady. By the way, did you find out who was in your apartment?"

"You don't have to worry, Mrs. Fieldworth. It was my partner. He came by to feed my fish."

"Well, next time you have to leave town, don't bother your partner. I would be more than happy to feed your fish for you."

"You're a living doll," John said as he gave her a kiss on the hand. Mrs. Fieldworth smiled as he left.

He walked across the street to his car and drove to the diner — an old railroad car that had been converted. The exterior was silver with round, porthole-like windows. The diner seemed out of place surrounded by so many tall buildings, but it was very unique, which drove up patronage. The service was good and the food even better. There were many regulars who came daily, and new customers came by word of mouth.

Walking through the front door, he went to the counter and sat down. "Gale, how are you doing?" he asked lightheartedly.

Gale had been a waitress at the diner for nearly ten years before she had married Sal, the owner. She continued to waitress from time to time because she really enjoyed serving others and talking to the customers. Whenever the staff was shorthanded, she pitched in. She was one of the bubbliest and most energetic people he had ever met — and one of the reasons people kept returning.

"Hey, look who has decided to grace us with his presence," she said to no one in particular, grinning at him.

"I've been busy, Gale," John replied apologetically.

"I've missed you." She poured him a cup of coffee. "So, what can I get you this morning, Doll?"

"A couple of eggs, over easy, toast and bacon would be great."

"You got it, Babe." Cracking her gum, she handed the order to the cook and then turned and placed a newspaper on the counter. "I know how much you enjoy reading when you eat. I'll be right back with your bacon and eggs."

"Thanks," John said, amazed at what a good memory she had. "You're the best."

"That's what they all say," she teased as she poured coffee at the end of the counter. "But I'm a married lady. Don't you forget."

As the jukebox crooned oldies in the corner, John picked up the paper and unfolded it. A second later, he nearly fell off his chair. On the front page was a huge photo of Regina. *$1,000,000 reward offered for the safe return of Regina Cavelli.* The small article under the photo said that her husband was offering the reward to anyone who could help him find his missing pregnant wife. He was quoted as saying, "I just want the safe return of my wife. No questions asked of the person or persons who find her. I pray she is all right. Her mother is beside herself with worry, and I will do anything to relieve her heartache."

John couldn't believe this. A horrible thought came to him. What if all the papers across the country picked up this story? She was going to be a hunted woman with an enormous price on her head. He was glad that she was safe and isolated in a monastery.

He lost his appetite. He slapped some money on the counter and started to leave.

"Hey, Johnny, where are you going? Aren't you going to eat?" Gale asked.

"Thanks, but no; I have to go. Catch you next time." He had to make sure that Regina was still all right somehow, that this headline hadn't disrupted her safety at the monastery. He was going to pay Father Thomas a visit.

Vinny opened his front door and picked up the paper. He didn't always get to read the whole thing, but he liked knowing what was going on in the world. People thought that because he was so big, he was stupid. But he liked reading the paper, so that had to say something.

He'd have to do a quick read this morning; he needed to get to Poppy Cavelli and let him know about the meeting. Last night he'd gotten in so late that he'd had only a few hours' sleep. His brain hadn't snapped into gear yet. He walked into the kitchen and started to make some coffee. This was definitely an extra-strong coffee morning. He picked up the paper and opened it on the counter.

First he checked the back page to see who had won last night's game. He enjoyed sports, but with his job he didn't always get to watch the games. Flipping the paper over, he looked to see what was going on in the rest of the world.

The huge picture of Regina splashed across the first page instantly caught his eye, and he shook his head. This wasn't good for her — and Poppy was going to have a serious problem with it. And if he was angry, imagine how Sophia was going to react!

It was going to be another long day.

Father Thomas stood at his front door, just staring at Regina's picture. He knew how upset Sophia would be about this. How could he tell her that her son-in-law had now put a bull's-eye on Regina's back? He heard her coming down the stairs and went in and closed the door.

"Good morning, Father. Isn't this a fine day?" she asked, smiling brightly.

"Good morning, Sophia. You're in a very good mood. Did you sleep well?" Father Thomas folded the paper in half to cover up Regina's picture. He wanted to break the news to her gently.

"Yes, I did. I want to apologize to you for last night. I realized I was being unreasonable. I forget you're a priest and that you see the best in people. Anyway, the important thing is that Regina is safe and away from these people. They will never be able to find her." She walked into the dining room, and Father Thomas followed.

Nancy had already set the table with coffee, juice, eggs, oatmeal, toast, and sausage. As they sat down, Father Thomas didn't know what to say to Sophia, or how to say it. Maybe he would just wait until after breakfast. This was the first time he had seen Sophia with an appetite, and he hated to ruin the optimistic mood she was in.

"Aren't you going to eat? This is delicious. I can't believe how hungry I feel. I haven't felt this way in a long time. Do you have the paper?"

Father Thomas swallowed the lump in his throat. He didn't want to spoil her mood. He had the paper still in his hand, half hidden beneath the table.

"Father Thomas, are you okay? You look a bit stunned."

"Sophia, um . . . why don't we just chat for a bit while we eat and you can look at the paper later?" He placed it face down on the table next to him.

"Sure, if you'd like."

When Stuart brought in Antonio's breakfast tray, he decided not to bring in the paper. Antonio sat up in bed as Stuart placed the tray on the bedside table. "Where's the paper?" he asked.

"I'm sorry, sir, but it has not been delivered yet. Why don't you eat your breakfast and I'll go out and get you one later?" Stuart wanted to protect him for as long as he could. He knew he would find out soon enough, but why spoil his breakfast?

Antonio just looked at him, and Stuart could tell by his expression that he knew he was lying. He was a terrible liar — always had been.

"What's in the paper you don't want me to see?"

"I beg your pardon, sir," Stuart replied with a straight face.

"I've known you for a very long time, Stuart. You always have the paper ready for me, and the delivery boy is never late. I know you're trying to hide something from me. Just give me the paper."

Stuart left the room and returned with the paper in his hands. Antonio was eating, and he held his hand out. Stuart just stood there.

"Give it to me."

"Sir, I . . ." He didn't know what to say to soften the blow, so he finally just handed him the paper.

Antonio looked at the picture of Regina, saw the amount of the reward, and his face went white.

"Are you all right, sir?"

"Take the tray away and get the car. We're going to pay my son a visit."

Regina heard a knock on her door. "Come in."

Brother Steven opened the door and slowly stepped inside. "Good morning, Regina."

"Good morning, Brother Steven." She noticed that he couldn't seem to look at her directly. She figured he wanted to tell her something but didn't

213

know how to do so. Her throat tightened. "Is there something wrong? Did the doctor call already?"

"No," he said, pausing. "I haven't heard from the doctor. This has nothing to do with that. The cleaning lady brings the paper to us in the mornings when she comes to work. I don't know how to break this to you, but I have something to show you and I know it will upset you. Promise me you will stay calm."

"I promise I'll try."

He handed her the paper.

Regina couldn't believe the large picture of herself on the front page and the amount of the reward Anthony was offering. "Oh, no." She looked up at Brother Steven and started to cry. "Do you know what this means? One million dollars! I'm not safe *anywhere*. If anyone recognizes me, they will surely turn me in for a million dollars!"

"Don't panic. The only people who know you are here will not turn you in. The brothers, the doctor, and I have been the only ones who have seen you. The doctor would never turn you in, not even for a million dollars. I have known him for almost twenty years, and he is most honorable. The cleaning people who work here from time to time have not seen you, so you need not worry. And besides . . ."

He was starting to ramble. Regina took a deep breath. "You're right. Thank you for showing me this. I need to be alone for a while, if you don't mind."

"I understand. If you need anything, don't hesitate to ask."

While they were eating, Sophia and Father Thomas talked about her boiling emotion toward Antonio and her past with him. She knew it was unhealthy for her to continue to carry all this hurt and unforgiveness. She had to forgive him, as well as herself, for what had happened between them so many years ago, but it was turning out to be much harder than she'd anticipated, perhaps because of one issue in particular. In her heart she knew that Regina belonged to Michael . . . but what if she was wrong?

"Father Thomas, I've prayed and asked God to forgive me for the hatred in my heart towards Antonio. The sad thing is that I am just as much to blame as he is. I have so much animosity towards myself. It's just been easier to blame him all these years. Michael worked always . . . I was lonely and wanted his attention. I was wrong."

She sat there quietly for a moment. Even though saying these words was like cutting open an old wound and scrubbing salt into it, she could sense its healing properties, too. Who else could she talk to about this? Who else was there to help her heal? Father Thomas was the only one she trusted.

"It's funny how, over time, events change in your mind when you look so hard for someone to blame. All those years away, afraid for Regina's life — afraid for ours. How do you go about trusting someone whom you hated for decades?"

"You're taking a step in the right direction. First you choose to forgive him, and then you need to ask God to forgive you for your sins in the situation."

Nancy interrupted him as she entered the room to clean up the dishes.

"Mrs. Palmetto, I'm so glad to see that you're eating this morning. It must be the good news about your daughter that has put a smile on your face."

"What good news?" asked Sophia.

Father Thomas quickly said, "Nancy, would you be so kind as to get us some more coffee?"

"No problem, Father. Right away." Nancy left.

"Father Thomas, why did you do that? She was about to tell me something about Regina."

"Sophia, I wanted to break this news to you gently." He took a deep breath. "Anthony has contacted the papers and offered a reward for Regina's safe return."

"A reward? What kind of reward?"

He picked up the paper and opened it for her to see. Sophia read the headline and couldn't believe her eyes. "A million dollars? He's gone insane. He'll have every crook and wacko looking for my daughter, hunting her down like a prized pig!" She got up from the table.

"Where are you going? Sophia, let's talk about this first."

She turned around and with a look of determination stated, "To see my son-in-law. I have to talk to him."

"I don't think you should go there alone. Let me come with you."

"No! He has no respect for anyone, not even you. I will not let you get involved any more than you are already. I will be fine."

Regina sat in her room, wondering what to do. Anthony had put a price on her head. A gigantic price. Most people would give her up for less than half that amount. She wished she could just knock his teeth in. What was she going to do?

She did feel safe behind the monastery walls, at least for the time being. She looked down at her stomach. It had grown more with each passing week — she loved every inch of it. She couldn't believe how quickly time was passing.

She smiled as she felt her child move within her. What a glorious sensation it was to feel life move. She loved this child more and more as time went on. She couldn't let Anthony get his hands on him — or her. Just like his father had done to him, Anthony would corrupt this child, and one day he would grow up to kill, steal, and destroy lives.

How much longer will I be able to hide? What kind of a life will I make for us? She knew that the doctor seemed a bit concerned about the baby, but she felt God's peace about the situation and believed that her baby would be fine.

Stuart pulled up to the penthouse. He got out to open the door for Poppy, but Poppy beat him to it.

"I will go park the car in the garage, sir, and be right back."

"No, Stuart, that won't be necessary. I want to talk to him alone. Just drive around the block a few times."

Stuart felt a bit unsure about the whole situation, but he relented. Through the years, Anthony had grown more and more devious, and Stuart was worried about what he might do when confronted by his father. "Anything you say, sir," he said at last, knowing the choice wasn't up to him.

The doorman recognized Antonio right away. "Good morning, Mr. Cavelli. Shall I buzz your son for you, sir, to let him know that you are coming up?"

"That's not necessary. I have already phoned him, and he is expecting me."

He lied because he wanted Anthony to be caught off guard. On the elevator, he thought about all that had gone wrong with his son. He couldn't help but blame himself. This life and the business that he and Anthony shared were all he knew. What a terrible example he had been for his son. How had it all gotten so out of hand? He had thought that if Regina married Anthony, he would be able to keep her close and watch over her, but instead he was beginning to see that he had caused her more harm, much more harm, than good. He had to put a stop to this right now.

He got off the elevator and found Anthony waiting for him. The doorman must have phoned ahead anyway. There went the element of surprise.

"Good morning, Poppy. Did you see the paper? I understand the wire services picked up the story, and it's running all over the country," Anthony said, sounding pleased with himself.

Poppy found it odd that Anthony was so anxious to talk about this with him. He must have known it would be upsetting to him. "Yes, that is why I am here."

"Come in. I'm so excited. I'm sure this is going to work. You'll see — she'll be back before you know it."

"Son, have you lost your mind?"

"What's the matter? Don't you want Regina back? Don't you want to be able to see your grandchild grow up?"

"Yes, I do want those things but not like this. You have placed a large price on her head. Every lowlife across the U.S. will be out looking for her. You just don't think things through."

"Yes, I do. Poppy, I just want my wife and baby back. I want to make things right between Regina and me. I want to be there when the baby is born. I want to be able to give him everything he would ever need. I don't want to miss out on anything. You must understand that, don't you?"

Poppy looked at Anthony and for the first time truly saw through him. "I don't know what went on between you and Regina, but apparently, she can't bear to stay married to you any longer. She has hidden herself well for a reason. I want you to call this whole thing off."

"I can't do that. It would look bad — I would lose my credibility."

"What credibility? You do remember what we do for a living! I made a mistake in forcing you two to marry," Poppy said, genuine sorrow in his voice. "I see that now."

"But you were right about us. Up until now, we have been very happy. I'm about to become a father. What's wrong with that?"

"I want this hunt for Regina to stop before she gets hurt. If she wants to stay away so badly, don't you think she will resist getting caught? What if somebody tries to force her to return and something happens to the baby? What will you do then? No, I want the search to be called off. It was a bad idea, son."

"I can't. This is the best way to get her home," Anthony insisted.

"I disagree. She must be scared or else she would not have gone. She wouldn't have left her mother right after Michael's death. If a divorce is what she wants, then that's what she'll get. She'd come back if she felt safe, and apparently, she doesn't."

"Wait a minute — who said anything about a divorce? She's about to have my baby! Whose father are you, anyway? Why do you care more about her than you do me? What are you accusing me of?"

Anthony had a hard time understanding what was going on here. He could feel his breathing labor and his jaw tighten. First his old man had made him marry the woman he had always hated — and now he was changing his mind. All he had heard for years now was, "When am I going to be a grandfather?" But now that he was going to be one, Poppy wanted to let him off the hook, as if the marriage from hell had been nothing more than a business meeting they could always reschedule. Well, things had changed. This would be handled on Anthony's terms now. He was in control.

Antonio waited a moment, looking longingly at his son. "I am your father. I love you very much. Anthony, you don't want to be married to her. If you did, then you wouldn't run around with other women. You can stop pretending."

Anthony stared at him. "I'm not the only guy who fools around from time to time. It doesn't mean anything. I love Regina now and my unborn child."

The doorman's buzzer rang. Anthony walked over to the intercom and picked up the phone. "Yeah. Sure, send her up." Turning back toward Antonio, he said, "I guess my mother-in-law has seen the paper also. She's on her way up."

"Sophia has come to see you? You better not upset her. Listen to me — I want you to be nice."

"I'm always nice, Poppy."

Anthony opened the door and greeted her warmly. "Sophia, how good it is to see you up and about. Please come in. My father is also here visiting me."

Sophia was surprised to walk into the living room and see Antonio sitting on the couch. He looked different. She wasn't quite sure what it was about him, but something had changed. He appeared as if he were about to get up, and Sophia motioned for him to sit back down. She turned toward Anthony. "I won't be here very long. I've come to ask you to retract that reward you placed on my daughter's head."

"It seems you and my father are playing the same record."

She was surprised a second time. Antonio wanted the reward retracted as well? Why? "Anthony, please don't do this. Why don't you just forget about Regina?"

"I'm sorry, but I can't do that. She's my wife, a fact both you and my father seem to forget. First I'm thrown into this marriage and now everyone wants me to just forget about her and my child. I don't think so."

Sophia tried to stay calm because she didn't want to make things worse. "Anthony, please, I beg you to call off the reward. You are inviting all sorts of people to search for my daughter. Can't you see that she could get hurt through all of this?"

Anthony enjoyed having his father and Sophia begging him to do something he had no intention of doing. And right now, this game was giving him much more pleasure than he had been anticipating. His role was one of care and concern, and he thought he played it well. He enjoyed pretending that he loved Regina, when all he really wanted was her head on a silver platter.

Poppy spoke up for the first time since Sophia had entered the room. "Son, if you don't call this off, I'm afraid I will not authorize the release of the funds."

Anthony looked at his father and laughed.

"What is so funny?" Poppy demanded.

"Poppy, I don't need you to authorize anything. I have my own means."

"Where did you get that kind of money?" Poppy demanded.

"I have invested wisely," Anthony smugly replied. "And I'm glad, because now I can use that money for the safe return of my wife and child. I can't think of a better way to spend a million dollars. I would think the two of you would be thrilled that I would go to such lengths to bring Regina back."

He glanced at his watch. "Wow — look at the time! I would love to stay and continue to visit with you both, but I'm already late for an appointment. Feel free to stay and enjoy the coffee that's on the table."

"Anthony, this conversation is not over. We will talk again." Antonio stood up. "Come, Sophia. I will make sure you return safely to St. Mary's."

To his surprise, she didn't refuse but left with him.

John sat in Father Thomas' study, waiting for him. He felt nervous and wasn't even sure why. As Father Thomas entered the room, John stood up and greeted him.

"I'm sorry to keep you waiting," Father Thomas said.

"No problem. Thanks for seeing me on such short notice. You probably have seen the paper this morning, right?"

"Yes, I have. Let me assure you that she is perfectly safe where she is."

"I know; it's very secluded. I just want to make sure she's fine. She's alone and probably worried about all of this, if she's even found out about it. Will you contact Brother Steven and check on her for me?"

Father Thomas noticed that the concern in this man's voice went beyond that of a police officer, or even a friend. He couldn't help asking, "Tell me, Detective, do you get this personally involved in all your cases?"

John felt himself begin to blush. "I, uh . . . well, not as a rule . . . Um, it *appears* that I have let my personal feelings into this case more than I should have, but . . ." Why had he just said that? Inwardly, he groaned. His emotional state was not the issue here, but John had just moved it into the limelight, completely unintentionally.

"You've come to care for Regina deeply, haven't you?"

"More than care for. I've fallen in love with her, Father." There. He'd said it out loud again. Each time that happened, he experienced more freedom. It seemed to flow more easily. He wished it were Regina listening to him instead of this priest.

"I see. And how does Regina feel about you?"

"I'm not sure. She's such an honorable woman. She doesn't like me talking about my feelings for her, so she doesn't want to talk about her feelings for me, either. Even though her whole marriage is a sham, she stays faithful to her vows."

Seeing the look in Father Thomas' eyes, John started shaking his head. "I didn't intend for this to happen. I don't plan to do anything about my feelings. I have too much respect for her to act on them." John realized he was probably saying too much. "Will you please call?"

Father Thomas studied him a moment and then slowly nodded. "Yes, I will." He picked up the phone and dialed the monastery's number. "Good day. This is Father Thomas. I'm calling to speak to Brother Steven. Is he available? Thank you. Yes, I will hold."

He looked at John and, with his hand over the mouthpiece, he said, "Brother Steven and I have developed a code in which to talk so that we don't cause any suspicion in case the phones are bugged."

John thought to himself that this priest had watched too many mob movies. It seemed he was enjoying playing the part of a spy.

"Steven, good to hear your voice. How is everything?"

"Oh, we are all doing well. So much is going on in the news lately. Our newest brother loves to track information on the weather. We're also having a bit of trouble with our roof over the barn."

"What seems to be the problem?"

"The roofer said that it's too small for the barn. He will get back to me as to whether or not we have a serious problem."

"I see. I hope it all works out." Father Thomas continued to chitchat for a few minutes about other things. Finally, he said, "I will talk to you soon. Have a nice day, Steven." He hung up the phone.

"How is she?"

"It appears there are some difficulties with the baby. It's too small, and the doctor is running tests."

"Is that it? Does she know about the reward?"

"I think so, but to tell you the truth, our code confuses me a little."

They both laughed.

But then, growing more serious, Father Thomas continued, "Detective Nelson, it would be best for you and for Regina if you do not come here anymore. I don't know if the church is being watched, and I don't want any suspicion to arise."

"You're right. I just didn't know what else to do."

"Well, I have found that prayer always works for me."

John smiled. "Yes, it appears to work for Regina also." The longer he sat here, the more he was starting to feel uncomfortable. He couldn't believe that he had told Father Thomas he was in love with her. What had he been thinking? "Thanks for your time. If you hear anything, please let me know. I just want to help."

"Yes, I know. Don't worry — she's going to be just fine. Her and her baby."

Chapter 14

Kelly usually left the door open when she did her work in Regina's office. Today, the door stood open about a foot as she sat at Regina's desk and, wearing her headset, argued with one of the restaurant suppliers.

"I'm trying to tell you that Mrs. Cavelli is gone, and I'm in charge of the restaurant. If you have a problem with that, I could have Mr. Cavelli give you a call and ask why my clean tablecloths and napkins aren't here yet. Oh — well, good. I knew you would see it my way."

Rolling her eyes, she hung up and pulled off the headset. Anthony Cavelli's name was a powerful thing to drop around the city. On principle, she didn't like to use it very often, but with Regina's disappearance, it had become more necessary.

As she took out the checkbook to pay bills, somebody knocked. She looked up to see Anthony Cavelli in the doorway. The sight of him standing there startled her in such a way that her heart skipped. Instantly, her throat tightened, and she could barely breathe.

Anthony always intimidated her. It was the way he looked at her that creeped her out — as if he wanted to devour her.

He clapped his hands. "Bravo, Kelly, bravo! I didn't know you could be so clever. I mean, using my name like that to get what you want."

She stood up nervously. "Mr. Cavelli, I'm sorry if I did anything wrong. I've been having some trouble with people trying to take advantage of the fact that Mrs. Cavelli is gone."

He walked across the room and stood next to her. "I'm not angry. You haven't done anything wrong." Leaning toward her, he asked, "So what are you working on?"

Stepping around the desk, she put her back to him as she opened the filing cabinet and responded, "I was about to pay some bills. Why don't you take a look? I've been keeping very good records." She could feel his intent and tried to distract him from getting too close to her.

"Oh, I'm sure you are. I have no doubt about your . . . ability."

He came around the desk and stopped just behind her. Her face flushed as she heard him sniff her neck. "You smell nice. What fragrance are you wearing?" he asked softly.

Kelly was not comfortable with this. At all. But she didn't know what to do. She wanted to avoid doing or saying anything that would anger him — she'd seen for herself how rough he could be with Regina. She felt a lump forming in her throat and couldn't seem to move. Fighting to control her emotions, she finally forced the words. "Mystery. It's new on the market."

He laid his hands on her shoulders and slowly turned her to face him. "You've been doing a great job taking my wife's place."

The warmth from his hands and the crooning tone of his voice made her want to vomit, but she lifted her chin, determined to stay strong. Taking a deep breath, she blurted, "I'm only taking her place *here*, at the restaurant, because it's my job." Her statement came out a bit more forcefully than she had intended, but she was not sorry she had said it. She found strength to wiggle away from him and sat back down at the desk.

She hadn't liked the direction that conversation was going. He didn't look very happy, either, but she didn't care. "I'm sorry you haven't found Mrs. Cavelli yet, but I'm sure she's all right." Pretending to reassure him, she gave him a brief smile and then continued to work, as if everything was normal.

Out the corner of her eye, she saw him smile at her, a smug look on his face. Kelly didn't appreciate the way his eyes scanned her body as if he had X-ray vision. As she scowled down at the checkbook, he came and sat at the edge of the desk, looking at her intently.

"Kelly, I want to talk to you about something. Stop what you are doing and look at me."

She set the pen down and looked up.

"Do you know where Regina is?" he asked calmly.

The question caught her off guard. Why did he think she knew something? "No. I have no idea."

He leaned down toward her. Placing his hand under her chin, he lifted it up and whispered, "You wouldn't be lying to me now, would you?"

"My mother raised a smart girl, Mr. Cavelli. I don't lie and especially not to you. I haven't heard from her."

He moved his hand up and began to stroke her face softly with his thumb. "You have such a pretty face. I would hate to see anything happen to it."

He slowly pulled his hand away, and Kelly knew she wasn't hiding her fear very well. She didn't know where Regina was and hoped he believed her. At last, he stood up and headed toward the door.

"If you do hear from my wife, you will tell me right away." Kelly didn't respond. "You understand me, right?"

"Yes, sir. I understand quite clearly."

"Good. Keep up the good work. You're running this place as smoothly as Regina did. You fill her shoes very nicely." He paused one last time and added, "I hope that kid of yours is in good health." He smiled at her as he left the room.

Relieved, Kelly sagged in her chair and hoped he never came back. She could leave town, but then who would take care of the restaurant? Regina had given her a job when no one else would; she couldn't leave the place in Anthony's hands. She would just have to be careful not to be caught alone again.

She hoped for Regina's sake that she stayed far away from him.

Silent, Antonio sat two feet away on the other side of the car, looking out the window and waiting for Sophia to speak. She didn't know what to think about the changes in him. She found it even harder to believe that they had actually agreed on something. Maybe Father Thomas was right and the man truly *had* had a change of heart. She finally broke the quiet.

"I'm glad we finally agree on something."

"I truly want what is best for Regina. I have to do something to help her, and if I help her, it means I'm going against my son. I see that now."

"Your son is out of control. I know you don't believe this, but he *is* responsible for Michael's death *and* for my house blowing up. I know it like I know the sun will rise tomorrow. I know it here," she said, pointing to her chest.

He rubbed his temples with both hands, as if a headache was beginning behind his eyes, and whispered, "I have not found any proof of that. If I do, I will make sure he never hurts you or your family again. I promise."

Sophia felt sorry for him, because he was so blinded by love for his son. At the same time, she didn't know what to think now, because he seemed to be softening. For so many years she had hated him. This change was confusing to her.

"Antonio, you couldn't even stop him from doing the damage he has already inflicted on my family. How are you possibly going to stop him in the future?"

He looked at her, seeming to not know what to say. It was the first time she had seen him at a loss for words.

"Can't you see that he's the reason she left?"

Frowning, he glanced out the window again, and she pressed, "She ran for her life and is trying to protect her child. Do you want to see your grandchild grow up in this environment? Regina will be fine as long as Anthony stays away from her."

For a minute, it seemed like he wasn't going to respond. But then, finally, he turned his head and looked at her. His eyes were glassy and his emotions on edge. She had seen him this way only once before, when he had found out she was pregnant. Quietly, he said, "I'm beginning to see that. I've tried to convince him to let her go . . . to divorce her. It didn't work."

Sophia was shocked. After all, it had been Antonio's insistence that they marry to begin with.

"Why? Is it because you think Regina is your child?" Her question not only clearly surprised Antonio, but it startled her as well.

"I thought you didn't want to talk about that ever again." Sophia kept silent. "I love Regina. Over the years she has held a special place in my heart."

He paused, not sure if he could continue. "I owe you an apology. I used you all those years ago. I didn't realize I fell in love with you until it was too late. I couldn't leave my wife; she was going through such a hard time. Besides, you were so angry with me. I'm sorry for the pain and suffering I have caused you. Please forgive me."

He turned his head so she couldn't see the tears forming in his eyes. He didn't understand why he was feeling remorse so deeply. This had never happened before. The last time he had cried had been at his wife's funeral. Now it was happening more often than he felt comfortable with.

Sophia could not believe what she was hearing. She was truly moved by his sincerity, and the words stuck in her throat.

"I forgive you," she managed quietly, and without warning, she felt as if a heavy weight had lifted from her shoulders.

His voice seemed to quiver a bit as he said, "Thank you."

John got back to work, his mind still on the one person he couldn't seem to shake from his thoughts. His disquiet had been bad enough when all he'd wanted to do was clear Sam's name, but now, with him worried about Regina's life, it was worse. Anthony Cavelli needed to be put away where he couldn't hurt anyone else.

When the phone rang, he grabbed it on the first ring. "Detective Nelson speaking."

"Hey, John. It's Bobby."

"Bobby, I'm so glad you called. Do you have good news for me?"

"I don't know yet. I found out who was working the case, and they want to meet with you. You know, exchange information. Can you come down here?"

"Yeah, just tell me when."

"These guys are anxious to speak to you. Can you come now?"

"No problem. I'm on my way." He hung up the phone. This could be really promising. He tried to contain his excitement. *Just in case.* He didn't want to be disappointed.

Just as he was about to leave, the captain and Frank came by his desk.

"Nice of you to join us, Nelson," the captain said, folding his arms. He was a big guy, and when he wanted to be intimidating, he could do a fair job of it.

"I have to go. I'll be back later."

"Where are you going now?" the captain demanded.

Lowering his voice, John replied, "I have a friend at the FBI, and he's set up a meeting with the guys working on the Cavelli case. I'm going to see if we can work on this thing together."

"Since when do they want our help?" Frank was obviously irritated.

"Well, they didn't really ask. I did. Anyway, they're waiting for me."

"Go with him, Frank, and I want a full report when you get back," Captain Merrill commanded as he walked away.

"Do you mind if I tag along?"

Even if he did mind, the captain had given him an order. John only hoped that Bobby didn't have a problem with it. "Let's go."

Regina had been pacing around her room for an hour. She hated waiting. Brother Steven had promised he would get her as soon as the doctor called, but patience, apparently, was a virtue she had yet to develop. She had to believe in her heart that this child would be fine — and she did, but it was so hard to put aside the little, nagging doubts that tried to take hold in her mind.

She sat at the desk with her head in her hands, took a deep breath, and started to pray. As she poured out her heart to God, she lost track of time and jumped when the knock on the door finally came. She got up and ran to open it, hoping for good news. To her surprise, the doctor was standing there next to Brother Steven.

"Dr. Franklin, what a surprise! I thought you were going to call us."

"I thought it would be better if I came in person. May I come in?"

"Please do." Regina's room was very modest. It had a bed, a small desk, and two chairs. She motioned for the doctor to sit down. "Brother Steven, please — come in, too."

"I don't want to invade your privacy. I can wait out here."

"Please stay. I could use the moral support."

He came in and sat in the other chair. Trying to breathe calmly, Regina took a seat on the edge of the bed. She didn't like the expression on their faces. Apparently, Brother Steven already knew what was going on.

"I gather by your expressions that this isn't very good news. Please just tell me that my baby is going to be okay." She felt desperate. *Not this, too, God,* she thought.

"Regina, during the ultrasound, there were some heart abnormalities, and the amniocentesis is abnormal."

"I see."

"You will need to have a fetal echocardiogram by a physician who is specially trained in fetal cardiac evaluations."

"Are you saying I need to see a specialist? Can't *you* run the fetal echo . . . cardio . . . whatever test?" Regina's mind felt scattered as fear and confusion crept in. Hadn't she been through enough already?

"I'm afraid not. Our small hospital is not equipped for it. This is very specialized testing done by very few doctors in the country."

"What type of doctor do I need to see?"

"You'll need to see a perinatologist who specializes in problems with congenital heart defects in utero. He will be able to take care of you and your baby."

Brother Steven finally spoke up. "I tried to explain to the doctor how dangerous it would be for you and your child to see a specialist. It would mean trusting someone else."

Regina stared at the floor, trying to process what was happening. "But I have to do what is best for the baby. Who do you recommend?"

"Well . . . this is where Brother Steven objected. Dr. Jacob Weinstein is the best, but he's located in New York."

"Can you imagine?" Brother Steven interrupted. "I told him you can't go back there."

"Would it be possible for Dr. Weinstein to come here and do the tests?"

"I'm afraid not. As I mentioned earlier, we aren't equipped for that. It would be better if you went there."

"No," Brother Steven protested. "I say we bring the doctor and his equipment here. If you go to New York, someone might recognize you."

"Could we go somewhere halfway and meet him?" Regina asked.

"I could ask, but if you don't want to be seen, trying to arrange for him to fly to another hospital on a specialty call would probably cause more attention for you than your going to New York."

"If he can keep my presence quiet and I have contact with no one but him, then I'll have to risk it. I just want my baby to be healthy, and if the best chance of that is Dr. Weinstein, then I say let's go."

"I can't believe this is happening," Brother Steven said. "What am I supposed to tell Father Thomas? I don't think this is a wise decision."

Regina looked at him with determination in her eyes.

Brother Steven sighed. "Fine. But if you insist on going through with this, then I insist on coming along."

"I promise I will make the arrangements for you personally so that no one will know about your trip," the doctor said. "Please don't worry. Dr. Weinstein has been practicing medicine longer than you've been alive. He has a fine reputation and is well-respected. He's an old friend from medical school. I know we can trust him."

"You have been very helpful, Dr. Franklin. I appreciate all that you're doing for me. I don't know how to thank you."

"You just take care of yourself and your baby. That will be thanks enough for me."

Father Thomas found that he could no longer concentrate on his paperwork. Sophia had been gone for a long time now — much longer than he had been anticipating — and with each passing minute, he grew more and more uncomfortable. He should have insisted on going with her. If she didn't come back soon, he would go after her.

He heard the front door open and then close, and he left his study to see who it was.

"Sophia! I'm so glad you're back. I've been so worried about you since you left. Tell me what happened."

Sophia just looked at him and shook her head. "Why don't we go and sit down?"

They took a seat in the living room. She sat quietly for a moment, trying to gather her thoughts.

"I just witnessed something I thought I would never see."

"What's that?"

"Antonio Cavelli drove me home."

Father Thomas blinked in surprise. He couldn't imagine Sophia in the same room as Antonio, much less sharing a car.

"He was at Anthony's when I got there, trying to reason with him about the reward, but that isn't the amazing thing. He told me he was sorry for the past and asked me to forgive him."

Father Thomas raised a brow as a slight smile went across his mouth. He had prayed that God would touch Antonio, and now it appeared the Holy Spirit had been answering his prayer.

"I saw tears in his eyes. I've never once heard that man say he was wrong, much less apologize to anyone. The crazy thing is that I really do believe him. He wanted to help. He told me he tried to convince Anthony to divorce Regina."

"Divorce? I don't understand."

"He says he agrees that this marriage is dangerous for her and that she would be happier without his son. I guess he truly cares for her. I don't believe that his tears or his words were intended to mislead me. After I agreed to forgive him, I felt a tremendous weight lift off my shoulders."

The two of them sat there in silence, trying to comprehend what this might mean. Father Thomas didn't know if he should voice the question that naturally came to mind on the heels of her story.

Sophia brought it up without his prompting. "You're probably wondering if Regina is his or not?"

"That's none of my business." He paused for a moment. "But yes, I admit I was wondering."

"I wonder also. I really don't know for sure. Michael didn't need or want a blood test to prove Regina was his child. He loved her and accepted her as his own. I believe in my heart that she is Michael's, but I don't know for sure."

"I see."

"You must think poorly of me, don't you, Father?"

"No, Sophia, I don't. But let me ask you this — do you want to know the truth? Do you ever plan to tell Regina that Michael might not be her father?"

"No! I can't do that. I would feel like it tainted Michael's memory in some way. Regina doesn't need to know this. Besides, I'm not even sure. Why cause her unnecessary pain to find out?"

"What do you plan to do, then, about Mr. Cavelli?"

"I don't know. Maybe he's the only one who can help her. We'll just have to wait and see what happens for now."

So that Bobby could give clearance at the gate, John called from the car to let him know Frank would be joining them. The FBI complex was located out on Long Island in a secluded area that was not easily accessible. They drove up to the gate and were greeted by the guard, who checked his list and examined their badges. On the other side of the gate, they found a parking spot, entered the building, and met Bobby at a second check-point.

"Hey, John. Good to see you."

As they shook hands, John grinned and said, "Good to see you, too. You look great. Hey, this is my partner, Frank Holstrum."

Bobby extended his hand again. "Nice to meet you."

"Nice to meet you, too."

"All right, then. Let's go upstairs."

On the elevator, Bobby tried to give them some background information about the agents assigned to the case. They were two by-the-book kind of guys who had been on this case for a couple of years, starting back in the Antonio Cavelli days. They allowed John to continue to do what he was doing because it didn't interfere with their case and they hadn't wanted to stop him after his brother's death.

Bobby took them to a small conference room on the fifth floor. The room was painted beige and had a picture of the FBI director on the wall.

The oval, rosewood table seated ten and was surrounded by black-leather, padded chairs.

The men they had come to see were standing across the room by a small, square table that held a water pitcher and glasses. When John and the other two entered, the agents set their drinks down and walked over.

"I'd like you to meet Agents Norman Harris and James Wilton. These are Detectives John Nelson and Frank Holstrum."

The men exchanged handshakes and pleasantries. After the introductions, Bobby excused himself and left the conference room.

"I understand you've come here for our help. Why now?" Harris asked.

Dressed in his everyday casual attire, John was beginning to feel pretty out of place in front of these guys who wore dark suits and ties. He felt as if he was back in high school trying to explain himself to the principal. "We've hit some obstacles in the case, and we're at a dead end."

"Oh, the black book, huh?" replied Wilton.

John was a little shocked he knew about that. It was supposed to have been top secret in his department. "How did you guys find out?"

"We have our ways. You should have given us a copy in the first place, and this wouldn't have happened. But that's over now. Your big problem is the informant."

John and Frank glanced at each other.

"Do you also know who it is?" Frank snapped. "You seem to know everything else."

Harris looked at Frank and then back at John. "We don't know who it is. Say, do you fellows want some coffee? Great! Holstrum, why don't you give me a hand?"

Frank gave John a puzzled look. "Sure, if you like."

After they left, Wilton looked matter-of-factly at John. "So, Detective Nelson, how much do you trust your partner?"

What? It was so quick and to-the-point that a minute passed before it registered. But then it did, and John felt his ire rise. True, the idea of Frank being the informer *had* crossed his mind, but everything had crossed his mind — it was his job for things to cross his mind. His suspecting Frank was one thing, but who did this guy think he was?

Frank and the captain were the only people who knew what was going on, but wondering if the captain was the informer was as crazy as thinking it was Frank. Wilton must not realize how stupid his implication really was.

"What are you getting at? That Frank's the informant? If you have proof, then show it to me."

"I wasn't trying to insinuate anything. After your brother's death, we started taking a closer look at your department. Someone had planted those drugs in your brother's place. There was no sign of forced entry, so it was someone your brother trusted enough to allow inside. We don't believe he would have allowed any of the Cavellis' men into his apartment."

He had captured John's attention, but the idea of Frank being guilty was ludicrous. "Go on, Agent Wilton."

"I'll make you a deal. You call me Jim, and I'll call you John."

"Okay, Jim. I'm listening."

"We believe your brother was killed, even though the evidence suggests a suicide. Someone had to know the police would come to that conclusion. Tell me, who do you think could stage something like that? A policeman — that's who. Now, you know why you haven't gotten anywhere with your case, don't you? It's because Cavelli gets tipped off."

"Really?" John interjected sarcastically. "Tell me something I don't know."

"Well, I didn't know how much you had told him. Bobby told us at first only you were coming, and we still don't know who's working for the Cavellis. Now, I didn't say it's Frank, so don't get excited, okay? And there's the other matter."

"What other matter?"

"Mrs. Cavelli."

John could feel his face redden. How much did this guy know?

"We know you helped her get out of town. She must have been the one who gave you the copy of the black book in the first place. She's the only one who could have gotten access to it. We've tried sending guys in undercover, but Cavelli lets no one get close to him. He's the only one who knows who the informant is."

"So, what do you want from me?"

"Well, when you contacted Bobby, we saw this as an opportunity to pool our resources. We need Regina Cavelli."

"Out of the question."

"She got close enough once before; she can do it again. This time it would be under controlled conditions, and we would protect her fully. We don't know where she is, but you do, don't you?"

"Even if I did, I wouldn't ask her to do that. You don't know what he's done to her. He'll kill her if she comes back. You know you can't fully protect her, and I won't allow you to do this."

"You fell for her, didn't you?"

It took a great deal of effort, but John managed to keep his mouth shut and not say something he'd regret. He decided not to even answer the question. "Look, she's a good lady and deserves to be safe. We can't ask her to risk her life and the life of her child to do this."

The door opened, and Frank and Harris stepped back into the room. Immediately, Frank could tell that John was upset and gave Jim a frown.

John stood up. "Look, thanks anyway, but we have to get going."

"Don't you want to stay for your coffee?" Harris asked.

"No, thanks." John shook their hands as he said, "Thanks for your time, and we'll let you know if we make any progress. You can do the same. Good day."

Down the hall, Frank asked quietly, "You want to tell me what went on in there while I was gone?"

"It was nothing. Big waste of time. They've got nothing concrete to help us. They were on a fishing expedition."

On the way home, all Antonio could do was think about Regina and Sophia. He hoped Sophia realized how sincere he was and how he wouldn't hurt her daughter, not for anything in this world. All these years, he'd considered Regina his own, and he just couldn't stop now. Maybe she wasn't his; maybe she was. A blood test wouldn't change his feelings for her.

His mind raced in so many directions, but he had to admit, through it all he felt peaceful. It had started when he'd gone to see the priest . . . Maybe they were right when they said that confession was good for the soul.

As Stuart pulled into the garage, Vinny greeted them.

"Oh, Vinny, I'm sorry. I forgot you were coming. Let's go into my office and talk."

"That's okay, sir. I saw the paper this morning. You must be upset."

"Yes, I am. I'm curious as to where he got that kind of money. I don't believe he's invested *that* well. Do you have any ideas?"

"I might, sir."

As they walked inside, Vinny thought to himself how much Poppy seemed to be changing lately. *Did he really just apologize for making me wait?* Being considerate of others was something the Cavelli men weren't exactly known for. He didn't know what to make of it.

They went into the study and sat down, Poppy behind the desk and Vinny in the chair opposite him.

"So what happened last night?"

"Seems like there's some trouble with his informant. They got into an argument about whether or not he is going to continue to work for him."

"Did you see who it was?"

"No, it was dark. But I know I've heard that voice before. I tried to think who it might be, but I can't seem to place it. Sorry. Anthony did get a box from the cop and put it in the trunk. I don't know what's in . . ."

Vinny stopped. *You've got to be kidding me.* He couldn't believe he had forgotten about the box in the trunk of *his* car. He jumped up and ran out to the garage, throwing the trunk open.

The box was still there. It had been early, early morning by the time he had driven Anthony home. Anthony had been drinking and must have forgotten about the box, too. Vinny grabbed it and took it inside. Poppy came out into the hallway to see where Vinny had gone.

"Look — I forgot that I still had it in the trunk of my car."

"Well, let's have a look, shall we?"

Regina couldn't believe she was packing her things to go back to New York. Something about that just seemed inherently wrong.

She glanced at the red wig lying on her bed. Walking over, she picked it up, fit it over her hair, and then adjusted it so that the bangs weren't crooked. Looking in the mirror, she saw very little change in her appearance. Red hair, brown hair — it didn't make much difference. How was she supposed to fool anyone? Her picture had been plastered on the front page of every newspaper across the country. Maybe a pair of sunglasses would help hide her facial features more.

She heard a knock on the door. "Come in."

It was Brother Steven. "Dr. Franklin just called. He's made all the arrangements for the flight and the testing. He even booked a room in a hotel near the hospital. He assures me that Dr. Weinstein will keep your appointment very confidential. He will have you in and out in no time. He promises me you won't even have to wait in a waiting room. No one will know you're his patient."

Regina could hear the anxiety in Brother Steven's voice. He had not mentioned a word about himself, but when she thought about how much he would be in danger, too, her stomach went into knots. "I've been thinking. It might be better if I go to New York alone. I don't want to put your life in danger. If we're caught, I'm afraid of what Anthony might do to you for helping me. He has no sense of right or wrong. It doesn't matter that you're a monk; he would kill you in a second and not lose any sleep over it."

Brother Steven thought about that for a moment. He looked into her hazel eyes and saw again all the pain and hurt she carried within her. He couldn't allow her to go on this journey by herself, no matter the risk. Anthony was just as capable of killing her as he was anyone else.

"It would look better if you were traveling with a 'husband' rather than by yourself. People are looking for Regina Cavelli alone, not Mr. and Mrs. Jones. Besides, I wouldn't be able to live with myself if I let you travel alone in your condition. God will protect us. Please, let me do this."

"You are a kind soul. I'll never forget the compassion you've shown me, Brother Steven."

"You know you can't call me by that name if I'm pretending to be your husband. Dr. Franklin registered you under the same name you used when you had the test done at the hospital — Mrs. Alice Jones. I guess that makes me Mr. Jones."

"So, am I supposed to call my husband Mr. Jones?" She chuckled.

Brother Steven shook his head. "No. Let me see . . . How about . . . Philip Jones? You can call me Philip. I've always liked that name."

"Okay. Mr. and Mrs. Philip Jones." Her smile began to fade, and Regina paused, studying him carefully. Taking his hand, she asked, "Are you sure about this?"

"Very sure," Brother Steven replied. "We have an early flight. I know it's still early tonight, but you'd better get your rest."

Regina nodded slowly, her look growing more and more far away.

He wanted to reassure her somehow. Frowning, he said, "You know it's going to be all right — the baby, the trip. We'll be back here before you know it."

"I'm sure you're right. Thank you. I just wish I could see my mom and . . . never mind."

"And maybe Detective Nelson?"

Regina put her head down. She felt ashamed for thinking about him, but she couldn't seem to help it — she missed him. "Yes. But seeing them would be too dangerous. I'm positive that my mom's being watched carefully." She glanced at him and sighed. "You know, you're right. I do need my rest. I'm feeling very tired all of a sudden." She walked over to the door and opened it. "Thank you again for all your help."

Brother Steven smiled at her. "If you want to talk, I'll listen."

"I'll be fine. Good night, *Philip.*"

"Good night, *Alice.*"

Checking up on Regina's assistant had been more entertaining than Anthony had anticipated. He had to remember to do that again soon. Maybe next time he'd find her a little friendlier.

Sitting in the back seat of the car, Anthony stretched out his legs and folded his hands behind his head. He felt like everything was finally starting to go his way. The whole reward idea was brilliant. He'd like to see her stay hidden, with a million reasons motivating people to find her. He started to smile.

Then he remembered.

He sat up quickly. The box — and the evidence he had to destroy. He'd left it in his trunk.

"Hey, Mario, let's go home. I need to check up on something."

Poppy emptied the box all at once. "What is all this stuff?"

"I don't know. But these copies look like pictures of a book, and the writing looks like Anthony's."

"Why would my son have a coded book? These other papers look as if someone was trying to figure out what the codes mean."

A thought began turning in Vinny's head. "You know," he began carefully, "this might be copies of the black book he keeps with him all the time."

"What black book?" Poppy asked.

"Your son has a small black book that he's always writing things in. He keeps it in his pocket. I've never seen him put it down." Vinny shook his head. "I wonder how the cops got a copy of this."

Poppy looked at him, wondering that as well, and then it struck him. "If he never leaves this book lying around, then the only person that could get access is Regina. She would be the only person close enough to make copies of it without him knowing — maybe while he was sleeping or in the shower."

"Do you think that's why she left? You think Anthony found out about it and figured out she betrayed him?"

Poppy started to pace, looking at all the pages on his desk. "Of course. If Anthony knows she betrayed him, then . . . she wouldn't be safe." His voice tightened. "We have to find her first. I'm the only one who can protect her and the baby."

"What do you plan to do about Anthony, sir?"

"I don't know. But I'm sure he'll be missing this soon. Go and give it to him."

Vinny stared at him. "That's it? Sir, aren't you a bit curious about what's in here? What does it all mean?"

"Vinny, even after all he's done, Anthony is still my son. I blame myself for the person he is. What would you want me to do? Give it back to the cops? I can't do that. I can't be responsible for my son going to prison. I have to handle this my way. Now go."

Vinny put everything back in the box and replied, "You know he will probably destroy all of this. We might never get this chance again."

"Yes, I know."

With that, Poppy left the room. Vinny picked up the box and walked out to his car. Perhaps Poppy wouldn't do anything about this, but, glancing at his watch, he thought it wouldn't be a bad idea if he made a copy for himself before giving it back to Anthony.

Anthony hated being stuck in traffic. He swore beneath his breath and then said, "Tell me, Mario. How come whenever I'm in a rush, we seem to hit traffic?"

"I don't know. It looks like an accident up ahead. If I can get to the next corner, I know a shortcut."

"Okay, fine."

Crossing his arms, he sat back against the seat and tried not to lose it. He couldn't remember how much he'd had to drink last night, but apparently, it'd been a good amount because he couldn't even remember getting home, much less leaving the box in his trunk.

When he was frustrated like this, he had learned to focus on lighter things, things that would make him happy. Right now, he couldn't think of anything that would make him happier than getting his hands on his wife. Thanks to his cop friend, he knew what she'd been up to. He had thought she would be smarter than that. She must know that if he caught up with her, her life was over.

But somehow, even though she was gone, she'd still managed to have his own father wrapped around her little finger. What was that about? He didn't want to give her a divorce — he wanted to give her a funeral. He chuckled to himself at the thought of being the grieving husband. He looked really good in black.

Vinny spotted a copy center and pulled up in front. For a long moment, he just sat there and looked around to make sure he was alone. He felt nervous all of a sudden — a feeling he was not quite used to. He opened the trunk and took out one set of the copies, glancing around again just to be on the safe side.

As he walked into the center, the young woman behind the counter smiled at him and asked, "Can I help you, sir?"

"Yeah, I need a copy of these pages, and I need it right now."

"Well, I'm in the middle of something. Can you wait about fifteen minutes? I can do it for you then."

"No, I need it now. I don't have much time." He reached for his wallet. "I tell you what. If you stop what you're doing, I'll make it worth your while." He pulled out a twenty-dollar bill and set it on the counter. She just looked at him, so he dropped another twenty-dollar bill on top of the first.

The young woman looked at him and then at the forty dollars and then decided that for forty dollars, she could afford it. "No problem. It will take just a couple of minutes." She picked up the money and slid it into her pocket.

Mario pulled into the parking garage underneath the penthouse and parked alongside Anthony's car. Anthony didn't wait for Mario to open the door. He just jumped out and popped his trunk with the button on his key ring.

And then stood there shocked. The trunk was empty.

"Where is it?!" he yelled, slamming his hand on the open lid.

"Where's what?"

He tried to think of where it could be. But there wasn't anywhere else! He didn't remember much from last night, but he did remember putting it right here. How could — and then it came to him. "Oh, man, how stupid. We took Vinny's car last night." He let his breath out and laughed a bit, to calm his nerves. "Boy, am I relieved. Vinny must still have it in his car. Do you know where he is?"

"No, I haven't seen him all day."

Anthony took out his cell phone and dialed.

Vinny answered, "Yeah."

"Where are you?"

"I'm running an errand for my grandmother. You need me?"

"Yeah, I need you to get to the penthouse ASAP. You have your car, right?"

"Of course, Boss. Is there a problem?"

"Not if you get here soon." Anthony hung up.

Anthony must have remembered. He didn't say it, but Vinny knew he didn't have much time. He had to get to the penthouse, or he would have too much explaining to do. "Are you done yet?"

"Yes, sir, I just finished. Here you go."

Vinny handed her another twenty to pay for the copies. "Keep the change."

"Thank you, sir. Do come again."

Before he left, he turned around and said, "Just forget you ever saw me."

She raised her brow, as if that wasn't quite the exit she'd been expecting, and then replied, "No problem."

Chapter 15

At 36,000 feet, Regina sat in the window seat, and Brother Steven slept in the seat next to her. Every so often, she couldn't help but chuckle because he made funny snorting sounds, like he was whistling through his nose.

At least he could rest. She had so much on her mind that she could barely even close her eyes. She had tried reading and praying, but her thoughts kept racing in different directions. It felt like her head was going to explode.

Looking out the small window next to her, she could see the familiar skyline approaching. She had thought it would be a long time before she saw the city again, but right now, despite the dangers and the silly red wig, she felt relatively safe coming back to New York. She'd thought about this. A woman on the run didn't just turn around and come back; Anthony would never suspect she'd try to sneak back into the city with the price he'd placed on her head.

But, then again, maybe she was just deceiving herself.

For the hundredth time, she prayed no one would recognize her and then laughed as she pictured herself with her red wig and sunglasses. She felt a bit self-conscious being outside among people. Every time someone looked at her, she felt like a million-dollar price tag was waving above her head.

The flight attendant came over and interrupted her thoughts. "Excuse me, Mrs. Jones, but do you need anything?"

"No, thank you. I'm fine." The woman had been so kind, taking extra care of her because of her pregnancy.

"We will be landing shortly. You might want to wake up your husband. He'll have to buckle up."

"Thanks. I will," Regina replied.

The attendant smiled at her and continued down the aisle, seeing to the needs of the other passengers. Looking at Brother Steven, Regina thanked God again for this kind man He brought into her life. Even though she hated that he was involved in this mess, she felt safer because she didn't have to do this alone. She put her hand on his arm and shook him gently. She almost called him Brother Steven but stopped herself just in time.

"Philip. Philip, it's time to get up. We're about to land."

He opened his eyes and yawned. "That didn't seem to take a very long time."

"That's because you slept most of the way," she teased him.

They heard the pilot on the intercom. "Ladies and gentlemen, we are about to begin our descent. Please pay attention to the seat belt signs, and secure your trays and seats in the upright position."

"Are you ready?" Brother Steven asked.

"As ready as I'll ever be." She saw the concerned look on his face and tried to reassure him. "I'm fine, really. I'm sure no one will recognize me under this very fine wig." She patted it and smiled. "I'm more worried about you."

"Hey, this is like an adventure for me. I get to be a husband and father-to-be. Not too many monks get to do that and stay a monk!"

As the plane descended, Regina's thoughts began to pull, again, toward a certain train that had been carrying them along for several days now: no Anthony, her dad still alive, John the father of her baby and the three of them leading a normal and happy life. She felt guilty about her feelings for John, but no matter what she tried, they remained. Time and distance hadn't changed them. She could push them aside with prayer, but they kept coming back. As long as she was married, however, regardless of the circumstances, she would not do anything about her feelings. She just had to pray for strength.

The bumpy landing jolted her thoughts back to the present. They'd brought only what they'd carried on the plane, which made moving through the terminal easier. She'd been to Kennedy Airport many times and knew her way around. However, she'd never been there pregnant before, and it wasn't too long before she realized that some things got in the way of a quick and easy exit. She had to find a bathroom and knew she couldn't wait until they got to their hotel.

"Brother . . . Philip, I need to find a restroom. There's one right over there. I'll be right back."

"I'll wait for you over there by the newspaper stand."

Regina walked into the restroom and was relieved to see that no one was in the first room. She would be thrilled if she could just get in and out without any interaction with people.

As she was taking care of business, she heard two women come in. They took up station in front of the sinks and started talking. She decided to wait a moment before exiting the stall. At first, their conversation seemed innocent enough. They talked about the everyday kind of things: kids, husbands, etc.

But then one of them said, "Did you see the paper today? They ran another ad with the picture of that missing mobster lady."

Her hand on the door latch, Regina felt her heart stop.

"Imagine being married to a guy like that," the other said.

"Yeah, a million dollars for her return — how romantic is that? He must really love her to cough up that kind of dough. I can't imagine my husband offering a hundred dollars for me, much less a million." They both laughed.

"Well, I can't imagine my husband offering *ten* dollars." They laughed even harder.

Regina remained in the stall. She took a deep, calming breath. If these women knew the truth about Anthony, they wouldn't be talking like this.

"I wonder what happened to her. You think she ran away instead of someone snatching her?"

"You never know. But I tell you the truth — I wouldn't mind running across her. A million dollars would go a long way for someone like me."

"I hear ya. But she's probably a million miles from here if she doesn't want to be found. Are you done with your lipstick?"

"Yeah, I'm done. Let's go."

Regina exited when she lost the sound of their footsteps. She quickly washed her hands and left to find Brother Steven. "Let's get out of here."

"Are you all right?"

"Yes, I just want to get to the hotel and off the streets." If these two strangers were having a conversation about her, then all of New York could be talking about her. She suddenly doubted the logic of coming back here. She hooked her arm through Brother Steven's and walked with her head down. Right now, she wished she could just disappear into thin air.

Antonio woke up with Stuart's hand on his shoulder. "Sir," the man said quietly, "I'm sorry to wake you, but you have a visitor."

Only half-hearing him, Antonio opened bleary eyes and mumbled, "Stuart, what's wrong? Did I oversleep?"

"No, sir. I'm sorry to wake you, but someone is here to see you."

Antonio pushed himself up and looked over at his clock. It was only about eight in the morning. Who could be visiting him this early? "Who is it?"

"Mrs. Palmetto."

Instantly, he was fully awake. What was Sophia doing here? Something must be terribly wrong. "Tell her I'll be right down."

He grabbed some clothes, dressed quickly, and finished buttoning his shirt on his way down the steps. He found Sophia standing by the living room window.

"Sophia, what is wrong?"

Without a word, she turned around and handed him a newspaper. He unfolded it and immediately saw Regina's picture. This announcement was even bigger than the first Anthony had placed. It took up two whole pages. His son seemed to be going for more sympathy — this picture was of Regina in her wedding dress. What a true manipulator.

Antonio slowly walked over to the couch and sat down.

"Sophia, I don't know what to say. You must believe me. I didn't know anything about this. What Anthony is doing is wrong. You must know I don't approve."

Sophia sat down beside him. "I never thought I would hear myself saying this, but I believe you."

Despite the situation's tremendous misery, at her words Antonio experienced his first moment of true happiness since learning he was going to be a grandfather.

"But you need to do something about this," Sophia pressed. "Anthony is endangering her life."

"He apparently has not thought this through. You would think that he would care enough about his own unborn child without starting a witch hunt for his wife."

Turning her head away from him, Sophia stood from the couch and walked back to the window. She didn't know if she should tell him the truth or not about how that unborn child had come into being. Maybe if he knew, it would motivate him to put a stop to this. Somehow that monster had managed to convince him he cared for Regina.

"Is something bothering you? Please tell me what it is."

On the other side of the room, Sophia sat down on the loveseat and said, her voice strangely calm, "Antonio, I have something to tell you. I know this will upset you, but I think you should know the truth. Regina has made me promise never to bring this up to anyone, but I have to tell you about the baby."

The doorbell rang. Both of them startled.

"I wonder who that can be?" Antonio asked.

Stuart walked by the living room on his way to answer the door.

Antonio called to him, "Just get rid of whoever it is." He focused his attention on Sophia again, his face serious, and urged, "Go on. What about the baby? Is there something wrong?"

Before Sophia could respond, she saw a familiar figure in her peripheral vision. Anthony. She looked up, and he glared at her, as if Antonio wasn't even in the room. His gaze was so strong that she felt her throat constricting. The darkness in his eyes went beyond mere color; it was as if a demon was leering at her, waiting for an opportunity to pounce and destroy her.

"Good morning, Poppy. Sophia, how interesting to see you here so bright and early. It's nice how you two have become so chummy lately."

"Anthony, what do you want?"

"Well, Poppy, I've come to talk to you about our last conversation. If I had known you had company, I would have come later."

Tightlipped, Sophia said, "I was just leaving."

Antonio stood up. "Wait, Sophia. You were about to tell me something."

Knowing that Anthony would be hanging on every word, Sophia had had enough. She just wanted to leave. She was having trouble catching her breath.

Anthony watched her.

She felt the fear rise up inside of her and fought to keep her voice from shaking. "We can talk later. It's important that you talk to your son."

As she walked past him, Anthony said sweetly, "Say hello to my wife for me, will you? Tell her how much I miss her."

"Anthony!" Antonio yelled.

She turned and looked Anthony right in the eyes. "I don't know what game you're playing, but I'm not interested. Because of you, I haven't seen my daughter or spoken to her in a very long time. You're not helping by putting a price on her head."

She left, having had the last word.

Anthony shrugged his shoulders. "What's her problem?"

Gathering his thoughts carefully, Antonio sat back down. He was in shock. He felt as if he was living in a bad dream. What Sophia said couldn't be right, could it?

There was a very important question beginning to build within him. It had begun a few days ago as merely a vague impression, hardly worth his notice. But now, especially with this morning's display, it had formed completely. The one question, the one that Antonio almost felt frightened to ask, needed to be voiced. He had to know for certain how far gone Anthony was. He loved him more than life, but how far could his love carry their relationship?

Anthony began to twitch beneath his father's gaze. Clearing his throat, he said, "Well, Poppy, you look like a man with something on his mind. You have something you want to say to me?"

Antonio looked at him carefully, trying to decipher his thoughts. Frowning at him, he asked, almost hesitantly, "Do you hate me?"

Anthony's expression indicated that was the most ridiculous question he had ever heard. "What is that woman filling your head with, Poppy? How can you ask me such a question? You're my father — I love you. I'm just not the type of guy who goes around saying that kind of stuff all the time."

"If I ask you to do something for me as your father, would you do it?"

"Do you even have to ask? Of course, I would."

"First, I want you to know that I love you more than anything in this world. You are my only son. But I care also for Regina and my grandchild. There is nothing more I want in this world than to have them home safely. This million-dollar reward is not the way to do it. I'm asking you to call it off."

Anthony sat down to think about it for a moment. Maybe he shouldn't have taken that second ad; it seemed to have pushed his father over the edge. How could he answer him without giving in to his demands and appearing weak?

"You know, Poppy, you're wrong about me and Regina. She got upset with me the day she left because I wanted her to move back home, to be with me, and she wanted to stay in her mother's house longer. I guess we disagreed about that, and you know how pregnant women are . . . very emotional. She got mad at me and became very irrational. She started blaming me for her father's death again."

He paused dramatically. "I tried to convince her I had nothing to do with it, but she wouldn't believe me. This whole thing is a big misunderstanding. That's why I'm trying so hard to bring her back. Both you and Sophia seem to think that I hate my wife and would cause harm to her. But I'm hoping she sees the ad and will come home herself. I want her to see how much I care for her and how valuable she is to me."

Antonio had never seen his son this emotional before. He wasn't sure what to make of it.

Tears filled Anthony's eyes. "If I take back the reward, I'm afraid she'll think that I don't care and that I don't love her." He placed his head in his hands and began to sob.

Disturbed, Antonio sat down beside him and put his arm around Anthony's shoulders. "I didn't mean to upset you. I thought maybe Regina . . . but it doesn't matter. You should have talked to me about this earlier. You can't get her back this way; you're only going to scare her. Besides, there are crazy people out there right now who would do anything to find her, and that's not a good thing. What if she gets hurt while someone is trying to bring her back? You were right about this — she will come back on her own. Her mother is here. Do you think she would keep the baby away from her grandmother forever? When she does return, we will clear this all up."

"I guess you're right, Poppy."

"Good. It is settled then. You will retract the reward."

Anthony hated wasting such a brilliant emotional performance and still not get his way. He loathed giving ground, but he had no choice. The only thing left to do was see if he could put off retracting the reward for a couple of days. "Yes, I will."

"Why don't you stay for breakfast?"

"I'd like that. Thanks."

John sat at his desk, still annoyed at his conversation with Jim at the FBI. Imagine the nerve of that guy, asking him to involve Regina in her condition. He felt like he was on an emotional rollercoaster. He would be upset at Jim Wilton one second and then two seconds later be worried about how Regina was getting along and if everything was okay with the baby. It was funny how much she was always on his mind. Eventually, he was going to have to figure out a way to see her again or go crazy in the process. One or the other.

The phone rang. He was surprised to hear Father Thomas' voice on the line.

"Hey there, Father Thomas. How ya doing?"

"I'm fine, Detective, but I need to see you right away." He sounded rushed and tense.

"Is there a problem?"

"Can you come over here sometime today? I really don't want to discuss this with you over the phone."

As his concern for Regina increased exponentially, John replied, "Sure, I have some time. I can be there in about an hour. Is that all right?"

"Yes, that will be fine. I'll see you then."

John couldn't help but wonder what was up. During their last conversation, Father Thomas had told him it would be better if John didn't go to the church anymore. He felt it would be safer for Regina that way, just in case the church was being watched. Now he was requesting that he come over to talk to him — there had to be something wrong.

John grabbed his jacket and headed for the door.

"Hey, John!" Frank called out to him. "Where are you going?"

With barely a pause, John replied, "I'm going to visit my mom. She's not feeling well, and I'm going to check up on her. I'll be back later. Cover for me." He didn't know what made him lie — it just slipped out.

"Sure, no problem. I hope she feels better."

"Thanks, man." John left feeling like a jerk. Yet another fable to add to his growing list. He still didn't believe Frank was the informer, but lying was easier right now than telling the truth. Or risking the truth, depending on how you looked at it. Sometimes he just didn't know what to think anymore. That FBI guy had gotten him all confused. He decided to find a different way to the church, in case he was being followed.

Frank was doing some paperwork when John's phone rang. He normally didn't pick it up for him, but since he was covering for him, he decided he would. "Detective Nelson's desk."

"Hello, this is Mrs. Nelson. Is my son there?"

"Oh, hi, Mrs. Nelson. This is Frank."

"Hello, Frank. How are you and that lovely family of yours?"

"We're all fine."

"Well, that's good to hear. Is John around? I need to speak to him."

"You just missed him. But he's on his way to see you."

"He is?"

The question struck Frank as a little odd. John had just told him he was going over there because she wasn't feeling well; she sounded fine on the phone. "How rude of me not to ask you how you're feeling."

"Oh, I'm fine. Never better, actually. So I guess I'll see my son soon. He must be planning a surprise visit. He does that from time to time. Well, it's been nice talking to you, Frank. Say hi to your beautiful wife for me."

"I will, Mrs. Nelson."

Frank could not believe that John had lied to him again. Why would he do that? Did he suspect him of something?

And where was he *really* going?

Sophia walked into the rectory feeling hopeless and helpless. Her heart ached for Regina. This was a time when a daughter needed her mom, and yet in their horrible situation, neither could be with the other. She prayed that one day, it would be different, that she could see her grandchild grow up. And that one day, they all could live without fear.

Father Thomas walked into the room and greeted her. He must have been able to read her expression, because he asked, "Sophia, are you all right?"

"Yes, it's just that . . . It doesn't matter. I feel like a broken record when I talk to God. Sometimes I wonder if things will ever get better. Anthony just made everything worse. I'm afraid he'll never go to prison for his crimes, and I feel so helpless and frustrated."

She noticed he didn't answer. He usually told her that everything would be fine and that Regina eventually would be able to return safe and without harm. But this time, he didn't. Her stomach tensed. "Is something wrong, Father Thomas?"

"Come and have a seat. We need to talk."

Vinny sat in his apartment, staring at the pages in front of him. It looked as if the cops had been pretty close to decoding Anthony's book. If they had succeeded, Anthony would probably be in jail right now.

Thinking about who the informer might be, Vinny knew it was a cop with a lot of access. Someone who knew how to get around in the different departments at the police station. What in the world should he do with the information he now held in his hands? This was Anthony's life and reputation here. It was obvious that Poppy Cavelli didn't want to do anything, but what could Vinny do? Anthony would kill him just for having made a copy. So where did that leave him? Regina had risked everything to get this information to the police.

Vinny stared at the pages and scowled. Some of the orders he had followed were probably written down in here. If the police had been successful, no doubt Vinny would be sitting in the cell next to Anthony's right now. If he was smart, he would just burn this and forget about it.

The sound of the doorbell startled him. He quickly slid the pages underneath the couch. Getting up, he went to look through the peephole and saw the last person he'd ever expected to see on his doorstep. Anthony had never done this before. If he needed him, he just called. Vinny hadn't even realized that Anthony knew where he lived. He took a deep breath and prepared himself for anything.

He opened the door and smiled. "Hey, Boss, what brings you here?"

Looking very serious, Anthony asked, "Aren't you going to invite me in?"

"Sorry, Boss. Sure, come in. I'm just surprised to see you. You've never dropped by before. Is there something wrong?" Vinny tried not to sound as nervous as he felt.

Anthony came in and looked around Vinny's simple apartment. It wasn't decorated much, since Vinny didn't spend the majority of his time here. The front door opened to the living room. There weren't any pictures hanging on the beige walls, and the simple furniture consisted of a television, an old couch, a coffee table, two lamps, and a recliner. None of it matched.

"Do I need to give you a raise?"

"I don't understand the question, Boss. You're very generous."

"What do you do with your money? It's apparent you don't spend it on furniture or clothes."

Vinny didn't know how to respond to that. He simply said, "I don't need much to make me happy. I'm usually never home. I guess I just never got around to it."

"Lighten up, man. I'm kidding."

"You want a drink, Boss?"

"No. Why don't we sit down and have a chat?"

Vinny knew exactly what Anthony was doing now. He had showed up unannounced like this to throw Vinny off guard. He had seen him do this before, and none of those situations had turned out well.

They sat down, Anthony in the recliner and Vinny on the couch.

"You know me pretty well, don't you? You know I have the ability to figure out when someone is lying to me."

"Yes, Boss."

"Then answer me this: Who are you working for?"

The question threw Vinny for a second, but he knew he couldn't afford to hesitate. "I don't know what you mean — I work for you."

"Are you sure?"

"Yeah, Boss. Why don't you believe me? I've done everything you told me. I would never betray you."

"That's good. Would you do anything I ask without question?"

"Yes." Vinny definitely did not like the direction this conversation was heading. He had thought they were beyond Anthony's needing to test his loyalty. He couldn't help but wonder what had happened for Anthony to doubt him.

"Good. I believe you. I have a job for you. It's not pretty, but you're the only one who can do it. Some people might not have the stomach for it, but I need to know where your loyalty lies. You do spend lots of time watching my father for me, and I want to make sure he hasn't won you over."

Anthony got up and sat next to him on the couch. Vinny knew that if he wanted to see another day, he would have to be very convincing. This test was going to be tricky to pass.

"It's because of your closeness to my father that you're the only one for this job." Anthony took out a small plastic bag from his jacket pocket and handed it to Vinny. "This is the stuff I bought to use on Regina but never got a chance to. I want you to start putting this in my father's food. You think you can handle that?"

"Yes, sir, if that's what you want me to do."

"It's not like it sounds. I don't want you to kill him. He is my father after all. I just want him off my back. If he's sick and in the hospital, then he won't be bothering me. I'm hoping to locate Regina very soon, and I have plans for her that he will just get in the way of."

Vinny felt the heat in Anthony's eyes. He made sure with everything in him that he had no reaction to what Anthony said. "Whatever you say, Boss. When do you want me to start?"

"Right away." Anthony got up. "Remember — just a little bit. I want him sick, and that's all."

Vinny walked him to the door, experiencing a wide range of emotions but specifically gratitude that Anthony was leaving. He closed the door behind him and then stared at the packet in his hand. He couldn't believe that Anthony would do this. He couldn't believe that he would ask him to put Poppy at risk.

Vinny walked over to the couch and removed the copy from its hiding place. He looked at it and then at the packet and knew what he had to do. He had done many awful things in his life, but sometimes you had to draw a line. He was getting too old for this stuff. He had to find a way out.

Before he went over to Poppy's, there was something else he needed to take care of. He pulled his cell phone from his pocket, looked up a number in the phone book, and dialed. He had never thought that one day he would call upon this childhood friend.

The man answered, and Vinny found himself feeling extremely grateful a second time. "Hi, it's Vinny. I know it's been a long time since we talked. I need your help. Can you meet me? Good. Do you remember where we used to play as kids? Yeah, meet me there. Can you go now? Great. I'll see you in about twenty minutes."

Vinny hung up the phone, not believing what he was about to do. He took the first page from his copy and folded it, pushing it down into his back pocket. The rest of the copies he placed inside one of the couch cushions, zipped them up, and left for his meeting.

Chapter 16

Sophia faced Father Thomas, disturbed and incredulous. "Are you sure about this?"

"Yes, I'm afraid so. We really need to pray."

"Oh, Lord! Why is this happening? I mean, hasn't she gone through enough? Haven't we all gone through enough?"

"Sophia, I understand your frustration, but this is a time to press in and pray. God has His hand on her. He will keep her and her baby safe. It will all work out in the end."

Sophia wasn't sure if she could buy that this time. After her run-in with Anthony this morning, she felt like her emotions were hanging by a thread. She was just so angry — at this whole situation. Yet, at the same time, she knew he was probably right. As much as praying didn't appeal to her right now, it couldn't hurt. "Father, I'm sorry. I don't mean to be negative. I'm sure you're right."

Their conversation was interrupted by the backdoor bell.

"Oh, good. I believe it's Detective Nelson. I've asked him to come over. I think he can help."

"Do you really think that's a good idea? I mean . . . I've seen the way he looks at her. I think he has a personal interest in my daughter that extends beyond his doing his job. Those feelings might get in the way, and *nothing* can be allowed to go wrong with this."

"I know he does, but I don't think they'll get in the way."

Nancy showed John into the living room and slipped out again as Father Thomas rose to greet him.

"Thank you for coming."

John shook his hand warmly and then walked over and greeted Sophia. "Hello, Mrs. Palmetto. It's nice to see you again."

Trying to smile, Sophia shook his hand.

Father Thomas asked, "Would you like something to drink?"

"No, thank you. I'm fine. The truth of the matter is I'm curious about why you asked me here. The last time we met, you told me it would be a good idea not to come back here. I'm sure you wouldn't have changed your mind unless it was important. What's going on? Regina's not in trouble, is she?"

"Well, yes and no. There is a situation that you should know about, and it does concern Regina and her baby. I received this letter from Brother Steven today. He wanted me to know that there are some complications with Regina's pregnancy. The baby isn't developing as the doctor would like, so he wants her to see a specialist. Unfortunately, the best one for the job is located here in New York."

"Are you saying that Regina is coming *here*?"

Father Thomas looked at him and shook his head. "I'm afraid the circumstances with the baby prompted her to make this decision. Brother Steven is traveling with her, and they are going to stay near the hospital. According to this letter, they're probably already in town."

Sophia watched John, waiting for his reaction and prepared to judge it. He appeared disturbed and even a little distraught at this new and unexpected development. She could see it in his eyes and frowned, wondering again if his obvious feelings for her daughter were going to be a problem.

But what could she do, at this point? Regina needed him.

"Does the letter say where they're staying?"

"Yes, and that's why I've called you here. I'm worried that even though she's in a disguise, she might be recognized. Sophia and I would like you to keep an eye on them while they're here to make sure they stay safe. I'm afraid they've bitten off more than they can chew."

"I agree. This isn't the smartest move on their part. I can't believe they would take this risk. What is she thinking?"

Sophia interjected, "How about Anthony? Do you think he would have Detective Nelson followed?"

"I'll be careful. I'll make sure no one is following me." He looked at her, concern forming a line between his brows, and said, "I wouldn't do anything to place your daughter in further danger. Nothing at all."

Apparently, he thought her coming back to New York had been a crazy move, and in Regina's defense, Sophia said, "The baby must be in great danger. She wouldn't have taken this chance except to save her baby." She paused for a moment, searching for the right words. "Detective Nelson, I know you have feelings for my daughter. I hope that won't interfere with your job."

She regretted saying it as soon as the words left her lips. He glanced away as he adjusted his position on the chair.

"I'm sure Detective Nelson can help protect Regina; after all, he's the one who brought her to safety."

Now Sophia felt even worse about her statement. Father Thomas was a consummate diplomat trying to make everyone feel at ease.

"It's okay, Father Thomas. I can understand her concerns. You're right, Mrs. Palmetto, about my having feelings for your daughter. But let me reassure you that I won't let them get in the way of protecting her. If you want, I can arrange to get someone else to watch over her."

Sophia thought about that for a moment. His honesty was refreshing and unexpected. She just wanted Regina to be safe. "Father Thomas is right — there is no one else we can trust to keep her safe. Just promise me you'll make sure she gets back to safety as soon as all her tests are done."

"Don't worry. I will. Father Thomas, where is she?"

Father Thomas handed him the letter. John glanced over it, read the hotel's address, and then said his good-byes.

When he got out to his car, John just sat there for a moment, trying to sort his emotions so that his mind would be clear when he saw her again. Part of him was upset with her for endangering her life like this, but the other part was bursting with anticipation, regardless of the circumstances. She was here. In New York.

Now he would need to disappear for a while so that he could protect her without causing anyone at the precinct to be suspicious. This would be very tricky, especially after what had happened last time. He took out his cell phone and pressed Frank's number on his speed dial.

"Hey, Frank. It's me."

Just the sound of John's voice made Frank's blood boil, but he wanted to see how far he would take his lies. "How's your mother?" he asked, knowing the answer to that question.

"She could be better. I'm going to need to take some time off to help her out. I thought that maybe you could relay that information to the captain for me."

Frank shook his head. He couldn't believe it. Not only was he lying to him, but now he expected him to cover for him, too. Partners? Was that what they were? Hardly. John had changed so much lately, and Frank just couldn't take it anymore. "Just stop it! Do you think I'm stupid? I thought we were more than just partners. Why are you lying to me?"

"Frank, take it easy. What are you talking about?"

"Your mom called right after you left this morning — that's what I'm talking about."

John hesitated. "I see."

"'I see'? Is that all you have to say to me? What's with you, man? Why don't you trust me enough to tell me what's going on?"

"Frank, it's not safe to talk over the phone. Meet me outside the station. I'll swing by and pick you up. We can talk then. I'll explain as much as I can. I promise. I should be there in about thirty minutes. Will you be there?"

Frank sighed. "Yeah, in thirty minutes. I'll be waiting."

Vinny pulled into the parking space, turned off the car, and for several minutes sat there in silence, looking around. The park had more trees than he remembered. The open field where he'd played baseball and the giant wall — well, when he was younger it had seemed giant — where he'd played handball. He watched as the kids played on the same slide he'd played on when he was a child and wondered what would have happened if he'd made different choices in his life. He found himself meeting someone he thought he would never talk to again; it kind of made him think a little differently about things.

Smiling to himself, Vinny looked around again, carefully this time, as he climbed out of the car. Obviously, this wasn't going to work if anybody was following him. He walked down the path until he reached the horse trail, and, taking a shortcut through the trees, he came to an old, abandoned shed. Somehow he had known it would still be there.

So had his friend. The man was leaning against the side, waiting for him. He turned around when he heard Vinny approaching.

Vinny spoke first. "Hey, Jim. Good to see you."

Jim Wilton walked up and shook Vinny's hand. "It's good to see you, too, old friend. I couldn't believe it when you called me. The last time our paths crossed was about five years ago. Remember?"

"Yes, I do. A lot has happened since then. I'm glad you came. The last time I saw you, I had to pretend I didn't know you; Anthony Cavelli was standing right there. I'm sorry for that."

"Hey, I understand. I wouldn't want your boss to know we had grown up together. That would be dangerous. So why am I here?"

Vinny had butterflies in his stomach and wasn't sure he wanted to get to that just yet. "You know, Jim, as kids, you were my best friend. When you moved away when you were ten, it was such a sad time for me, but I'm glad we kept in touch — for a while, anyway. You know, I think moving saved you from the path I'm on, and all the other guys we hung out with. Most of them are dead now."

"Vin, did you bring me out here to relive our childhood, or do you want to tell me something?"

"Yeah, right."

Jim sighed and studied him. He could tell he was very troubled about something and struggled to tell him what it was. He felt bad about being short with him. "I do remember how close we once were." He hesitated and then said, "I always felt guilty about the path you took, like it was my fault because I left. When I first saw that you were involved with Cavelli, I thought that maybe if I had been there, you would have chosen a different path. I guess it made me mad when you chose to dismiss my attempts at helping you."

"It's not your fault. But I'm in trouble now, and I need to know that you're still the honest kid I knew. Are you?" Vinny looked at him.

"I'm not sure how to take that, but I guess that working for the people you work for, that's a reasonable question. Yes. You can trust me."

Vinny started pacing back and forth in a small circle, staring at the ground. He was thinking, processing this situation, and hoping that he wasn't inviting a bullet to his head. Finally he looked into Jim's eyes, past the surface, and searched for the same kid he used to know and trust. And he found him.

He pulled out the folded paper from his pocket and handed it to him. Jim looked it over, a bit puzzled.

"What is this?"

"It's a page from Anthony's black book."

Instantly, Jim was nearly beside himself. Was Vinny talking about *the* infamous black book — the one he'd heard about? If this was from *that* book, then he'd just struck gold. "How did you get it? Where's the rest of it? Are you going to hand all of it over to us? Why are you doing this?" The questions stormed out of him. He couldn't believe his luck. He knew what handing over that piece of paper meant to Vinny.

"Hey, slow down. It's a long story that I really don't have time now to get into. I have my reasons. I brought this paper over to show you that I'm serious about turning against Anthony. I didn't want you to think it was some type of trap. Do you want my help or not?"

"Yeah, we want your help. Are you sure about this? If he finds out what you're doing, you know what will happen to you."

"Yeah, I know. I'll bring you the rest of it and explain what's going on. Can you meet me tomorrow?"

"Anywhere, anytime — you name it."

"Good. Let's say here at seven a.m."

"Great. I'll be here," Jim said enthusiastically.

"Just one thing. You can't let anyone know that I'm helping you, and I mean *anyone*." Vinny looked Jim in the eyes. "If I find out you told anyone, my cooperation stops immediately. You understand what I'm talkin' about?"

"I understand completely. I'll see you tomorrow then."

John pulled up in front of the precinct, and Frank was there waiting for him. His partner got into the car and immediately demanded, "Do you think I'm the informer? Is that why you're shutting me out?"

The question threw John off guard. He pulled away from the curb and responded, "No, I don't. How can you think such a thing? I trust you."

"Then what's the problem? Why are you lying to me?"

Taking a right at the first corner, John said, "I'm sorry about that. I have to do something, and I promised I wouldn't tell anyone, not even you. This is something I have to do, and it has nothing to do with me trusting you. I'm asking you as my friend not to ask me any questions about this. I need to take off for a few days. Can you cover for me with the captain? Tell him I'm sick or something."

Frank didn't say anything.

"Please, I'm asking you to trust me. I'll tell you everything as soon as I can."

"I don't like it, but I'll cover for you."

"Thanks, man. I owe you for this."

John pulled back in front of the police station. "You're a good friend."

"Yeah, a better one than you deserve. Just promise me you'll be careful and watch your back, since you won't let me do it."

"I promise."

Frank got out of the car and watched as John drove away. John was grateful that it had gone as well as it had. He'd thought Frank would fight him more, but he was glad he hadn't.

Antonio was troubled by his earlier visit with Sophia. She had wanted to tell him something and hadn't gotten the chance because of Anthony's unexpected visit. After Anthony left, Antonio decided that he would go to the church to see her.

He wanted to know what she had to tell him about the baby; maybe she'd heard from Regina and was afraid of saying anything in front of Anthony. He was relieved she was starting to trust him again and valued that more than he could express. The last thing he wanted to do was anything that would misplace that trust.

Hopefully, her news wasn't bad.

On the other side of things, his breakfast with Anthony had been pleasant and productive. It had been a long time since he and his son had been able to spend any time together without it ending in some sort of dispute. At this point, Antonio didn't know what to make of anything — of Sophia, of Anthony, of their opinions about one another as well as Regina. But one thing he was certain of: He hated the tension that built between him and his son, the distrust he felt toward him. If there was any possibility at all that Anthony was right and all of this really *was* just a misunderstanding . . . Well, that needed to be made clear.

Stuart pulled up to the church.

"Stuart, just wait for me outside, please. I'll try not to take too long."

"That's fine, sir."

After Antonio got out of the car, Stuart sat there and scratched his head. He couldn't believe that Antonio had just said he'd try not to take too long. He had even used the word *please*. He'd been so polite lately, and considerate, that Stuart wondered if this was the same man he had worked for all these years.

Antonio walked to the door and knocked. Nancy answered, and this time, she didn't seem surprised to see him. "Mr. Cavelli, who are you here to see?"

"I need to see Mrs. Palmetto, if she's in."

"Come on in and have a seat in the living room. I'll let her know that you're here." She pointed in the direction of the living room and left.

Antonio sat down on the couch, feeling slightly apprehensive. He waited for a few minutes and then as Sophia entered the room, he rose to greet her.

She sat down with him on the couch and wasn't exactly sure what to say. She knew why he was here, even though he had yet to say a word. He waited for her patiently.

She still was not certain if she should say anything about this, but finally, she began, "Antonio, I know why you're here. I'm still not sure I'm doing the right thing, but I've seen changes in you lately, and . . ."

"And what, Sophia? You can tell me whatever it is. If it's about Regina and the baby, I want to know. All I want to do is help."

"Are you sure about that? This concerns Anthony."

"Anthony?" Antonio paused, as if considering something, and then he leaned forward and replied earnestly, "If you're talking about what happened on the day she left, he told me about the fight they had. I know she still thinks Anthony had something to do with Michael's death, but he didn't. He truly does love her, and he promised me he would retract the million-dollar reward. So you see, it's all going to be fine. Once she's home, I'm sure this misunderstanding between them will be resolved. I know my son is not perfect, but he's trying."

Sophia realized how sincere he was being. He truly wanted to give Anthony a chance; he wanted to believe there was hope. This would break his heart, but he had to know the truth. If Regina was ever discovered, he had to be convinced about Anthony's deceptive ways, or else she would end up dead.

"Antonio, I know this will be hard for you to hear, but it is the truth. I would never make up something like this. Promise me you will not interrupt me until I'm done telling you what I have to say."

"I promise." Antonio took a deep breath.

"I know you love your son and believe in his sincerity, but he has you fooled. He doesn't want to be married to Regina, and he wants out of their marriage as much as she does. She is an honorable young woman and is trying to live up to the vows she made before God. I don't think you realize that he made her pretend to be happy around you. They pretended. She married him only to save Michael's life — and that's the bottom line on her part. Anthony's reasons I'm not sure of. Maybe he just wanted to please you."

As she neared the topic she had promised never to speak of, she dropped her voice until it was not much more than a whisper. "Anthony and Regina had an agreement about the physical part of their relationship."

She noticed the frown deepening on his face and knew he wasn't happy about this. And he hadn't even heard the worst of it yet. She had come this far; she couldn't go back now. He had to know the truth. "Anthony has had many affairs, a fact that doesn't bother Regina. They had an agreement about that also, if you catch what I'm saying. He is always discrete so that you don't find out." She wasn't quite sure if Antonio was following her; he was beginning to get a glaze across his eyes. "This part might be hard for you to believe. One night he came home very drunk and . . . and he . . ."

"He what? Just tell me."

"He raped her." There. She said it. Finally she could breathe again.

"He raped her?" Antonio repeated.

"Yes. I'm sorry; it's the truth. He's verbally abusive and at times has gotten physical. It was no longer safe for her or her child to stay there. She had to get away. She's not coming back — ever."

The color drained from his face. He suddenly stood from the couch. "I have to go."

"No, wait. Please listen to me. I'm telling the truth!"

He walked out the door. She prayed that she had done the right thing.

Antonio jumped in the back seat of the car, slamming the door. "Take me home."

Stuart was startled by the sudden change in his disposition. He wondered what had happened to make him so angry.

The ride home was quiet. Stuart knew from years of working for him that when Antonio got quiet and his eyes squinted like this, he was angry and getting angrier. Stuart wanted to say something, but he knew it was better, and safer perhaps, to keep silent.

Antonio replayed what Sophia had told him over and over in his mind. He had done some terrible things in his life but never anything like this. He couldn't believe his son was capable of such a thing. He couldn't believe that he and Regina had lied to him all these years, making him believe they loved one another. No, he couldn't and wouldn't believe it. He didn't know why she would lie to him, but when he calmed down, he would find out.

He arrived home to find Vinny waiting outside, his arms folded as he stood on the front stairs. Knowing the man had a reason for being there, Antonio climbed out before Stuart could open the door and demanded, "What is it, Vinny?"

"Sir, we have to talk. I've been asked to do something you should be aware of."

"What is it?" The last thing he needed right now was more bad news.

"Let's go inside. You'll need to sit down."

Antonio couldn't believe this. What could be so terrible that he had to sit down to hear? He led the way to the living room and sat on the sofa, trying very hard to keep his cool. Vinny didn't sit. Instead, he paced back and forth — something he did when he needed help thinking.

This entire day, everyone had seemed to feel it necessary to tell him things he didn't want to hear. Now even Vinny was having a hard time formulating words, and Antonio's patience ran thin. "Just tell me what it is!"

Vinny jumped. Well, he didn't have to wonder anymore what mood Poppy was in. How was he supposed to tell this man that his son wanted to poison him? Not kill him — that had to count for something — but just get him out of the way.

Not knowing what else to do, he took the plastic bag out of his jacket and handed it to him. "This is arsenic. Your son gave it to me today. He came to my home and wanted to know how loyal I was to him. He wants me to start putting this in your food."

Vinny's words impacted Antonio with such force that he felt like he had been physically hit in the head with a baseball bat. His world came crashing down around him, and he whispered, "My son wants me dead?"

"No, sir, he doesn't — he made sure I knew that. He just wants you sick enough to go to the hospital so that he can have free rein with you out of the way."

"Go home, Vinny. I need to be alone and think about a few things." He could barely speak. "Why don't you come back later after I have thought this through?"

"Yes, sir, if that's what you want. I'm sorry."

On Vinny's way out, he told Stuart to keep an eye on him. He was worried about leaving him alone after such bad news.

Antonio sat on the couch in shock. He couldn't believe what was happening. If Vinny was right — and Antonio had no reason to believe he would lie to him — then Sophia must be right as well.

And if Sophia was right, then there was only one decision for Antonio to make: Anthony had to be stopped.

He had been blinded by his love for his son. He wanted to believe in him. He wanted there to be hope, for both of them — but now he realized Sophia had been right about him all along. His son had crossed a line no one should ever cross.

He took a deep breath to push down the lump in his throat. But who was he kidding? His son had crossed *many* lines he shouldn't have.

Now, he had to think of a way to handle the whole situation. Trying to decipher these new developments, he began to wonder, *What —— are you surprised Anthony turned out this way?* The boy didn't know any better. Antonio and Antonio alone was to blame for choosing this life not only for himself, but for his son as well. No wonder Regina ran for her life! He had to find her and protect her from Anthony at all costs.

His thoughts rattled all over the place, and whatever his next step, he knew he had to be careful. If Anthony knew Vinny had betrayed him, Vinny would be killed. Antonio had always appreciated Vinny, but now especially he didn't want him to suffer, because he'd been decent and told him the truth. And in light of today's conversation, Antonio didn't want to imagine what would have happened if Vinny hadn't been decent.

For several minutes, he couldn't get his thoughts in order. But then, quite suddenly, he remembered Dr. Gino Giovanni. Gino's father, Carmine, had worked for Antonio for years, and after the man had died saving his life, Antonio had always felt responsible for Carmine's family. He had made sure his wife and children were provided for. Gino had genuinely appreciated not having to pay for his schooling, and seeing his gratitude, Antonio had gone a step further and made sure he always had some spending money; he'd wanted him to be able to concentrate on his schoolwork and not be distracted by working part-time. When Gino had expressed interest in becoming a doctor, Antonio had insisted on paying for medical school, something that had barely made a dent in his assets. The young man hadn't had to struggle financially as some of the other medical school students had.

Antonio decided to give him a call and see if Gino could help him. He went into his study and looked up Gino's number. As he dialed, he felt nervous and didn't understand why. *If my son finds out about . . . any of this . . .* He closed his eyes, feeling like he was dying. *Why . . . ? What if this phone is bugged?* He wasn't sure if Anthony would do that, but he didn't want to take chances. If a son would poison his father, there was nothing he wouldn't do. He didn't want Gino to get caught in the middle of all this.

"Mercy Hospital."

"Hello. May I please speak to Dr. Gino Giovanni?"

"Hold on please, and I'll connect you to his office."

There was a pause, and then: "Dr. Giovanni's office. May I help you?"

"Yes, this is Antonio Cavelli. I would like to speak to Dr. Giovanni. Is he available?"

"Oh, Mr. Cavelli, he's with a patient, but if you hold on for a moment, I'll tell him you're on the phone."

Antonio tried not to call Gino too often, but he was amazed on the warm reception he always received whenever he did call. Maybe Gino had told his staff about him.

After waiting for a few minutes, he heard Gino come on the phone. "Hello, Poppy."

"Gino, it's so good to hear your voice. How are you and that charming wife of yours?"

"We're great! She's due any day now. We're very excited."

"That's wonderful. I'm glad to hear such happiness in your voice." His words didn't line up with his tone. His heart was breaking over all that he had learned about Anthony.

"Is something wrong, Poppy? You don't quite sound like yourself."

"You're amazing, you know. Gino, I would like to meet with you when you have some time. I need to talk to you about something very important."

"I always have time for you. Let me check my schedule." There was a pause while Gino did so. "How about four thirty today? Is that good for you?"

"Yes, that is fine. I'll meet you outside the hospital, and we can go for a drive."

"Great! I'll be there."

Antonio started to feel better about this whole thing. He had a plan, but in order for it to work, he would need Gino's help. He just hoped that his friend wouldn't mind bending the rules a bit to help him out.

John's cell phone rang while he was driving to the hotel. He answered it and heard a voice he hadn't expected on the other end. "Agent Wilton, I wish I could say it's nice to hear your voice . . . Hey, how did you get my number?"

"You forget I work for the FBI."

"I don't think I'll ever forget that. I have nothing to say to you, and I don't care to hear any more idiotic ideas you may have."

"Look, just grow up, would you? I have some information I thought you might be interested in. If you are, then why don't you meet me at the bureau tomorrow morning, say around eleven? If you show up, I know you mean business about the Cavellis. If not, then I guess I know where you stand."

The next sound John heard was the dial tone. Jim Wilton had hung up on him. *How rude was that?* John thought. He wondered what had happened since they had spoken last. Maybe he'd be able to get away tomorrow long enough to see what he had to say.

He pulled into a parking space about a block from the hotel. He climbed out of his car, and seeing that no one was following him, he walked into the hotel and took the elevator to the third floor. All the way up, he planned what he would say to her. To Regina. The conversation ran smoothly in his head.

When the elevator opened, he stepped off and walked down the hall until he reached door number 610. He took a deep breath and knocked on the door. A few seconds passed. Then the door opened a crack, and an arm came out and pulled him inside.

"What are you doing here?" Regina demanded, very indignant.

"What am *I* doing here? I have a better question for you — what are *you* doing here?" John was just as indignant. This was not going as he'd planned.

"How did you find us?"

"Father Thomas told me where to find you."

"How did he know?"

"I wrote him a letter," Brother Steven said from behind her.

Regina whirled around. "Why? Don't you know what could have happened if it got into the wrong hands?"

John suddenly noticed that there was only one large bed in the room. That kind of disturbed him, and he wondered what sleeping arrangements they had come up with.

"I was hoping that Father Thomas would send John here. I knew that if we ran into trouble, I wouldn't be much help. I'm just concerned for you and the baby. Please don't be angry with me. I did what I thought was best."

"How could you? Now even more people are involved — whatever happened to being discrete?"

"Regina, I'm sorry. I thought this was best. But it's done now. Let's move on. You getting upset is not good for you or the baby." Brother Steven put his hand on her shoulder, and John watched his every move, scowling. "I'm sorry if I upset you. That's the last thing I wanted to do."

"Okay." Regina paused. "Maybe you're right. Next time, it would be a good idea if you would talk to me first. Don't leave me out of the equation when my life is on the line."

"You're right. Forgiven?"

"Yes. You're forgiven." Turning back to John, she asked, "Does anyone besides Father Thomas know you're here?"

"Just your mom." Then in a much softer tone, he asked, "How are you doing?"

"I'm fine, but the baby could be better. I go to see the doctor tomorrow at five a.m. to run the fetal echocardiogram. The hospital isn't as busy then."

"You do know that this is a bad idea . . . There are people out there, just hoping to run into you. Do you realize the price Anthony has on your head?"

"Yes, I do, but do you realize that I could lose this baby? If there was a chance that I could have saved him but did nothing, I just couldn't live with myself. I have to do this."

Just looking at her brought his feelings back to the surface. He felt like a schoolboy and found himself staring. "You look great. I've missed you." Clearing his throat, he continued, "I promised your mom that I would look after you and Brother Steven. Please don't fight me on this. I know this room isn't very big, but I'm going to spend the night here and go with you to the hospital tomorrow."

"You can't come. It would look suspicious."

"I'll stay out of the way, but I *am* coming. Don't argue, okay?"

Brother Steven chimed in. "It's probably for the best, Regina. I know I would feel safer if he was nearby."

Regina sighed. "Fine. It seems that this is out of my hands." Looking around the room with a frown, she said, "Where do you suppose you're going to sleep?"

"He can sleep with me on the floor," Brother Steven said.

"That will be fine." John was glad to hear Brother Steven was sleeping on the floor, but why he had been concerned that *Brother* Steven would sleep anywhere else was beyond him. He had not been thinking straight for a while now. "So is there anything good on television? Or would you rather play cards?"

For the first time, Regina smiled at him, beginning to relax, and John felt himself melt through the floor.

Antonio's limousine pulled up in front of the hospital. Gino was waiting for him.

"Poppy, it's so good to see you," he said as he climbed into the back seat.

"It's good to see you also, Gino."

"What's wrong that you can't talk to me on the phone? It's not your health, is it?"

"No, my health is fine — for now."

"For now? I don't understand. What is going on?"

With a frown, Antonio began, "So much has changed these past few years. Today, I found out some very difficult things about my son."

Gino glanced out the window and didn't reply.

"You don't seem very surprised. Do you also have some horror stories you could tell me about Anthony?"

"Poppy, I love you, and my family is forever grateful to you for all that you did for us after my dad died. He always spoke highly of you. I don't want to add to your pain."

Antonio dismissed that with a wave of his hand. "It doesn't matter. I found out that my son is only pretending to be in love with his wife. He got drunk one night and raped her — my grandchild . . ." It pained him to even think about it. He shook his head and determinedly continued, "Now one of my men tells me that my own son wants to poison me with arsenic, so that I get sick and he can have free rein to run the business. Is it any worse than that?"

Gino was silent for a moment. He was horrified that Anthony would risk Poppy's life, but what was he supposed to say? He could see the pain Poppy was in and didn't want to add to it. What good would it do to tell him that Anthony resented Gino and his family? That he hated that Poppy had taken care of them after his father had died? What good would it do to tell him how he'd tried to intimidate his mother and hit on his sister? It had gone on for only a short period of time, and then he had stopped, for whatever reason. A few years had passed since and nothing more had been done, so perhaps it was best that Gino kept the stories to himself.

"No, I have nothing to tell you about Anthony, but I'm not surprised, either. I'm sorry that it caused you pain. What is it that I can do for you?"

"Well, if he wants me out of the way, what can I do to fake being poisoned? I want him to think his man is doing as ordered and that I landed in the hospital. But he won't believe it just on face value. I need you to help me convince him. I need you to be my doctor, but if it will get you into trouble, then don't do it."

"No one has to know you're faking it. Just don't tell anyone I'm helping you. For you, being your doctor is the least I can do. If the hospital needs your room, I can arrange for you to be moved to a private nursing home that I know of."

"Good. Then let's get started."

Chapter 17

The precinct was especially busy for four thirty in the morning, Frank thought. *Must have been a full moon last night.* The neighbor's dog had woken him, and he hadn't been able to get back to sleep, so he'd decided to come in a couple of hours early to catch up on some paperwork. He figured he might as well do something constructive with his time, and with John leaving him in the lurch, he didn't want to fall too far behind. He wasn't sure yet what he would say about John's absence today, and he was still mad that his partner didn't trust him enough to tell him exactly what he was up to.

The office was noisy, even this early in the morning. Frank tried to tune it out as he yawned and finished his coffee.

Suddenly, he heard the captain's voice behind him. "Hey, Frank."

Frank nearly jumped out of his skin. He wasn't expecting to see him so early — and he still didn't know what to say about John. "Morning, Captain."

"You're in kinda early. What are you up to?"

"Just trying to keep up with the paperwork." Frank smiled.

"How come your partner's not here helping you out?"

Frank looked at him and said, "He called me last night; he's not feeling very well. He has a sore throat and a fever. I think he's going to the doctor today."

Captain Merrill returned his look. For a second, Frank thought the jig was up, but then the captain said, "That's too bad. How are you boys doing on your case?"

"About the same. Nothing new to report. It seems the trail is getting cold, but we don't intend to give up."

"Good. I'm glad to hear that. If there's anything new, let me know."

"Yes, sir. You bet. You'll be the first to find out."

The captain walked away, leaving Frank feeling a bit unnerved. He couldn't believe John would ask him to lie for him and then not even tell him why. What had happened to trust? The whole thing probably had to do with Regina Cavelli. The last time John had lied to him, it'd had to do with her. He wondered if John knew where she was. If he did, that would certainly explain all the secrecy again.

Maybe there was a way he could find out what John was doing.

He had to know for sure.

Father Thomas looked out his study window to see Sophia walking in the garden. The worried look on her face concerned him. It seemed to rarely leave her these days, and he knew high stress wasn't good for her health, much less for her soul. Maybe there was something he could say to help. He opened the door that led out onto the porch and walked over to join her.

"Good morning, Sophia. I thought I was the only one who woke up at the crack of dawn."

"I had trouble sleeping, and I decided to just get up early and pray."

Feeling like he was intruding, Father Thomas hesitated and then turned back toward the house. "I'm sorry. I didn't mean to interrupt you."

"You don't need to apologize. I'm done. I was just thinking."

"You look very troubled."

"Regina, Antonio . . . the whole thing." She glanced at him. "I told Antonio how Regina had become pregnant. He didn't take it very well. I don't think he believes me."

Father Thomas shook his head, saying, "Sophia, why would you do that?"

"With Regina being back in the city, I was afraid that she would be found out and that Anthony would get his clutches on her again."

"She's in good hands with Detective Nelson."

"I know." She paused for a moment then continued, her voice sounding like it was about to break, "Antonio is blind to the truth about his son. I can't let him believe the lies that Anthony is telling him. Regina and the baby's life are at stake."

She started to cry softly. Father Thomas placed his arm around her to comfort her.

"I know I shouldn't take these matters into my own hands but leave them in God's. But . . . I guess I'm not as strong as I should be."

This woman had become very dear to his heart. Father Thomas pulled his arm off her shoulders and took her hand with both of his own. "Sophia, you are like a mother to me. I care for you deeply. There isn't anything I wouldn't do for you or Regina. Crying doesn't mean you're weak; it just means you're upset. Why don't we go inside and talk over some coffee? Okay?"

"Yes, I'd like that."

Anthony rolled over to look at the bedside clock again. Five in the morning already. He usually wasn't awake this early, but he'd had trouble sleeping. Rarely was he anxious about anything, but what he'd asked Vinny to do was bothering him. There was no going back now. He didn't like the fact that Vinny hadn't done as he was told yesterday, and now that he'd made this decision, he wanted to get his plan moving.

He picked up the phone and dialed Vinny's number. After several rings, a very sleepy Vinny finally answered. "Huh-lo?"

"It's me. Wake up!" Anthony yelled into the phone.

That seemed to jar him more awake. "Hey, Boss. Is something wrong?"

"Yeah, I want to know if you plan to carry out my latest order? Last time I checked, I was still the boss."

"I know that, sir. Your dad wanted me to come over later this morning, because he wanted me to have breakfast with him. I was figuring on doing it then."

"Really . . . That's good. Remember, don't over do it. I don't want him dead, just sick."

"Yeah, Boss, I know. So you're sure about this, then?"

"Are you questioning me? Nobody questions me. You just do what you're told. I don't need some second-class hood questioning my orders!" He hung up the phone. *The nerve of that guy.*

He threw back the covers and climbed out of bed, trying to think. Grabbing the phone again, he dialed another number. "Yeah, it's me. I want to know what kind of progress you're making with my wife."

The informant was not happy to hear from Anthony, especially at the precinct. "I told you to never call me here! It's too risky," he whispered.

"And I told you that you work for me and not the other way around. So answer my question. Where is she?"

"I don't know, but something is up. Our friend is not at work today. I don't have any proof, but I have a suspicion he might be with her."

Anthony didn't like the sound of that at all. "Are you nuts? What gives you that idea?"

"Well, the last time something like this happened, I believe he was with her. He's a very responsible kind of guy. I hate to say this, but I think he's falling for her."

Anthony clamped his mouth shut to keep from yelling into the phone again, but he couldn't contain the rage that statement instantly boiled inside of him. "You don't know what you're talking about. She's pregnant with my kid — what man would be stupid enough to go after anything that belongs to me, unless he had a death wish! Are you just trying to tick me off? Besides, if he is with her, then where are they?"

"I'm not sure. But I don't think he's left town. What if she's here? Maybe she sneaked back."

Anthony thought about that for a moment. "No. That's crazy. This city is big, but not that big. Why would she risk coming back here?"

"I don't know. Maybe she misses her mom or maybe she's sick. I don't know. But it wouldn't hurt to comb the city for her one more time."

"Yeah, okay. Maybe that's not a bad idea. I'll get some guys on it." Anthony hung up without saying good-bye. He wasn't the type to say good-bye, because he enjoyed having the last word in a conversation. Not only that, but he was still mad at that dumb cop's insinuation about Regina and another guy.

He dialed Mario's number this time. "Get up!" he yelled into the receiver. "I've got a job for you, and it's a big one. Are you awake?"

"Boss? Yeah, I'm awake. I think."

Anthony was getting impatient.

"What time is it?" Mario mumbled.

"Listen to me, you moron. I've got an important job for you and the boys."

"Sorry, Boss. I'm awake now. What can I do for you?"

"I want you to gather the boys and do another sweep of the city for Regina. I want you to pull some extra guys, because I want all the boroughs covered. Follow her friends, mom, anybody she might go to for help. I want it done now — *today*. You understand what I'm saying?"

"Yeah, Boss. Loud and clear."

Anthony hung up and felt himself begin to smile. Today might turn out to be a really good day. If he both found Regina and put Poppy out of commission, then he would have a reason to celebrate tonight.

It began to dawn on him that he didn't know what to do with Regina after he'd found her. He'd probably have to stash her away in the old warehouse. It had an office and bathroom. He could get a bed in there and some guys to watch her, with a doctor on standby for when she delivered the baby.

He would tell Poppy she'd died during childbirth . . . maybe that he'd found her and she'd died right after giving birth. That would be a beautiful thing. How could Poppy possibly get mad about that? Women still die during childbirth. Anthony knew Poppy would be so happy about a baby, he would soon forget about Regina.

With his mind finally at ease again, he decided to go back to sleep.

John watched from a distance as Brother Steven stood nervously outside the examining room, waiting on Regina. He kept twisting a candy wrapper with his hands. It seemed as if she'd been in there forever. John kept alert, watching carefully as nurses, doctors, and other hospital staff walked the halls. He'd made sure the door Regina entered was the only access to that room; he didn't want to take any chances of someone getting to her from a different angle.

But why was he being so paranoid? Anthony didn't even know she was in the city.

His thoughts traveled to last night. He hadn't been able to keep himself from watching her as she slept. She was . . . perfect. She'd looked so peaceful. Her beauty amazed him because it was as if she didn't see it, which made her even more beautiful, both inside and out. What he really admired was the strength she possessed to deal with the circumstances that surrounded her. She didn't complain and didn't delve into self-pity. Most people would dwell on their troubles, but not her.

The truth was, he enjoyed being with her no matter the situation — and that was the issue. For that he felt guilty. But he'd promised her mother that he wouldn't let his feelings get in the way of his job, so he constantly redirected his thoughts.

He noticed Brother Steven sitting down in a chair in the waiting area. He watched as he opened up a book, but John couldn't see what type of book it was from this distance. Brother Steven just sat there reading, and slowly, John began to notice a change in him. He started to calm down and sit still. He finally closed the book, and with his elbows on his lap and his head in his hands, he sat there quietly. It appeared as if he was praying.

It seemed that this praying thing helped people relax. He'd seen it with his sister, with Regina, and now with this monk. Filing it away in the back of his head, John kept watching the door.

Vinny arrived fifteen minutes early for his meeting with Jim. He was anxious to get this all over with, and he had to go over to Poppy's and see what the plan of action was.

He wouldn't be able to tell Poppy about Jim Wilton and copying Anthony's book — Poppy wouldn't understand. He knew he was doing the right thing, but he felt awful about the whole situation. It felt like he was betraying Poppy in some way, but Poppy had a soft spot for Anthony that blinded him to the truth, and his son's activities had to stop.

Vinny frowned at himself. What was up with this? He had to be developing a conscience or something. He walked to the shed and was surprised to see Jim already waiting for him.

"What are you doing here so early?" Vinny asked.

"Same as you, Vin. I guess we're both a bit concerned about this. So do you have it?"

Looking around to make sure no one was lurking anywhere, Vinny swung the backpack off his shoulder and pulled out the stack of copied pages. His hands shook slightly. He stared down at the pages, knowing that the moment he handed this over to Jim, life, as he knew it, would change. One day, no matter what he said now or agreed to, he would have to sit in a courtroom, face Anthony, and testify against him. He knew he would have to go into hiding for the rest of his life and never see his family again.

Sensing his hesitation, Jim said, "Vinny, you're doing the right thing. This man you work for is a monster. He has to be stopped."

Vinny looked up at him.

"You know you're doing the right thing. Don't you? I always knew that there was good in you."

Feeling like he was moving in slow motion, Vinny held the copy out to him. Jim extended his hand slowly also, and Vinny watched him. This seemed surreal.

Jim placed his hand on the copy, but before Vinny let him have it, he said, "I want you to promise me something."

"That depends on what it is."

"No. If you can't promise me this, then I won't hand this copy over."

Assuming he knew what the promise was, Jim said, "You're concerned about jail time. Well, if you testify, then we can work out a deal."

"No. It's not about me." Jim looked at him curiously, and Vinny continued, "Poppy Cavelli has come to mean a lot to me. I don't want to see him hurt. I don't know if there is anything in there that would convict him of any wrongdoing, but he's an old man now, and he's changed lately. I want you to promise me that you will let him live out the rest of his days in peace. And I mean no jail time."

Jim took a deep breath. That, obviously, was not the request he'd been expecting. He let go of his corner of the copy and rubbed his chin. He didn't appear to know what to say. "If you testify and back up what we decode, then I'm sure we can probably make a deal about the old man."

"Thanks."

"If you don't mind my asking, why do you care what happens to Antonio Cavelli?"

"He's been real good to me. He looks beaten and defeated lately. You don't know what Anthony has planned for his own father. I just don't want to see him hurt anymore than he has been already."

This time, without any hesitation, Vinny handed him the copy, and Jim took it. Vinny could see the obvious relief on his old friend's face.

"Vinny, thank you."

Vinny didn't respond; he didn't have anything to say. He just shook his head.

"Hey . . ." Jim started to say as Vinny walked away. "I'll be in touch."

Vinny waved to him as he left. He'd become the one thing he'd thought he never would be — a rat.

Much to John's relief, Regina finally came out of the examining room. Her "husband" Brother Steven walked over to join her. He couldn't make out their conversation with the doctor, but a few moments later, they shook his hand and began walking up the hall toward him. John followed them into the elevator.

"So what did he say? Is everything okay?" John asked the second the elevator doors closed.

Regina looked at him and for the first time, he noticed fear in her eyes. "The doctor is concerned about congenital heart disease," she whispered. "He says my pregnancy is at risk because the tests were not as conclusive as he wished. Some heart abnormalities are not detectable prenatally. He doesn't want me to travel at this time, so I have to stay here so he can keep an eye on my progress, and if anything happens he'll have the right equipment."

John looked at her in disbelief. "But you can't stay until the baby's born. It's too dangerous."

"I know, but I don't have a choice now, do I? I can't endanger the life of this child. I've come this far; I have to do everything I can to save him or her."

Brother Steven spoke up. "Regina's right. We came here at great risk to save this child. What good would all that do if we leave and something else goes wrong?"

John shook his head. One thing he'd learned about Regina was that she was a strong woman. If she made up her mind about something, nothing he said would change it. But this was a horrible decision to make. "If you're insisting on this, then I guess that will leave me with no other option than to take a leave of absence from the force."

"You can't do that, John, not on my account. Wouldn't it cause suspicion?"

Before he could answer her, the elevator doors opened. Putting some distance between them, John waited until Regina and Brother Steven walked out first.

A nurse reporting for work was coming toward them, but she was looking into her purse and not paying attention to where she was going. Regina, with her head down, didn't see her either, and before John could do anything, they ran right into each other.

The purse dropped out of the nurse's hands and hit the floor, its contents scattering across the tiles.

Regina was so startled that she stared straight at the nurse for a second. *So much for not giving anyone eye contact,* John thought, scowling. The nurse stared at Regina, too, and then started apologizing over and over again for bumping into her. As Brother Steven knelt down to help her pick up her things, she said, "I'm so sorry for not looking where I was going. I'm late for work, and I couldn't find my badge."

"It's okay. No harm done," Regina replied quietly.

John stepped off the elevator and started to help Brother Steven pick up the nurse's belongings lying all over the floor. He couldn't believe how much stuff this lady had in her purse. He saw her badge and handed it to her, saying, "Here you go, ma'am."

"Oh, thank you so much for all your help. I should be more careful. I feel terrible for bumping into you, especially in your condition."

Brother Steven spoke for Regina. "Oh, that's okay. No harm done. Let's go, Dear." He stood and took Regina by the arm.

Regina glanced down at the nurse's badge and read her name — Maria Malotti. That sounded so familiar to her, but she couldn't place from where.

Her heart pounding, she quickly walked away with Brother Steven, hoping that hadn't been some sort of horrible mistake.

John stayed behind for a moment to make sure everything was okay with the nurse. Her purse now in hand, she looked at him and said, "You and your friends are very nice. Thanks for helping me pick up my things. You don't expect that from New Yorkers."

"I don't know those people. I just got off the elevator with them and saw what happened. I thought I would help."

"Well, thank you."

"You're welcome."

John walked away and got close enough to Regina and Brother Steven to watch as they entered the hotel. He made sure they weren't being followed.

Nurse Maria Malotti took the elevator to the fifth floor. She put her things away, reported for duty, and then went into her first patient's room to check on her.

Inspecting the woman's IV, she said, "Hello, I'm Maria, and I'll be taking care of you today. If you need anything, just buzz me." She smiled and ran into the doctor as she exited the room. "Oh, Dr. Weinstein, I'm so sorry. I just keep knocking into people today."

"That's okay, Maria. I'm fine."

She was being such a klutz this morning! First that pregnant lady and now Dr. Weinstein.

She thought about that pregnant lady again. She had seemed overly startled, even a little frightened, when they'd run into each other. Maybe she was just shy. But the weird thing was, her voice had sounded vaguely familiar. Maria thought she'd seen her someplace before, but she just couldn't place it. Oh, well. It didn't matter. She'd better keep her mind on her work. She had enough to distract her today.

Poppy sat at the table and ate his breakfast, not saying much to Vinny. He was still shaken over the fact that his son wanted to poison him. Finally, because he had to, he said, "So when are you supposed to start putting that stuff in my food?"

"Now, sir." Vinny cleared his throat. "Anthony called me early this morning. He was upset that I hadn't started yesterday."

"I must be a terrible father for my son to grow up hating me so much."

"No, sir, I don't think that's it at all. I think Anthony loves you, or else he wouldn't hesitate to kill you. He just wants to be in charge of things and do things his way. He wants to get rid of Regina and doesn't want you to try to stop him."

There was silence for a few minutes.

Vinny couldn't help but notice how distracted Poppy was today. "Excuse me, sir, but do you have a job for me?"

"Huh? Oh, yes. I do. I spoke to Gino yesterday. He explained to me the symptoms of being poisoned with arsenic. He says a small dose would produce abdominal pain, nausea, or vomiting. So if you were supposed to give this to me during breakfast, then I guess I'm supposed to get sick today. I'm sure Anthony will either visit me or call me later to see how I'm feeling."

"Eventually, he'll want you to see a doctor. What will we do then? I'm not really going to give you this stuff, and a doctor would know that you're faking it."

"That's where Gino comes in. He'll convince Anthony he can't find anything wrong with me. Luckily, arsenic doesn't show up in a person's blood or urine. The only way it shows up is in hair and nail analysis."

"Looks like you've done your homework, sir."

"Yes, I've done my homework." Poppy frowned. "Well, let's not talk about this anymore. Just enjoy the rest of our breakfast."

"Yes, sir." As they ate, Vinny tried to steer the conversation to anything but Anthony.

John hated leaving Regina and Brother Steven alone at the hotel, but he had to find out what information Jim Wilton had. He arrived at the FBI complex and was escorted to Jim's office this time. Jim stood from his desk to greet him.

"John, I'm so glad you came." He extended his hand and John took it.

"To tell you the truth, you've got me curious," John stated.

Jim pointed to a chair opposite the desk. "Have a seat."

As John sat down, Jim tossed in front of him a copy of something that looked mighty familiar. John picked it up.

"Do you recognize this?" Jim asked, looking as if he were about to smirk.

John's eyes widened, and he sat straight up in his seat. "Where did you get this?"

"Well, I can't say who gave it to me, but let's just say someone working for Anthony intercepted it and made a copy. Our guys are working on it right now."

"I don't believe it! This is the best news I've had in a long time."

"I knew you'd be pleased. But this has to stay between us. You can't let anyone else know we have this. It would endanger the life of my informant."

"Are you accusing my partner again?"

"Look, it could be anyone in your department. Do you want to help us out or not? That's the question you need to answer. Because if you do, it means that no one, not even your partner, can know you're working with us."

At this point, John wanted Cavelli put away so badly that he was willing to do just about anything. "Okay, you've got a deal."

"Good! Now, you need to be honest with me and tell me everything you know. Do you know where Regina Cavelli is?"

"I told you to keep her out of it."

"I don't want to put her in it, but maybe I can help you to keep her safe. You can't do it alone twenty-four seven."

John thought about that for a moment. Unless he wanted to cause suspicion at the precinct, he probably could use Jim's help in watching Regina and Brother Steven; leaving them alone for long periods of time wasn't something they could afford to do, and yet he couldn't stay away from the department, either.

"Come on, John. What do you say?"

"Fine . . . I'll work with you. But are you sure you guys don't have any leaks?"

"Look, the guys who work on my detail are always being checked and rechecked, even me. We can be trusted. So what do you know?"

John took a deep breath and decided that at this point he was going to trust this man. He wasn't sure why he should or what proof he had to support that conclusion; it was just a feeling he had. In all his years of being a cop, he'd developed an instinct about people. He was right 99 percent of the time, and he knew he was right this time, about Jim, even though it kind of annoyed him to admit it. "Well, I do know where she is. She's in the city."

"Which city?"

"This city."

"You've got to be kidding me. I don't believe it. For how long?"

"Just a couple of days. She's having trouble with her pregnancy and is having some tests done by a specialist. He wanted her to stick around, so she can't travel. I've been keeping an eye on her since yesterday, but if I don't get back to work soon, the informant, whoever that is, might notice and get suspicious."

"Do you want my help?"

"Yeah, but she doesn't trust anybody. You can imagine that the life she's led makes her a bit skittish. I'll have to talk to her and Brother Steven first."

"Who's Brother Steven?"

"He's the monk helping her out. She was hiding out in his monastery. It's a long story. I'll talk to her, and if she agrees, I'll call you."

"Are you sure she's safe where she is?"

"Yeah, for now. We've been very careful."

John stood up and shook his hand again. He thanked him for his help and left, hoping he'd done the right thing. Something inside of him told him he could trust this agent, and that, to say the least, kind of surprised him.

After he left, Jim sat in his chair and looked over his file on the Cavellis. He couldn't believe that after all these years, this case was finally progressing.

And to think that Vinny would be the reason for it. After all these years of praying for him and hoping to see a change take place, this was very encouraging on several different levels.

He knew he could trust John, but he still wasn't sure who the informant was. Until they found out, they would need to proceed with caution in order to keep both Regina Cavelli and Vinny safe. He said a prayer and thanked God for His help on this case.

Stuart came into Antonio's study and said, "Excuse me, sir, but I thought you would like to know that I saw your son's car pulling up to the house. He's outside talking to Vinny."

Antonio stood up from behind his desk and replied, "Thank you, Stuart." As Stuart left, Antonio went and lay down on the couch, preparing himself both mentally and emotionally. He heard footsteps coming down the hall and knew they belonged to his son. He started to groan softly, and his look of pain wasn't hard to pull off, because Anthony had hurt him more than he had ever been hurt by anyone before.

"Poppy, are you all right?" Seeing him lying there, Anthony rushed over to the couch and knelt down beside it. He seemed genuinely concerned, and Antonio had to look away.

"I'm not feeling very well today. Must be something I ate."

"Maybe I should call the doctor to come over and see you."

Sitting up slowly but still holding his stomach, Antonio replied, "Don't be silly. My stomach feels funny — I'm a little nauseous, but I'll be fine. I think I'm going to go up and rest in my room."

"Let me help you upstairs."

Anthony did so and then helped him change into some pajamas and tucked him into bed. And the whole while, Antonio couldn't help but feel contempt toward him. Here his son was, acting as if he cared. His hypocrisy was astounding. How could Antonio have been so foolish and blind when it came to him? He would have to use this time to think of a way to stop him before he could hurt anyone else.

"I'll go and get you some toast and tea. I hear it helps settle the stomach."

"No, that's okay. I don't want you to trouble yourself like that."

"It's no trouble. You're my father, and I love you. I'm glad I stopped by. This way I can help take care of you and make sure you get better."

"Why don't you have Vinny do it? This way you can stay up here and visit with me. I think Vinny is still here."

"Sure thing. I'll get Stuart on the intercom."

Before long, Vinny came into the room, carrying a tray with the tea and toast. Looking at him, Vinny gave him a subtle nod — and Anthony knew he must have mixed more of the arsenic in the tea.

"Here you go, sir. I fixed this up myself, just like my mother used to do." He set the tray on the nightstand and then put the mug directly into Poppy's hand.

Poppy took a sip. "It's hot, but it tastes good. Thanks, Vinny. Why don't you wait downstairs while I visit with my son?"

"Yes, sir." Vinny left.

"He's a good man, Anthony. Thank you for loaning him out to me. I really appreciate his help."

"No problem, Poppy. It's my pleasure. That's why I'm here — to make your life easier."

Anthony's smile sent chills through Antonio's entire body. Could this man standing before him really be the son he raised? Antonio could almost swear that Anthony's face looked different. Maybe it was just his eyes. Whatever the change, he didn't like it.

Antonio continued to sip his tea while his son looked on, trying to hide his smirk with a concerned smile.

Chapter 18

Just in case the rectory's phones were tapped, Brother Steven insisted on going to the church to give Father Thomas and Sophia an update on Regina in person, which left Regina and John alone for a while. She listened in quiet disbelief as John explained to her what had happened in his meeting with Jim Wilton.

When he had finished, she stood and started to walk slowly through the room, trying to think. "I don't know about this, John. Are you sure he can be trusted?"

"Yes, I'm sure. I have this feeling. I can't explain it, but I know that we can trust him. He somehow got a hold of a copy of Anthony's black book and will be working on it. I'm not sure how he got it, but it has to be one of Anthony's men who intercepted it somehow. That's actually a good thing for you, because it means you won't need to testify. Once we have something on him, we can arrest him, and you can go back home and be safe."

"I don't know . . . I don't know if I'll ever be completely safe from Anthony." She sat down on the bed again and then, feeling drained, proceeded matter-of-factly, "Even in jail, I don't think he'll give up on getting me. He resents me for so many things. He resents being married to me, and he resents the way his dad cares for me. He resents the fact that I breathe."

Just in case John wasn't getting the message, she glanced at him and then said, "He wants me dead. That's when he'll finally be content. I've tried praying for him, but his heart is so hard and unyielding. I just don't want this child to grow up in an environment that could produce another Anthony. One of him is enough."

She paused and searched for the right words. Leaning forward, she studied John's eyes, trying to read what was happening on the other side of them. She hated putting this into words; voicing it made it sound so much more real and frightening, but she knew she had to. "If something should happen to me, would you promise me that Anthony will have nothing to do with raising this child? Will you help my mom get the baby to safety?"

"Don't be silly. Nothing is going to happen to you."

"For a cop, you just don't get it, do you? Don't you know Anthony at all? Do you think that prison would stop him from continuing business as usual? I used to think that if he were in jail, I would be safe. I guess I was being naive. After my dad was killed, I began to realize that not even prison would be able to harness his evil." She remembered and felt sick to her stomach. "The way he looks at me — never mind. I guess I'm warning you not to underestimate him. My life will never be the same. I'll have to live somewhere else or . . ." Her eyes stung, and she started to weep softly. "Or else he'll kill me, and then my baby would be without a mother."

Regina felt John's arm go around her, comforting her. Leaning against him, she closed her eyes and found herself being drawn into his strength. Here in his arms, she was surprised to feel her fear begin to drain away until, even though the battle still raged, she had never felt so safe. His hand tenderly caressed her cheek, and he wiped away her tears. With his thumb on her chin, he lifted her face upward, his touch as gentle as it could be. His eyes, full of compassion, seemed to penetrate her soul as he held her even closer. In this surreal moment, she knew he felt her pain. She wasn't sure how that was possible. All she knew was that with everything within her, she wanted to feel the touch of his lips against hers.

The baby's kick startled her back to reality. She suddenly realized how close their lips had come, and she pushed herself up from the bed.

"I'm so sorry, Regina. I didn't . . ." John seemed at a loss for words.

What had she been thinking — getting caught up in the moment like that? "There is nothing to be sorry for, John. I wanted you to kiss me as much as you wanted to. But nothing happened . . ." She paused. "Even though we both wanted it to. I know how you feel, and you know how I feel; let's not fool ourselves about it anymore. Our trying to avoid the issue isn't working. I . . . I just . . ."

"That's fine. I understand. I promise I won't let that happen again."

Regina's mind had a hundred thoughts sprinting through it: What if things were different? What if she was married to John instead of Anthony? What if Anthony found her? What would happen to her baby if Anthony got his hands on him?

She felt like crying again. "You know, I'm as much to blame as you are. It's so hard to do the right thing at times. I'm not perfect; if I was, then I wouldn't need Jesus. It's as much my fault . . . I should know better. I . . ." *Great. Go ahead and over explain yourself, Regina.*

She stopped talking as the door opened, and Brother Steven walked into the room. His steps slowed just inside the door, and as he looked from one of them to the other her face began to burn. "Brother Steven — what are you doing back so soon?"

"I'm sorry. I forgot the ultrasound picture. I wanted your mother to see her grandchild. I got halfway there . . . Am I interrupting something?"

Not much could have made her feel more embarrassed. The way he looked at her, she knew he knew exactly what was going on. Or what had been *just about* to go on.

"I was telling Regina about Agent Wilton and trying to convince her that we can trust him."

It was sweet for John to try to cover what was really going on. She thought about letting it ride for a moment, but then, with a grimace, she decided the better route was just to be open and honest. "John, it's okay. I told Brother Steven that I — the truth about our feelings for one another." Looking at Brother Steven, she said, "Everything is okay, though. Really. I got upset, and John comforted me, and anyway, everything is fine now. There is really nothing to worry about."

"I see." That was all Brother Steven said.

Reaching into her bag, Regina pulled out the baby's picture and handed it over to Brother Steven.

"I'm sure your mother will get a kick out of this." Before he left, he added, "Are you sure everything is okay?"

They both chimed, "Fine."

"Well, then, I'll see you both later."

When the door had closed again, they looked at each other. Regina spoke first.

"We'll finish our conversation when this is all over with, and I'm free to speak to you openly. Can we agree on that?"

"Yes, that's fine." After an awkward pause, John said, "Do you want to play gin rummy again?"

"I guess you're not tired of me beating you?" Regina asked, trying to smile. It ended up not being all that hard.

"Well, I feel a bit of luck coming on."

"You're going to need more than luck to win."

So they sat down at the table and started playing cards. They talked about everything, from sports to their favorite foods — anything but their feelings.

Slowly, Regina began to relax. She felt at ease with John, much more at ease than she felt with anybody else, even her mother. As she looked at her cards, she replayed the day in her mind. She did that whenever she felt comfortable and at peace. For some reason, focusing her thoughts relaxed her even more.

Her thoughts floated to the nurse she'd run into — literally run into. She'd looked so familiar. *I wonder if we've met somewhere before?* She knew she'd seen her before, but where? That smile stood out the most to her — she'd seen that smile before.

Staring at her cards, she frowned as the likeness came to her gradually. Mario smiled like that whenever he was being coy and trying to smooth talk his way through a situation. She frowned harder. *Mario?* Mario had a sister who was a nurse. She remembered meeting her at a party.

The color started to drain from her face. Her cards dropped onto the table.

"Regina, what's the matter? You look pale."

When she didn't answer, he said her name again, more loudly this time. "Regina!"

She snapped out of it and looked up at him. "The nurse today."

"What nurse?"

"The one that bumped into me. I remember where I've seen her."

"You've seen her before?"

"Yes, but just a few times. Her name is Maria Malotti — as in Mario Malotti's sister."

"Mario Malotti as in Anthony's right-hand man?"

"Yes, Anthony's Mario."

They both looked at each other. John got up from the table and went to the window, pulling the curtain back and peering down at the street six stories below.

"Do you think she recognized me?" Regina asked, her stomach twisting.

"No, it doesn't seem that way. She was in a rush. How well do you know her?"

"Not very well. I've spoken to her at parties, but I haven't seen her in a couple of years. I guess that's why I didn't recognize her at first. I don't think . . . she got a good look at me."

"Let's not take any chances. Why don't you pack up your things, and I'll pack for Brother Steven? We need to find another hotel. The hospital has this address so they can contact you."

"Okay. Maybe that's not a bad idea."

Poppy seemed to have gotten worse after drinking his tea. He was now in the bathroom vomiting. He wouldn't allow Anthony in there with him.

"Poppy, are you all right?" Anthony asked through the door.

Gino had told Antonio that he had to make himself throw up; he couldn't fake it, as he'd wanted to, because in order to make this as realistic as possible, he needed to be able to show the obvious physical stress vomiting produces. It wasn't easy for him, but Antonio eventually managed to produce the desired effect. He opened the door and staggered out. "I'm not sure what's wrong with me. I just don't feel well."

"That's it. I'm calling my doctor to come over here and examine you."

"No — I don't know your doctor. Help me get dressed. I want you to call Gino. I'll go see him."

Anthony didn't like the sound of that. He hated Gino and his siblings. They were too goody-goody for him, and his father had practically adopted them after their father had died.

Well, it didn't really matter; arsenic couldn't be easily traced unless you were looking for it. "Okay, Poppy, whatever you want. I'll call Gino."

Sophia answered the door for Nancy, who was sick today and had stayed at home. "Hello. May I help you?"

"My name is Brother Steven. I've come to see Father Thomas."

Sophia smiled and glanced over his shoulder to make sure there wasn't anyone lurking about down the street. "Please, come in." He entered and she closed the door behind him. "I'm very happy to meet you. I'm Sophia, Regina's mother."

"Oh, Sophia! It's good to meet you. Your daughter has talked about you often."

"How is she? I can't begin to thank you for all that you've done for her."

"I've brought something for you." He took out an ultrasound picture and handed it to her. "We thought you might like to see a picture of your grandchild."

Sophia took the picture and just stared at it. This tiny little baby was her grandchild. She could make out a head and some fingers and the baby's feet. As she studied the black-and-white image in her hand, for the first time, she actually allowed herself to think of this child as her grandchild and not a child conceived through rape. She became so excited that she forgot they were still standing in the entryway. "Please, forgive me — where are my manners? Come in and have a seat, and I'll get Father Thomas for you."

She led him to the living room, and Father Thomas walked in before she could go searching for him.

"Greetings, Brother Steven. It's so good to see you again." He gave Brother Steven a friendly hug.

Sitting down in the living room, they began to visit. Brother Steven tried to catch them up on Regina's condition and how she would have to stay longer until it was safe for her to travel.

Only partially listening, Sophia looked at the picture of her grandchild and felt her heart ache. So tiny, so vulnerable. The sound of Father Thomas and Brother Steven's conversation faded into the background of her thoughts. If Michael were here, things might be different. He always seemed to know what was best. *O Lord, protect this baby — and my baby. Will I ever see this precious child?* Worry began to fill her.

"Are you sure that Regina is all right?" she asked Brother Steven.

"Yes, she's fine. Your daughter is a very strong and courageous woman."

"I only wish I could see her for myself."

Father Thomas interjected, as she'd known he would. "Sophia, you know that would be dangerous. We're not sure if Anthony is having us watched. You don't want to take the chance of leading him to Regina now."

"I know. I just miss her so much." Sophia looked at the ultrasound picture again, and a tear rolled down her cheek. She held the picture out to Brother Steven. "Thank you for bringing this to me. It means so much that I can share in this in a small way."

"Regina wants you to keep it."

She thought about that for a moment. "I don't think that's a good idea. I can't take the chance of someone finding it. Please let Regina know how much it meant to me."

Brother Steven took the photo back and placed it in his pocket. "Well, I should be getting back. I've probably been gone too long already."

"Can't you stay a little longer, Brother Steven? We haven't seen each other in such a long time."

"No, I think I've left them alone long enough already."

Sophia thought that was an odd thing to say. "What do you mean by that? Is there something going on I should know about?"

"Oh, no, I just mean . . . I just think it would be a good idea for me to leave now before they worry about me." Rising from the chair, Brother Steven extended his hand to Sophia, saying, "It was a pleasure to finally meet you."

"It was nice meeting you also."

After saying their good-byes, Brother Steven left.

Mario sat in his car across the street. He wasn't alone; he had a couple of the guys with him. He'd been wondering who that was who had entered earlier, and now he watched as both Sophia and that priest gave the visitor a very friendly, smiling good-bye at the door.

"I wonder who that guy is. Hey, Joey, you stay here with Tony and watch the church. I think I'm going to follow that guy and see where he goes."

The two men climbed out of the car as Mario watched the priest's visitor get into a cab. He started his car and followed the yellow taxi down the street.

Regina waited in the car while John checked them out of the hotel. He handed the clerk an envelope for Brother Steven and then carried the bags out and put them in the trunk. Sitting in the driver's seat, he said, "Don't worry. I left a note for Brother Steven telling him where we're going to be. I don't feel comfortable waiting for him any longer."

"I just feel bad leaving without him, but I guess you're right. We shouldn't take any chances."

"He'll catch up with us soon."

Anthony had discovered early in life that money helps you get what you want, when you want it. Like privacy. He had yet to be disappointed in that belief. In Poppy's private room, Anthony sat in the chair by the window and waited for Gino to come see his father.

"Poppy, you don't look very well," Gino said when he entered the room. He had Poppy's chart in his hand and read the history and physical taken by the triage nurse.

"Wow. Is that what they taught you in medical school — how to state the obvious? Aren't you glad your money was so well spent, Poppy?"

Anthony didn't think Gino did a very good job of hiding his hatred of him. Frowning at him, the doctor coolly answered, "Anthony, it's *always* such a pleasure to see you. I'm glad to see you haven't lost your flair for words. Now, if you don't mind stepping outside, I'd like to examine your father."

"As a matter of fact, I do mind. He's *my* father, and I wanna stay."

Poppy spoke up at this point, his voice sounding old and rather weary, "Anthony, please don't give Gino any trouble. Just wait out in the hall with Vinny."

Anthony didn't like getting dismissed. One day when the old man was gone, he was going to settle things with a lot of people, and this quack was one of them. Glaring at Gino, Anthony left.

Gino whispered, "How are you really?"

"I'm fine. I just hate throwing up." Antonio sighed, feeling so sick at heart that it wasn't all that hard for him to sit here, helpless in a hospital bed. "Thank you again, Gino, for all your help."

Gino shook his head. "I can't believe we're having this discussion. Have you decided what you're going to do about your son?"

"No. I can't go to the police; I have to take care of this my way. This buys me some time to think."

"Poppy, your son is trying to kill you. You can't just sit by and let him."

Gino didn't understand. "He's not trying to kill me."

"Oh, that's right — he just wants you to get sick enough so that you can stay out of his way while he plans who knows what."

Antonio's look stopped him from going any further.

"I'm sorry, Poppy. It's just that Anthony has done so many evil things, and it's getting worse as he gets older. He has got to be stopped."

"Gino, you forget that I'm not an innocent old man. I've done many things that I now regret. Many things that I should be in jail for. Let me see if I can redeem my son; if I can change, maybe he can also."

"With all due respect, Poppy, you're wrong. On your worst day, you look like an angel compared to the things your son has done."

Unfortunately, Antonio suspected that Gino was right. Still, he had a hard time accepting it. He just didn't know what to do with him, but he had to do something. "I know you're right in what you're saying, but he's still my son. I blame myself for the man Anthony has become. He didn't have a very good example growing up. Now, let's get to the matter at hand — how long do I stay here?"

Gino couldn't believe the huge, gaping blind spot Poppy had for his son. For everyone's sake, he hoped this kind old man saw more clearly one day soon. It was useless to argue now. "Well, I'll run some tests and send you home tomorrow."

"Good. Bring Anthony back in and tell him that."

Mario watched as the priest's friend walked into the hotel. Hanging back, he followed him inside and watched him go up to the front desk from across the substantial lobby. The clerk handed him a note, and after reading it, he looked worried. He quickly walked back out of the hotel and hailed another cab.

That cab stopped at another hotel about fifteen blocks away. Mario watched as the man went inside. Assuming he was going to meet someone here, Mario pulled up to the parking garage and tossed his keys to the attendant, as there was no parking spot available. By the time he got inside, the man was gone. Muttering beneath his breath, Mario went up to the clerk to see if he could find anything out.

"Excuse me, but a friend of mine just came in here. He was wearing a green shirt and tan pants."

"Oh, you mean Mr. Jones?"

Mario shook his head. "Yes, Jonesy. I thought that was him. I haven't seen him in a long time. Can you tell me what room he's in? I would love to catch up on old times."

"Well, sir, if you tell me your name, I'll phone him. We aren't allowed to give out the room numbers of our guests."

"I see." Mario took out a hundred dollar bill and placed it on the counter. "But you see, I would like it to be a surprise."

The clerk's gaze darted through the lobby to see if anyone noticed what was going on. Mario took out another hundred dollar bill and placed it on the counter. The clerk's eyes grew. He wrote the numbers down on a piece of paper and slid it across the counter. Mario picked it up, left the money on the counter, and said, "Well, that's okay if you can't tell me. I'll come back later. Thank you."

When no one was looking, the clerk grabbed the money and shoved it in his pocket.

Mario took the elevator to the sixth floor and got off. This was a nice place, with rich carpets and fancy chandelier lights. He noticed that at each end of the hall were a couple of plush chairs, a little table, and a large green plant. Starting toward the opposite end, he found the room about midway, which was perfect. Continuing to the end of the hall, he took up residence in one of the plush chairs and waited. From here, he could watch pretty openly, yet not be close enough to be recognized.

Anthony and Vinny waited in Poppy's room while he was taken to another floor for some tests. As they were waiting, an attendant came by with Poppy's dinner. He left the tray on the table and when he'd gone, Anthony looked at Vinny and said, "Do you have any on you?"

"Any what, Boss?"

"Don't play stupid with me." He walked over to Vinny and searched his pockets. He found the plastic bag in his jacket. "This is what I'm talking about."

"Do you really think that's a good idea? I mean, he's already kinda sick, and we don't want to go overboard."

"When will you learn not to question me? I know what I'm doing." Anthony took a pinch of the powder and dropped it in Poppy's tea. Tying the bag shut, he chucked it back at Vinny.

His timing, as always, was perfect. Moments later, the young, noticeably pretty nurse wheeled Poppy back into the room and helped him into his bed. "It looks like your dinner has arrived." She uncovered the meal and continued, "Now you eat, because you need to keep up your strength."

She paused when she saw Anthony, leaning up against the wall with his arms folded, and as she took him in, she began to smile a slow, sultry sort of smile that he had seen several times in his life. Not from her, but from those like her. Anthony appreciated the way she practically salivated looking at him. He smiled at her in return, and raising an eyebrow, she said, "Now you make sure your father eats up."

"Oh, I will," Anthony responded, mentally removing her purple scrubs until only the stethoscope around her neck remained. When the image in his head combined with the look in her eyes, he made a quick decision and said, "Hey, Vin, why don't you help Poppy eat? I'll be right back."

Turning his attention now to his father, he said, "Poppy, I want to ask the nurse some things. Vinny will help you. I'll be right back." He kissed his father on the forehead and then left the room with the nurse.

Vinny turned around in time to see Antonio lift his teacup, and he hissed, "Don't drink that! Anthony put some of that stuff in it." He grabbed the cup from him and emptied the contents in the sink.

Antonio sat there in the bed and stared at him for a moment. "You mean he put that poison in my tea personally?" He'd done it right here in his hospital room? His son was truly determined to hurt him. Perhaps prison wasn't such a bad alternative after all; it seemed Anthony was leaving him no choice.

A short time later, they were both startled by a knock on the door. Sophia stepped into the room. She smiled, just a little, when she saw them, and Vinny figured she must not have met Anthony in the hallway.

"Antonio, are you okay? I called your home and Stuart told me you were here."

At her question, his composure changed. His face whitened, and he turned to Vinny and said, "Why don't you wait outside while I visit with Sophia?"

Vinny nodded and left the room.

"Sophia, please come closer so that I may whisper to you."

He looked terrible, so much so that she felt a little sorry for him. It didn't take a rocket scientist to know that no matter what his symptoms were, his son was somehow at the root of his problem.

She approached him and leaned in to hear what he had to say. A look of horror came over her face as Antonio began to tell her about Anthony and the arsenic. When he'd finished, she stepped back and looked at him for an eternity, trying to sort her thoughts and come up with a response. She couldn't believe a son would do such a thing to his father. She'd never expected Anthony would try to hurt Antonio. He had truly gone off the deep end to do such a thing.

At last, she simply said, "You see, if he would do this to you, whom he loves, what wouldn't he do to my daughter whom he hates?"

"You're right." His voice cracked. "I see that now, and I've been a fool. Let me help Regina. Let me send some of my most trusted men to help keep her safe and guard her wherever she is."

"You can't even protect yourself from him; how in the world will you protect Regina?"

"Maybe you're right, Sophia. But I do promise you this: If something goes wrong and Regina is found by Anthony, I will do whatever it takes to get her back to you safely. I mean *whatever* it takes. Do you understand what I'm saying to you?"

Before Sophia could respond, the door swung open, and Anthony stepped into the room. When he saw her at his father's bedside, he nearly hissed, "It seems every time I turn around, you are talking to my father, Sophia. You should really go home — my father needs his rest."

"I would love to go home, but unfortunately it blew up."

Anthony smirked at her comment. "That's right. It's unfortunate how accidents happen. You still need to leave."

"Why don't you let your father decide if he's too tired for my visit?" Turning to Antonio, she asked, "Are you getting too tired? Would you like me to leave?"

"No, I'm not too tired, Sophia, but Anthony, why don't you go home? I'll be fine here, and Vinny is outside. You can come back later if you wish. Or tomorrow."

He what? *He* was being dismissed? Again? *Yeah, right.* Anthony wasn't about to let his father get rid of him a second time today, especially in favor of this woman. "I think I liked it better when Michael was alive, and you didn't even talk to my father."

"Anthony! How dare you be so insensitive! Now apologize to Sophia."

That tone of voice was one Anthony hadn't heard since he was a little boy. Again his father favored this woman. Anthony was sick and tired of being second place to so many people — they weren't even blood relatives. Glancing at Sophia, he tried not to sneer as he said, "Sorry." He went over to his father's bedside and kissed him on the head. "I'll see you later, Poppy."

Not looking at Sophia, he walked out of the room.

Mario sat at the end of the hall and aged. That was how slowly the time seemed to crawl by. Someone had left a newspaper folded on the other chair, and he flipped through it, growing as bored as he'd ever been as he waited for the funny little man to come out of room 610. Finally, two hours later, he heard the elevator doors open, and a guy wearing a suit stepped into the hallway. He looked in Mario's direction, and Mario lowered his head, pretending a dedicated interest in his paper.

The suit approached one of the doors mid-hall — it appeared to be the one holding Mario's interest — and disappeared through it. A short time later, a second man came out and walked to the elevator.

This second man looked vaguely familiar. Mario decided to get a better look; he tossed the paper on the table and headed for the elevator. As he got closer, he suddenly recognized the guy and hurriedly bent down, hiding his face as he pretended to tie his shoes. The elevator doors opened, and he heard the man say, "Do you want me to hold the elevator?"

Mario shook his head, and he heard the doors close.

So what did this cop and the funny little man have in common? Were they friends? But who was that other guy? He took out his cell phone and called Anthony.

"Boss, you won't believe what I just saw. We need to talk. Where are you? That's good. I'm in the city also . . . Yeah, I know where that is. I can be there in about ten minutes. I'll see you then."

John was grateful when Jim came to relieve him. He should really get back to the precinct before the captain thought he was dead. That, and he had some research to do. *Maria Malotti.* Sister of Cavelli's right-hand man. He was going to see if anything came up on her. Regina was probably safe, but at this stage of the game, they couldn't afford to take any chances.

Walking out to his car, he thought again about how he couldn't wait until this whole mess was over with.

Maria was at her station, finishing up some charts before her shift ended so that she could go home. She was so looking forward to going home and taking a hot bath. It had seemed like today would never end, and the weirdness had all started when she'd bumped into that pregnant lady. It had all gone downhill after that.

That woman still reminded her of someone. She could almost picture her, except with different hair. Who in the world did she remind her of? She hated it when she couldn't remember things.

Anthony had to wait for Mario at the restaurant, and it didn't improve his mood any. He hated waiting for anything. Mario should have known that.

And apparently, he did. He started apologizing the minute he came through the door. "I'm sorry, Boss, but I had trouble finding a spot to park, and the garage across the street was full — "

"What did you want to see me about?"

"Well, I was watching that priest's house, and I saw this funny little man come out, and I decided to follow him."

"Why did you do that?"

"Well, he seemed so chummy with Sophia and that priest when he left that I took a chance and followed him. Anyways, he goes to the city, and I followed him to a hotel downtown, and then right after he gets there, he leaves again."

Anthony was getting bored with this. He had a date with his father's cute nurse coming up, and he didn't have time for all of this chatter. "Get to the point before my hair goes gray."

"Yeah, well, I decided to keep an eye on him when I saw that cop coming out of his hotel room after this other guy in a suit goes in there. What do you suppose that means?"

As Maria was getting into her car, it suddenly dawned on her who that woman reminded her of: Regina Cavelli.

Regina Cavelli? That couldn't have possibly been her; she'd been missing for a long time now. But what if it *was* her? She knew Anthony had been looking for her. Maybe she should call Mario. It would look good for her brother if he found his boss' wife — if that was, in fact, who the pregnant lady turned out to be.

Not only would it make her brother look good, but it might make Anthony take notice of her. He would be so grateful. She wondered if that reward was still available. She wouldn't bring it up because that would be tacky, but she sure wouldn't turn it down if it was offered.

Anthony tapped his fingers on the table, trying to decide if Mario's little goose chase was actually something or not. Looking at Mario closely, he asked, "Are you sure it was Nelson? Did he see you?"

"Yeah, I'm sure it was him, and he didn't notice me. If he did, he would've said something."

"I had a conversation with our friend at the precinct, and he thinks the cop is with Regina. If that's true, then maybe she's in that hotel room."

Mario pulled back a little, frowning. "Boss, she's not the smartest lady ever, but she's smart enough to never come back here. That would just be stupid."

"True. It'd definitely have to be — "

Mario's cell phone suddenly started buzzing. Anthony scowled at him, annoyed at the interruption, but with a nod gave Mario permission to answer it.

"Yeah . . . Maria, not now. I'm in a meeting. Okay, make it quick. What? Are you sure?" He shot a quick look at Anthony. "Thanks, Sis. I'll talk to you later, all right?" Hanging up, he shook his head and said, "That was my sister, the nurse. She thinks she bumped into Regina today at the hospital."

Seriously? Anthony straightened. "Is she sure?"

"No, not a hundred percent, but it sure did look like her."

That was the best news he'd heard in a long time. "Well, maybe she's not as smart as we think. We better get to that hotel and see if she's really hiding out with your funny little man."

John arrived at the precinct to find his partner doing paperwork. Frank looked up as he approached his desk, irritation in his eyes. When he saw it was John, without pause he went right back to his paperwork.

John felt like groaning. "Frank, come on. Don't ignore me. I want to thank you for covering for me. I wouldn't ask if it wasn't necessary. Aren't you going to talk to me?"

"Talk to you. Why? I don't believe anything that comes out of your mouth. We're supposed to be partners, yet you treat me like a stranger. You don't tell me anything that's going on, like I'm somebody who can't be trusted. I'm really tired of it, and I want you to know that I'm through covering your . . ."

Frank looked up, about to finish that sentence with some choice words, but then he paused. "Captain."

John turned around. Captain Merrill was standing right behind him. "Hey, Captain."

"How are you feeling, John?"

"I'm better, sir. I'm sorry I haven't been in, but I was really sick."

"I tried calling you, but there wasn't an answer," the captain said.

"Maybe you called when I was at my doctor's appointment. I didn't get a message."

"I didn't leave one. Well, your partner here has been carrying your weight for long enough. Why don't you catch up to speed and see what you can do to help him with all the backlog?"

"Yes, Captain." John watched as the captain walked away, and when the man had disappeared back into his office, John, wishing he were somewhere else, looked down at Frank again. All he saw was animosity looking back at him. How long were they supposed to keep this up? Now that the FBI had a copy of Anthony's book, the corner had been turned and it was only a matter of time now before this case was closed. Maybe there was a way he could show Frank he trusted him without revealing too much. He'd have to think about that. "So," he said finally, "what can I do to help?"

Sitting in the overstuffed chair by the window, Regina was trying to read a book she'd found in the desk about baby animals, but the situation made concentrating incredibly hard. With a sigh, she closed the book and looked around the room.

Brother Steven was playing solitaire at the table. He'd been such a big help in this whole ordeal.

And John had been right about Jim Wilton. As she looked at him across the room, she could sense there was something trustworthy about him, even though she didn't have any logical reason to trust this FBI man. He was a perfect stranger to her. She watched as he took a little book from his pocket and thumbed through it.

She was a bit curious, so she asked, "What's that?"

He shrugged. "Just my pocket Bible. I always carry it with me. I was just praying . . ."

Regina found that interesting — a tough FBI man reading the Bible. She smiled at him. "You're a Christian?" she asked.

Jim looked puzzled by the question. "Yes?"

"Well, this is a small world. So am I. Were you praying for me?"

"Well . . . um, yes, I was. I always pray for the people involved in my current case."

Before she could continue the conversation, his cell phone began to ring. "Excuse me," he said to Regina and answered it. "Hello."

And that was the end of the last normal conversation he had all day.

The man on the other line said, "Hello. You don't know me, and you might think this is crazy — but I need to speak to Regina."

That was the last thing Jim had been expecting to hear. He didn't recognize the phone number; it definitely wasn't local, and he felt his face turning white as all the possibilities raced through his head. Who had his number? "I'm sorry, but you have the wrong number. I don't know anyone by that name."

Before Jim could hang up, the man said, "Please, don't hang up. God gave me this number and said that I could use it to reach a young woman named Regina. I have a verse for her . . . if you wouldn't mind telling her to read Proverbs 27:12."

"Who are you? How did you get my private number?"

"Sir, I assure you this is not a joke. Whether you believe me or not, I had a visitation from an angel who asked me to pray for Regina. As I was praying for her, God gave me this verse and your number. Please, just read the verse." The man hung up.

Regina looked at Jim, concern lining her forehead, and asked, "Who was that? You look a bit upset."

Jim wasn't quite sure what to do. Never in his life had he ever gotten a phone call quite like that one before. Yes, God had given prophets of old messages for other people, and he'd heard fantastic stories of miracles of yesteryear, but . . . now?

But how else could this man have gotten his number? With very little exception, nobody knew he was here, this involved. Could it possibly be a God thing? He decided to check out the Scripture the man had given him.

"What are you doing?" asked Regina.

"One minute." After reading it, he looked up and tried to explain. "Well, the craziest thing just happened. That phone call was . . . for you, actually. A man was asking for you." He instantly could see the fear in her eyes. "No, don't be afraid; he told me that *God* told him to call you and that *God* told him my phone number. He said to read Proverbs 27:12. So I looked it up, but in looking at it, it's not making that much sense."

"What does it say?" Regina asked.

"Well, it says, *'The prudent see danger and take refuge, but the simple keep going and suffer for it.'* But I don't really get it. I mean, you are in hiding already. So even if it meant something . . . what?"

Regina thought about that for a moment. "That's very odd."

"To say the least."

"But if that *was* some kind of prophet or something, maybe God is trying to tell us something," Brother Steven said quietly, taking his time as he processed. "Weren't you just praying for Regina? Maybe He's answering your prayers. Why don't we all pray and ask God what it means?"

Regina hauled herself out of the chair and stretched her hands out to them. As they held hands and prayed, she felt something shift in the air. It was a bonding. The only way she could describe it later was that this FBI man, who had been a stranger only a few hours before, became her brother in Christ.

As Anthony and Mario arrived at the hotel, Mario asked, "Boss, do you think we need to call for backup?"

"The day you and me can't handle Regina, a funny little man, and some other geek, we might as well call it a day."

"So what are you going to do to her, Boss?"

"She's still pregnant, so for now nothing. But that's a good question."

"How about the abandoned warehouse you have in downtown Brooklyn?"

"Yeah, I've thought about that before. Call Joey and tell him to get some things ready, like a bed and some food. That way she can give birth there, too."

Mario stepped back outside to make the call, and Anthony decided to go and see if he could get any help from the goofy-looking kid behind the front desk.

"I'm getting a bad feeling," Regina said. "I feel like something bad is going to happen."

The others nodded their heads in agreement.

That was it, then. Jim said, "Let's get out of here. I think we should move to another hotel."

"Is that necessary? I mean, I already moved once today."

"Yeah, I think it is. You're right — I feel like God is trying to warn us about something, and we shouldn't ignore that. If God would go through the trouble of contacting some stranger to get a message to us, don't you think we should listen? Get your things together." Jim didn't want to take any chances.

Reading the young man's nametag, Anthony said, "Excuse me, Tim, but I was wondering if you could help me with something."

"Yes, sir. What can I do for you?"

"My wife is staying upstairs on the sixth floor because we had a fight. I messed up, and I'm afraid she won't open the door if she sees me standing there. I was wondering . . . would you be kind enough to come upstairs with me and knock on her door?"

The young man hesitated. "I'm sorry, sir, but that would be against our rules of privacy. I can't do that for you."

Anthony reached into his back pocket and removed his wallet. He took out two one-hundred dollar bills and put them on the counter in front of the young man.

Tim looked down and saw how much money was there, but he didn't want to take the chance. What if this was some kind of test the owner set up? Who puts two hundred dollars in front of someone to just knock on a door?

"What about John? Will you be able to contact him and let him know we left? I mean, he's the one who checked us in. Who will check us out?"

"Don't worry about that, Regina. I'll have John come back and check you out of the room. We're not stopping anywhere near the lobby. We're getting out of here as quickly as possible."

"I'm sorry, sir, but I can't help you," Tim said.

Anthony placed another two one-hundred dollar bills on the counter. He could tell that made a difference to this punk kid. "Look, I would appreciate it greatly if you helped me out."

"Sir, I could get fired for this."

"If you do, I'll give you a job with my organization. What do you have to lose?" Anthony gave him a big, toothy smile to reassure him as the kid took the money, crammed it into his pocket, and grabbed his master key card. "Thank you so much. You're helping to save a marriage."

Regina, Jim, and Brother Steven stepped into the elevator, and Jim pressed the button for the garage floor, where he'd parked his car.

Mario joined Anthony and Tim as they headed for the elevator. Anthony pressed the button and waited for the elevator to rumble down to the first floor. Why was there only one elevator working in this place? *What a dive,* he thought to himself.

Jim suddenly pressed the button for the second floor, and the elevator stopped, the doors sliding open.

"What are you doing?" Regina asked.

"Can you walk down the rest of the way?"

"I think so, if I take it easy."

"Good. I'll feel better if we get off this elevator and take the stairs."

"What's taking that elevator so long?" Anthony demanded.

"It's back on its way down; someone must have gotten on."

"Maybe we should take the stairs," Mario suggested.

"Here it is," Tim said as the doors opened.

The three walked onto the elevator. When they got off on the sixth floor, Tim rang the bell at door number 610. No one answered. So he said, "Open up please! I have a message for you from the front desk." Still no response.

Shrugging his shoulders, he said, "I guess she must have stepped out."

"Use your key to open the door."

"Sir, I really can get in trouble for that."

Anthony had enough. He was losing his patience with this pimple-faced brat. Nose to nose with him, he said, "Look, kid, I like you, but I need to get into that room. Either you open it up with that card of yours, or I'll open you up. You got me?"

As Anthony stared him down, the kid's breathing got heavy. He looked scared, which was the reaction Anthony wanted. Scared people always co-operated better.

Tim opened the door and then quickly walked away. Anthony and Mario stepped inside and searched the room. There was nothing out of the ordinary. People had obviously been there, but they were now long gone, and they hadn't left anything behind.

"Mario, call Maria and see if she can find out why Regina was at the hospital."

"Sure thing, Boss."

Chapter 19

By the time they'd checked into the motel last night, it was late and Regina had just gone to bed, completely exhausted. This morning, the sun had woken her up early, and for the last couple of hours, she'd been trying to occupy her mind.

Brother Steven walked back and forth through the room, praying.

Jim also paced and from time to time glanced out the window, as if he were expecting trouble. The phone call had unnerved them all just a little. Jim hadn't told John about it yet; he'd just given him a quick call late last night to tell him they'd moved again. Regina could only imagine what John would have to say when he did hear about it.

She looked around the small motel room. It wasn't much to speak of, especially when compared to the last hotel, but it was clean. There were two double beds, a small television, a couple of nightstands, a very small bathroom that had seen better days, and an old rotary telephone.

Not wanting to take any chances, Jim had found the remote motel just outside the city limits. Unfortunately, it was about an hour away from the hospital, which made Regina nervous. If something should happen to the baby, she hoped she wasn't too far away from help. Jim had his reasons for coming this far; he'd tried explaining them to her, but that hadn't gone very well.

The silence broke as Jim suddenly picked up where they'd left off last night. "Regina, listen to me. I've been doing this for a long time. You can't stay in the city. It was too risky and you're too easy to find. I don't think you should even give the hospital your phone number."

"Why? How are they going to contact me when the test results come in?"

"You can call and check daily. They don't need your address or number. After what you told me about Maria Malotti, you can't take any chances. If you remembered who she is, it's a good possibility she'll remember you."

"I'm concerned for my baby. I risked so much coming here for help. We don't even know if we were really in any danger."

"You're right, of course. We didn't have any hard proof. Coming from an old FBI guy like myself that probably sounds ridiculous, but from a position of faith — we did the right thing. You have to trust me if I'm going to protect you and the baby."

Regina hated to admit it, but she knew he was right. This whole situation was getting out of hand. She tried not to give in to despair, but at times it was difficult. "Fine. You win. Have you contacted John again to tell him about the phone call?"

"No, but I'll do it now."

"Thanks." Regina sat on the edge of the bed. She was so concerned for the baby and their future that her stomach was in knots. How had she ever found herself in this situation? Her thoughts began to dredge back toward the past again, and she forced herself to think of other things. So far, dwelling on the past hadn't done her any good; it only depressed her. She needed to keep her mind focused on the present.

While Jim phoned John, Brother Steven came over and sat beside her. "Hey, it's going to be okay." As if he could read the conversation going on in her head, he added, "You have two very determined men looking after you to make sure you're safe. What could go wrong?" He smiled, trying to reassure her.

"You don't know my husband. I've made him look bad in front of his people. I had the nerve to leave him, and I'm sure that by now he must know that I'm the one who gave the copy of his book to the police. Anthony believes in a very warped type of justice, and he won't rest until he gets it. I'm safe until this child is born and after that . . . all bets are off."

"He would really kill you and leave your child . . . his child without a mother?"

Regina could easily read Brother Steven's troubled look. He didn't have much of a poker face.

"Without hesitation." She placed her hand on Brother Steven's and looked at him. "I think it's time you return home. You've been so helpful up until now, but I couldn't live with myself if you somehow got caught in the crossfire."

"No, I'm staying until you have the baby, and I can take you back to safety," Brother Steven insisted. "You can't change my mind."

Vinny helped Antonio out of the car and then up the walk and into the house. Anthony followed them home in his own vehicle.

"Poppy, I'm so glad you were cleared to come home," he said as soon as they were inside the house. Antonio didn't answer him. "Why don't I help you up to your room?"

"No! Stuart can help me. I really don't need to be babied by *you*!"

"Whoa, Poppy — are you upset with me in some way?"

Apparently, Antonio needed to get his emotions in check. He couldn't allow himself to lash out like that at Anthony. If he kept exploding like this, his son would back off, when Antonio needed to keep him close until Regina was found. Biting his tongue and swallowing his pride, Antonio tried to encourage him.

"Anthony, forgive your old father. I've been so sick, and the doctors can't even tell me why. I'm just frustrated, but not at you. You've been so good to me through all of this. Why don't you get back to work and take Vinny with you? I won't need him the rest of the day."

"Okay, whatever you say." He gave his father a kiss on the cheek. "Vin, come on. We have work to do."

Vinny acknowledged Poppy with a nod. When they got outside, Anthony stopped short. "Look, there is lots going on today. I have to go pay Mario's sister a visit."

Somewhat confused, Vinny repeated, "Mario's sister? Which one . . . Maria or Anna Marie?"

"Maria."

"What for?"

"What is this — Twenty Questions? I'll explain on the way. Let's take your car. I'll leave mine here, and you can send one of the boys to pick it up later."

"Anything you say, Boss."

Antonio watched them talk from inside the house. Then, tightening his jaw as Vinny and Anthony got in the car and drove away, he couldn't help but feel contempt for his own son. Anthony was responsible for Michael's death, Sophia's home being destroyed, raping Regina — all Anthony. Why hadn't he seen it coming? In some ways, he was glad Anthony's mother wasn't alive to see all of this. It would break her heart to see what their son had become. This whole mess was Antonio's fault; he just had to make it all right again. He felt the weight of it.

Stuart came up behind him. "Sir, is there anything you require?"

The burden of his circumstances was more than Antonio could bear at the moment. He heard Stuart's question but hesitated slightly before answering. "No, thank you. I'm fine. I just need to be alone to think some things through."

It was seven in the morning and John was still at home when Jim's call came in. Jim told him about the odd phone call yesterday and also that he'd be able to call on another agent if John couldn't get away. And that was good, because there was no way John could leave the precinct today without causing suspicion. The captain was already fuming at him for all the time he'd missed. He also had to try to mend fences with Frank. He felt like he'd really blown it.

And on that note . . . how bad would it really be if he were to tell Frank a little about what was going on? Not all the details, just a few. Enough to get John out of hot water with him. He'd been thinking about it, and he knew he could word things in such a way that Regina wouldn't be compromised.

He looked at the phone for a minute and then, making the decision, he picked it up and dialed Frank's house. "Hey there, Lynette. How are you, Sweetie? . . . That's good. Is your dad still at home? Good. Can you get him for me?" He waited for only a couple of minutes, but it felt like ten. "Look, Frank, we need to talk. Can you meet me at the Fifth Street Diner in about twenty minutes? Please — it's important."

After a long pause, Frank finally agreed.

"Good. I'll see you there."

Mario wasn't finding his sister very cooperative. He had to convince her to help them out with this, or else he knew that Anthony would come try to convince her himself. That was something he was afraid of because Anthony was very unpredictable. And this was Mario's kid sister. He'd always looked out for her, and now he'd gotten her into a mess.

"Look, Maria," he said, following her into her living room, "you have to find out where she's staying and what doctor she's seeing there."

"It's a big hospital, Mario. How am I going to find that out? I'm just a nurse. Besides, she probably used a fake name — it's like finding a needle in a haystack."

Why was she being so difficult? It wasn't like he was asking her to go through the entire hospital with Regina's picture, asking everybody she met if they'd seen her. "You don't know Anthony Cavelli. When he gets it into his head that someone can help him with something, he doesn't let it go." Mario knew she hated it when he told her what to do, but this was important; she had to understand that.

"Mario, you're being ridiculous. He's always been very nice to me."

"He's my boss and believe me when I tell you that there's a side to him . . . I don't want to have to . . ." He sighed. How was he going to convince her without telling her exactly what kind of man he worked for? She'd always looked up to him, and for that, he would protect her from this no matter what he had to do. "Maria, listen to me. I'm serious." He took her by the shoulders and looked into her eyes. "I love you. You're my baby sister. You have to find a way of getting that information."

She stared at him, and relief washed through him as he saw he'd finally gotten through to her. "Mario, you're scaring me," she whispered. Her voice quivered. "What if I can't do that?"

The doorbell rang.

"I'm not expecting anyone. It's probably a salesman." She walked over to the front door and looked through the peephole. "Oh, my God! It's Anthony Cavelli!" Her eyes wide, she looked at Mario like a frightened little girl. "What is he doing here?"

"I don't know. He's probably here to talk to you. I told him I would handle it. Don't just stand there — open the door!"

Maria took a deep breath and opened the door. Anthony stood there with a flashy smile on his face, and Vinny was behind him, looking the way Vinny always looked — like he was about to kill someone. The way Anthony studied her made her feel uneasy. Maybe it wouldn't have just a few minutes ago, but Mario had scared her. There was a lump in her throat, yet she managed to say, "Mr. Cavelli, please come in."

"Thank you, Maria, but you can cut out that mister stuff and call me Anthony."

Vinny entered behind him.

Mario looked uncomfortable, Anthony thought. It must not be going well, so it was a good thing he'd come by. Mario was usually very good at getting people to cooperate, but Anthony figured he might be a little soft this time because it involved his sister. Mario was one of the most ruthless men he knew — except where his sisters were concerned. His father had been killed when they were young, and Mario had always looked after them. "Mario, how's it going?"

"Good, Boss. Maria wants to help us out. We were just figuring out how. It's all going to work out."

Anthony had never seen Mario so flustered. What was up with that? He watched him shoot a glance toward Vinny, and frowning, Anthony filed that away for future reference. Something had been going on between Mario and Vinny lately. They didn't seem to be getting along at all. For a moment, he wondered what had caused it, and then he wondered if there was a way he could possibly use it to his advantage.

"Did you come up with anything?" he asked the sister calmly.

"Not yet, but we're working on it." Mario chuckled, trying to keep the mood light. Anthony looked at him and then at Maria and wasn't happy with what he saw. Mario was usually smooth, pretty sly. But he had yet to allow his sister to say a word, and it struck Anthony that he was lying for her — a very, *very* bad move for Mario to make. Apparently, he needed to be reminded who was boss here, even where his sister was concerned. "Mario, why don't you and Vinny wait outside for me? I'd like to talk to Maria alone."

"Boss, please — she's my sister."

And there it was. Anthony was annoyed and didn't try to hide it. "You can trust me with your sister, man. I just want to talk to her."

When Mario still balked, Anthony stepped up to him and glared, making a promise that didn't have to be voiced. Mario looked away. "Now step outside."

Leaving her alone in here was like knowingly leaving a baby in a snake's nest. Mario hated this, but what could he do? He'd run out of options here. There was no telling what Anthony would do to her, what he would say, and Maria looked so frightened. Mario had to leave her, per Anthony's orders, but he'd be keeping a very close ear to the door.

He looked at her as he passed and squeezed her hand to reassure her that everything would be okay. Vinny opened the door and motioned for Mario to go first. He looked a little smug, Mario thought.

"Would you like something to drink, Anthony?" Maria said.

He heard her voice shake. She was nervous, and he knew how to use that. Exactly what had Mario told her about him? "Sure. Anything cold would be good."

He followed her into the kitchen area. It was small, with a refrigerator, a sink, and a four-burner stove and oven combination. There wasn't room enough for more than two people. He stood in the doorway and watched her as she pulled a glass from a cabinet and filled it with iced tea.

"You know, I'd forgotten what a beautiful woman you are."

She didn't say anything as she handed him the glass.

As Anthony took the drink from her, his fingers touched hers instead of the glass, and he kept his hand there, on top of hers like that. Knowing what he was about, she looked away and tried to keep her heart from sprinting. With his other hand, he gently lifted her face.

Her right hand still trapped beneath his, he placed the drink on the counter and then moved closer to her until his face was barely a handbreadth away. In a soft and seductive voice, he said, "I understand you've seen my wife."

So much for keeping herself under control. Stuttering, she answered, "I think it was her. It was just a . . . a brief encounter." Maria wasn't sure if she was more afraid or excited at this moment. This was the closest she had ever been to such a powerful man. Her heart raced, and she could barely breathe.

Anthony began to stroke her face with his thumb, his hand still cupped under her chin. He leaned in until he could smell her perfume and discovered it worked pretty well for her; she was an attractive woman. "I'm confident that you will be able to find out where she is and what doctor she saw, no matter how difficult it is. I have faith in you."

Releasing the glass, he put his hand on the small of her back and drew her against him. He felt her breathing getting heavy. He could tell she was attracted to him and afraid of him at the same time, and he figured he could get further with sugar than with vinegar. Most women would do anything for him if he asked.

"All I want is the chance to see my child and raise it. She's trying to keep me from doing that. Do you think that's right?"

All Maria could do was shake her head.

"You'll help me then?"

She nodded.

Anthony leaned down. She closed her eyes as he kissed her. He kept his eyes open to judge her reaction. Slowly, he took a step back and watched as she opened her eyes, her face flushed, and when she looked at him, he knew he had her right where he wanted her.

Maria couldn't believe what had just happened. Anthony Cavelli had kissed her. She couldn't wait to tell Mario. All kinds of thoughts rushed through her mind: thoughts of a kiss leading to other things, better things — not only for her but for her brother, too. "I'll do everything I can to get you that information," she whispered.

"Good. I knew you wouldn't disappoint me. Maybe when this is all over with, we can talk more about that kiss."

His comment made her face warm, but she felt like he had enjoyed kissing her as much as she had him. A woman knows when a man wants her. Why wouldn't he want her? She was beautiful and she was smart — at least, that was what she'd been told all her life.

"I'm going now. When will you be able to get back to me with the information I asked for?"

"I go back in today, and I'll snoop around for it. The fact that she's pregnant narrows the list of doctors she could have seen, and I know someone in registration who might be able to help us out."

Suddenly she was just full of ideas. Anthony smiled at her. "I'll talk to you later then."

He winked at her and walked toward the door. He opened it to find an anxious Mario, who quickly walked into the apartment and froze when he saw his sister standing there smiling. His expression was actually pretty pitiful. Anthony smirked at him.

"What?" Maria asked her brother.

"I've never seen such a big smile on your face before. What's up with that?" He glanced at Anthony and frowned.

Mario sounded quite serious, but she brushed off his concern. "Nothing. I promised I would help." Maria was not about to let him rob her of this moment. You would think he'd be pleased it went well, instead of just standing there like a sourpuss.

When John arrived, Frank was already at the diner, sitting in a booth by the window and drinking coffee. As he walked in, John saw the same look of hurt and mild aggression in his eyes that he'd seen at the station the day before.

"Hey, Frank," John said as he slid into the booth. Frank didn't respond. "Look, I know you're mad at me for keeping you in the dark, but I have my reasons. It's not because I don't trust you."

"Ha!"

"Hey, man, I trust you with my life."

"Really . . . but not Regina's."

"It's not my decision; it's hers. You can't imagine how hard it's been for her. She's running for her life and to protect her baby."

"It's not only her baby, John — it's Cavelli's kid, too. That's something you wish wasn't true, isn't it? Maybe you wish it was yours."

That stung. And it made him mad. "Hey, knock it off. You really don't know what you're talking about. She's not that kind of woman. I have found her to be nothing but strong and good . . . and honorable."

Frank and John just stared at each other.

"I can see it in your eyes," Frank said. "You really have it bad, don't you? And that, my friend, is what will get you killed."

John knew he was right, but he wasn't about to admit that to him. He tried to steer the conversation in another direction. "She's having trouble with the baby. She's in hiding, and I'm just trying to help her stay away from Cavelli. He'll kill her if he finds her."

Frank looked out the window when he spoke. "If you don't want my help, then fine." He got up. "But know this — we're through as partners. I'm putting in a request for a new one. Someone I know will trust me."

"Frank, please don't. Sit down. I'll tell you whatever you want to know about it, except where she is. Is that fair?" John didn't want to lose Frank over this. He'd been a good, faithful partner and friend. He didn't know what he would have done after Sam died, if it hadn't been for Frank and his family. "Please, just give me another five minutes. I deserve that much, at least."

Frank hesitated. Finally, with a glare, he sat back down. "Okay . . . five minutes. Why don't you start at the beginning?"

So John told Frank everything from the beginning. How he'd gotten involved with her and how he'd helped her escape New York. How she was back now and why. He even broke down and told him his feelings for her. Once the truth came out he felt better, like a load had been lifted from his shoulders. The only part he left out was where she was now and Jim Wilton's involvement. He'd made promises to them about that.

"You're forgiven," Frank said.

"Thanks, man." He wasn't sure if this had completely fixed the issue, but it was a start.

Sophia kept peeking out the window. She'd seen two very suspicious-looking characters across the street and was trying to figure out if they were the police, Anthony's men, or Antonio's. She didn't know who they belonged to, but she knew they belonged to somebody.

As time went on, things seemed to be getting more and more out of control. At this stage of life, she should be enjoying herself with Michael; he should be here to share in the joyous event of the birth of their first grandchild. But that wasn't a possibility anymore, which broke her heart every time she thought of it. Her husband was gone, her daughter was running for her life, and she had no home. How joyous could a baby's birth be when he'd been conceived out of hate and his father was trying to kill his mother?

She had found that bitterness was something she fought daily, sometimes hourly. She tried so hard not to let it get to her, but it was like trying to climb a ten-foot brick wall. Her feelings for Antonio were only adding to the confusion. All those years of hating him, and now he might be Regina's only hope.

Slowly, she allowed herself to wonder what would happen if she knew for sure who Regina's father was, but what good would that do now? It would only serve to taint Michael's memory and add more hardship to Regina's already insane situation.

"Sophia, are you all right?" Father Thomas asked.

She was so deep in thought she hadn't heard him approach. Turning from the window, she said, "Father Thomas, I think we need to be very careful; there are two men out there across the street in a parked car. I can't really get a good look at them so I don't know who they are."

"You mean, are they friend or foe?"

"Yes, that's exactly what I mean." She sighed. "When is this all going to end?"

"I wish I had an answer for you, but I don't. We just have to keep praying that it all works out for the best."

Sophia thought about that for a moment. She was almost ashamed at
how small her faith had become lately, and yet, at the same time, she felt so
weary of pursuing something that didn't seem to be pursuing her in return.
"Do you think that's going to be enough?"

"In my line of work, I find that praying is always the best option. And
in this case, I know it's the best thing for you and your daughter."

"I understand why *you* would feel that way, but I'm not so sure."

Father Thomas took her right hand in his. "It's okay. I can be strong for
both of us, but in any situation, the power of prayer strengthens when two
or more are gathered in His name."

Sophia rolled her eyes, not caring if she appeared childish.

"Trust me. I've seen it work. So have you, actually. It couldn't hurt now,
could it?"

Sophia felt as if she had to try something — anything at this moment,
even if it was something that seemed to have failed in the past. Desperate,
she decided to give it another try. "I guess you're right. Some days I believe
that more than others."

"Let's pray now . . . together, for Regina. Will you join me?"

Sophia knew there was power in prayer. She did know that, even at
times like these when she wanted to avoid the very thing she knew would
help. Why was that? She wished she knew. She went beyond what her heart
wanted to do and answered, "Yes, I'll pray with you." So they joined hands
right there and started to pray.

Maria felt so very nervous as she walked into the hospital. There were
three really good doctors who Regina would probably have seen if she were
having complications with her pregnancy, which seemed to be what Mario
and Anthony were thinking. She just had to figure out which one she had
seen that day. Maybe she could narrow the list a bit.

Dr. Paulus dealt with several issues with complicated pregnancies, so it
was possible Regina had gone to him. Then there was Dr. Fisher, who dealt
mostly with infertility problems, and since Regina was already pregnant,

he probably wouldn't have had her as a patient — probably. Then there was Dr. Weinstein. He was world renown for his advances in his field.

So those were Maria's best possibilities. If she were Regina, who would she go to?

Probably Dr. Weinstein. Maybe she should start there. If not, then Dr. Paulus would be the next choice.

She had a good guess where to start, but figuring out which fake name Regina was using was going to be the hard part. First, Maria would have to get Dr. Weinstein's patient list, which wasn't going to be easy, and then she would have to pick it apart, name by name, and she wasn't looking forward to that.

But then again . . . maybe getting the list wouldn't be *that* hard. She thought of Ricky, who worked in registration. Ricky had been attracted to her for a while. Now would be the time to cash in on that, if she had to, but hopefully, she could think of a less distasteful way than giving him any of her favors. If he could print out a list of patients Dr. Weinstein had seen that day, that would certainly help. Maybe Mario could track down each one to see who was a phony.

She walked over to the registration desk on the fifth floor where Dr. Weinstein's office was located. She saw Ricky and gave him a big smile. "Hi, Ricky. How are you doing today?"

"I'm fine," he stuttered and after a second or two remembered to add, "How are you?" Maria knew she made him nervous.

"Well, I need to see the list of patients seen by Dr. Weinstein last Tuesday."

"You . . . do? Why?"

"I need to recheck one of the charts that Dr. Weinstein mentioned to me, and I can't remember which patient it is, and . . . Can you do this or not?" Maria smiled at him coyly.

Ricky looked at her for a moment. "You don't work for him — why would you need to recheck a chart?"

"I guess you haven't heard. I'm being transferred next week, and he wants me to review this particular case in order to . . . um, get familiar with the types of patients he sees." Maria knew she was blowing it. Ricky was too smart for a lame excuse like that. *But the things we do for love,* she thought.

He was hesitant. "Maybe I should call Dr. Weinstein myself and see if that will be all right."

Maria looked around and saw that most of the staff was out to lunch. She stepped behind the desk and leaned against Ricky from behind. She whispered in his ear, "Ricky, I would really appreciate it if you would do me . . . this favor. I don't want Dr. Weinstein to think I can't handle a simple request. He might change his mind about my coming to work for him. I would hate to lose that extra cash."

"A favor?"

Maria leaned down, close enough for Ricky to smell her perfume and feel her chest move up and down with each breath she took. "Yes, but I wouldn't expect you to do one for me without my doing one for you." She placed her hand on his back as she whispered softly, "If you give me the printout, then maybe later tonight you and I can go have a drink."

He swallowed. "I don't know. I don't want to get in trouble. I don't want to lose my job."

Maria started to move her hand slowly along his spine, greatly hoping she was wearing him down.

She was. "Okay, but you can't tell anyone I did this."

Victory was hers. Anthony would be proud. "It'll be our little secret. So may I have it now?"

"No problem." Ricky glanced down the hallway and saw that they were alone. Frowning to himself, he printed off the patient list and handed it to her. "So what time tonight?"

"How about six thirty, when my shift ends? We could meet at the bar across the street." Later, she would have to come up with a way to bow out of it.

"That'll be great."

Maria walked to her desk and called her brother. "Yeah, it's me. I've got the patient list. Yeah, I know. You're welcome. So you'll come by and get it? Good. I'll see you then."

She was relieved. She really didn't want to disappoint Anthony. Not only that, but he'd scared her a little, the way powerful men do — at the same time, she couldn't help feeling attracted to him. His position was irresistible. His dark brown eyes glistened when he smiled. His touch sent goose bumps throughout her entire body. No one had ever made her feel this much excitement before. It went beyond his chiseled features.

But Mario would kill her just for thinking about it. Maybe she should forget about that kiss and find herself a nice, safe doctor to marry.

Her nose wrinkled. Unfortunately, that thought really didn't appeal to her. She knew what kind of man Anthony was, but she didn't care. She started to fantasize about maybe becoming the next Mrs. Cavelli. Now, that would be something!

She looked down at the list. Nobody seemed to stand out. A horrible thought came to her. What if she wasn't on the list? What if the doctor knew he had to keep her identity a secret?

Well, that wasn't her problem now. She'd done her part.

Captain Merrill was on his way into the diner as Frank and John were leaving. He frowned when he saw them. John was beginning to get used to that expression. "Hey, what're you guys doing here?"

"We were just having a bite to eat," John said and then, as the captain turned and spat some nonverbal daggers in his direction, he wished he'd let Frank answer instead.

"Well, I hope you're ready to get back to work, Nelson."

Frank replied, "Of course, Captain."

John glanced at his partner but didn't say anything until they were alone outside. "Why did you do that? You know I'm not going back now. I have someplace else to be."

"Now, that wouldn't have created too many questions, would it?"

"Yeah, I guess you're right. What will you tell him if he goes back in and I'm not there?"

"Don't worry about it. I'll come up with something."

Frank had told him he was forgiven, and apparently he'd meant it. John was relieved to have his partner, and his friend, back again. "Thanks, man."

At the office, Anthony's cell rang. "Yeah. Good. Now, you look over the list and check out each name. One of them has got to be hers."

Closing his phone, he smiled to himself, satisfied with the way Maria had come through for him. She was so eager to please. He remembered her kiss and looked forward to taking that a step further. She was a nurse, she was Italian, and she knew her place; it was a combination that was hard to beat in his book. Maybe eventually she'd even make a good mother for his kid. He'd have to give that some more thought, especially since he found himself without a steady right now. His kid was going to need a mother after Regina was taken care of.

The phone rang again. "Yeah." He straightened in the chair. "Really . . . That's interesting. I want you to follow him. He'll lead you to where she is. Nice job. You've earned a bonus with this one. Call me when you know for sure."

He hung up and grinned. Today was almost too good to be true. But he'd always known everything would work out to his advantage. Things always did. Always. Even if they resisted at the beginning.

Regina couldn't hide from him forever. She should have known that.

"Hey, Boss," Vinny said from the couch, watching him. "You got some good news or something?"

"Yeah, you could say that. Vin, why don't you get me some coffee, okay?"

"Sure. I'll be right back."

Vinny left, and Anthony made a phone call. "Joey, it's me. I want you to go to that old warehouse I have downtown . . . Yeah, that's the one. I want you to get it ready like we discussed earlier. You understand? Good."

Vinny pulled his thumb off the intercom the second Anthony hung up. Moving quickly, he went over to the coffee urn, poured a cup, and returned. "Here you go, Boss."

Anthony didn't say anything. He just took the cup from Vinny and sat back down in the overstuffed chair. Vinny wondered what he'd meant by getting the warehouse ready. Ready for what? What was he planning now?

Regina sat in the bathroom, the only place she could go without every-one staring at her as if she were about to break. There was a large frosted window in here. It was oddly shaped and weirdly placed, as if the bathroom had a screen door once many years ago. Twice today so far, she'd come in here, opened the window just enough for fresh air to come in, and tried to think.

She needed to be alone. There were days she just got so tired of running and hiding. There were times she just wanted to give up. Then she would think about the baby and knew she would do anything to keep him from Anthony. But this morning, it felt as if something bad was about to hap-pen, and there was no way of stopping it. John and Jim were doing their best to keep her from getting caught, but the possibility of that happening still remained — which led to Brother Steven and the reason she was sit-ting in the bathroom.

She had to convince him to go home. If they were caught, Anthony would kill him without a second thought, and she couldn't live with that possibility; she couldn't allow that to happen. He wanted to stay and help so badly — it would hurt him to be sent home, but she knew she wouldn't be able to close her eyes again until he was away from here.

Resolute, she opened the bathroom door. Brother Steven was sitting on the bed, watching television. He didn't watch television at the monastery and seemed to enjoy just about anything, even commercials. He was grin-ning at one now, and she hated to interrupt him, especially with this.

"Brother Steven, we have to talk."

He picked up the remote and pushed the power button. In the sudden quiet, he looked up at her and asked, "Sure, what about?"

Regina went over to him and put her hand on his shoulder. "I'm afraid that it's time for you to go home."

Jim's replacement, a serious young man named Patrick Maine, was sit-ting on the other side of the room. He'd looked over when he'd heard the seriousness in her voice, but when he heard the reason for it, he nodded at her, letting her know he agreed with her decision.

Brother Steven, on the other hand, did not. "Regina — we've talked about that. I'm staying here until you can come back with me."

She sat on the bed next to him. The mattress sagged beneath her extra baby weight. "I'm not sure when that will happen, and I can't take the chance of your getting hurt. I've made a decision. If you don't go back, I'll go to Anthony and end this."

She could feel Patrick stiffen up all the way across the room, but she ignored him.

Brother Steven gave her a look, knowing how empty that threat really was. "You wouldn't do that."

"I will not allow anyone to be killed on my account. Do you hear me? If it means keeping you safe, I would go back to him in a heartbeat. You have to leave. Please, if you care about me, then go home."

Brows lowered, Brother Steven looked at her closely, as if studying her resolve. She meant every word, perhaps some more than others, but it was still difficult for her to keep his gaze. She knew how disappointed he would be.

"Please, Regina, let me stay."

"No, it's for the best. You have to go. I've thought about this, and yes, maybe my threat to go to Anthony is unfounded, but the thought of you getting caught in the crossfire . . . It's too much for me to bear. You must go back to where you belong."

She searched his face, hoping she was getting through to him.

"Okay. You win. I'll go back, but you must understand it's under protest."

Regina smiled a bit at his choice of words. "I understand. Thank you. It's a load off my mind."

Brother Steven started to pack.

Taking a deep breath, Mario walked into the office. Anthony and Vinny had just finished some Chinese food. The leftover containers were still on the table.

Leaning back in his chair, Anthony asked, "Well, did the list lead to anything?"

Mario didn't know what to say. Getting his sister involved was the last thing he'd wanted to do. No, they hadn't found anything — so what was he supposed to say? He hesitated until Anthony started to frown and then said, "No, Boss. All the women on the list checked out. Sorry. Maybe the doctor's in on it, and he's helping her cover her tracks. If you want, I can go pay him a visit. If he knows something, I'll get it out of him."

He wanted to divert the attention to anybody else, especially if Anthony went on a tirade.

For a moment, Anthony didn't say a word, but by the expression on his face, Mario knew he was angry. His mouth twisting, Anthony stood up and said, "Let's go."

He sounded almost calm, which made Mario more concerned than ever. "You okay, Boss?"

Vinny got up. "Where are we going?"

"You guys ask a lot of questions. If you must know, we're going to visit the priest. I know he knows something. If he doesn't, then Sophia does. One of them is going to get me Regina back, if it's the last thing they do."

Vinny didn't like the tone of Anthony's voice. When Anthony was angry and shouting, he was dangerous enough, but when he was angry and calm, he inspired a new level of fear for anybody who dared cross him. Vinny didn't like this at all. Maybe he could make a quick call to Jim and have him warn Sophia and the priest. "Hey, Boss, could I hit the john first?"

"Hold it. We don't have time for that now."

Vinny drove Anthony in his own car, while Mario followed behind. This wasn't looking good. Somehow, he had to call Poppy and let him know what was going on. If Poppy showed up, Anthony wouldn't be able to do anything.

John arrived at the motel, pulling into a parking spot by the main doors and looking carefully around him. He knew he hadn't been followed, but these days he couldn't help but feel a little paranoid. *Goes with the job, I guess.* He waited for a moment or two, and when the coast proved to be clear, he exited his car, went to the room, and knocked on the door. The agent Jim had sent looked through the window, and John held up his badge to identify himself.

The man opened the door. "I'm Patrick Maine," he said.

John entered, closing the door behind him. "John Nelson. I'm here to relieve you."

John saw Regina sitting on the second bed and smiled at her. Then he noticed the packed bag lying next to her. "What's with the bag?"

"Brother Steven has agreed to go home," Regina informed him.

"It's not my idea — it's hers. She's afraid I'll get hurt," Brother Steven said, squeezing out the last few words as if they were hard for him to say.

John could see the disappointment on his face. "Regina's right. We have her well covered."

"I've made flight arrangements. I was getting ready to call a cab."

"Why don't you drive him, John?" Regina asked. "I'd feel better knowing he got there safely."

Why would anybody need to escort Brother Steven out of town? He studied her a moment, trying to read her, but apparently, she didn't want to be read. She seemed happy to see him, but beyond that, he couldn't see a thing. Whatever reason she had for asking, he was willing to accommodate her.

"Well, if Agent Maine doesn't mind staying awhile longer, then I'll do it."

"No, I don't mind. I wasn't expecting you for another couple of hours anyway."

"Let's go then. I'll see you later." He smiled at Regina again, and she smiled in return.

John and Brother Steven left for the airport.

As Anthony and Vinny pulled up to the church, they noticed Poppy's car parked outside. Stuart was sitting in the driver's seat, and he appeared to be sleeping.

"I wonder how long Poppy's been here. We can't go in there now. Go down to the corner where Poppy won't see the car when he comes out. We'll wait there."

For more than an hour, Sophia, Antonio, and Father Thomas had been discussing how Anthony could be stopped; *arguing* perhaps would be a more accurate description. Sophia had heard Antonio explain ten million times how he was the only one who could adequately protect her daughter. He and his list of reasons — good reasons, some of them — were sounding like a broken record, and she couldn't take it anymore.

Finally, she said, "Look, Antonio, I know you mean well. I really do believe you, but I don't know where she is."

Father Thomas nodded. "Mr. Cavelli, it's the truth. We don't know where she is. She's being guarded by a police officer and FBI men, and we don't know where."

During the last hour, Sophia had watched Antonio's face grow more and more haggard. Though she was annoyed, she was also a little concerned for him, especially as he pleaded, "But you can find out if you want to. Please, I beg you. Before it's too late."

Sophia and Father Thomas exchanged a glance.

"It's your decision, Sophia."

Part of her couldn't believe she was even considering this, but Antonio had been right about one thing in particular: He was the only person who had any level of control in this situation. Anthony, in some strange, twisted way, did respect him. "Let me talk to the detective, and if he agrees to your help, then he'll tell you where she is. That's the best I can do. He won't tell me, should Anthony try to pressure me. If I knew where she was, it could endanger her."

Antonio nodded. "Fine, fine. That seems fair. Why don't you ask him? We . . . we just cannot delay any longer."

Anthony's cell phone rang. "Yeah."

Instantly, his entire demeanor changed. From the driver's seat, Vinny watched him grin and was relieved that something appeared to have distracted him. But his relief lasted only a moment.

"Oh, really? Does he know he was followed? Good job. Did she leave with them? Good. I want you to stay there in case they leave again. I'm on my way; I'll take care of this personally. You done good."

He flipped his phone shut and turned to Vinny and Mario, who had joined them and was eagerly leaning forward in the back seat. "We're in luck, boys. I just found my wife. Mario, you follow in your car."

Vinny couldn't do a thing. The situation was out of his hands. Anthony typically didn't leave any witnesses, which meant anybody with Regina right now was as good as dead.

John dropped Brother Steven at the terminal and started to head back. It would be easier now that he was gone. One less person to keep an eye on. One less person to make Regina feel uncomfortable when she and John were together.

John glanced at the clock on his dash and mentally calculated when he'd be getting back. Once he'd relieved Agent Maine, he would be able to have Regina all to himself again. The thought sent some unexpected butterflies through his stomach. It felt like he hadn't been able to talk to her alone in months, which was ridiculous, considering he'd only known her for that length of time.

The phone interrupted his anticipation. "Hello? Sophia, is something wrong? Well, I was on my way back to see Regina. I have to relieve the agent watching her . . . Can't you tell me on the phone? Okay, then. I'll be right there. I'm at the airport so it'll take me about thirty minutes."

With a sigh, John ended the call and then placed one to Jim. "Hey, it's me. Something has come up, and I'm going to be late relieving your agent . . . Can you let him know? . . . Thanks, man. I'll check in with you later." *I hope this doesn't take very long.*

Agent Maine got off the phone with Jim.

"Is something wrong?" Regina asked.

"No. Detective Nelson has to make a stop. I guess you're stuck with me a little while longer."

Regina smiled. "I find you to be pleasant company. Do you play gin rummy?"

"Yeah."

"Do you want to play? It helps to pass the time."

He shrugged. "Why not?"

As Regina got the cards out of her bag, she said, "I'm sure in your line of work you play lots of cards?"

"Yeah, but let me warn you — I win often."

Regina let out a chuckle. "Well, prepare to taste defeat."

At Anthony's signal, Vinny pulled over a block from the motel and parked behind a car whose driver appeared to be waiting for them.

"Wait here," Anthony said as he got out and talked to the other driver.

Vinny looked carefully at the back of the driver's head. It was getting dark out here, but he knew he'd seen that guy somewhere before. The car also looked familiar. Where had he seen that car?

Then it came to him — he'd seen it the night Anthony had met with his informer on the police force. It was the dent on the left side that triggered his recall first, and then he remembered the car had been a dark blue Taurus, like this one.

Anthony returned. "Leave the car here, and we'll go on foot and give them a surprise. I found out which room."

He signaled for Mario to join them. As they walked past the other car, Vinny caught a glimpse of the driver just before the man turned his head. He had chills when he saw him. It couldn't be him. When he heard the car start, Vinny turned quickly and got a better look. The driver saw Vinny looking at him, and suddenly face to face with the man, there was no doubt in Vinny's mind who that was.

Agent Maine's phone rang again. He answered it and immediately handed it to Regina. "It's for you. It's Jim."

Regina took the phone. "Hello?"

"Regina, I just got a call from that man who called us at the hotel."

Her heart jumped, but somehow, she wasn't all that surprised to hear him say that. She'd known something was wrong — she'd felt it. "What did he say this time?"

"That you were in danger and that you have to leave where you are immediately. I . . . well, I think you should do it."

"If you think it's best. I'll do whatever you say."

She handed Agent Maine the phone. He listened to Jim and then hung up. "Let's go." He stood from the small table where they'd been playing cards and looked through the blinds. Instantly, he tensed. "Looks like we've got company."

She froze. "We what?" *So soon?*

"Three of them. The only other way out is through the bathroom window." He handed her his car keys and cell phone and started pushing her toward the bathroom. "Go out the window and take my car out of here. If they mean trouble, I'll hold them off."

"What about you?"

"Don't worry about me. Now just go!" He shut the door after her, and she locked it.

The window was nearly floor to ceiling, and it was already open a crack from when she'd been debating what to do with Brother Steven. She shoved it up as far as she could get it, kicked the screen onto the grass, and ducked outside. Agent Maine's car was parked in the rear lot. As she climbed into it, her hands shaking, she became aware of how much God really was watching out for her. Of all the motels, of all the motel rooms, she happened to have one with a window that used to be a screen door. If it'd been any higher off the ground, she never would have made it.

They approached the room slowly, staying away from the window. Mario quietly went to one side of the door, Vinny to the other, guns drawn, silencers screwed on. Getting a nod from Anthony, Vinny blew the lock off and Mario broke the door open with his foot.

Agent Maine had taken cover, the best he could, behind a turned-over table. With gun drawn, he yelled, "FBI! Drop your weapons!"

Anthony motioned for Mario to move in. They had played this game before, and Mario had never feared it, even the first time, when he was just a boy. Jumping into the doorway, he shot before he'd steadied his hand and put a bullet in the agent's shoulder, a mere inch above his target. He hissed an oath and yanked the trigger back as the agent returned fire and hit him solidly in the chest, the force of the bullet driving him back against the doorframe. *What?* Completely surprised, Mario dropped his pistol and clutched his chest, feeling warmth run across his fingers. *What . . . ?*

Vinny had heard Mario's shout. When Anthony added one of his own and then dove into the room, he knew something had gone wrong.

Anthony never missed, and he didn't miss this time. He fired once and put a bullet in the middle of the agent's forehead. Helping Mario to the floor, Anthony shouted, "Mario! Mario, hold on, man. We'll get you to a doctor. Vinny, go get the car!"

Vinny turned and started running for the street. But then he slowed. Just across the parking lot, Regina was in a car about to go out the entrance. When she saw him, her eyes shot open. Picking up his pace again, he motioned for her to go, and she put tracks down as she accelerated onto the street.

He ran to the car and flew back to the motel. But Mario was dead. Anthony stood over the agent and made sure his man wasn't going alone. He fired two more shots into the agent's head.

He looked up at Vinny and ordered, "Put this trash in the trunk and Mario in the back seat. He's gone now." His voice heated. "She's going to pay for this."

Vinny did as he was told.

Chapter 20

John arrived at the rectory. He immediately spotted Cavelli's men across the street and cursed beneath his breath, wishing Sophia had been more specific in her phone call. He didn't have time for games with these guys. Opening his door, he got out, went up the walk, and rang the doorbell.

Sophia answered the door. "John," she said, appearing a little rattled. She glanced over his shoulder at the car across the street, and he wondered how long the guys had been there. "Thank you for coming. Please, step inside."

She led him to the living room, where he found Father Thomas and, much to his surprise, Antonio Cavelli sitting down.

John grimaced. *You've got to be kidding me. What sort of game is he playing now?* Before anyone could say anything, he demanded, "What is this gangster doing here?"

Father Thomas answered. "John, it's not what you think. This man has gone through many changes in the last several months and is here to help."

"Help with what? Getting Regina killed by putting her back into the hands of his son? Yeah, that'd be helpful."

"John, you don't understand," Sophia said quietly.

He looked at her in disbelief. Had he landed in an alternate universe somehow? She actually supported this? He thought she hated the guy.

She went on, "I know this might be hard to swallow, but this man loves Regina and has come to face many truths about his son. Now, sit down and listen to what we have to say."

Only out of respect for her did John do as she asked, but he wasn't about to let his guard down. He knew this was a trap and fully expected him to make a condemning move at any moment. Antonio might be a few years older now, but John knew he still had a few tricks up his sleeve.

Antonio cleared his throat. "Detective Nelson, I understand your distrust of me, but I assure you, I'm here to help." John didn't say anything — yet — so Antonio continued. "My son needs to be stopped. There are things I've learned about him that have shocked me. I believe he will harm Regina if he ever finds her."

"Really? That's funny. A killer is surprised he raised a killer." John couldn't help himself. He hated this man and didn't trust him.

"John! Please let him finish," Sophia pleaded.

"It's okay, Sophia. Detective Nelson has no reason to believe anything I say. I am what he says I am. I have killed and ordered others to kill for me. I have stolen, lied, cheated, and other things I'm now not proud of doing. I guess I will have to take what is coming to me when this is all over, but that isn't my concern right now — Regina is my concern. You may not believe me, Detective, but I would willingly take a bullet for her. She's a bright, charming, and beautiful young woman who has stolen my heart. I only want to see her and my grandchild safe, and I assure you that if it means helping you put my son away, I will."

John sat there in silence, trying to digest what he'd just heard. Had he truly just heard Antonio Cavelli confess to murder? They'd been trying to put this guy away for years, and he'd just confessed? And if that wasn't enough to process, had he just said he'd help put his son in prison, too, and actually sounded sincere about it?

"Is this some kind of sick joke?" John held up his hand. "Just a second — let me see if I've got this right. You're telling me that not only are you willing to help us put your son away, but you also just admitted to several crimes, ones that would put *you* away for a very long time. I find all of this hard to believe. Impossible, actually. I don't have time right now for games. I have somewhere I have to be. I don't understand you people. You trust this gangster to help Regina? Are you all crazy?"

John stood up, but Sophia gently placed her hand on his arm. "Please, if you won't listen to Antonio, then listen to me. Believe me when I tell you that he isn't here to harm Regina. He wants to help, and I think that right now, we could use all the help we can get. Isn't that right? She's my daughter, John. Do you honestly think I would endanger her life in any way? Please, listen to him. He can stop Anthony."

Before John could answer, his cell phone rang. "Excuse me, but I have to get this." He jerked his phone from his pocket and barked into the mouthpiece, "Hello!" The second he recognized the frantic voice on the other end and understood what she was saying and realized he hadn't been there when she'd needed him the most, he felt a level of horror that he hadn't experienced since learning of his brother's death. "Are you all right? Where are you? . . . Are you hurt? . . . Where's Agent Maine? Okay — calm down."

Everyone was looking at him. Sophia was as white as a sheet. He didn't want to say who was on the phone, but he could tell all of them already knew.

"John, that's Regina, isn't it?" Sophia whispered, sliding to the edge of the couch. She reached out to him, as if she thought she could touch her through the phone.

He didn't have to answer.

"Is she okay?"

"I don't really know how to answer that," he replied, moving the phone away so Regina couldn't hear him. He leveled Antonio with a glare. "I hope you're happy, because your son just found his wife."

Sophia nearly screamed.

"But she's all right," John added as quickly as he could. "She's fine. Unhurt. She escaped out a window."

Sophia stared at him, wide-eyed. Antonio came to his feet, rubbing his hands together. Father Thomas looked heavenward as if he was praying. John tried to calm down and not upset Sophia any more than she appeared to be.

Antonio suddenly spun toward him. "I have a cabin in the Pocono Mountains, and Regina knows where it is. Tell her to go there. She'll be safe. It hasn't been used in years, and there isn't anyone around for miles. Tell her the key is hidden in the same place."

For a moment, John didn't know what to do. This was Antonio Cavelli. *The* Cavelli, the one who had raised the son and taught him everything he knew. He'd be a fool to trust him. And yet Sophia seemed to have changed her mind about him, which spoke volumes because she knew exactly what her daughter had been through.

Sophia wouldn't trust this man unless she knew something about him that John did not. He decided he would put his faith in her judgment. "Regina," he said into the phone, "I'm here with your mom, Father Thomas, and Antonio Cavelli . . . Yes, please listen carefully and trust me. Good, I'm glad you do. Now, I want you to go to the Cavellis' cabin in the Pocono Mountains. Yeah, that's right. I'll meet you there. Try to stay calm. You know what the doctor said. Good. I'll be there as fast as I possibly can."

John hung up and pointed the phone at Antonio. "I trust Sophia — you I don't trust. Let me warn you. If anything happens to her because you're playing both sides of the fence, I will come after you and jail won't be my objective. Do I make myself clear?"

Antonio didn't seem bothered by John's response. "I understand. I'll write down the directions for you."

"John, what happened?" Sophia asked nervously.

Forcing his voice to calm, he told her, "She's fine, just shaken up a bit. Anthony somehow found out where she was hiding. She was able to get away, but she's worried about the agent who was watching her. She could hear gunfire but isn't sure what happened." He lifted his phone again. "Excuse me. I have to report this."

John dialed Jim's phone and told him what had happened. "Call me when you find out . . . Don't worry about her; I'm going to her now."

Antonio placed his hand on John's shoulder. Ignoring John's stare, he handed him a piece of paper with directions scribbled across it. "Please make sure she's safe." He pulled his hand away and said firmly, "I assure you, I won't allow Anthony to endanger her. I know you don't believe me, but I'm ready to cooperate in any way."

"I'll have to get back to you on that," he said abruptly, heading for the front door.

"You won't be followed. I'll take care of Anthony's men outside."

Sophia followed him to the door. "John, please be careful." Her voice broke. "She's all I have left."

"I know, Sophia. I promise you that I would die first before letting anything happen to her or the baby."

Sophia believed him. She knew this man would do anything for her daughter. His determination eased her panic, just a little. He would protect her at all cost. Regina was blessed to have such a man looking after her.

Trying to breathe deep, calming breaths, she closed the door after him and walked back to the living room. "Antonio, are you sure Anthony won't find her?"

"I'm positive. He would never think to look there. She'll be safe until we find a better place for her."

He studied her a moment, then he stood from the couch and went to her side. "Thank you for trusting me," he said quietly. "I will not let you down. I will not let Regina down. And I will stop my son, even if I have to testify against him myself."

Sophia never thought she would see the day when Antonio admitted to all the evil he had done. And now the man she had hated the most was helping save her daughter.

"Excuse me for a moment while I take care of those guys outside."

Gripping the steering wheel with both hands, Regina kept looking into the rearview mirror to see if anyone was pursuing her, tears streaking down her cheeks. She had no idea where she was driving.

"Get a grip, Regina," she said out loud, barely able to talk.

Fear welled up inside of her. She couldn't think straight, but she knew she had to calm down and get a sense of where she was. Where was she supposed to be going again?

She said a little prayer. A few seconds later, she saw a sign and realized she was heading in the right direction for the cabin. Relief flooded her. How was that even possible? It had to be a miracle, too.

Twice now a strange phone call had come out of nowhere, and this time she knew for sure it had saved her life. What was that all about? Obviously, God was watching out for her. But who was this man who kept calling? The Lord's wonders amazed her, and now things were happening that she couldn't explain. Her thoughts traveled in every direction. She was worried about Agent Maine.

She started to pray again, and over the miles, the tears stopped and her mind began to clear. It was going to be okay. It was. God hadn't brought her this far to abandon her now.

But why was John with Poppy? Why had Vinny, one of Anthony's right-hand men, signaled her to go? What in the world was going on?

She would have to wait for the answers until she saw John. Maybe he could fill in all the gaps.

Anthony drove Mario's car back into the city while Vinny headed out to the "burial grounds," as Anthony called it, to get rid of the two bodies in his car. He couldn't believe what had happened. There was nothing he could have done to save that FBI agent, and he was sure glad it hadn't been Jim.

Vinny let his breath out and wondered, *What am I doing?* With a groan, he pulled his foot off the accelerator and tried to think that question all the way through. What was Jim going to say about all of this? Vinny hoped he'd believe him when he explained what had happened. There had been no way for him to stop Anthony; that agent was fated to die, just by being there.

So . . . what was he doing? What *should* he be doing? He couldn't go and bury Jim's man out in the middle of nowhere. He probably had a family. Vinny just couldn't go and make the guy disappear. He couldn't do it. He'd started to lose the stomach for this job. It had to come to an end.

He pulled to the side of the road, and for nearly ten minutes, he just sat there in his car. Would Jim believe him when he told him what had happened? That was a big, big question. Would Anthony find out he'd betrayed him? Vinny didn't know what to do. But at least Regina had gotten away. Poppy would be pleased with that.

Maybe he should just go and bury the bodies.

The more he thought about it, the more he knew that wasn't a good idea. It wasn't like he was going to get away with this — Jim was going to know he'd been there because Regina had seen him. Vinny sat there debating and finally decided to make the call. He took out his phone and dialed.

"Hey, Jim, it's me . . . I know. Yes, I was there. I have the bodies with me. Yes — bodies. Your agent killed Mario, and Anthony killed your agent . . . I'm sorry. There was nothing I could do. It happened so fast. I had no opportunity to call you. What do you want me to do now? . . . Fine, I'll bring them there for you." Vinny listened as Jim expressed his concern. "Don't worry about that; Anthony went back to the city."

Vinny wasn't sure he'd survive all of this, when it was finally over, but he couldn't turn back now. He was heading in one direction and would have to live with the consequences, just as Mario had. He couldn't believe he was gone. Mario had always thought he was completely indestructible.

In the middle of washing dishes, Maria heard her doorbell ring. Wiping her hands, she went to the door and looked through the peephole, grinning when she saw Anthony standing on the other side. She took a deep breath and checked her hair in the mirror.

She opened the door with a big smile. But her smile faded as she noticed the expression on his face. "What's wrong?"

"Can I come in?"

"Where are my manners? Of course. Please come in and sit down. Would you like something to drink?"

"No, thanks."

Anthony walked slowly to the couch, as if he'd just finished a marathon and each step was painful. He motioned for her to come and sit next to him, and she did so tentatively, knowing by the look on his face that he had bad news. The normally smooth Anthony hesitated as he searched for the right words. The longer he faltered, the more worried Maria became.

"Something terrible has happened," he whispered at last.

"Is it Mario?"

"Yes. I'm afraid he's been killed."

Maria's face turned white. Tears welled up in her eyes. She sat there, trying to breathe and trying to process. She'd always known the life her brother led would one day get him killed, but she'd tried not to think about it. The tears rolled down her cheeks. "How?" was all she could manage.

"We found where Regina was hiding. The agent guarding her opened fire, and Mario got hit and went down."

Looking Anthony in the eyes, she asked coldly, "And is this agent dead?"

Anthony raised a brow. "Yes, I made sure of it."

"Good. Where is my brother?"

"I told Vinny to bury him. We couldn't leave him where he was, and if we came back with him . . . Well, you know, the cops would find out what happened. I guess they'll figure it out anyway, but this way they have no proof."

"So what am I supposed to tell my mother? Am I supposed to tell her that her only son is dead, and she has no body to bury because that would incriminate you?!"

She got up from the couch. "Why did you come here? If it wasn't for your stupid wife, my brother wouldn't be dead!"

Anthony was taken aback by Maria's forcefulness. This was a side of her he hadn't seen before, and he hadn't known it existed. "I came out of respect for you. I thought you and your family deserved to know what happened to him. He served me loyally for many years."

"And this is how you repay that — by burying him like some piece of garbage without his family there to say good-bye?" She glared at him, pointed to the door, and said, "Get out of my house!"

Anthony stood up. This wasn't going the way he had imagined it would. He had to do something before she got out of hand and did something stupid. "Listen. You have to be smart about this. I came here because I care about you. I could have led you to believe that he had just left town, and you never would have known the truth. Instead, I came here at great risk to myself."

He walked over to her and put his hands on her shoulders. She jerked away.

"Don't touch me," she said with disgust.

"Look, if it will help you, then get angry at me. But it wasn't my fault, and I did exact revenge for him. I cared for your brother also. Don't turn away from me. Let us help each other through this."

He put his arm around her. She started to struggle.

"Get off of me! It's all your fault!" She cried and started to pound his chest with her fists.

Anthony didn't let go but drew her closer to him. "It's okay. Let it out. Let me help you."

She began to weep, and Anthony pulled her against him. She laid her head on his chest, and he held her gently as she sobbed.

John was about halfway to Antonio's cabin when his phone rang. "Talk to me. Jim, what happened? . . . I'm so sorry. How did you find out?"

He couldn't believe what he was hearing. He listened as Jim told him about Vinny and how he'd been working against Anthony for weeks now. He also told him about Mario and Agent Maine. But what nearly caused him to go off the road was what Jim told him about the informer.

"Are you kidding me? That has to be a mistake. He didn't see him — he couldn't have!" He had to swerve to stay on the road and for a second sincerely considered pulling over before he killed himself. "What do you want me to do? I don't agree! Man, you can't ask that of me . . . Yes, I know . . . You're right . . . Okay, I will *not* let on that I know, but . . . Yes, I know what's at stake here. I'll talk to you later." He ended the call as quickly as he could.

Oh, no. John couldn't believe it. Not that. Through this entire case, he had tried to consider every possibility from every angle, but he hadn't *really* considered . . . How was he supposed to do this? How was he supposed to pretend he didn't know what he knew? How was he supposed to go to work and face someone he used to trust? How was he supposed to look him in the eyes and listen to more lies?

He didn't have any answers, and his questions piled up. More and more of them. He wasn't sure if he had it in him to pretend like that, but as he'd told Jim, he knew what was at stake. He had to do it.

When his fog lifted, he realized he was almost to the cabin. He looked again to make sure he wasn't being followed. Paranoid, he looked in his rearview mirror a few more times before turning onto the mostly concealed private road. He drove until he reached a gate. A tall brick fence surrounded the property. He rolled down his window and pressed the button on the intercom.

A soft voice asked, "John?"

"Yes, it's me."

"Pull in behind the house."

The gate opened and he drove through. The road continued for about another mile. He finally caught sight of the house, surrounded by enormous trees. "I guess Antonio Cavelli was right," he said to himself. This wasn't the easiest place to find. If you did somehow manage to stumble across the private road, you'd still have to conquer the beast-like gate and travel another mile before reaching the house.

He pulled in behind the house where he saw the other car parked. Regina was waiting by the back door. He got out of the car, and she practically ran to him. He reached out and held her in his arms, and she just wept.

"It's okay. Everything is going to be okay."

Not enough time had gone by for Vinny to have buried two bodies and then returned, so he went to see Poppy before reporting back to Anthony. Just in case Anthony came by, he pulled in the driveway and around to the back of the house, hiding his car from the street. He rang the back doorbell, and after a few moments, Stuart came and let him in.

Stuart didn't say a word as he ushered Vinny into Poppy's office, where Poppy was sitting behind his desk and looking into space.

He noticed Vinny standing there and came alert. "What happened?"

"Anthony found Regina. I didn't have time to call you — he wouldn't let me out of his sight. We got to the motel where she was hiding, and she slipped out the back way. I saw her and made sure she left."

Vinny hesitated. "There was an agent there, and he shot Mario — he's dead. Anthony returned fire and killed the agent. It happened so fast. I had no time to stop it. I . . ." He glanced away. "I know I failed you."

"No, you haven't. It's tragic about the agent and even Mario, but at least Regina got away safely. That's all that matters. You did your job well. Thank you."

Somber about the whole situation, Vinny didn't tell Poppy about Jim, or that he'd handed the bodies over to the FBI. He knew he wouldn't understand.

"Regina got away, but I don't know where she is. Anthony doesn't know, either. I think I'll go home after I call Anthony, if that's okay with you." He was feeling the need to get away for a while.

"That's fine. It's been a long day for everyone. I'm sure Regina is somewhere safe."

"I hope so. I'll let you know what Anthony does next."

"Good. Go home and get some rest. You look like you could use it."

Vinny left.

For a long time, Antonio sat there and pondered the day's events. Regina should be safe where she was; Anthony hadn't gone there in years, and for a variety of reasons, Antonio knew he'd never think to look there.

But now, the hard part began. He would have to cooperate with the police, which meant he'd probably have to spend the rest of his life in prison. But he'd recently had something of a change of mind about that. It really didn't matter anymore. He couldn't lose Regina and his grandchild. They were the only ones who mattered.

Frank sat on his couch, watching an old movie. Annie and the kids were visiting her mother's, and he was happy to have the house to himself for once. Today had been an extremely taxing day. The peace and quiet were soothing. He must have been dozing off, because he was startled when the phone rang. He jumped and looked around, half expecting someone to be there.

Running his hand over his face, he picked up the receiver. "Hello."

"Hello, Frank."

Immediately, Frank recognized the voice on the other end, and he wasn't happy that he'd called him at home. "I thought I told you to never call me here. What if one of the kids answered, or my wife?"

"Ahh, your lovely wife. I hope she's enjoying her visit with Mom."

Frank held his breath, gripping the phone so hard that it trembled against his ear. How *dare* he do that to him. "How did you know that?"

"I know plenty. I know where your wife is, but the question is, Do you know where my wife is?"

"Look, Anthony, I'm tired of playing games with you. I'm done! Find yourself someone else to do your dirty work. Do you understand?" The silence on the line was so complete that it started to unnerve him. "Are you still there? Did you hear what I said?"

"Oh, I'm here. I heard you, but I'm having trouble believing you just said that to me. Do you have any idea what happened today? I lost one of my best men. I almost had her, but she slipped . . ." Frank heard his voice tighten and sensed how furious he was. " — slipped away again. Now, we both know who she's with, don't we?"

"Yes."

"You know what you have to do. Let's not have anymore of this foolish talk about our business arrangement being over. We both know that's never going to happen. After all these years, don't you think I have enough on you? If I go down, you go down with me. Now, what would that pretty wife of yours think about that?"

"You leave her out of this!"

"Oh, I'll be glad to, Detective, so long as you remember who you're dealing with." Anthony hung up.

In his quiet house, Frank slowly reached over and hung up the receiver and wondered how he'd ever gotten himself into this mess. Leaning forward, he dropped his head into his hands. He'd been leading this double life for so long now. And he knew Anthony was right. There were things he'd done, many things, that wouldn't just hurt his family — they'd be decimated. All of them. He would go to prison, for the rest of his life, and they'd go on with their broken lives and try not to remember him.

If they ever found out what he'd done.

He couldn't let that happen, no matter what. It had been so simple in the beginning. Too simple. He should have known better. With Anthony's every request, he'd been further compromised. Finally he had committed the ultimate betrayal, and in that Anthony unfortunately was right: There could be no turning back now.

He heard the key in the door, and he quickly leaned back into the couch as if he'd been watching television the whole time. The movie had ended, and there was some shampoo commercial on. A second later, the kids came bursting into the room.

"Hey, Dad!" they called in passing as they ran up the stairs to their rooms.

Annie stepped into the living room, shaking her head and saying, "Your kids are really something."

"So how come they're my kids only when 'they're really something'?" Frank teased her.

She rolled her eyes and plopped down next to him. "Oh, you know what I mean. We go over to visit my mother, and what does she do? She spoils them. I swear that's not the same woman who raised me." She laughed, but then her expression changed as she looked at him more closely. "Hey, are you okay?"

"Oh, yeah. I guess I'm just tired. It's been a long day." He placed his arm around her, pulling her close to him, and Annie turned toward him and rested her head on his chest. "Mmm . . . I'm feeling better already. Why don't we turn in early tonight?"

"Why, Detective Holstrum, are you propositioning me? I'll have you know I'm a happily married woman."

That brought a smile to Frank's face. "You know, Annie, I really do love you. There isn't anything I wouldn't do for you. I would give up my life to protect you."

"What brought all of this on? Why so serious all of a sudden?"

"I just want you to know that I love you. Don't ever forget that, no matter what happens."

"Yeah, I know. I love you, too." Leaning against him, she whispered in his ear, "Now let's go upstairs, okay?"

"Okay."

"Are you coming back to bed?" Maria called.

"Yeah, I'm coming. I just had to use the phone." Anthony walked into the living room and stopped just inside the doorway, looking at her. She was a beautiful woman. Once again he had managed to control a situation that was getting out of hand, and to be honest, it hadn't been a hardship on his part. "Are you okay?"

"No, but I will be. You're right, you know, but I don't think the rest of the family will be as understanding of your lifestyle as I am. That being said . . . I don't think it's a good idea to tell them the truth about Mario." She joined him at the doorway.

"Are you sure?"

"Yes. I am now." She took his hand and pulled him back toward the bedroom.

Regina and John sat at the dining room table, eating the meal she'd prepared in silence. He had gone out and brought back some groceries and supplies. The house hadn't been used in years, and even though Poppy had never turned off the utilities, Regina didn't feel comfortable using any of the food she found in the cupboards. Only God knew how long some of it had been there.

"So how long are you staying?" she said, feeling a need to break the heavy quiet.

"Until morning. Jim will be coming here to stay with you."

"Are you okay?" Regina asked softly.

"Yeah, I just know what Agent Maine's family is going through right now."

"I've said a prayer for them."

Choosing not to respond, he dropped his gaze to his food and went on eating. It appeared to Regina that God was not something he wanted to discuss.

"So, Vinny is working with the FBI?"

"Well, it appears to be true. He grew up with Jim and apparently had a change of heart. So has your father-in-law, seemingly. What's up with that?"

"I wish I knew. I always knew he cared for me, and to tell you the truth, it used to creep me out. But coming here was a really good idea. Anthony always hated it here. I don't know why."

John got up and put his plate in the sink, feeling sick to his stomach. He couldn't believe that Frank was the informer. He hadn't told Regina about that yet, and for a minute, he stood there not moving and just looked down at his plate that was still filled with food. He felt a gentle hand on his shoulder and turned around. She had such kind eyes. The one good thing out of all this craziness was that he had met her.

"You look upset, John. Is there anything I can do?"

"I didn't tell you everything. I left something out."

"What?"

"I know who the informer is. Vinny saw him at the motel. Apparently, he'd followed me there, so it's my fault this whole thing happened."

"It's not your fault."

"Oh, yes, it is. I'm a cop — I'm trained to know if I'm being followed, but apparently I'm not trained to see my own partner. I even sat there and told him . . . more than I should have, trying to patch things up, because I didn't realize the truth."

"Oh." She hesitated. "I see. I'm so sorry." She stepped away.

He noticed her discomfort and assumed he knew what it meant. With a sigh, he walked away, heading toward the living room, and she followed him.

"John, it's going to be okay."

"No, it's not. I almost got you killed, and I'm supposed to be the one protecting you. I made such promises to you, to your mother, and I failed every single one of them." He paused for a moment. "I'm going to let Jim and the FBI handle your protection from now on."

Regina didn't know how to answer that. Feeling miserable at the thought of his absence, she said, "If you think that's best. I will miss you, though."

"You will?"

"Yes. You know why. I don't need to say it, do I?"

"It might help."

"If I say those words out loud . . . It just isn't right . . . I mean . . ."

John walked over to her and looked her straight in the eye. "Are you trying to say you love me? You don't have to, you know. I already know that."

She looked down at the floor.

"I know because I happen to love you, too. That's why I need to stay away for now. Once everything is over, we can pick up this conversation again."

Regina lifted her gaze and smiled, suddenly feeling a little shy. "I would like that very much."

Chapter 21

Antonio hadn't slept well last night. He sat and sipped coffee in his study and knew that very soon now, everything would be coming to a head. How had life gotten so complicated? Eventually he would have to face his son with truths that would destroy their relationship forever. Never had he wanted to pick sides, but Anthony had left him with no choice.

Try as he might, he'd never understand why Anthony hated Regina so much or why his son hated him. It might be too late for Antonio to redeem the wickedness he'd done in his life, but . . . he had to try.

He was so involved in his thoughts that a minute passed before he noticed Sophia standing in the doorway. "Sophia, what are you doing here?"

"I've come to see if you're okay. Are you?"

She was concerned for him. Despite the pain in his heart, hearing her say that was like a breath of fresh air, and he waited a moment before he answered, wanting to savor the sensation. "I guess I'm as good as could be expected. Anthony will hate me forever when this is all over with . . . but I guess that's the price I'll have to pay to keep our daughter safe."

He realized what he'd said, but this time she didn't correct him. Seeing the tears in her eyes, Antonio got up and went to her. "Sophia, what's wrong?"

"Antonio, are you doing all of this because you believe Regina is yours?"

He hesitated slightly before answering her. "Yes . . . partly."

"I don't know if she is, but you can't ever tell her the truth. She loved Michael so very much. She's been through hell . . . This would be the straw . . ." No longer able to hold back the tears, she didn't finish her sentence.

Looking away from her, Antonio walked over to one of the chairs facing his desk and sat down. "I can live with that if I have to; all that really matters is that she's safe. She is the mother of my grandchild, whether she's my daughter or not." He glanced at her; she was still crying at the doorway. "I guess I have to stop fooling myself into thinking that I'll ever know for sure. I guess you don't want to find out who she really belongs to, do you?"

Between her sobs, she answered, "No, I don't care who her biological father is. Michael is her dad and forever will be. I don't mean to hurt you. I know you're giving up everything to save her, and I'll always be grateful for that, but it doesn't change anything. I want you to understand that." She came to him and sat in the other chair, placing her hand on his. "Promise me, as long as you live, that you'll never, ever tell Regina what happened between us."

He pulled his hand from hers. What she just had asked . . . He hated to make a promise like that. The thought of it caused an old hope inside him to loose its grip and begin to die. "If I promise this, will you promise me something in return?"

"It depends on what it is."

"Promise me that no matter what happens to me, you will tell our grandchild about me and how much I loved him before he was even born."

"Yes, I can do that for you."

"Then, I, in return, will never tell Regina about us."

"Thank you." She smiled at him through her tears. Wiping them from her cheeks, she pulled in a deep, shaky breath and looked him in the eyes. "What happens now?"

"I'm not so sure. I guess the FBI will contact me today at some point, and they'll move in to arrest Anthony. No doubt, I will also be in jail. Once the organization is dismantled, you and Regina can settle anywhere you want. To tell you the truth, I'm more frightened for Anthony than myself. I worry he might resist arrest and get himself killed in the process."

Antonio knew that Sophia couldn't offer him any comfort when it came to Anthony; he expected nothing from her, and she kept her silence.

After a long moment, she slowly stood. "I have to go. Thank you for all you've done. I'm sorry that things couldn't have been different."

"Sophia, wait. Please, don't go. Let's talk some more. Would you like a coffee?" He knew he sounded desperate, but he didn't care.

Compassion filled her eyes. "Okay. I'll stay."

Regina sat at the kitchen table, her head down on the top of it and her eyes closed. How did everything get so crazy? She wanted to cry, but she didn't have any tears left in her. She didn't notice when John entered the kitchen. She heard him clear his throat and looked up.

When he didn't say anything, she asked, "Is Jim here yet?"

"No, but he will be soon."

"Does the FBI have enough to take Anthony in?"

"Yes. Now it's a matter of making sure that Vinny will do his part and testify. Without his testimony, the case will be weak. Also, there's the matter of my partner. Only Vinny saw him, and they need more proof to make the case against him solid. I guess that's where I'll come in. They might wait and coordinate the whole thing so that neither case will be jeopardized."

John noticed she'd become distant, almost detached. "Hey, are you all right?"

"No, not really. I never understood all the killing that went on around me. Anthony will blame me for Mario's death. I'm as good as dead."

John knelt down beside her. "Hey, don't say that. I'll never let anything happen to you. Know that I would — "

Regina interrupted. "You would die first, just like Agent Maine. I can't let all of this killing continue. Innocent people are dying because of me. That is the one thing I knew I couldn't . . . I can't tell you how — how much this has got to stop."

"Regina, you're talking foolishness. In this line of work, that's the risk you take, and Agent Maine was no different. He knew the risks involved with his job. This is not your fault."

She looked at him, her eyes empty. In a suddenly and completely blasé voice, she answered, "Yes, I know. You're right. It's just that I feel horrible about all that's happened. If I hadn't sent Brother Steven home, he'd be dead, too. The important thing is that he's safe, and so are you." She looked over at the back door. "If you have to go, you can. I'm sure Jim will be here very soon. I'll be perfectly safe by myself."

John didn't like the way this was going. She was acting a little weird. But he didn't have to reply to her odd suggestion because he'd already let Jim through the gate.

Someone knocked on the door.

"It's Jim. I'll let him in."

"I'm going upstairs for a nap. I really feel tired. Thank you for listening to me and for being so understanding."

"I'm sure we'll see each other again soon. This'll all be over before you know it."

"Yes. You're certainly right about that."

She got up and left the kitchen. He watched her go and frowned, sensing something was wrong but not sure what it was. Maybe she was just tired, like she'd said.

Opening the door for Jim, he asked, "Anything new?"

"Plenty. Where's Regina? I think she might be interested in hearing this, too."

"She went upstairs to take a nap. I don't know, man. She's acting strange this morning. This whole thing's getting to her."

"I'm sure she'll be fine. She's been through so much in the last twenty-four hours. I'll talk to her later."

"So what's going on?"

"Let's sit down."

Jim seemed a little keyed up for coffee, but John thought he'd ask anyway. "Want some coffee?"

"No, thanks. Okay, here's the deal. I'm certain Vinny will testify against Anthony. From what you tell me about Antonio Cavelli being willing to work with us, we'll have more than enough to put Anthony away for a very long time."

"That's great. What about Frank?"

"Well, that's a bit more tricky. We don't have any hard evidence that he's actually Anthony's mole. We only have Vinny's word, which is good enough for me, but it's probably not good enough for court. So if we move on Anthony right now, Frank might just slip through the cracks."

"Well, Regina can't keep hiding. She's having trouble with her pregnancy."

"I understand that. But at the same time, we can't let Frank get away with what he's done."

"I know he played a substantial role in Agent Maine's death, and I understand that the Bureau wants him to pay for that . . . but what about Regina?"

Jim was silent for a moment. Grimacing, he shifted his weight in the chair, and John mentally tensed, sensing the agent was about to say something he wasn't going to like. "Look, John, I'm not so sure I know how to say this, but we think this has been going on for some time now. It seems he's been helping Anthony for years. And we believe he's the one who set up your brother."

John stood. Firm, he said, "No way. He may have lost his mind, and he's done some terrible things, but he couldn't be responsible for my brother's death. He's . . . he sat with me at the funeral. He sat there and comforted —" He forced his voice to stay calm. "No way can that be true. He had to have started working for Anthony some time after that, because he couldn't have . . ."

"I'm sorry, John, but I'm afraid it might be true."

"What evidence do you have? Prove it to me."

Quiet, Jim watched him, apparently hearing what John was trying to keep hidden. "Well, I've been debriefing Vinny, and his evidence is convincing . . ."

His voice trailed off. Cocking his head, he stood up. "Did you hear something outside?"

"No. What?"

"I could've sworn I heard a car start."

A second later, they heard the rumble of tires spinning through gravel. They both looked at each other and then raced to the door. Regina was gone. Agent Maine's car was already a hundred yards down the road.

They ran for their cars, but Regina had planned for that — she'd cut holes in their tires, deflating two on each vehicle.

"You don't think she went back, do you?"

That sick feeling returned to John's stomach. It was worse this time than it'd been last night. *Oh, Regina,* he thought. "She was acting so funny. She blames herself for Maine's death. She didn't take it very well. H-how soon can you get someone to pick us up?"

"I'm working on it," Jim said, punching buttons on his speed dial.

Sitting at Maria's little dining table, Anthony was actually enjoying the breakfast she'd cooked up for them. It wasn't bad. He was impressed. Sensing his satisfaction, she smiled at him from across the table.

The question he now faced was what to do with her.

"Breakfast is good. Thanks for cooking."

"My pleasure." She looked over at him again, and the smile slowly slid off her face.

"Hey, what's the matter?" he asked.

"I can't believe that we got together because of Mario's death."

"If it makes you feel better, I think it would have happened eventually. Now, you have to be strong. Remember what we discussed last night?"

"Yes, I remember. I promise I'll be absolutely perfect."

"Good." Anthony hoped that was the end of it. He didn't have time for a high maintenance woman in his life right now. Sure, her brother was dead, but everyone suffers loss.

His cell phone rang. He answered it while lifting his coffee mug. "Hello?" Coffee spilled all over the table. "Are you for real? To what do I owe the pleasure of this call?"

"Don't you dare play games with me," Regina said, fighting to keep her voice calm. "I don't want to see anyone else get hurt. I am prepared to come back, but I have my terms. If they are not met, I'm hanging up right now, and you'll never hear from me again. Will you promise me that after the baby is born, you'll let me help raise him?"

He didn't answer.

"Well?"

"I'm thinking."

"Not funny. If you want me to come back, then you have to give me your word that no one else gets hurt because of me. The second thing is that you'll let me raise this child."

This time, there was no hesitation. "Fine. You have my word."

Anthony hoped she bought it, but he couldn't believe she'd be that stupid.

"I'm not sure I believe you." She paused. "I'm on my way to the penthouse now. I should be there in a couple of hours. I will be calling your father to ask him to meet me. I want him to know that I'm coming back."

Anthony didn't like the sound of that. He'd have to think of a way to deal with it. "Great. I'll see you then."

He closed his phone. Maria was looking at him.

"Who was that?"

Anthony wasn't sure how he wanted to play this. Should he tell her the truth or lie to her? Which would be more beneficial to him? "You won't believe this, but that was Regina."

"Regina? Are you serious?" She didn't appear happy to hear that at all. Grabbing a handful of napkins from the counter, she started attacking the coffee spill with vengeance.

"Yeah, she said she's coming home. Do you believe that?"

Maria was obviously having some trouble hiding her concern, and Anthony inwardly smirked. Poor kid. Afraid she was losing him already.

"I see. So after what she's done, you're going to let her come back like everything is okay?"

"Now, I didn't say that, did I?"

"No, but what *do* you say about it?"

He looked at her and then laid his phone on the table. Standing up, he reached over and gently stroked her face. "You're beautiful. Last night changed things for me, but I have a kid to think about. That's all I want from her. You understand me?"

Her expression changed again. "Tell me what I can do to help."

"She may think she's coming home, but she's not. If it weren't for her, your brother would still be alive." Anthony figured it couldn't hurt to fuel

Maria's fire. "Before she gets to the penthouse, I'm going to have the boys pick her up. I need you to play nursemaid to her. I understand she's having trouble with the baby. It would be good to have a nurse around in case of an emergency."

Anthony tugged the coffee-stained napkins from her hand and pulled her against him. He held her in his arms and then, with care, kissed her softly. He felt her hungry response and purposely began to pull away. One thing he knew how to do was charm the ladies. Leaving Maria wanting more ensured that she stayed primed and ready for whatever he needed next.

"Do you think you can do that for me?"

"I'd do anything for you," she replied, her breathing growing ragged as she leaned against him.

"Good. I gotta go and make some preparations. I'll have one of the boys pick you up and take you to the warehouse." He kissed her cheek and then pushed her away.

With Anthony in her home, Maria felt like she was living in a dream world. That aura of danger and mystery he carried only added to his appeal, and it wasn't hard for her to ignore the faint misgivings she had about all of this. As soon as he was gone, however, she started to wonder about some things — such as, what *did* he have in store for Regina after the baby was born? Was it a question she dared ask herself? She blamed Regina for what happened to Mario, but it wasn't like she was blind to the truth; Regina wasn't the one who had pulled the trigger.

Angry and terrified, Maria had said and thought some things that, now, she was realizing were wrong, at least in part. Wasn't that what happened to people in the heat of the moment? Mario was dead, and there was nothing that could bring him back. Could she live with not telling her family the truth? Was being with Anthony worth living a lie? She did want him — badly, and probably at any cost, if she admitted it.

But some questions had complicated answers.

The phone rang in the rectory, and Father Thomas answered it. When he heard John's panic, his heart started to race. He doubted John was a man who panicked very often. "Calm down, John. What are you talking about?"

"Regina's gone. She sliced our tires and took off in one of the cars. I'm afraid she's heading back there."

Father Thomas felt like he'd been punched in the gut. "What would make you think that?"

"She blames herself for the agent's death — but I need to speak to Sophia. She has to call Antonio Cavelli and let him know."

"She's not here, but I'll call her. Is there anything I can do?"

"Well, do what you do best, Father." John hung up.

Father Thomas did just that. He fell to his knees right there by the phone and started to pray for Regina. "Lord, I pray that You would keep her safe and that she wouldn't do anything foolish. Give her wisdom; clear her mind from confusion. Protect her and her unborn child." He got up, opened his phone book, and looked up Antonio Cavelli's number. He knew that was where Sophia had headed this morning.

Antonio and Sophia were still talking when Stuart entered with the phone in his hand. He held it out to Antonio. "Sir, you won't believe this, but it's Mrs. Cavelli."

Sophia gasped. Antonio jumped up and grabbed the phone. "Hello!"

"Hello, Poppy," Regina said softly.

"Regina, are you all right?"

"Yes, I am, but I want you to do me a favor."

"Anything."

"I want you to meet me at the penthouse."

"What penthouse?"

"Mine."

"You must be joking. You can't do that!"

"I know what I'm doing. Please, just meet me there. I'll be there in about an hour." She hung up.

Sophia stared at him, her face white. "Did I hear you correctly? Is Regina going back to her penthouse?"

"Yes."

"Is she crazy? Why would she do that?"

"I don't know. She hung up on me." The phone rang again. "Hello! Regina —"

"No, it's Father Thomas."

"Look, Father, I can't talk right now."

"Is Sophia there? I need to speak to her. It's important."

Antonio handed her the phone.

"Hello?"

"Sophia, I just got off the phone with John. He's worried about Regina."

"I know — she just called here; she's going back to her penthouse."

"John said she was acting weird and blames herself for the agent's death."

"Well, that's just absurd. Look, Antonio and I are heading for the penthouse to meet her. Will you meet us there? Surely Anthony wouldn't try anything with all of us there."

"I'll be there." He hung up the phone.

Antonio took her arm. "Sophia, I don't think that's a good idea. Let me go alone. I don't want you to get hurt if there's any trouble."

"I'll be fine. I need to do this."

He didn't want her to beg him. He saw the desperation in her eyes and felt himself giving in. "All right, but I need to make a phone call first. Do you mind telling Stuart to get the car, and then you'll wait for me outside?"

"No problem."

Antonio dialed a number he now knew by heart. "Vinny, we have trouble. I need you to find out what Anthony is up to. Regina is planning on returning to the penthouse, and I'm afraid he might try something."

What in the world was Regina thinking? So much had been done to keep her safe — why would she return? Vinny couldn't believe it.

Well, it seemed like the moment had finally come for him to jump off the fence. It was time for him to take a side. He hoped he'd be able to follow through and do the right thing. For once in his life, he had to do the right thing. He didn't want to end up like Mario — dead, without ever doing anything good for anybody.

He had just started getting dressed when his phone rang again.

"It's me, Vin," Anthony said. "I need you to pick up Maria and bring her to our warehouse downtown."

"The one on Fifth Street?"

"Yeah, that's the one." He hung up before Vinny could ask him why.

That was weird. Why did Anthony want Maria to go to the warehouse? It was dirty, out of the way, and . . . The truth began to dawn on him. Regina was coming back, and Anthony knew it. But why Maria? What did she have to do with all of this? *Of course.* The pregnancy! It all started to come together. Anthony was setting up the warehouse to keep Regina there. Vinny knew he'd better call Poppy, and Jim, and let them know what was going on.

The FBI had sent a car for John and Jim, and the ride back to New York had been very quiet. John knew that, somehow, he'd failed Regina, and he figured Jim felt that way, too, though they didn't discuss it. This was the last thing he'd ever expected to happen.

They were still about an hour away when Jim's phone rang.

"Hello." He glanced at John and mouthed, "It's Vinny." Raising his voice again, he said, "Go on . . . Are you kidding? I know where that is. Okay, I'll get things going." He hung up and told John, "Vinny said Anthony's planning on keeping Regina hostage at an old abandoned warehouse he owns downtown."

"So, are they there now?"

"No, but Anthony will be soon. If he sees us before we can move in, he might hurt her in a panic. We have to get him before he gets to the warehouse. I have some men staking out the penthouse, and I'll call for some backup at the warehouse. I think we should head there first."

"Why not go to the penthouse first?"

"It's just a hunch. I don't want to waste any time. Trust me, okay?"

"Okay. But so help me, if he tries to hurt her, I'll . . ." He couldn't finish the sentence.

"It'll be okay. We won't let that happen. My men will not advance if she's in harm's way. They know what they're doing."

Anthony was waiting at the penthouse when the doorbell rang. Right away, he knew it wasn't his wife. If she had somehow managed to get past his men, she would have just used her key. He opened the door to find not only his father but Sophia and the priest standing there as well. "Well, well, what an interesting cast of characters."

"We're here because Regina called," Poppy said.

"Come in. She phoned me, too. I was expecting only you, Poppy, but you've brought your newfound friends as well. Interesting company you keep nowadays."

They entered. Sophia and Father Thomas stayed quiet and barely looked at him. Apparently, they'd decided to let Poppy do most of the talking.

"I'm here to make sure you don't try anything," his father said.

"Poppy, what would I try? I'm very excited to have my wife return. She can now have our baby here, and I can be a part of it."

"Humph!" Sophia exclaimed.

Anthony turned to her and, with ice in his eyes, sweetly asked, "Is something wrong, Momma Sophia? Do you doubt after all these years how much I love your daughter? Do you actually think I would harm my un-born baby?"

Antonio placed his hand on Sophia's shoulder, cautioning her. She didn't know if she'd be able to keep quiet, but she heeded Antonio's warning and tried to keep her voice calm. She didn't want to make things worse for her daughter. "Regina has been gone for a long time," she said smoothly. "We're all on edge and desire the same thing, and that's for her to be safe. So let's sit and wait together. She should be here very soon."

Anthony glared at her and then smiled at her in a way she found highly irritating. Evil dripped from him like water from a faucet. It made her hair stand on end. She didn't want her daughter or grandchild anywhere near this beast. Once Regina got here, she would take her away forever. The cops would come and arrest Anthony, and it all would be over. The thought of him behind bars put a smile on Sophia's face.

So they all stood looking at each other, waiting.

Driving down the street, Regina was gripped by fear. *Brave,* she kept repeating in her head. *Be brave. Be brave.* She had to overcome the terror of her flesh because she had no other option. She couldn't allow anyone else to die because of her. *Be brave.*

It was dark inside the parking garage. Her nerves were shot, and she felt like someone was watching her. She pulled into her spot next to Anthony's car and gripped the steering wheel with white-knuckled hands, searching the dark but not seeing anyone.

Wait. She thought she saw something, a quick turn in the shadows, and a lump formed in her throat. She wasn't sure she wanted to get out of the car now, but Poppy was waiting for her upstairs — she was going to be fine. Anthony wouldn't dare try anything with Poppy here.

She took a deep breath and opened the door. As she stepped out of the car, she seriously began to regret her decision. But she couldn't just stand here. There was no turning back now. Seeing no one, she carefully closed the door, looked around again, then started heading toward the elevator.

The second she came around the back of Agent Maine's car, Anthony's back door swung open, and a man jumped out. She felt her heart stop. "Jimmy!" she shouted, trying to lurch out of his reach. "What are you doing?" He grabbed her with an iron grip, and she pleaded, "Don't, Jimmy! Don't do this!"

He ignored her. Anthony's car started as he hauled her into the back seat with him. Even before the door had closed, the driver was peeling out of the parking space.

Regina hadn't thought she had any tears left. She was wrong. Had anybody seen that? *Oh, please, John . . .* Even if somebody had been watching, it had happened so quickly that nothing could have been done. Her only hope was that Jim had gotten his agents in place and that they would be following.

Maybe she could talk her way out this.

"Jimmy," she whispered, trying to swallow her tears, "what are you doing? Anthony's expecting me."

"I'm following orders." He pushed a button on his phone, waited a moment, and then said simply, "It's done," and hung up. Looking at Regina, he said nothing else.

"Please, tell me where you're taking me."

He wouldn't answer her.

She started to pray.

Flipping his phone shut, Anthony looked at everyone and said, "That was one of my associates. There's a problem I have to attend to."

"Now?" Antonio asked. His concern elevated. "Regina will be here any moment. I thought you said you wanted to see her?"

"I do. This won't take me very long. I tell you what. Why don't all of you stay and wait for her? I'm sure she's a bit leery of seeing me anyway. This way, she'll be comfortable, and I'll be back before you know it."

Antonio didn't like the sound of this. Anthony must have pulled a fast one and somehow trapped Regina before she could get here. He pictured the parking garage below and figured he knew what had happened. Why hadn't he been expecting something like that?

"Okay, Son. That's a good idea."

Sophia and Father Thomas looked surprised.

Anthony gave his father a kiss on the cheek, as was his custom. "See ya later."

When the door had closed behind him, Sophia demanded, "What was that all about?"

"I think he has Regina," Antonio said calmly.

"What makes you think that?" asked Father Thomas.

"Someone close called me earlier and told me he believed Anthony's preparing an old warehouse we own for Regina. My man was ordered to bring a nurse there. Why else would Anthony need a nurse at an old warehouse we don't use?"

"Oh, no!" Sophia cried out. "We have to go!"

"No, it's not safe for you both to go. Let me go and handle this. No matter what Anthony's done, he won't kill me. I'm the only one who can save her."

"I'm going. She's my daughter."

"What good will you do her if you get hurt? Please, let me handle this." Ignoring her expression, Antonio headed for the door. He touched his right pocket and felt his gun there. He never carried one, but this morning he'd taken it out of his desk, just in case. He turned around and said, "Father, please make sure she's safe."

Father Thomas nodded. Antonio left.

Sophia whirled around. "Give me your keys!"

"No, I can't do that. How could I live with myself if you got hurt?"

"Then come with me. We have no time to argue; we have to follow him. Look, I promise I won't get out of the car. I just want to be there for Regina when Antonio brings her out. I haven't seen her in so long. Please, we have to hurry."

Father Thomas looked at her in such a way that Sophia suspected he knew her true intent. But then he said, "Okay. But you promise you're not going in, right? That could ruin the whole rescue. People could die, Sophia."

"Yes, I promise." She felt slightly guilty lying to him. But only slightly. She was desperate.

Jim got off the phone. "He's got her."

"How?"

"They grabbed her as soon as she got out of the car. My men saw Anthony leave, and then Antonio left shortly after. It looked like everyone was heading in the same direction. But don't worry — we're almost there."

"Why didn't your men grab him?"

"I'm not sure, but I intend to find out."

Jim leaned forward and tapped the driver on the shoulder. Without a word, the driver reached over and turned off the siren, which they'd been using to clear traffic.

"How much longer?" John asked.

"Maybe twenty minutes."

"I hope we're not too late."

"I'm praying the same thing."

John shot him a funny look. Before meeting Regina, he'd never suspected how many people actually thought prayer worked. He wasn't sure what was going to help her now, but at this point he'd try anything.

Anthony was almost there when he decided to call on Frank.

Frank was at the station. "Detective Holstrum here."

"It's me."

"I thought we agreed you'd never call me here."

"Don't get up in my face. I need you to meet me downtown at my warehouse."

"Why?"

"I can't tell you, Frank. It's a surprise. Just meet me there. You remember where it is, don't you?"

"Yeah."

"Good."

Before Frank could answer, Anthony hung up.

Frank was very aware that this could be a trap. He checked his gun and then slid it back into the holster. He glanced around the office and then grabbed his jacket and headed out the door.

Chapter 22

Jimmy wouldn't answer any of her questions. Regina had no idea where they were going, and she was scared sick, but she managed to get her tears stopped and now refused to give Jimmy the satisfaction of knowing how frightened she really was. Toward the beginning, she'd considered throwing herself out the door, but even panicked, she'd realized how ludicrous that idea was. She would hurt the baby.

They pulled up to what appeared to be an abandoned warehouse. A two-story garage door opened, and they drove inside. The door immediately lowered behind them.

As the car pulled to a stop, Jimmy opened his door and got out. Regina remained in the car, waiting with her hand pressed flat against her stomach. As if the baby sensed her distress, he moved about, sending his little heels into her ribs. She tried to breathe as normally as possible.

Now that her initial hysteria had passed, she was amazed at how calm she appeared. Even though her heart raced, her hands weren't shaking. It wasn't all that difficult to pull in slow, deep breaths.

Jimmy opened her door, and she carefully climbed out, looking around for a way of escape. This first room was about fifty feet long and nearly empty, with exposed beams and air ducts overhead. The only doors were the garage door they'd just come through, a small door beside it, and then a door painted red in the left wall. Nothing allowed for a getaway or even a hiding place, and even if she did somehow manage to escape, the nearby buildings were boarded up, and nobody was out here who could help her. In her condition, how far could she expect to get?

Jimmy took her through the red door which opened up into the main body of the warehouse. Boxes, newspapers, and dirt were strewn everywhere. It looked as if the place hadn't been used in years. A large, chain-link cage stood against the far wall. There was a hospital bed in it.

Her arm trapped in his vise-like grip, Jimmy started pulling her toward the cage.

"You're hurting me." He didn't answer. He practically threw her into the cage and then swung the door shut behind her, locking the padlock.

"Jimmy, please don't do this. I'm about to have a baby. Jimmy!"

He looked at her and walked away, going to sit in a chair next to the red door they'd just come through.

Counting slowly to five, Regina reached out and gripped the chain-link wall with one hand, steadying herself. The other hand went back to her stomach, as if she could somehow protect the baby from the filth they found themselves in. This would not be a good place to give birth. The cage floor was covered with dirt and litter. It felt like it was only fifty degrees in here.

She heard footsteps approaching. The room was huge and mostly empty, except for some crates stacked in lopsided towers. There was a large, dark area on her left that she couldn't see into. Everything echoed, and whoever was coming wore heels, which made her wonder. Who wore heels in a dirty place like this?

Two shadowy outlines appeared in the darkness, growing more succinct and visible as they came toward her. One was Vinny. She saw him and tried not to show any relief. *Oh, thank You, Jesus.* The other was Maria Malotti. Regina wasn't all that surprised to see her.

Maria stepped up to the cage. "Well, well — we meet again. This time without your wig."

"What are you doing here, Maria?"

"I'm here because Anthony asked me to be here. He wants me to help keep an eye on you. I'm a nurse, and you're going to need one soon."

Vinny took his normal position in the background, folding his massive arms and not saying anything. Regina wasn't sure if Maria knew her brother was dead; she'd been a Cavelli long enough to know that people around Anthony sometimes disappeared without the families ever being told the truth.

Maria glared at her. As Regina looked into her eyes, all she could see was hate staring back at her. What had she ever done to this woman? She'd bumped into her at a hospital — that was it. No matter what, Regina was resolved to stand tall and strong. She'd started to return her glare when suddenly the truth clicked into place, and she realized what the issue was.

Anthony had gotten to this woman. She had joined the long, long line of beautiful women who thought they belonged to him, and he to them, and Maria wanted Regina to know how little property she, the wife, had left. *If you only knew,* Regina thought.

As if she'd heard her, Maria sneered at her, her mouth twisting as if she was about to say something else, but she didn't. Regina didn't care what this poor woman thought she belonged to. She spoke first.

"It's cold in here. You think I could get a sweater or a blanket?"

"I'll see what I can do," Vinny said. He walked over to Jimmy. His voice echoed through the expanse. "She's cold. Why don't you see if you can get her a sweater or a blanket?"

"Why do I have to go?"

"Because I'm telling you to go." Vinny took another step in Jimmy's direction, just one, and Jimmy instantly jumped to his feet.

"Okay, okay. I'll go."

"Give me the key."

Reluctantly, Jimmy took the padlock key out of his pocket. But in the middle of handing it to him, the red door swung wide, and Anthony stepped into the room. The air caught in Regina's throat. She hadn't seen him in months and abruptly discovered she hadn't been quite emotionally prepared.

He grabbed the key from Jimmy's outstretched hand, saying, "I'll take that. Where do you think you're going?"

"Vinny told me to get a blanket."

When Anthony glanced at him, Vinny shrugged and said, "Well, Boss, I thought it wouldn't be good for the baby if she was cold and uncomfortable."

Anthony nodded for Jimmy to go. As the man left, Anthony's attention turned to his wife. He slowly walked over to the cage. She felt each step as he approached. His eyes narrowed as he examined her face. The darkness in his gaze seemed stronger than she had ever seen it, and she had to remind herself to keep breathing again.

Hate dripped from him as he said, "So you think you can make the rules around here?"

Regina hadn't anticipated Anthony double-crossing Poppy. She had nothing to lose now. Unless God rescued her, she knew she was dead. As that was the case, she decided there was no longer any reason for her to be cautious. She moved to the fence to show she wasn't afraid.

"Why are you doing this, Anthony?"

"I think you know why." He walked up to the cage and leaned against it right next to her. "It's not that hard to figure out. You're a smart woman. Supposedly. You tell me."

Anthony always liked making his prey ill at ease, but Regina was past playing those games with him. That was really what they were, anyway. Feeling a renewed sense of boldness, she decided to lay it all out there. "I'm guessing as soon as this baby is born, you're going to kill me."

Anthony started to clap. "Bravo. You're smarter than you look."

"I hope your new girlfriend's okay with that." Regina looked at her over his shoulder. She wagered that Maria had never been a part of the family business before. She was a nurse, a care provider, and Regina hoped her heart hadn't changed that much, that there was still some softness left.

She could tell that what Anthony said had startled her a little. Maria tensed and stared at him as if trying to decide whether that was true or not. Was that confusion Regina read on her face? Anthony turned to her and extended his hand. Tentatively, Maria reached out and took it. He pulled her close, slid his arm around her, and kissed her passionately for what seemed like an eternity.

Regina thought about laughing. What did he expect her to do — get jealous? She just didn't see where this was heading until Anthony said, "Regina, I want you to meet the mother of my child."

Then she got it. Anthony wanted to replace her, and he actually thought she'd be upset about it. She did laugh then. "You think that Poppy will allow you to get away with this? You *must* be crazy."

Without warning, he banged his hand on the cage, and she flinched. "I'm not crazy!" Pointing his finger at her, he shouted, "Because of you, her brother is dead! You have to pay for that. That child is mine, and it's a shame you died giving birth to it — at least, that's the story I'm telling."

Regina laughed again.

"Stop that! What's so funny?"

"The fact that you think your father is stupid enough to buy that."

"He'll be upset you're dead, but he'll have his grandchild to comfort him. You know how much that means to the old man," Anthony said smugly.

"Anthony, you'll never get away with this. Your father knows I was heading for the penthouse and what I was up to. You've made a very bad mistake."

"Shut your mouth, or I'll shut it for you!"

Anthony whirled around as the red door opened again, and Antonio Cavelli stepped into the room. Regina had never been so happy to see him.

"Anthony! What is going on here?" he demanded.

John and Jim pulled up to the warehouse. At first, the street appeared empty, but then an agent materialized at Jim's door. *Where in the world has he been hiding?* John wondered as they climbed out of the car. He started to see agents popping up around buildings and from behind dumpsters. There were at least a dozen of them.

Jim asked, "What's the status?"

"Well, sir, she's inside. But before we could make a move, Anthony Cavelli, and then his father, went in."

"Pull back your men in case anyone else wants to stop by."

He spoke none too soon. John, Jim, and the agent crouched down behind the car as a black sedan approached. It was Sophia and Father Thomas. The latter appeared to be upset about something. His expression was the closest thing to a glare John had ever seen on a priest before — not that he'd known many of them, of course. To his surprise, both of them got out and immediately went through the door of the warehouse as well. What was this — a convention?

"What are they doing here? We have to go in. There're too many civilians in there. Someone's going to get hurt," John said.

Before Jim could answer, they saw another car approaching. John recognized it right away, and for a second, he couldn't move. Jim reached up and yanked him back down as the car pulled to a stop behind Anthony's.

It was Frank. John had been holding onto a faint, struggling hope that maybe there was some explanation somewhere. Like Frank had just happened to be at the wrong place at the wrong time. Or that somebody had set him up. But now, John watched him and felt the last of his hope crumbling away.

Climbing from his car, Frank looked around cautiously, pulling his gun as he slowly approached the warehouse door. He opened it and entered.

"Get her out of there now!" Poppy demanded, as if Anthony were a disobedient toddler who knew better.

Anthony was shocked to see his father. How in the world had he found him? And what was he supposed to do now? He looked at Poppy and then at Regina in the cage and slowly came to the realization that the jig was up. He'd come so close to realizing his dream of freedom, but there was no way he was getting it now.

"Now, Anthony!" Poppy repeated.

Without saying a word, Anthony stormed over to the cage door. His hand hesitated on the lock. He slowly unlocked it but then kept the padlock firmly in his grip, his breathing growing labored. As long as this padlock remained on this door, he was still in control.

"Anthony!"

He really didn't have a choice.

"Step away from the cage, Son."

Anthony spit on the ground in disgust, glared at his wife, and then did as his father ordered.

Poppy held out his arms to Regina — with a longing in his eyes that was pathetic. It was disgusting. Anthony wanted to puke. He felt his father's eyes on him and tried to keep himself under control. *Don't you worry, old man. Your time's coming.*

"It's okay, Regina. Come here, my dear."

Right then, Anthony hated her more than he'd ever hated her in his life. She neared him cautiously and was just about to step past him when the red door opened again, and in walked Sophia and Father Thomas.

When Sophia saw her daughter, she shouted and held up her arms. "Regina!"

Poppy turned. In that instant, Anthony made a decision. He spun around, grabbed Regina's arm, and heaved her in front of him. As she cried out, he slammed his forearm around her neck and held her firmly against him.

"No!" Sophia screamed.

Anthony pressed the muzzle of his gun to Regina's head. "Don't anyone move, or I'll shoot her! You know I will."

"Anthony, what are you doing?" Poppy demanded, still talking to him like he was only three years old. "Put down that gun!"

"No! I'm done with this. I can't live like this anymore. I'm taking her away, and no one is stopping me. Maria, come to me!"

Maria didn't know what to do. This whole thing had started horrifying her. If he would put a gun to the head of his pregnant wife, what would he eventually do to her?

"I . . . I can't do this," Maria whispered.

Anthony twisted toward her, and in the split second he wasn't looking, Antonio pulled his gun out of his coat.

"Anthony," he said, leveling the pistol at his son.

Maria sucked in her breath and started backing away.

Anthony saw the gun in Poppy's hand and laughed. "Are you kidding me, old man? Come on, Poppy. Are you really going to shoot me? You should be careful — you might hit your precious Regina. I don't think you're that good of a shot."

"Anthony, Son — let her go and put down your gun."

Out of the others' line of sight, the red door quietly swung open, and Anthony smiled when he saw Frank. He had nothing to fear now. With a smug expression, he pulled his arm away and let Regina go. She ran toward her mother, and as she did, Anthony lifted his gun and trained it on her backbone, right between the shoulder blades.

Antonio was horrified. He'd seen the complete lawlessness in his son's eyes, and knowing he was going to pull the trigger, he jumped forward and shoved Regina out of the way. She tripped headlong and landed on the concrete. Antonio heard a loud *crack*, and the bullet slammed into his chest, spinning him around. He dropped to the ground beside Regina.

Sophia rushed to her daughter, crying, but through the haze in Antonio's eyes, Regina appeared to be fine. She managed to crawl over to him and hold his head in her hands.

"Poppy, speak to me! Anthony, what have you done? You shot your own father!"

Anthony just stood there with the gun hanging limply at his side, a look of horror on his face. He stood as stiff as a statue and stared at Poppy on the floor. Vinny came and stood behind him, putting a hand on his shoulder. Whether it was for protection or for control Regina couldn't tell.

Hearing a commotion on the other side of the door, Frank ducked behind a crate as John, Jim, and the other agents rushed into the warehouse.

"This is the police! Drop your weapons!" John shouted, gun in hand. He saw Anthony standing there and Poppy on the floor, bleeding.

Anthony turned and looked at him. His voice hollow, he whispered, "I didn't mean to shoot him." Then his attention went to something lurking behind a stack of crates, and he yelled, "None of this would have happened if you did your job!"

John spun around and saw Frank trying to hide. "Why, Frank," he said, attempting to sound surprised, "what are you doing here?"

Frank froze. And then he straightened and casually motioned with his gun. "I followed Anthony here, but the shooting happened so fast, I couldn't stop it."

Anthony had a complete breakdown. He yelled something unintelligible and growled, "Don't listen to him — he lies! He works for — "

Frank pulled the trigger. Anthony caught the bullet right between his collarbones. His eyes shot open, and he grabbed his chest, saw blood on his fingers. "For me," he managed and then toppled face-first onto the concrete.

Jerking up his pistol, John yelled, "Frank, drop your weapon!"

Frank looked at him and frowned, pretending to be confused. "Hey, man, I was just doing my job. He still had a gun in his hand. He was going to shoot Regina when Antonio Cavelli got in the way."

"It's over, Frank. We know you've been working for Anthony all this time."

"No, man, you got it wrong. I wouldn't do that. You would believe this gangster? Come on — you know me."

Looking at him over the barrel of his gun, John repeated quietly, "Frank, throw down your weapon."

Vinny stepped over Anthony, bent down, and checked for a pulse. There was nothing. The man was dead. "You didn't have to kill him," he told Frank as he straightened. "I saw you at the motel."

No. Frank thought of all the faces in his family — his wife, his children . . . *No.* It was over.

"I won't go down like this," he yelled and shoved the muzzle of his gun under his chin. Before he could pull the trigger, Jim Wilton put a bullet in his shoulder, and the gun popped out of Frank's grasp. Weaponless and bleeding, he sagged to the floor.

On the outskirts of his vision, John saw Vinny going over to check on Poppy. Regina was trying to comfort him. John recognized Maria Malotti from the hospital. She was kneeling beside Anthony's body, staring blankly. FBI agents swarmed the room.

But to John, all the action and emotion seemed like background noise. Everything was part of his peripheral vision, except for Frank.

John picked up his former partner's gun off the floor. Frank just sat there, holding his shoulder. He looked up as John slowly approached him.

"Just finish the job, man," he said. "I can't go to jail. Think what it would do to Annie and the kids."

"Maybe you should have thought about them before you started working for Cavelli. I think you made your decision a long time ago." He paused. "I just want to know one thing, Frank."

"You want to know why?"

"No. I don't care *why*." John looked directly into Frank's eyes, seeing him for the very first time. All his anger and fear channeled into one question that burned inside his heart. "Did you kill my brother?"

Poppy was bleeding badly. The bullet must have hit an artery.

"Hold on, Poppy," Regina pleaded as Vinny applied pressure to the wound. *Oh, God . . .* "Help is on the way."

"Are you okay?" Poppy asked her, quiet.

"Yes, I didn't get hurt." Her voice broke. "Thanks to you."

"At least I did one good thing with my life. That's all I wanted . . . redemption."

Feeling helpless, Regina looked up at Father Thomas, tears in her eyes. Despite Vinny's efforts, the flow of blood wouldn't stop. It was all over his hands and soaking through the dirt on the floor.

"Please, Poppy. Hold on. Help is coming."

She started to cry in earnest. For most of her life, she'd hated this man, but now his head was on her lap, and he was dying. He had saved her life. She didn't understand why he would have done that. Maybe she had been wrong about him, and if that was the case, then she had wasted years of her life and lost all the memories she should have made.

"Don't cry, my dear. Just don't forget to tell . . . my grandchild I love him."

"You can tell him yourself, Poppy."

Father Thomas started to administer Antonio last rites. On her hands and knees, Sophia wept. She'd loved this man at one time, and now he'd laid down his life for her daughter. She didn't think of the bad things that had happened between them, only the good.

By the time the ambulance arrived, there was nothing the paramedics could do. He was gone.

Frank stared up at John, standing there with his gun by his side. "Would you shoot me if I told you the truth?"

"I need to know what happened, Frank. I deserve that much."

"You deserve nothing," Frank said coldly. "But I'll tell you the truth if it'll make you happy. I mean, life's all about making you happy, right, partner?" His expression changed slowly, maniacally. John had never seen that expression on Frank's face before. It was pure evil, and with it, the atmosphere in the room changed. He felt the temperature drop. "You know he didn't kill himself. You've always known that, but I was the one who set it up to look that way. It was easy. He didn't even see it coming."

Bringing up the gun, John took aim at Frank's head, right between the eyes, and cocked the hammer. He had thought he hated Anthony, but he couldn't even begin to describe the revulsion he felt toward this man he'd thought was his friend. He had never *wanted* to kill anyone before this moment.

Jim came up behind him. "No, John, don't do it. He's not worth it," he said, calm. "Just give me your gun. It's over. It's all over."

Tears stung John's eyes, and his hand began to shake. He couldn't believe what he'd just heard. He couldn't believe Frank had fooled him all those years. *You killed my brother?* He stood there, trying to think, and in that moment, he noticed the friendship bracelet Lynette had made for him, tied around his wrist. That made him think about Annie and the rest of the family. Jim placed his hand on John's shoulder, and John just couldn't bring himself to pull the trigger. It wasn't because he had any semblance of respect left for Frank, but he did for his family. He lowered his hand.

The paramedics came over to Frank and started working on him. Jim read him his rights as he handcuffed him to the stretcher. John turned around to survey the scene. So much had happened in such a short period of time. Anthony and Antonio Cavelli were dead. Vinny and Maria didn't appear very comfortable as the FBI battered them with questions. Regina stood by her mother in tears as she watched them cover Antonio's body.

As he stared at her, her tears suddenly stopped, and her eyes widened. She pressed her hands on her belly, as if she was surprised to find she was pregnant, and then a second later, she bent over and cried out in pain.

John ran to her. "Are you all right?"

"No, I think something's wrong. Ma, help me!"

"We need some help here," John yelled to the paramedics.

The paramedics working on Frank came over to aid Regina. They helped her onto a stretcher. "Don't worry, ma'am; we'll get to the hospital in no time," one of them tried to reassure her.

"Please, don't let anything happen to my baby." Regina winced and then cried out again, her hands on her abdomen.

John had never felt more helpless. He held her hand and whispered to her, "You're going to be fine, and so is the baby. I'll be there the whole time. You don't have to go through this alone."

They took her away.

"Jim, I gotta go with Regina. Can you clean up this mess without me?"

"Sure. You go. Tell her I'm praying for her."

Father Thomas grabbed his arm before John could take off. "I'll drive. You look too upset."

They left with Sophia and followed the ambulance to the hospital.

The hospital was only ten minutes from the warehouse, but it was the longest ten minutes in John's life. By the time they arrived, Regina was in labor. They sensed it wasn't going smoothly, and their tension escalated when Sophia wasn't allowed in the delivery room. All the doctor stopped to tell them was that Regina was in shock. "Complications," he said.

As time went by without further word, John thought he would go insane. He watched as Sophia and Father Thomas sat quietly with their eyes closed. He guessed they were praying. It looked like it was helping them, but was it helping Regina?

The doctor finally came out in his blue scrubs. John didn't like the expression on his face.

"What happened? Is she all right?" he asked, not really sure he wanted to know the answer to those questions.

"Are you her husband?" the doctor asked.

"No, I'm . . . just a close friend. This is her mother."

The doctor nodded to her and then looked at all of them. "The baby is fine. It's a boy."

John briefly closed his eyes, relieved. That had to lighten Regina's heart, despite the rest of the day's events. She had been so concerned about the baby.

"And my daughter — how is she?"

"I'm afraid there were some complications. She lost a lot of blood. We have her stabilized now. We're running some tests, and we're very hopeful she'll recover."

John stared at him. "You're very what?"

"Doctor, what are you saying?" Sophia pleaded.

With compassion in his eyes, he said, "I'm so sorry." Choosing his words carefully, he continued, "She's slipped into a coma. She's not responding to treatment as we would like, but she's not in any immediate danger. We're doing everything we can and hoping for the best."

Words could not describe what Sophia felt just then. The doctor's prognosis hung there in the air like something bent on killing her. With tears in her eyes, she whispered, "When can I see her?"

"As soon as we bring her to a room. You can see your grandchild in the meantime. He should be in the nursery down the hall to your right."

They slowly walked to the nursery window. As they approached it, Sophia thought, *This should be the happiest day of my life. Instead, Michael isn't here to see his grandchild, and Regina is in a coma.*

It wasn't fair.

She took a deep breath and then, as courageously as she could, she looked through the windowpane, searching for her grandson. A nurse was hanging a sign that read "Boy Cavelli" on his crib. He was red and crying.

"He's so beautiful," she whispered. "I pray that Regina will get to hold him very soon."

"So do I, Sophia," Father Thomas replied. "So do I."

John couldn't take it anymore. He just walked off, wandering around the hospital aimlessly. He came upon the hospital chapel, and knowing he needed something, he opened the door and went in. There were five red-cushioned pews, an altar, and a wooden cross hanging on the wall. He wasn't exactly sure why he was there, but he knew he was angry. He walked up to the altar and glared at the cross.

"Why? Can You tell me why? All she ever wanted was to have this child. And now she can't even see her baby. Isn't it enough for You to take everything away from her? Do You need to take her, too?"

"John."

John turned. He was breathing heavily and had tears in his eyes. He hadn't heard the old man come in. Running his hand over his face, he looked at him and demanded, "Do I know you?"

"No."

"How do you know my name?"

"I know your name because God sent me here."

The old guy had to be crazy. *John* hadn't even known he would end up here, and he didn't have time, or the patience, for this. In answer to his prayer, God had sent him a crackpot. *Figures.* So upset he couldn't think anymore, he started toward the door.

But before he could make it out, the man said, "God sent me here for you. He knows that you love her."

John slowly turned, giving the old man his full attention. *Who is this guy?* "Love who?"

"Regina, of course," he said matter-of-factly.

"How do you know . . . ? Who told you about . . . us? What kind of sick game are you playing, mister?"

"God told me. I've been praying for Regina for months now. God told me to come here and find you. He knew what would happen. He wanted your attention, John. He wanted your heart. Don't be afraid. I'm not crazy, and I speak the truth. Do you think all the Christians you have in your life right now are there by coincidence?"

John's vision blurred, and he blinked to keep his tears at bay. He didn't know what was wrong with him, but he couldn't seem to move. He just stood there, looking at this funny old man and the love and compassion he expressed when he spoke. All that had happened — Frank, the Cavellis, the baby, Regina — it had taken its toll on him. John felt as if he was finally at the end of himself and was unsure if he could keep God at arm's length anymore.

"Now is the time to let go of your anger at God and at man for things in your past, so that you can live a full life in the future."

John was having a hard time controlling his tears. *What's wrong with me?* he wondered again. He sucked in a deep, trembling breath and said, "You think . . . I'm mad at God? That's just . . ."

"Aren't you?" the man asked quietly.

John broke. He didn't remember falling to his knees, but he suddenly found himself there, unable to stop the tears this time. His tough New York City cop persona melted away, and he started sobbing like a baby in front of a stranger. The old man walked over to him and, kneeling down beside him, he told John about redemption and forgiveness. He told him about God's great love and sacrifice in sending Jesus to die for his sins. John wept as he asked God to forgive him. He then, with a lump the size of Texas in his throat, forgave Frank for killing his brother.

Hours passed. Hours of talking and praying.

For the first time in maybe his entire life, John began to feel peaceful. He never thought he could feel this way. He had asked Jesus into his heart, and the hole that was there was filled. John thanked the old man for spending so much time with him. As he started to leave, John followed him.

"Hey, I don't even know your name."

The man smiled at him, as if he found that request a little amusing. "My name isn't important. You learned the only name you needed today, and that's Jesus. Maybe one day we'll meet again." He walked out of the chapel, and the door swung shut after him.

John turned around and looked at the cross one more time. This time, anger wasn't in his heart but peace. He glanced at his watch and noticed how late it was. He had to go and see Regina.

Walking up to the maternity ward, he asked a nurse which room she was in, and going inside he found Sophia and Father Thomas beside the bed. They were praying. He didn't want to disturb them, but they looked up at him as he entered.

Father Thomas wearily smiled and said, "You look different. Are you okay?"

"Yeah, I'm fine. How is she?"

Sophia murmured, "About the same."

John walked over to the bed and closed his eyes and started to pray silently. He didn't know if he would be any good at it just yet, but he wanted to give it a shot.

Father Thomas and Sophia just looked at each other and then continued to pray as well.

As the minutes turned into hours, the three of them took turns staying by her side. Praying. Listening. Watching. Hoping that she would take a turn for the better and come out of it.

About six o'clock the next morning, Sophia had nodded off in the chair beside the bed; Father Thomas was looking out the window, arms folded behind his back, and John was at Regina's side. He held her hand, stroking her hair. *God, I know You love Regina. With all that is holy, please — let her wake up. Her son needs her. Her mother needs her . . . I need her.*

Just as he was praying those last few words, without warning, Regina moved her head and groaned. Instantly awake, Sophia jumped from her chair and grabbed Regina's free hand.

"Darling," she whispered, "can you hear me?"

Slowly, Regina started to blink her eyes and then looked up to see all of them smiling at her.

"Regina, are you okay?" Sophia asked. "Father Thomas, could you go get the doctor?"

He left quickly.

Standing beside the bed, John stared at her, feeling a dopey smile on his face and not caring if it made him look like an idiot. Tired, relieved, happy, peaceful — he was in love with this woman, and he was pretty sure that any second now, he was going to start floating off the floor.

A few minutes later, the doctor returned with Father Thomas and said, "If you all don't mind stepping out for a moment, I'd like to examine our patient here." After a little while, he met them in the hallway and said, "It's a miracle. She's fine. She's still a little weak, which is to be expected, but all signs of trauma have disappeared. I'll be back to check on her later."

"Thank you so much, Doctor!" Sophia said. "Can we go in and see her now?"

"Yes. She's asked to see her baby. I'll have the nurse bring him."

As soon as they entered the room, Regina asked quietly, "Is Anthony dead?"

No one answered until John finally replied, "Yes, he is."

"Darling, don't worry about that now," Sophia said, taking her hand. "You have to get stronger for the sake of your beautiful son. He looks just like you."

"Do you know what you will name him?" Father Thomas asked.

"Yes. I knew if it was a boy, I wanted to name him after my father, but after what happened at the warehouse, I know his middle name: Antonio. Are you okay with that, Ma?"

"Yes, Dear. I think it's very fitting to name him after his grandfathers."

The nurse brought in the baby and placed him in Regina's arms. The moment she touched him, tears started running down her face. This tiny, innocent child would never know his grandfathers, or his father. She had never wanted to see Anthony dead; she had just wanted to be safe from him.

Now she was.

She looked up at everyone and said, "Do you mind if I talk to John alone?"

"Of course not, Dear. We'll be back later to see you." Sophia kissed her on the head and then kissed little Michael, who turned his head in the blankets and cooed. She gave John a special, knowing little smile and left with Father Thomas.

"He's really beautiful, Regina."

"Thank you. You look different. Something about you has changed."

"Yes, it has. I found that peace I've always seen in you."

Regina smiled. "You mean you've accepted Jesus?"

"Yes."

"How?"

"It's a strange story that I'm sure you're not going to believe."

"Try me."

He sat on the edge of the bed and started to tell her about the old man and all the things he'd known about him and Regina. Her eyes were wide the whole time.

"Crazy, huh?"

"Actually, no, it's not. Twice I've had a strange man call me and warn me of danger."

"Really? He did say he'd been praying for you for months. I bet you it's the same guy."

"God works in mysterious ways."

She smiled at him again and then looked tenderly at the little bundle in her arms. John was about to say something else, but then he paused, watching her. She was so beautiful, and seeing her like this, at complete peace for the first time since he'd met her, his heart filled and then overran its borders with the love that he'd been storing up for her. Suddenly unable to breathe, he swallowed the lump in his throat and cleared it.

Regina looked up at him, a light in her eyes.

"Regina. I just want you to know that I'm here for you. I don't want to rush you. You've been through so much. Looking at you now, Michael in your arms . . ." He wasn't sure if he could continue. Her slow smile encouraged him. She reached out one hand and he held it. "I love you."

He said nothing else, but for the first time in months, his heart and his mind were serene.

"And I," she said softly, "love you back."

Epilogue

Seven months later, Regina was in the nursery of the home she'd bought out on Long Island. After the deaths of her husband and father-in-law, she'd sold the penthouse and moved out of the city. The restaurant she'd given to Kelly. She'd done a great job when Regina was on the run, and she couldn't have bestowed it on a more grateful recipient.

Money was not an issue. She had more than she could ever need, and all she really wanted to do was raise her son fulltime. He was crawling and getting into things these days. Because of everything they'd been through, she was so grateful that God had given her this chance to raise him. Little Michael was taking a nap in his crib just a few feet away, and she loved to watch him sleep.

She sat there until the doorbell rang. Going to the front door, she saw that it was John and stepped outside. His arms came around her waist and pulled her in close. Sliding her arms around his neck, she stood up on her tiptoes as he tilted his head down. Her lips welcomed his. Every time she kissed him, it was like the very first kiss — warm and passionate and safe.

"Hello, Beautiful," he said as he handed her a red rose.

"Oh, John, you're so sweet." She smiled.

He held on to her tightly, kissing her softly on the neck.

She swatted his shoulder. "Now, now — let's not start that out here. What will my neighbors think?"

"Who cares about neighbors? Let them talk." He laughed but obliged her. They walked into the living room and sat down on the couch. "How's my favorite little guy doing?"

"He's great."

"Good, good." He sounded slightly distracted. "And where is he?"

"He's taking a nap . . . Why?"

A quirky smile on his face, he got down on one knee and held her hand.

"John, what are you doing?"

"Regina, I love you more than life, and I love Michael. You two are my world. Will you allow me the privilege of being your husband and Michael's father?"

He pulled out a little box and opened it up. Inside was the most beautiful antique ring Regina had ever seen. It took her breath away.

"This belonged to my great grandmother." He paused, looking deeply into her eyes. "Make me the happiest man in the world — marry me."

Regina's heart filled with joy. "Yes! A thousand times, yes!"

He got to his feet, pulling her up with him, and kissed her until she could barely breathe. She never wanted him to let her go. "John," she whispered, "you've made me so happy. I want to thank you for giving me time to heal these past few months. You never once pressured me. You stood by me, and for that I love you."

He moved a strand of hair out of her eyes, touching her cheek. He held her face in his hands, and Regina thought she would melt at that very moment. "I promise you that I will love you all of my life. And," he added, then paused to kiss her again, "it's not just you, you know. Michael has captured my heart, too."

"Let's go tell our son the good news."

He winked at her. "Okay, then let's set a date as soon as possible. I don't want Michael to be an only child."

Never in her dreams had Regina thought she would be this happy.

In a tiny cabin just outside a small Tennessee town, a familiar elderly man was sleeping beside his wife. Suddenly, he was awakened by a presence in their room.

He jolted up and saw a tall, angelic figure at the foot of his bed. It took a minute before his head cleared, but when it had, he leaned forward and asked, "Who is it this time?"

Acknowledgements

I want to thank all my friends who, through the years, read the rough drafts of this book. I thank especially Linda Addison, Lynda Meyers, and Gwen Wierman for all their help in the early stages of this project.

I want to thank Patty Mapes, who introduced me to Lauren and was so helpful in this self-publishing endeavor.

I want to thank Lauren Stinton, who made editing fun. You are my favorite editor. Even though you're the only one I've worked with, you're still my favorite.

I want to thank Sherry Claussen and Jennifer Troutman, who helped by being extra eyes in the final edits of the book.

I want to thank Tom Marsh for his fine work on the cover.

I want to thank Dianna Clark, whose artistic gifting is responsible for the photo on the back cover.

I want to thank my daughter, Lisa, who was the very first person to read my early story. Thank you for encouraging me to actually attempt to write a book.

I want to thank my son, Tom, whom I love. I appreciate all of your encouragement throughout this project.

I want to thank my husband, Tom, who encouraged me to finish what I started when I wanted to quit so many times. Thank you for believing in me and helping see this project through until completion. I couldn't have done it without you.

Finally, I want to thank God, who inspired me and helped me with the direction of my story. Without His creativity, this book would not have been written.